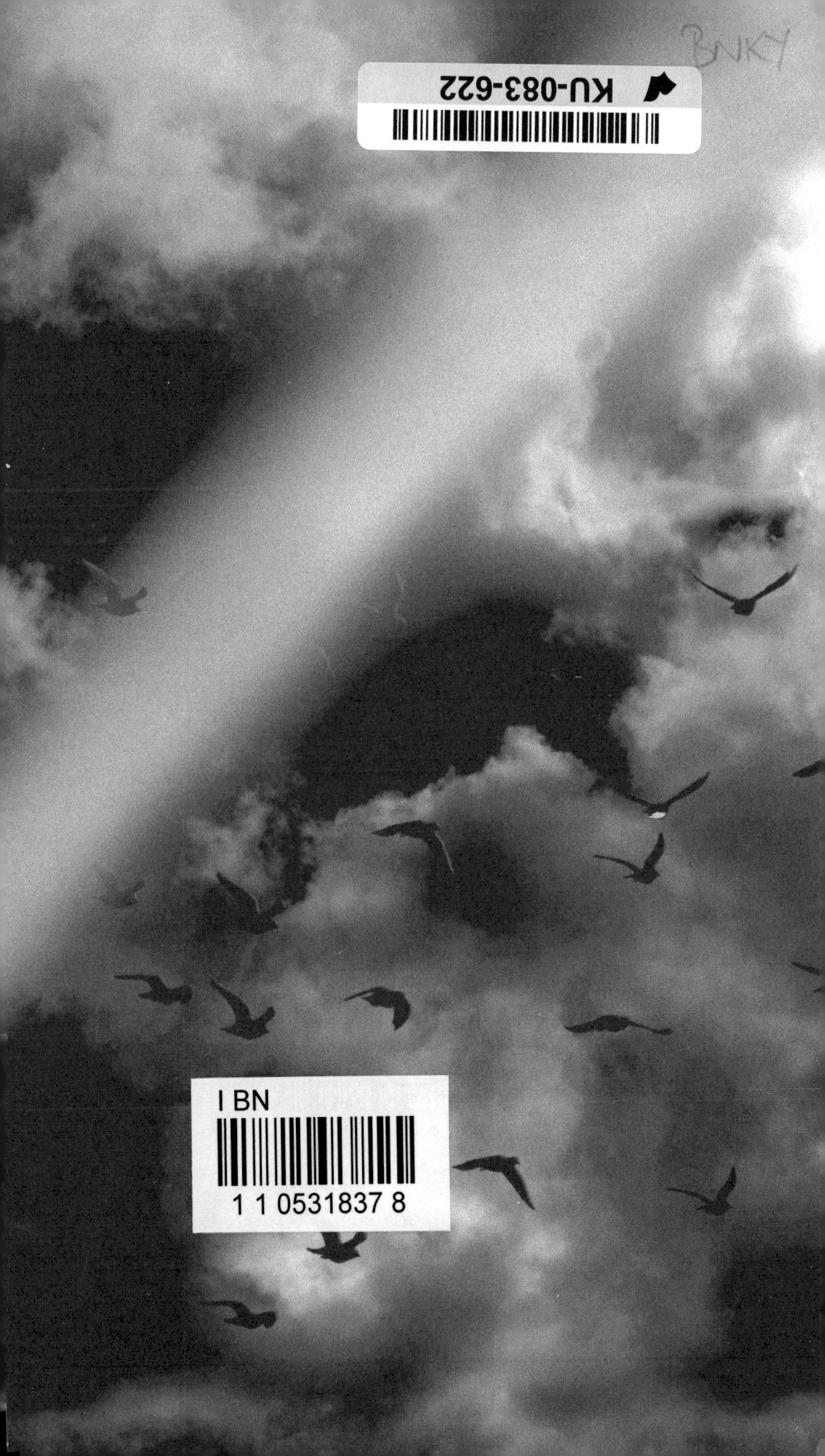

FROM THE AUTHOR OF

'ULTIMATE JUSTICE'

WHITE GATES ADVENTURES THREE

WINDS
AND
WONDERS

EXPLORE AMAZING NEW WORLDS
AND DISCOVER YOURSELF...

TREVOR STUBBS

Matador
9 Priory Business Park,
Wistow Road, Kibworth Beauchamp,
Leicestershire. LE8 0RX
Tel: 0116 279 2299
Email: books@troubador.co.uk
Web: www.troubador.co.uk/matador
Twitter: @matadorbooks

ISBN 978 1785893 353

British Library Cataloguing in Publication Data.
A catalogue record for this book is available from the British Library.

Printed and bound by CPI Group (UK) Ltd, Croydon, CR0 4YY
Typeset in 12pt Aldine401 BT by Troubador Publishing Ltd, Leicester, UK

Matador is an imprint of Troubador Publishing Ltd

This book is dedicated to all those for whom life is a struggle. I pray that, even as they are surrounded by hardships of many kinds, they may yet perceive the powerful, but gracious, hand of God, and be transported – if only for a fleeting moment – to a place where all they can utter is: "Wow!"

By the same author

Fiction
The Kicking Tree
Ultimate Justice

Non-fiction
WYSIWYG Christianity: Young People and Faith in the Twenty-First Century

At the beginning, all was formless and empty,
and the dark was deep.
Then the Creator spoke.
Her Spirit, Her Breath, and Her powerful Winds, fell upon
the chaos.
There was an explosion of new order.
The laws of nature came into being, dimension upon
dimension.
Light illuminated the darkness.
Life and love followed.
All was wonderful beyond measure.
Finally, She created a race of people with bodies, minds and
hearts designed to explore, discern, feel and love all that She
had called into being.
And, then, She, who is all-love, touched the people she had made
with Her Winds, so that they, too, grew, knew and spoke.

[Based on the first chapter of Genesis]

"Earth's crammed with heaven,
And every common bush afire with God;
But only he who sees, takes off his shoes –
The rest sit round it and pluck blackberries."
Elizabeth Barrett Browning

1

A bby felt a shove from behind as the year sevens and eights pushed forwards towards the bus stop. She hated getting on this bus these days. Now in year eleven, she was an adult compared to these youngsters mostly below shoulder height, but they didn't care how senior she was – they continued to push. The bus arrived and Abby stumbled aboard, touched her pass and headed straight up the stairs. She found an unoccupied seat halfway down the upper deck – hot and stuffy in stark contrast to the dank, windy, British winter, which seemed to have been going on for ages. The windows were steamed up, and Abby put the flat of her hand on the wet pane and cleared a small space to look out on the dull, darkening town. Brown-uniformed children squealed as a wave of water, thrown up by the bus, surged across the pavement that divided the road from Renson Park. A gawky, spotty youth, with half of his shirt hanging out of his trousers, fell into the seat beside Abby.

Yuk, she thought, *not George Geoffrey Walters (a.k.a. Gee-gee)!* She was convinced that he hadn't showered since last term. Apart from the smell (which some of her friends said she only imagined), he fancied himself, and gave the impression that Abby should appreciate the honour of him sitting next to her. Some of her friends reckoned that Abby had a thing against boys in general. Was there something wrong with her? Did she fancy girls? Or, worse still in their imagination, perhaps she was frigid. Obsessed as many of them were with the opposite sex, it had never occurred to them that it was perhaps *they* who were the ones with the problem! But Abby knew that, given the right boy, her heartbeat quickened. Such a boy was Bandi Smith, and this weekend she was determined to seek out the white gate at the bottom of her garden, and step through it into Woodglade on Planet Joh – literally light years from drab Persham – into the warmth of the cottage garden and Bandi's welcoming arms.

Abby got off at the stop before hers. George was becoming unbearable. She had removed his wandering hand twice and he had now made to put his arm around her. As if the problems of being editor of the school student magazine weren't enough! Shouldering her bag, Abby battled the wind up the long road that led to the vicarage. Walking round to the side door, she turned the handle and pushed. It was unlocked.

"Hi Mum," she called. Her mum was somewhere else in the big, detached house that went with her father being vicar of St Augustine's, Persham. Her dad had held the position there for the past ten years. Abby went straight to her room, offloaded her bag, and headed for the bathroom. Peace at last. This was the one place no-one could bother her – except her mum. The landline phone rang, and her mother called up the stairs, saying that a reporter wanted to talk to her.

"I'm in the loo!" she yelled. "Tell them I'll ring them back."

"He says he'll hold on."

"Just put the phone down, Mum."

"Abby, this is getting too much," said her mother, when Abby at last felt hungry enough to head for the kitchen.

Indeed it was. Abby had deliberately left her mobile on her desk in her bedroom because it hadn't stopped bleeping all day. It was all to do with the election. Persham, in the English Midlands, was the subject of a by-election, and the head of the senior school (years ten and eleven) had suggested that they hold a "mock election" as an exercise for the students to amuse themselves with in the run-up to the real thing. It was meant to be an adjunct to the social education bit of the PSHE course. Abby had volunteered to be the "political editor" for the student magazine and had sought interviews with each of the candidates. The mainstream political parties had school societies – Consoc, Labsoc, Greensoc and Libdemsoc – who had each fielded a candidate, but, in the spirit of British politics, there were others who had put themselves forward. The head had intervened to prevent any extremist candidate, but had happily allowed a couple of innocuous eccentricities, among whom was one guy (ironically, considering he campaigned for a bonfire, his name actually was "Guy") describing himself as the "Burn-Your-Underwear Freedom Party".

Guy's main theme was that underwear was an imposition on the masses by a conspiracy between those who wished to control the populace, and those who made money out of unscrupulous manufacture and trade. His "straplines" were "Freedom from Restraint" and "Independence from Underpants". In his interview with Abby, he had called upon all young people to declare themselves free from the restraints that society (manipulated by the powerful) placed upon them, and to symbolise this by publicly burning their underwear. He even named a day and place within the school grounds. Seeing where this was going, the head of the senior school immediately invoked his powers and forbade the event. But, of course, this was speedily claimed by the candidate as evidence of the oppression under which they were all languishing. The teacher had played straight into the young man's hands and given grist to his campaign. Guy wrote a letter to Abby who faithfully published it for all the students in the school to read. Abby was enjoying this as much as the rest.

It might have stopped there had it not been for two things.

The first was that a father of one of the school children, who owned a patch of waste-ground near to the school offered it to the Burn-Your-Underwear Freedom Party for them to use for their bonfire on the appointed date. The second was that the Consoc candidate withdrew her candidacy and called on her supporters to vote for the BYU Freedom Party. Abby faithfully wrote two articles to inform her public (the school students) of the developments. Everyone was having fun.

But this story was too good to remain inside the school. Already it had engaged the attention of the parents, one of whom was the chairman of the local Conservative Party, who were desperate to win the real election. He was incensed by the abdication of the Consoc candidate and was trying to get someone else to stand. This gave a real level of importance to the mock election. His interest, combined with the idea of an underwear bonfire, caught the attention of the local newspapers, and then, since this was a by-election in a marginal constituency, the whole nation. National reporters and photographers mingled among the local press for every angle on the story.

Abby was a deep-thinking girl and recognised there was a seriousness to this. Encouraged by her father (a philosophy enthusiast as well as a vicar), she pointed out that, in fact, many people aren't free. It might not be so much to do with underwear, but there *was a* conspiracy among the powerful to dominate people. Exploitation was real and Abby wrote an editorial to this effect.

Now the national media were after Abby as well as Guy. An attractive sixteen-year-old with long blonde hair, who also happened to be the daughter of a local clergyman, was irresistible! What started out as a bit of fun had now gone crazy. Her mother said (appropriately) that "those who play with fire get burned." Now this was the latest reporter who wanted to interview Abby. The last one wasn't just interested in the question of whether or not Abby was going to burn her own underwear, but what her views were regarding Karl Marx.

Abby gathered an armful of clothes, which she shoved into a shoulder bag, and picked up her phone. She texted friends to say she would be away a couple of days and went down the stairs two at a time.

"I'm going to see Bandi," she declared.

"What, now?" asked her mother.

"Yes, *now*. If that reporter rings again, tell him I'm away for the weekend and non-contactable. That won't be telling a lie."

"Oh, Abby. There are reporters at the front gate and a funny-looking man that I think is hiding a camera has just dodged behind a hedge."

"I'll go out the back. I'll be careful."

Abby looked out of the kitchen window. The white gate she wanted was clearly visible to her (but not to her mother or anyone else) and its position was not visible from the front of the house.

"I just want a day or two to think about this. I know I must go to school, but tomorrow is Saturday, so even if I don't come back till late Monday I'll only miss a day. Tell them I'm... oh, tell them anything you like – except about the white gates."

"Oh. Abby. You take care."

"I will. I'll be much safer on Joh than I will be here."

"That," said her mother, "is a fact. Give Bandi and his family my love." She took Abby in her arms.

Abby went to the back door, then turned and said, "And, Mum, don't dispose of my old underwear. I might need something to burn!"

"Abby!"

But Abby had already gone through the back door and was

stepping, head down, across the grass towards the far hedge. It was still raining, but just before she reached her white gate, a shaft of sunlight broke through and she looked up. There, vibrant and strong in front of the dark grey clouds, was a brilliant rainbow – the full spectrum of colour from vivid red to iridescent violet arced over the dark row of houses that lay beyond the vicarage. Abby smiled. Despite everything, there were shattering moments of beauty even in this dull Midland town. She turned and waved toward the kitchen window where her mother was watching. She pointed to the sky, and while her mother took in the glory of the rainbow, Abby disappeared through the hedge.

2

Jalli came out of her dream. In her half-waking state she felt Jack beside her, and then listened for her daughter's breathing. She couldn't hear it. She panicked. She sat up with a start and looked across at where the cot had been since they first transferred Yeka out of her Moses basket. It wasn't there, and then she remembered. Yesterday they had moved her into her own room for the first time. Jalli felt stupid, then cold, as her goosebumps retreated and her sweat evaporated. She shivered. Jack awoke.

"Jalli. What's wrong?"

"Nothing."

"But you're sitting up and you're shivering."

"I just panicked when I couldn't hear Yeka. I'd forgotten we'd moved her."

"Lie down and I'll warm you up."

"No. I must go and check on her."

"No. I'll do that. I'll go and see if she's awake. If she is, I'll bring her to you. And then I'll go and put the kettle on."

"Who could want for a better husband?"

"Since you ask, no-one," smiled Jack, as he sat up and kissed his wife. "Good morning, Jallaxanya."

"All formal, are we?"

"No." Jack stood at the cottage bedroom window and drank in the scents of the dew-laden lawn with its bench under the tree which was now coming into bud. "Just recalling how far we have come since we first met. That was nearly twenty-five years ago."

"Don't remind me!"

Jack put on his dressing gown and tiptoed into Yeka's new room. Remarkably, she was still asleep. She was their fourth child and they had named her after Jalli's mother, Mahsnyeka. Jalli had only a vague memory of her mother because she had died, along with her father and all the rest of her family, in the torrent of water from a fractured dam above their village on Planet Raika. Jalli and her grandmother, Momori, had only survived because they had been out of the village at the time. Momori had taken her granddaughter to the city because she had fallen and broken a front tooth, and the doctor had recommended she attended the hospital to make sure there was no other damage. She had had the X-ray and was declared fit. She would only have to put up with the gap a few years before the adult teeth grew. But Jalli and her grandma had had to bear much more than the temporary loss of a front tooth.

Momori invested all her love into her granddaughter and they never parted until Momori died some two years ago. Her death had been a significant event in their lives. There was an emptiness in White Gates Cottage, but that was now mitigated by this new little girl, who had just moved into her great-grandmother's room.

When Jalli and Jack realised that a new baby was on the way, they had decided, if it was a girl, to name her after her grandmother, Mahsnyeka, and great-grandmother, Momori. Mahsnyeka Momori was rather a mouthful, and from the day she was born she had become simply Yeka. And now, a little girl with a unique personality, she was beginning to be a major centre of attention at the cottage. Her older sister, Kakko, was twenty, but away almost as much as she was at home. Shaun, at nearly eighteen, was making an impression on Planet Joh with his impressive school record, and had become an indispensable part of his football team. Sixteen-year-old Bandi was a quiet thinker who, spurred on by his girlfriend Abby from Planet Earth One, worked hard at his school studies. Matilda, Jack's mother, was a proud nan. She had time for her family at the beginning and the end of the day, but spent most of the rest of it with her friends in the town. Teenagers and a baby were fine, but her friend Ada's front room, where the noise of knitting needles and the chink of teaspoons on saucers were the only things to be heard, was a welcome change.

Yeka's new room was the upstairs bedroom at the end of the house. Coming to her there, Jack thought the house was once again full, despite the fact that Kakko's downstairs bedroom was empty this morning.

Jack tiptoed back to Jalli and passed on the news of the sleeping child. He went down the stairs to put the kettle on. Matilda was already up.

"Yeka slept well in her new bedroom?" she asked.

"Still asleep. We didn't hear her at all last night. She's nearer to you now than to us."

"I had noticed! I thought I would be woken up."

"No. Yeka is a good girl. If she wakes, there is something wrong. She doesn't normally."

The kettle was just coming to the boil when there was an almighty howl. Yeka had awoken in a strange room and was wondering where her parents were. Jack heard Jalli get up and rush along the corridor saying soothing things as she went. They heard Yeka's cries transform into a low groan. Jalli carried her back to her own bed to suckle her. If Jalli followed the same pattern she had with the older three, she would nurse her at least another two months. Although she was no longer dependent on this for food, Jalli believed it was part of giving a child a sound, secure start in life. Both her mother and grandma believed in it, and Jalli followed Momori's guidance.

Although, as a baby, Jack had been bottle-fed from the start, he concurred with this approach. Matilda just said that it wasn't the custom where she lived when she was a young mother. It had been the exception rather than the rule.

Jack took the tea up to the bedroom. He put both mugs down on the chest of drawers. Then he took Jalli's and carefully turned. He did not approach but held the mug out in front of him. Jalli reached out to take the handle of the mug and put it down on the bedside table. Jack could navigate the house as if he could see but, in reality, he saw nothing. He hadn't been able to see since he was eighteen when he had been severely beaten in an assault while trying to protect Jalli. Jack could manage most things so long as they didn't move around, but little Yeka was not guaranteed to lie still in her mother's arms.

Jack collected his own mug, went round his side of the bed and put the tea down on his bedside table. He took off his dressing gown, and got in beside his wife and daughter. Yeka reached across and took hold of his thumb before coming up for air, and sliding between them.

It was the Joh equivalent of Saturday. Shaun's team was playing at home, so they knew he would not be up just yet. Bandi would probably be in bed for hours, although he would spend most of the time reading. He had taken to re-reading *Sophie's World* now he understood so much more English. Abby's family had given him a learning course, and this, combined with his frequent trips to Planet Earth One, and his nan's practising him, meant he was becoming quite proficient. The first time he read *Sophie's World*, Matilda tried to translate for him, but there were many English words she struggled to understand herself, let alone put into her second language. Abby's dad, Dave, suggested some English alternatives and slowly it began to make some sort of sense. Now, it was coming together. Knowing English was opening up a whole new world of study for Bandi. Even Pastor Ruk, who had a pretty good understanding of the cultures and literature of Earth One, could not read English – in fact, until Bandi had appeared with *Sophie's World* and then the Bible, he had never seen any book actually from Planet Earth One itself. Every time he saw Abby, he quizzed her about Christianity. A clergyman's daughter, notwithstanding, she could not begin to answer his questions at the depth he wanted. Sadly for him, her father did not have the privilege of moving between their worlds. The white gate was not there for him. But being the messenger had led to Abby asking questions she had never thought of before, and seeing her father struggle to find the words to answer them, too. Both her father and Pastor Ruk were men of convinced faith, a faith that gave them freedom to explore into the things of God and Her creation at depths that seemed to contradict what ordinary people took for granted. Abby did her best. She prayed that her father and Pastor Ruk would one day be able to meet – but for the moment it was not to be.

The white gates had again ceased happening for Jack and Jalli as they had done when Kakko was born. It was through the white gates that they had originally met – Jack from Persham and Jalli from Planet Raika in the Andromeda galaxy. They had made White Gates Cottage in Woodglade on Planet Joh their home. They had had adventures as two young people caught up in the magic of the ability to travel between planets, galaxies and probably even universes. This had stopped when Kakko was born, but when Bandi was fourteen they had wonderfully reappeared, and all the family had gone off, sometimes together but mostly in ones, twos and threes, on different trips. Each time they made quite an impression on the people they met. Kakko had even argued with the Prime Minister of the United Kingdom. But these days it was only Bandi who enjoyed a white gate. This had stood there permanently for him and Abby for almost two years, without the rest of them getting even a sniff of an invitation to an adventure.

Kakko, of all of them, was the most put out, while Matilda said she was quite past it and was relieved that it did not happen for her. She was sometimes heard to say, "We've had quite enough of the coming and going!" Shaun was wrapped up in the studies and opportunities that had opened up for him at home. Playing in mid-field he had become established as an important part of his team, even though he was still only eighteen. Football was not played professionally on Joh, but, for him, it was not a job but an absorbing passion. Jack and Jalli would have been astonished to see a white gate for themselves – white gate adventures and raising babies did not go together.

★ ★ ★

The peace of the morning at White Gates Cottage was gone. Shaun was up and taking an early lunch before heading off to the football ground. Kakko had come home, leading boyfriend Tam. With Kakko, there was no "low-key" button. She was either "on" or "off". She was off for a few hours at night but then was full-on throughout the day. Tam was always a pace behind, but was content to be in tow at all. In fact, he was the only one who could succeed in lowering Kakko's volume a little to help her reflect. In truth, Kakko adored him – they both loved each other dearly. Kakko loved Tam for his steady dependability, and because once she made her mind up about something she didn't do things by halves. Tam delighted in her enthusiasm – around Kakko it was always sunshine or a thunderous downpour, none of the persistent grey drizzle he had heard about that epitomised the weather in England.

★ ★ ★

Bandi was still in bed when Abby turned up with her bag and books. Bandi dressed in a minute and was in the kitchen to hear her tell the family about her problems.

"Well done," said Kakko.

"Well done?! The whole of the British Isles and beyond – the entire Twittersphere for all I know – is after *me,* and the school. The principal himself – 'he whom you never see unless the school is in crisis' – has demanded an end to the mock election and closed the student mag down. I am expecting a summons when I get back."

"So?" said Bandi.

"So, would you want to be at the centre of a tornado? Silent Sam could exclude me."

"Silent Sam?" queried Matilda. "Who's he?"

"The principal – Mr. Samuel Whitecastle, the head of the whole school of two thousand pupils. He's called 'silent' because he is mostly never heard or seen except at a year assembly once a term. So if he is involved…"

"But you're right," stated Kakko firmly. "Your friend Guy burning his panties has a serious point."

Jack couldn't help laughing. Then Abby joined in, and even Tam.

"What's funny?!" asked Kakko when she realised they were all laughing at her.

"You and Guy's panties," smiled Tam. "Do you remember how, in New London, that girl with the red stars on her skirt reacted when Zoe, I think it was, said about her young man seeing her panties when she was doing her gymnastics?"

"Oh, you mean Beth. It was something about being a cheerleader. She said they weren't 'panties' they were 'briefs', or something."

"'Panties'," said Matilda with authority, "are what Americans call knickers. They are only worn by females."

"Oh," said Kakko, "so Guy might not have any 'panties' to burn?"

"No," answered Abby, "I doubt he's the type."

"So what *is* he going to burn?" asked Shaun.

"I've no idea," said Abby, "I haven't seen them. Look, we're missing the point here, same as all those reporters."

"Yeah," said Bandi. "This 'Burn-Your-Underwear Freedom Party' is really about being free of oppression by big business, and domination by those who want to make money out of you."

"Exactly," said Abby.

"So why don't you just tell Silent Sam that you are standing up for those who have no freedom?" suggested Bandi.

"I knew a farmer once," said Jack, "who went bankrupt because he got a contract with a supermarket. It was alright the first year, but after he had become tied to the supermarket they told him much of his goods were not the right shape or size, and then they reduced the price. He couldn't make ends meet."

"Many of the old factories went, too," said Matilda. "And a lot of the underwear is made by people who work for next to nothing in sweatshops – a least it was like that when I was in Persham."

"Right," agreed Abby, "I think some of it still goes on. If not so much in Britain, it does abroad."

"So Guy has got a point," said Jalli.

"Sure. But the thing is, it has become more about bonfires and underwear, and less about the principle. The media just want to see girls burning their bras."

"They would," said Jack. "But it is an opportunity. What you need is an important person to come and make the point with you."

"The Prime Minister?" asked Kakko.

"*You've* talked to him. What do you think?" asked her mother.

"I don't think he wants to disturb anything to do with business. If he won't stop them making guns and war things because he is concerned about the economy, he's not going to address the thing about… what do you call them?"

"Sweatshops and supermarkets," said Jack.

"I agree," said Abby.

"What about your dad's boss… in the church?" wondered Tam.

"The bishop. I shouldn't think so."

"But you could ask him," said Jack. "And what about that man I met at the council who was talking about education for the blind. What was his name? Councillor… Councillor Banks. Look, let me write to him and suggest he gets involved. And you write about the principle, Abby. And get your friend Guy to meet him."

"You would do that? Write to Councillor Banks? That might work. His party lost control of the council this year, and he is in opposition now, so has nothing to lose."

"That I will do. If, Mum, you will take down my letter."

"Of course, son."

"And I doubt," continued Jack, "that Silent Sam – I mean, Mr Whitecastle – will actually exclude you. You have to have several warnings, and then suspension comes first anyway. And more importantly, holding a particular view on something is not a ground for exclusion. He can only do it on the grounds that he sees you as a disruptive influence. Mr. Whitecastle will, of course, be concerned about the press coverage, and perhaps he will ask you and Guy to cool it."

"But that would be bottling out," said Kakko, becoming more agitated. "I reckon you inflame it – literally. I'll give you some of mine to burn!"

"Kakko!" scolded her mother.

"But she's right," asserted Matilda. "If the world is listening to you and you have a point to make, I say make it! Mine are more substantial than any of yours and will probably make more smoke."

"I thought the bonfire had been cancelled," said Bandi. "Is it on again?"

"That depends on Guy. But he has a lot of people behind him. It is supposed to be in two weeks. The day before the election."

"Right. Let me write to Councillor Banks," said Jack. "And you write something up about the principle of this thing."

3

"I don't believe it," said Jalli, hurrying in from the garden with her baby in her arms. I was just out on the grass when I looked up, and saw Yeka pulling herself up on a white gate.

"What? A white gate for Yeka?" said Matilda, trying to get her mind around it. "But she's only *one*!"

"There can be no doubt about it. Both she and I saw it... and Jack's still at work."

"Hi," sang Jack, making his way to the kitchen, "talking about me?"

"Oh, Jack. I'm so glad you're home. I've just seen a white gate... and so has Yeka!"

"Goodness! They sent me home early. The college don't need all of us this afternoon. I thought, as the day was so nice, I could do a bit of work at home in the garden."

"Go and see if the gate is for you too... please," added Jalli in a worried voice.

"No problem," answered Jack. He put out his hand to reassure her. He got to the front door and was immediately aware of the gate.

"Me too," he called. Jalli visibly relaxed and subsided into a chair. Yeka wanted to go outside and continue to explore the new gate. As she tried to push past, Jack lifted her off her feet. She fought him to be put down.

"Not now, Yeka. Later," said Jack. Yeka shouted her impatience, but Jack held her tightly.

"Mum. What about you? Can you see it?"

"No. Not for me," said Matilda, who had gone to the dining room window to check a second time. "I can't see any new gate."

"We'll wait for the others," stated Jalli. "Anyway, I need time to come to terms with this."

★ ★ ★

Four hours later everyone had come home, and an excited Kakko, who had seen the gate immediately, had headed off to fetch Tam. Shaun and Bandi, it seemed, had to be content with staying at home with their nan.

Kakko returned with a patient Tam and, to his girlfriend's delight, was also to be in the party.

After another hour, they were all ready. Jalli had packed a bag of nappies, despite Jack reminding her that in the past they had never had to take anything. What they did find were robes like those they remembered from the *MEV Great Marton* in the first spate of their adventures. "Sass and... what was his name?" pondered Jalli.

"Matt. On the MEV."

"Yes. The mobile... mobile..."

"Mobile Emigration Village."

"You've got a better memory than I have."

"You have more to think about... Don't worry, wherever it is, they will have the wherewithal to look after babies – bound to have. If Yeka is to go, then she will be provided for."

"I guess so."

All five dressed in the flowing gear. Kakko smiled at the sight of Yeka. Wherever they were going, they made one-year-olds look cute. Jack explained that it could be the *Great Marton* – but, of course, that was just a guess.

"How long was it before it was due to arrive at their new planet?"

"Twenty-five years," said Jalli.

"Twenty-four years after you pressed the emergency button," Jack reminded her.

"So they must be arriving about now. Jack, we said we would remember them."

"And so we have – with a divine nudge. Thank you, God! If it is the MEV, we are going at an exciting time."

They emerged into the midst of a muddy, open-air music festival, exactly as they had the first time Jack and Jalli had boarded the *Great Marton*.

"Cool," whistled Kakko. "Not your spacecraft then?"

"Yes, it is. We were right. This stuff isn't real," said Jalli.

"A computer virtual reality programme," explained Jack. "Try talking to some of these people."

"Er, hi," said Tam to a guy in front of him. "Great music."

"Yeah," replied the guy. "Great music."

"Great weather," said Kakko to the girl with him.

"Yeah. Great weather," she repeated.

"The parrot's got her tongue," tried Kakko.

"Yeah," replied the girl. "The parrot's got her tongue."

"$E=mc^2$ today," teased Tam.

"Yeah man, $E=mc^2$ today."

"Told you," murmured Jack. "Not human. We need to look for someone human amongst this virtual reality experience." Kakko was prodding a girl's midriff with her finger. The figure just stood there. She felt kind of – well, not like anything really. Kakko prodded harder and stepped on her toe for good measure. "You enjoying that?" she asked.

"Yeah. Enjoying that," parroted the girl.

"OK, enough is enough. Don't abuse the programme," hissed Tam worriedly.

"We rather stand out in these clothes," said Jalli. "We

19

won't be difficult to spot." Just as she said it, an excited couple bounded over to them. They were in their early forties but Jalli recognised them instantly. "Sass, Matt?" she said.

"Yes," said Sass. "Fancy you coming back now! So great to see you."

"We were just indulging in some nostalgia with this MIVRE, but it is not like we remembered it. Guess we've grown up a bit. But it is so wonderful to see you!" Matt grasped Jack's arm. It was evident that he was blind. Matt stuttered, "Let's… let's… get out of here."

"Sorry, I can't see," Jack explained, "you'll have to guide me."

"How long have you…?" asked Matt.

"Not been able to see? Oh, decades. I'm quite used to it now. It's been so long I haven't ever seen my eldest. Let me introduce you. Matt, this is Kakko."

"Hi," said Kakko.

"Wow. You look the same age as your mother when she saved us all those years ago."

"Older," said Jalli. "I was only seventeen then. Kakko's twenty."

"My mum saved you?"

"Absolutely. We would have been taken over by space pirates if it weren't for her. She's a legend aboard this ship."

"My mum, a legend?"

"She will be forever remembered in the annals of our new world. Hasn't she told you?"

"She said something about being the only person unaffected by some stunner thing, and had to act alone."

"Indeed. She was extremely brave… and wise."

"Dad told us that, but he's prejudiced," smiled Kakko. Tam laughed at her.

"So now you know where you get it from, Kakko," said her father.

"Yeah, now I know where I get it from," repeated Kakko, distant in thought, as if she were one of the virtual reality people. Then, gathering herself back to the present, she said, "This is Tam, my boyfriend."

"Pleased to meet you." Matt took his arm. "And this is my wife, Sass."

Sass hugged Kakko. "Hi. And this is your little girl?"

"No-o! This is my little sister, Mahsnyeka – 'Yeka' for short."

"Wow, Jalli," said Sass. "How many children have you got?"

"Four. I have Kakko here, then two boys – Shaun coming up to eighteen and Bandi who is just sixteen – and Yeka, here, is one. What about you?"

"Two. One of each. Asida is fifteen and her brother Kwes is thirteen. You will meet them. Come, let's take some tea."

Matt and Sass led their five guests through the changing facilities to a smart apartment some floors below. The *MEV Great Marton* hadn't changed much. It had been kept as clean and bright as the day it had been made – the residents of the emigration village understood the importance of cleanliness in what was, after all, a restricted world, despite the large proportions of the vessel.

"Sit down." Sass showed them to a comfortable sofa that was showing the signs of age, but which had been carefully repaired. "Asida and Kwes are in class at the moment. They will be back in an hour."

Tam looked out of the window that extended down the side of the apartment.

"That's some planet," said Tam.

"Indeed. Its name is Earth Three… until we can think of something else. We're in the Tatania system."

"This is the planet you have been aiming for?"

21

"Yes, for forty-four years."

"You came aboard as babies?"

"We have known nothing else. Now we have arrived and, well, it's quite daunting to say the least…"

"We have established a base," explained Matt. "Those who have been down have said everything is good. But there is no intelligent life – never has been."

"That was the point, wasn't it?" said Jack.

"Yes. We were to colonise it. But that's not easy. We've been cosseted on this MEV all our lives. There, there is no construction – and plenty of things we just don't begin to understand."

"Like what?" asked Kakko.

"Moving air and flowing water. Dirt – "

"How can it be dirty if no-one has ever lived there?" asked Kakko, who never associated anything outside in nature as really *dirty* – for her, *dirt* was the mess humans left behind them.

"Perhaps you mean soil," suggested Jalli.

"Probably – I don't know what 'soil' really looks and feels like. In this case if it's the planet's surface, some of it is hard and rough, some is soft and made of rotted plant material."

"Yes. That's rock and soil," said Jack. "Of course, you have always grown your food using hydroculture."

"Correct. You remember well… We've decided that a few people at a time should go down and build a village, and discover how to live on the planet," explained Sass. "Each would stay just six months and then return. The plan is that, over the years, more and more will stay longer until we can develop as many things on the planet as we have on the MEV."

"A great idea," said Tam.

"The thing is, we're due to go next," said Matt nervously, "we were having a last fling in the MIVRE."

"The Multi-sensual, Interactive, Virtual Reality Experience," said Jalli, pulling Yeka's arms from strangling her and dancing her on her knee. Yeka had become rather clingy in this strange place with its odd smells.

"You remember well. But the thing is that this planet is not like the MIVRE."

"The mud on your feet doesn't just disappear when you turn off the programme," said Kakko. "Your MIVRE will seem tame once you have experienced a real planet."

"Don't scare them," said Jack. "I guess you're going to have to be really brave doing something we don't think twice about."

"Will you come with us?" asked Matt. "A new planet is nothing to you... I mean in comparison, is it?"

"I guess not. Of course we'll come with you," said Jalli.

"I think little miss here," said Jack, "would probably be happier there. She's used to the outdoors."

"There is nothing like the wind on your face," mused Jalli. "It's, like, a reminder of the presence of God. Sometimes She can be rough and demanding, but mostly She's gentle and kind."

"But She's always fresh," added Tam, "alive and invigorating."

"I believe we have been invited here today by the Creator precisely to go with you and help you over this hurdle," reasoned Jack. "I hope I shan't be in the way. It's when I'm not at home that not seeing where to go is at its hardest, so I can sympathise with you on this."

"Jack, you can never be in the way," assured his wife. "Besides, the gate wouldn't have been there for you if you weren't meant to come."

"Agreed."

★ ★ ★

23

Asida and Kwes were really excited to see them. They had been looking forward to the adventure. Missing school for six months was a bonus. It was like an extended holiday. It wouldn't be for forever, so they wouldn't get too far behind. But to have people to accompany them who knew all about how to live on a planet mitigated any anxiety they might have had. They took to Kakko and Tam immediately, and Yeka became Kwes's delight, as she played with her constantly. Yeka returned the interest, enjoying the attention.

That evening, the family were introduced to the MEV community. There was a new commander of course, Commander Juliet being long since retired. An apartment was made ready for them, and they quickly took to their new beds as they prepared themselves for the action that lay ahead.

★ ★ ★

Emerging from the shuttle onto the planet's surface was a massive deal for Matt, Sass, Asida Kwes and the others. They were standing on a rough beach between some trees and an ocean. Yeka reached forward to be put down, then turned to Kakko and said, "Bool."

"'Bool'…? Oh, you mean 'ball'." Almost from her first step, Kakko had encouraged her little sister to kick a ball. Yeka was being given a head start in the skills of football. "Sorry," said Kakko, "we haven't brought one."

The child began to pout a little but quickly spotted a beautiful, coloured rock. She trotted over to it and attempted to lift it. It was, of course, far too heavy for her, but Tam went over and helped her explore it.

"This is such a beautiful place," said Jalli, looking up from her children to take in a large bay bordered on one side by high cliffs made from the same bright-red stone as the rock that Yeka was now stroking. The rock was smooth and shiny – its irregular shape rounded by the action of the sea. Behind them was a stand of high trees topped with long leaves – not unlike giant banana plants from Earth One that Kakko had seen pictures of. But they weren't bananas, they were quite different in other respects. Behind these, there seemed to be a jungle of green undergrowth. Several metres along the beach, however, the undergrowth parted and a team of rather dishevelled, robed figures emerged. They were dressed in the same sort of attire that Matt, Sass and everyone else was wearing.

"Hello, there! So glad to see you," shouted the leading man.

"The first advance party," explained Sass to Jalli. "They were all volunteers. Half are due to return to the Village on the shuttle."

"Hi," shouted Matt. "So, all is good?"

"You *could* say that. It gets a bit easier after a bit. Hard work, of course, as you'll find out."

"But worth the effort?"

The man hesitated, then said, "The sunsets are beautiful."

"How's the agriculture going?"

"Hard on the hands. I'm not sure how much has germinated. You'll see for yourself."

"Er… Do you remember Jalli and Jack? They have come to join us."

"Jalli? Jalli the girl from God who saved the day?!"

"The very lady. She and Jack have returned together with two of their children and Tam, the boyfriend."

The planet dwellers crowded around. This was so exciting.

"They have been sent in answer to prayer," declared one of the men.

"Indeed," said Sass. "Look, the child has taken to this place straightaway!"

Yeka was at the seaside. She was stamping in the surf, sifting through the pebbles and dangling a colourful length of seaweed. Kakko had tied up her robes around her waist and was standing in the shallow water playing with her sister. Tam was explaining to Jack what could be seen.

"How many suns?"

"One. At least only one visible."

"It's warm, even in the shade. About 33°C, I would guess. Tropical?"

"Not exactly. It could be a temperate summer. The vegetation is kind of reminiscent of Joh. Different, but similar. Yeka seems totally at home."

Indeed, she was. The *Great Marton* people were gathering to watch her and Kakko – inspired by the immediate, innocent acceptance of this strange world.

"Where are you encamped?" asked Matt, who, probably by virtue of introducing the Smiths, appeared to be emerging as a leader of the new party.

The group led them off the beach into a clearing they had made in the scrub. Some of the trees they had cut down were arranged as frames for plastic awnings to form makeshift houses. Tam examined the timber. It was medium weight with growth rings. "Seasonal growth," he announced, "This place has a seasonal climate, not unlike Earth One, I would guess. A seasonal year on Earth One is exactly a standard year isn't it, Jack?"

"Exactly. Earth One is the planet that determined the length of a standard year."

"Well, as these trees are medium weight, from the distance between the rings, I guess the growing season is less than a standard year."

"That would make agriculture pretty straightforward," reflected Kakko.

"Look," said Jalli, "up there. See, a nest of flying insects. Could be pollinators."

"Yes," explained one of the grubby planet dwellers, "they attack those big flowers and even these little ones. But they don't bother us."

"Not sweet-smelling enough," said Kakko in a matter-of-fact voice. She had become aware these people were not as clean as they might be. They were not managing as well as she would have done in the bush. After all, there was not just the sea, but a small stream. Then, she added, noticing that the man had taken it personally, "The bees – they smell the nectar in the flowers."

"Ah, yes!" affirmed Matt. "After decades of artificial pollination in the hydro-halls of the MEV, we don't have to worry about that here. Nor the complicated artificial nutrient recycling we have got used to – here, it just happens in this 'soil'." He bent down with authority, gathered a clump of sand and squeezed it as if he was an old hand. With Jack, Jalli, Kakko, Tam and this brave little girl just beginning to walk, he felt emboldened. He was with people who were not fazed by the newness of it all.

The Johians, however, were not as unfazed as they seemed. But they sensed that they needed to keep strong for their hosts. Jalli and Jack conveyed that in their outward confidence, a signal that Kakko and Tam picked up on straightaway. Yeka, however, simply thought she was at the seaside. New experiences for young children are quickly absorbed in the standard way – most things are new to them. They feel their world is a safe place as long as their family are around them. Besides, some of the *Great Marton* women had started making a fuss of her and she liked to be played with. There is nothing like a baby to break the ice with new acquaintances.

They were soon unloading the shuttle. The newcomers were shown to frames built for them and new awning sheets were brought from the shuttle, and everyone joined in to lift them into place. Everything smelt new and fresh. The sap from the trees was quite pungent. As they set up their beds in this place, Jalli was suddenly aware of a joy inside her. This place was clean, bright and fresh. The oxygen levels were definitely good – but not too high – and the gravity ever so slightly less than on Joh.

"This is a beautiful place," she said.

"I can sense its beauty. If it looks as beautiful as it smells, then you could write a poem about it."

"*You* could. I'm not good at words," remarked Kakko, "but I like it here. You can see these people miss the ship, though. I mean there is absolutely no technology down here except a generator and a few tools. It would drive me mad after a bit."

"They miss the washing machines, that's for certain," said Tam.

"Why do they wear these clothes here? They're so... so... just not sensible," reflected Jalli.

"I wish I had my trousers," said Kakko.

"We could make some... I mean some better-suited clothes. That could be Tam's job while Kakko and I think about the agriculture," suggested Jalli.

"And you could also organise some walls to these houses. If there is going to be a winter, they'll need more than tents," added Kakko.

"But I'm not a builder – or a tailor," remonstrated Tam.

"You mean, you haven't done any building yourself... yet. But you have an advantage over these folk. You've seen buildings on Joh and, besides, you're pretty good at DIY. These folk have only ever seen pictures of houses or virtual ones on the MIVRE. Why don't you start with turf blocks between these timbers."

"They could certainly cut some better joints than they've

got. A gale will blow these things apart," said Tam, studying the frames.

"See, you've already begun to know where to start."

"But *I* shall be quite useless, I'm afraid," said Jack.

"Nonsense," barked Kakko. "You can look after Yeka."

"I can. But wouldn't we have been better without her, though? I mean, she'll just get in the way."

"Quite the opposite," said Jalli. "I've been watching the impression she's already made. You know, the Creator's very clever. As a very small child, Yeka's set an example of how to deal with things that are new and different. She's been the centre of attention. She's brought a sense of... how might you describe it?"

"Confident normality," suggested Tam.

"Precisely," said Jalli.

That evening, after staring at the star-studded sky, tracing the plane of the Milky Way galaxy and identifying the cluster of stars at its centre, their hosts pointed out landmark stars that lay on this side of it.

"That red one is Betelgeuse," pointed Sass. "We have to keep an eye on that because our astronomers tell us it could explode into a supernova at any time. We're safer on a planet surface if it does."

"And that bright one there," indicated Tam, "which is that?"

"That's Shedar. It's a double star – much nearer to us than Betelgeuse, on the limit of our capacity to travel with current technology."

"They're working on a fourth-generation intrahelical engine," said Kakko. "That would make it well within range."

"I can imagine a day when what took us fifty years will be reduced to a year or two," said Sass, "but probably not in our lifetime."

"Where's Andromeda Galaxy?" asked Jalli wistfully.

"Andromeda Galaxy? You can see it quite clearly... there, just at about eleven o'clock from Shedar. It's beautiful through a telescope... That's where your home world is, isn't it?"

"It is. I can't see it from Joh. At least, I don't think I can. To tell the truth, unlike you, because we travel using the white gates we really don't have any idea where in the universe we are – except I do know Planet Raika is in the Jallaxa system in what Earth One people call the Andromeda Galaxy."

"The Andromeda Galaxy is 2.5 million light years away. That means what you're seeing is two and a half million years in the past – rather a bit before you were born."

"I know. But if you can see it, then it still, kind of, feels like you have got a little nearer to your home world."

"Do you miss your planet?"

"Yes and no. Mostly, no. We've been back once. When I had been there a couple of days I got anxious not to get stuck there, so that means it's not really home anymore... Anyway, I don't have any living relative there."

"None at all?"

"No. All I had, since I was three, was Grandma. And now, my whole family are Jack and the children." Jalli gave a potted history.

"You know," said Sass, "you really are brave."

"She is," agreed Jack. "This is very local for me. I mean, the Sun system is on the same side of the galaxy."

"Oh yes, you can see it. You need a telescope, unless you've got really good eyes. It's in that group of stars..." said Matt, pointing at about thirty degrees above the horizon. "There, in the constellation of – "

"Just tell me," said Jack.

"Aah! Sorry, Jack. I forgot you couldn't see it – even with a telescope."

"No matter… I would think it would look like any other yellow star."

"Yes, nothing distinctive about it. It's the history that's important."

"Where's Earth Two, your home planet?" asked Kakko.

"It belongs to that bright star over to the left. We've radioed our news. We'll update it tomorrow. It'll take just under ten years to arrive."

"What will you tell them?"

"Why, all about *you,* of course. 'Jallaxanya the brave' is celebrated on Earth Two, too… especially in the Project Tatania headquarters."

"I'm flattered," said Jalli. "I wasn't brave. I just did what I thought I could do. After all, if I hadn't have acted, I would have been detected soon enough."

"But you still did it. And, without it, we would have all been prisoners, or worse."

"They're right, Mum. You're the heroine. You'll just have to accept it and stop trying to be so modest," put in Kakko.

Jalli was about to protest again when Jack squeezed her hand. "You rescued me, too," he said.

"It could have been worse than being prisoners," said Tam. "Do you remember the Thenits?" He told the story of the space cruiser, *Tal,* and her Sponron commanders.

"They wouldn't let me on the *Tal* at all," protested Kakko. "It was all left to the boys."

"We were not entirely useless," laughed Tam.

"Actually, though," she explained, "Tam can be quite a hero. Without him, I would have been rotting on a cliff ledge."

At the conclusion of that tale, their guests were enraptured. "You must write all your adventures down," they declared, "the 'White Gates Adventures'."

"One day… perhaps," smiled Jalli. "What do they call you

intrepid people… I mean, on your home planet. The 'Earth-three-ians' or something?"

"They call us 'the Tatanians' after Project Titania."

"That sounds good," said Jack.

"You're an Earthling, aren't you?"

"I was once. But when we got settled at White Gates Cottage, we have both become Johians – like our children."

"That's us," said Sass. "No going back. We come from Earth Two, but from the moment we left we became Tatanian. I guess, we've arrived on our home planet."

★ ★ ★

That night, the travellers lay on inflatable mattresses under blankets all brought from the stores of the *Great Marton*. Sleep did not come easily, except to Yeka.

"I can't help thinking I'm not the right guy for making houses and sewing clothes," sighed Tam. "If the Creator wanted someone to do that, He could have come up with a builder or a tailor."

"Maybe She sent us just because we are used to white gates?" suggested Kakko.

"Or something we don't know of yet," reasoned Jack. "Your mum was exactly the right person to resist the Wanulkan pirates, despite her not having any experience with a MEV from Earth Two."

"That's what's worrying me," said Jalli. "I have this awful feeling – a premonition – that something untoward is going to happen."

"Great," clucked Kakko, "I can't wait… Bring it on!"

4

T am was up with the birds, or whatever they were. As soon
as the first rays of sunlight glimmered in the sky behind
the camp, there was a cacophony of trilling and whooping.
It was amazing just how much noise the creatures were
making – presumably staking their claims for the activities of
the coming day. He stretched his arms high and breathed the
pure air into his sleepy lungs. Then he walked down to sit
on the beach and watched the morning stars gradually fade.
The ones they had talked about the previous evening, which
included the home worlds of Jack and Jalli, had long since set.

Tam looked across the bay to the far headland. Its distinctive
shape became clear against a brightening sky. Before the
darkness had completely gone, though, he thought he saw a
tiny, flickering light flare up at its base. He was just telling
himself that he had imagined it, when it came again, and this
time did not completely disappear. Kakko came to join him.

"What're you studying?"

"There, can you see it? A flickering glow… towards the
end of that promontory." But as he said it, Tatania's bright rays
struck the headland and bathed it in bright, yellow morning
light.

"What do you think it was?"

"I was just asking myself that… it was, like, someone just
lit a fire."

"No-one's ever lit a fire in this camp. They cook on that
solar-powered unit they that brought from the MEV."

"I know, it feels strange… I mean, camping with electrical gadgets. Whoever heard of a camp without a fire?"

"I guess they've never ever lit a proper fire. You wouldn't light a proper fire on a spacecraft – even in a MIVRE."

"Do you think *we* should light one?"

"Sure. Have you got any matches?" he joked.

"What do you think?"

"It won't be difficult, though. They have lenses. As soon as the sun's over the hill, I'll have a go… By the way, I'm not doing any sewing –"

"Good morning, you two." Jalli had spotted them and had come across with a couple of steaming mugs.

"I like the service," said her daughter, as she took a mug, and tasted it. "What's in it?"

"A kind of tea. It's new to me… Tam, I've been thinking… about the trousers. They've got piles of stuff they use on the MIVRE and they're bound to have tailors aboard."

"I was thinking the same thing. I don't feel I'm here to sew."

"But these robes are useless," stated Kakko. "I'd be better in just my undies."

"I know. We'll explain and order some easier stuff to wear," said Jalli.

"I'm all for the undies," laughed Tam.

"You would be," sighed Kakko with mock disgust, "but not for the right –"

"Smoke!" exclaimed Tam.

"What?" said Jalli, bemused.

"There," Tam pointed. "On the headland."

"Got it," said Kakko excitedly, "you were right."

"Right about what?" asked Jalli.

"Tam thought he could see a fire… before the sun shone on the place."

"And where there's fire," said Jalli, "there's generally –"

"People!" Kakko asserted. "Where's Dad?"

"Washing Yeka in the stream."

They made their way to the place where Jalli had left Jack with Yeka. She was busy playing in the shallow water. It was hard to decide which of them was the wettest.

"Jack," called Jalli. Yeka came splashing over to her mother, reaching out wet arms. Jalli found a towel and caught up her little daughter. "Jack," she said quietly, because they were now in the company of increasing numbers of Tatanians, "we've spotted smoke from the headland over the bay. We're not alone. I knew there was more to this than we saw yesterday."

"That certainly puts a new light on why we're here."

"What do we do?" asked Kakko, who was now taking a turn at drying her sister's feet.

"We'll have a word with Matt and Sass," replied Jack with a lightness in his voice. He did not want to spread consternation. He was aware that Kakko's face was one that betrayed all her emotions.

The breakfast was good, but was all from the supplies brought from the MEV. Jack touched Jalli's hand and asked Tam about the smoke.

"It's just a faint wisp now, but it's still there."

"Right." He then called to Sass, whom he had detected had just walked past him.

She turned. "Yes?"

"My family have seen something. Explain, Tam."

Tam explained about the fire and the smoke.

"So that means that almost certainly you are not the only intelligent beings on this planet… indeed, on this short piece of coast," said Jack.

"But our surveys showed it as uninhabited!"

"Intelligent life need not mean a developed civilisation.

Apart from the awnings being blue, would you be detectable from a planetary survey of the type you undertook? Suppose your houses had roofs made of leaves, or even turf, and you did not use electricity?"

"You're right. We wouldn't have picked that up. What do you suggest we do?" asked Sass.

"Call the people together. Let them see the smoke on the headland. Then, put that question to them."

Half an hour later, there was a group meeting. Those getting ready to leave on the shuttle had left their preparations for departure. There was consternation. Some immediately suggested they give up all thoughts of establishing a colony. They knew there were enough aboard the MEV who were disturbed by the challenge as it was. The knowledge that they would have to deal with – maybe even fend off – other intelligent beings would be one step too far. Matt appealed to the Johians. He felt sure that it was no coincidence that the Creator had brought them to them at that moment.

The official leader of the colony, properly called the Deputy Commander of Planetary Operations or DCPO, now spoke up.

"What would you suggest?" he asked them.

"Don't do anything without praying first," said Jalli quietly. "The Creator is just as powerful here as anywhere in the universe."

"Good thinking," said Sass.

As they prayed, Matt became aware that the Creator was calling them to act.

"I think," said Matt, "that we should attempt to contact these people. They may already know we are here. They could easily have seen the shuttle and the MEV is very visible in the night sky."

"The *Great Marton* will be over the horizon in an hour. We should ask the supreme commander," said the DCPO.

"Agreed," affirmed Matt. "But she's bound to ask us what we think we should do?"

"And she's not going to abandon the mission," said another. "She has been adamant all along that we should not bottle out. Fifty years ago, when we began, we were warned that this is how we would feel. They told us we would be completely 'institutionalised', or words to that effect."

"But they didn't anticipate any other intelligent life form," said one of the other men.

"No. But because something is intelligent, it doesn't necessarily mean that it is hostile..." spoke up Sass.

"I think you should light a fire of your own," said Kakko decisively. "A big one – with loads of smoke. Let them know you know they are here, and that you want to communicate. If they were going to be hostile, I think you would have been attacked by now."

"Do we have the technology here to light such a fire?" asked a member of the group.

"Of course," said a chemist from the first party. "We have the star. All we need is a lens if we use the right kind of material... I would love to light a fire – a great big one. Something much more impressive than the little flames we use in the lab," he added with childish enthusiasm.

"Yeah," said Kakko, "there's lots you can do here that you could never do on a spaceship – even one as big as a village."

"So, we light a fire. Then what?" asked Matt.

"Then we wait and see if, whoever it is, comes and investigates. If we make it a really smoky fire we're deliberately announcing our presence," said Kakko.

"And if no-one comes?" asked Sass.

"We make smoke signals with a blanket." Kakko demonstrated while everyone looked on, fascinated.

"If they still don't come, then we go and visit them,"

said Jalli. "It won't be so difficult because it is beach a lot of the way."

"I'm for making that suggestion to the supreme commander," said Matt.

"What about the rest of you?" asked the DCPO.

"It's a yes from me," said Sass.

"And us," chimed in Asida and Kwes. This whole planet thing for them was feeling cool.

"What if they don't want us here?" asked one of the first party.

"Then we leave… and find some other place to set up camp," said the DCPO. "We don't argue. We have no right to argue because they were here first. But, if you ask me, this place is big and empty enough for the both of us. Even when the second MEV arrives, there'll not be more than a thousand of us."

"I'm for it," said another. "We have a choice. We can either just pack up and go, or give this a try."

"What if they're violent?"

"It's unlikely. They'll probably be more nervous of us than we of them. In any case, we can defend ourselves long enough to get away. We have the shuttle here… I say we put this to a vote."

The company were hesitant at first, but, in the end, the confidence of their visitors inspired a near unanimous verdict. If a mother was sure enough to risk her little one-year-old – and especially a mother held in so much awe – then it must be the right thing to do. They couldn't, of course, see into Jalli's mind and heart. Her trust was based on her relationship with the Creator – but He had an annoying habit of testing it on too regular a basis. Jalli was praying hard, but silently.

The supreme commander was solidly of the opinion that the contact should be made. She was in no mood to abandon the venture at the first hurdle. Of course, *she* was safely aboard the *Great Marton*.

Remembering their experience on the clifftop of Johnson's island over two decades before, Jalli found some likely kindling, wood chips, brush and large green leaves. She ordered the company to collect a pile of these last two, while the scientist set up an apparatus for lighting the fire. He found a large, spare lens from a refracting telescope and a mount. Jalli built a little mound of dry pebbles as far down the beach as she could go, without getting the base of the fire wet. She then asked the scientist to warm up her 'nest' with his apparatus before she put some dry leaves and twigs under the concentrated heat of the sun. It took three goes trying different materials. The third flared up quickly, and Jalli concluded that those twigs probably had an oily sap. She placed more of the same wood across the small flames like spokes. Very soon they had quite a blaze, and when she was satisfied that it was big enough, they began putting on the brush and, finally, the leaves. The smoke was dense, yellow and acrid. Even the biochemist stood well back, retreating with his lens into the shade.

"If they don't see that, they're blind!" declared Kakko.

"Even if they are, they'll soon smell it," laughed Jack as he tripped and fell backwards, retreating from the fumes. Jalli picked him up and led him to safety. "You've done a good job there, Jalli," he affirmed.

"No point in doing things half-heartedly," she shouted above the shrieks of the Tatanians. The older ones were horrified, the younger ones dancing with excitement.

"None at all," agreed Jack. "What with the smoke, the smell and the noise, I think we have definitely drawn attention to ourselves."

During the next three hours, Tam took some of the younger Tatanians into the sea looking for fish, or whatever it was that might live there. He fashioned a hook and a lure and, using a line created for the purpose and imported from Earth Two (but which the Tatanians hadn't yet quite worked out how to use properly), he caught a sea creature. It was fish-like, but rather ugly-looking. Now, the thing was, was it good to eat? However, inspired by his success, the youngsters were soon learning to fish, too. Whether or not a person could end up eating these creatures, they were fun to catch. The second and third to fall for the lure were not so ugly as the first. The fourth was definitely beautiful with many colours. Tam called it a rainbow fish.

Kakko was teaching some of the women how to make dough twists. She took some of the bread dough that they had prepared for the solar ovens and twisted it around a stick peeled of its bark. She had dared to lick the stick carefully to see if it tasted OK. It was sweet, so unlikely to be poisonous. Then she took a brand from the fire that was now not so smoky and lit a new fire without the brush. The bread dough baked and, when it came away from the stick, she quickly slid it off onto a large leaf. As soon as it was cool enough, she picked it up and bit off the end. Delicious. There is something about cooking over an open fire that gives a flavour you can never get in an electric oven. She soon had half a dozen Tatanians crowded around the fire with sticks and dough. Everyone wanted to taste this new open-air food.

In the afternoon, Yeka was asleep. She had had a joyous morning playing on the beach. They had all had a good lunch. Then, one of the group came running up the pebbles.

"Beings," he yelled, "in boats."

Halfway across the bay, there were three small boats making a slow progress in their direction. They were near enough for the Tatanians to make out that each boat contained six or more of some sort of creature that knew how to handle a paddle. The men came forward into full view, while the women kept the children hidden at the back of the beach, all except Kakko and Jalli who were alongside the men.

As the three craft came closer, Tam said, "I think I recognise these people. They're –"

"Sponrons," declared Kakko.

"So, that is why we've been called," said Jalli calmly.

"Yep. Seems like it," Kakko concurred. "Tam, can you remember any Sponron?"

"I… I think so. It's been a while."

"Something like: *Gango es,* something …" volunteered Kakko.

"*Ganuigo, es mohindanes,*" said Tam.

"Which means?" asked Jalli.

"Hello, pleased to meet you."

"Well, that should do the trick."

"And the reply is: '*An ut mohindanan*' – 'I'm pleased to meet you, too'. And: '*Klumativan, Tam*'"

"'Your name is, Tam'?"

"Correct. '*Klumativan, Tam* – *klumatives, Jalli*'. 'I'm called, Tam – you're called Jalli'… Never imagined I'd ever use it again after we left One and his friends back in their home world."

"It's always useful learning a language. You never know when you might need it. What else can you say?"

"Not much. '*Dunanan. Dunanes?*' 'I'm hungry. Are you hungry?'"

"Well, I think you have mastered all the main things of life for a first meeting," said Jalli. "What about you, Kakko?"

"I've forgotten. I'm not clever like Tam."

"You are clever," protested Tam. "I couldn't begin with an engine like you."

"I get by. It's mostly bluff, though. Right now, I don't feel clever at all."

Jalli took note of her daughter's newly revealed apparent honesty. But she knew it wasn't true. Kakko was far more talented than she admitted to herself. She was able to think and act fast, and that was a gift if used wisely. She also had a true understanding of what was right and what was wrong, which is the key to integrity. And a person with integrity has the potential of being a great one, wherever she may find herself.

"Matt," spoke up Jalli. "We know this race. We have had contact with them on our world. Tam can say a few words."

The Sponrons pulled their boats up onto the beach about a hundred metres away. There were eighteen of them, Kakko counted. They were both male and female. They appeared to be armed with spears – fishing spears, Jack explained later (he had come across them when he was a boy on Earth One). The Sponrons walked steadily towards them, and then stopped when they were twenty metres away. Their spindly bodies were dressed in scanty, rough clothing made from tree materials, and their flat faces showed expressions of fear.

5

The male Sponrons stood slightly shorter than the average human and were probably half the weight. They would be no match in a fight. You could see they were nervous.

Tam spoke first. He wanted to dispel their fear. *"Ganuigo, es mohindanes,"* he said as confidently as he could muster.

It was as if the Sponrons had been hit by an invisible wave; their former stiffness began to dissolve. To hear their own language spoken by a stocky alien was the last thing they expected to hear.

To Tam's relief, one of the Sponrons replied. *"Udi ut mohindanem. Tian sent es."*

"Ut, tian es," replied Tam. It was coming back to him now, *'tian'* – 'peace' and *'tian sent es'* – 'peace be with you'. Tam stepped forward, pulling Kakko with him.

"Klumativan, Tam. Klumativa, Kakko." Kakko smiled as nicely as she could.

"I'm sorry, I can't remember much of your language," she said in Johian, but they seemed to understand. The Creator was probably providing a translation, just as She was for the communications with the Tatanians, and had done for Jack and Jalli from the start. But simultaneous translation or not, there is nothing to replace someone actually articulating another's home language. It builds immediate connections like none other. Introductions were soon made all round and Matt explained in a few words how they had come to be on the planet. He gestured towards the shuttle.

"We know," said a man that called himself Indit. "We saw your craft. We did not come because we were… But then you make smoke. That is a signal. We could not stay away – we had to make contact."

"*Dunanes?*" asked Kakko. She led the Sponrons to the camp. They relaxed totally when they saw the children. Treats from the shuttle were laid before them. The big eyes in the flat Sponron faces grew bigger still. It soon became evident that the Sponrons were not thriving.

All that morning, the Tatanians listened to the Sponrons' story. They had been the crew of a space cruiser that had malfunctioned. The engines had gone into overdrive – a facility that was only meant to last a few seconds. It appeared to have been similar to the one that Jalli had once operated aboard the *MEV Great Marton*. But instead of seconds, theirs had jammed and endured for hours, before the fuel – the helicates – was almost totally consumed and the engine was damaged beyond anything they could repair in space. Now virtually drifting – albeit at pace – all they had was ten per cent of main engine power. To add to their difficulties, they had travelled tens of light years off-course, and had no idea how they were going to continue. Unlike the MEV, they had not the capacity to grow enough food for indefinite existence.

They had sent a speed-of-light message in the direction of Ramal, their home world in the Medlam system. But the message was going to take around fifteen light years to arrive. Observing the nearest star to them, they spotted several planets. One of them seemed to be a good size for life and was in the Goldilocks zone. They decided it was their only hope. They struggled towards it and, eventually arriving in orbit, scanned its surface, and were delighted to discover a suitable atmosphere, seas and land with vegetation. They did not identify any signs of a civilisation, and they took the decision to try and land. They were only fifty in number and elected to stay together. Once they had left their mothership, there would be no going back – all they had were escape pods fitted with landing engines. Once on the surface, they could not take off again.

They had landed in the forests in five pods on the other side of the headland three summers ago. They had eaten all they brought with them after one year, but had learned to fish and had experimented with seeds, fruits and roots. They were fortunate to have got away with only a few bouts of sickness and diarrhoea, because they had some chemical testing kits. Indit pointed to one of the fish Tam and his party had caught.

"Do not eat that one. The colourful one is not good to eat… This one, though," he touched the ugly one with his spear, "is very good to eat."

"Thank you," said Tam. "We'll cook it."

"We'll show you the best way," said Indit.

It emerged that when the Sponrons noticed the *MEV Great Marton* approach and orbit the planet, they had first thought it might be a rescue mission.

"We no longer have radio. The batteries cannot be recharged. We just have to wait."

When they had seen that no attempt was made to contact them, and they realised the craft was not Sponron, they knew that the new arrivals were not meant for them. But they still had hope.

Sass explained, "We have come to stay. I'm not sure we can afford a round trip to your planet." She described how they were there to begin a new outpost. In ten years' time, they expected a second MEV to advance the colony.

"How do you know how to speak Sponron?" they asked Tam and Kakko. The next hour was spent telling them about Planet Joh's encounter with the *Tal*.

It turned out that one of the Sponrons thought he knew the commander of the *Starship Zon,* but news of the capture of the *Talifinbolindit* and the Thenits had not reached them. They were disturbed to learn of the way the Sponron commanders had behaved. They hoped the humans did not see their behaviour as typical of their species.

"No," said Kakko fervently. "I reckon us humans are probably much worse. I fear the human race displays many of the lowest traits of any species. Some of *us* are very bad indeed."

The Sponron commander looked a little alarmed.

"But not *all* of us... most of the time," continued Kakko.

Jalli could see a little fear rising again in the Sponron.

"What is your name?" she asked.

"Me? I'm Zorof."

"Mr. Zorof, you need fear nothing from us. Human beings are a mixture of traits, but those of us, who welcome the Creator to come and dwell in our hearts, have the hatred and selfishness replaced with love and generosity. Pray for us that we continue with Her always. You will be safe with any of the people here."

Soon, they were sitting together on the beach sharing the food. Tam and Kakko sat beside each other.

"I wish it were true that all those who *say* they let God in, actually *do*," whispered Kakko. "Some of the most terrible things of all on Planet Earth One have been done in the name of God."

"I know, Kakko, but we're not going to hurt these people, are we? And it's unlikely these Sponrons are going to meet anyone else that will take advantage of them out here – at least, not before they can learn something of what it means for us to be human. So, let's not scare them."

"You're right. The people of the *Great Marton* are not

exactly like the Spanish Conquistadors that Dad told us about. Though, apparently the sailor from the village called Marton in England, Captain Cook, 'lost it' on his last expedition. He became belligerent and ended up being killed by the natives."

"I don't see Matt doing that, do you? Or that deputy commander."

"Nah… Dad says *I've* got some of his qualities, so I must make sure I don't leave God out."

"Whose qualities?"

"Captain Cook's."

"I don't suppose Captain Cook had a partner with him on his voyages?"

"Not on his voyages. He was married with six children. They all lived in London in England."

"There you go. Not only have you your Creator with you, you have me. So, you're perfectly safe," teased Tam.

"Not if you go on like that. I might start with you."

"You started a long time ago. I just thrive on it."

"OK. Stop showing off."

"Why not? I just happen to have the most wonderful woman in the universe as my girlfriend."

"Good. Don't forget it."

"Don't worry, I shan't."

"OK, you two lovebirds." It was Jalli. "It's time to learn how to cook that ugly fish you caught."

The Sponrons stayed the night, sleeping on the beach for the few hours that remained after they called a halt to the sharing in the small hours.

At first light, it was time for the Sponrons to go home. Smoke signals had been sent to indicate that all was well, but they were aware that those that remained in the Sponron village would be anxious for them. It was agreed half a dozen Tatanians would return with them and help explain things. The

Sponrons were naturally keen to take Tam, Kakko, Jack and Jalli, but Jalli suggested they took only Tam or Kakko. After all, they were temporary visitors. But she did understand that they had a role to play. In the end, along with several Tatanians nominated by the DCPO, Jalli and Jack were chosen. Jalli sat her daughter on her knee. What was needed for this was wisdom and experience, and the Tatanians attributed this, along with courage and resourcefulness, to their long-standing heroes.

★ ★ ★

Within a few days, it was agreed that the communities would benefit from working closely together. The Sponrons had their years of experience in settling on the planet, while the humans had all the resources of a self-sustaining MEV in orbit, and the advantages of interplanetary communications. The Sponrons no longer felt so much in need of being rescued, because they had ceased to be isolated, and they had access to luxuries they could not have provided for themselves. Furthermore, these humans had come to stay. They agreed the planet should be called Enklon, which was what the Sponrons called it. In their language, it meant: 'surprise haven'. The sun star, for which the Sponrons did not have a specific name, was to retain its human name of Tatania. Sponrons and humans alike living on Enklon would be known as Tatanians, the interplanetary name already used in communications with Earth Two.

The human Tatanians were to remove their camp, and establish a new one next door to the Sponron village. A school was to be founded where each person would learn the other's language, and a training programme for the humans in the life skills needed on Enklon would be set up. Teachers for the children from both communities were to work side by side in language, maths, the sciences and history. Spirituality was a key element in the relationship. It consisted of a programme of inner explorations and testimonies to the encounters they had had with the Creator of whatever name. Both the Sponrons and humans believed that God, however revealed, was the Creator of life, of love and of peace.

The story of the hijacking of the *Tal* was an embarrassment to the Sponrons, until Jack and Jalli told of the evils they had come across on Raika, while Kakko was vociferous in her condemnation of what she experienced on Earth One. Perhaps all races throughout the universe were subject to the powers of darkness. "Intelligent beings," said Jack, "have need of a relationship with God. Without it, hope is much harder to find. I speak from experience. I wouldn't want you to meet the boy I was." Even now the thought of his 'kicking tree', and all that went with it, made him shudder with shame.

Over the week that followed, larger numbers of humans came down from the MEV. The astronomers from the *Great Marton* identified the Medlam system. It was fifteen light years away. More communications were sent and it was hoped that in thirty years' time they would get a reply. In the meantime they were happy to know that their families would have positive news of them.

"You know what all this means?" Jack said to Jalli. "If Ramal, the Sponron home world, is only fifteen light years distant, and Sponrons came to Joh by conventional space travel, albeit with polykatallassic engine technology, then –"

"Planet Joh is in the Milky Way and you might be able to see Earth One, Earth Two, Ramal and this planet from our garden."

"Probably not the planets, but certainly the stars around which they orbit: the Sun, Apha, Medlam and Tatania."

"And that means I could also make out the galaxy in which I was born," said Jalli.

"Can you see any galaxies from Joh? You haven't told me much about what you see in the heavens."

"It is all very different from Raika, but then, stars are stars. There didn't seem much to tell."

"When we get back, we'll get Bandi onto it... Would it make you happier to be able to see your home galaxy?"

"Of course. I don't know why, but I was thrilled to see Andromeda from here. I've spent a lot of time staring at it."

"Even though it's huge, hundreds of thousands of light years across, and you're looking at a time in the distant past? Planet Raika is barely a tiny speck of dust that could never even be detected from within most of its own galaxy. And Andromeda is supposed to have a trillion stars in it."

"I know. But it's still home. It's where I grew up."

Sass and Matt joined them as Jalli stared up at the sky.

"Homesick?" asked Sass.

"No, not really. Not for Raika, anyway. Home is where the heart is. I have no-one there."

"Apart from Mr Bandi," said Jack.

"He was my biology teacher," explained Jalli. "Most people don't keep in touch with teachers, anyway."

"Andromeda is on course to collide with us," stated Matt in a matter-of-fact way.

"Collide! When?"

"Well, 'merge' would probably be a better word. About three and three-quarter billion years. It could cause a few problems when that happens."

"Not soon, then?"

"I guess we'll be dead a year or two before it happens. Nothing to worry about."

"It's nice to think, though, that one day the Milky Way and Andromeda will become one," smiled Jalli.

"A kind of marriage."

"Yes. It's like Jack and I started something."

"Yeah," smiled Sass. "The Creator has certainly had a hand in it. As She has in bringing us together with the Sponrons. This is just what we needed. I hope She sends you next time we need something."

"It was good to be called. We are so happy to spend time with you again. And to see you settled, too. We shall pray for you. Now you know we are up there, somewhere, in this galaxy not too far away."

"Too far to visit without an IAS."

"IAS? Ah, for a moment I forgot that's what you called our white gates. A posh name: 'Immediate Access System'."

"We like our acronyms. Speaking of which, here comes our DCPO. He's come to thank you and propose a party."

"A party?"

"A thank-you party – for you. We are ashamed to say we were discouraged – some of us were ready to give up. We needed you to buck us up. We were praying – a few of us, that is – for God to help us. Our supreme commander and our leaders were becoming isolated, and the community was losing focus. Then you came to us and, within hours, things began to change. You brought your little girl, who clearly enjoyed being here. We had forgotten how we can learn from children. Then you connected us with the Sponrons. Without you, we would probably have fled…"

"A party? We don't need a party," protested Jalli.

But Jack saw the point. "That will be lovely," he said, "and then we must be off home. The shuttle is due to leave tomorrow isn't it?"

"But we thought we could have a party next week. A proper party with –"

"No," said Jack, "we have left our other children too long already. And we have jobs to go to. There's going to have to be some explaining when we get home in any case."

A gathering was called for that evening. Sometimes, the spontaneous can be just as good. In the end, it is the spirit that counts, rather than the bunting or cakes.

So Jack, Jalli, Kakko, Tam and Yeka were sent off home with the acclaim of two joyous races of people ringing in their ears. Not only were the Tatanians saying thank you to the Johians, they were celebrating their new, united community.

The shuttle pulled into the docking bay of the *Great Marton* and the five insisted on being conducted directly to the MIVRE bay. The supreme commander rushed in to wish them well and to add her thanks to the rest. The white gate shone brightly inside the bay, and no sooner had they bowed to the commander than they were standing in the garden of White Gates Cottage, looking rather out of place in their grubby robes.

"You never did get to make any trousers," laughed Kakko, kissing her boyfriend's cheek.

6

A bby returned to the vicarage garden feeling much more positive. Sure, she was going to be hauled before Silent Sam the next morning, but she felt that they were making a valid point and she wanted him to accept that – even if he disagreed with it. She was resigned to the fact that whatever the principal said would have to be obeyed – but perhaps, just perhaps, he might not think she was a wicked girl, just a principled one. It gave her courage, but it did not stop her knees wobbling. It crossed her mind that if she was being deliberately intimidated that was wrong. All intimidation is, by definition, a misuse of power. But she was getting ahead of herself – it might not be like that at all.

Abby mentioned to her father about the possibility of getting the bishop to make a statement.

"I shouldn't bank on it," he said.

"But isn't Christianity about standing up for the people that are being oppressed?"

"Yes. Indeed. That was in Jesus' manifesto in Luke, chapter four."

"Exactly. Something about 'setting free the oppressed'."

Dave nodded. "He was quoting Isaiah."

"So then, the bishop should approve of what we're doing."

"I am sure he would in principle, but –"

"How do I contact him?"

"I'll get you his office email address."

"Thanks, Dad. This will be great. Bandi's dad has good

ideas. If we have the bishop and his councillor friend, the principal will have to agree with us."

"My guess is, Abby, that your principal is more interested in taking the school out of the public eye rather than raising its profile even further."

"He's chicken."

"He's a pragmatist. You don't get to become a principal of a high school through being a campaigning idealist."

★ ★ ★

The interview with Silent Sam took just three minutes. It included the head of year as well as Abby and Guy. There was no discussion. The principal told them the mock election was abandoned, they were to drop any further campaigning, and the media were to be informed that they would be making no further statements. He would also be writing to the parent who had offered the venue to say there would be no event. A joke, he said, was fine, but now it had "got out of hand" and it had to stop.

Abby wanted to say that it was not meant to be a joke. But the head of year gave her a glare that said, "Don't argue with the principal!" She said nothing but lowered her eyes.

"Good," concluded the principal, "so now let's just concentrate on those studies, shall we?"

Guy nodded. Abby looked at her feet and thought to herself, *Let's just see if you change your tune when the bishop and Councillor Banks take up the cause.*

Outside the office, the head of year said he was sorry because he knew they had meant well. It had got them into trouble they didn't deserve, but he was sure it wouldn't go on their record. Abby was stunned at the weight of the establishment. Why were they all so mean? It didn't occur to her that it was precisely because she and Guy were gaining power themselves – the power of public opinion – that the authorities clamped down so hard. People who rule from the top down frequently prefer there to be no public debate. For Silent Sam, "control" was the name of the game.

"What are you going to do, Guy?" Abby asked when they were alone in the corridor.

"Nothing. Like the principal says, get on with my studies. I'm right behind in my work."

"But don't you believe in this? There are people out there getting exploited. We have a chance to speak out for them!"

"Yeah. Sure. But I guess we should leave them to campaign for themselves…"

"But they have no voice! They just have to take what they're given – you know that."

"And now we have no voice either, Abby. In case you hadn't realised, there is to be no mock election and the student mag is closed down. One day, when I've passed my exams and got on the ladder of success, I'll speak out. People will listen to me then."

"No, you won't! You'll just become a wimp looking after your own interests like them! We still have the interest of the newspapers. That's far more important than the student mag."

"Abby, it's over. You're just making a fool of yourself."

"And you know what? I don't think I care. Anyway, I've got a councillor involved – and the bishop."

"Oh, Abby. Just drop it! Now I've got a lesson… see you."

"Guy, you're a wimp!" But Guy was already heading off down the corridor.

★ ★ ★

That evening Abby had two emails. One from the bishop's office thanking her for her email and concern, but declining the opportunity to get involved. The bishop's secretary stated: "the bishop does not ordinarily join public campaigns."

Councillor Banks was not quite so curt, but he, too, felt it was inappropriate for him to get involved. He attached a proper letter.

Dear Miss Brook,

I was very interested to receive the letter from my friend Jack Smith who has contributed meaningfully to the inauguration of our new school for blind children.

I appreciate your concern and admire your passion for the campaign for equality in this country and beyond. However, I am not at liberty to become involved in your event. As you know, there is a really important by-election at hand with local issues that our candidate needs to address, and he does not feel that it is appropriate for him to become enmeshed in other things that may detract from the importance of the main campaign.

I do not want to discourage you from your very important concern for the marginalised, but we feel that talking of burning underwear at this crucial time is proving a distraction, and I would urge you and your friends to change your mind in the interest of a successful election, based on the real issues at hand.

However, the idea of seeking justice is a good one in the context of your school mock election. Keep up the good work. When you are of age, you could become a valuable member of our party. Politics is a good and worthy career, and you clearly have some of the necessary skills.

Yours sincerely,
Anthony Banks
Town Councillor.

Abby was incandescent. She was too angry even to talk to her parents for over an hour. She ignored the call for tea, and her father came looking for her. It took him five minutes to even work out what was wrong. When she eventually showed him the communication, he just sat in silence.

"Nobody cares!" sobbed Abby.

"They do. We do. Lots of people do."

"But nobody important! What about you? Are you going to say something in the church?" Her father looked down. "I think," he said, "this door has closed. Keep your powder dry until the next occasion."

"*Et tu, Brute?*"

"*Touché,*" smiled Dave, "but if it's any consolation, I am immensely proud of my daughter."

"Is anyone in this house coming for tea?" shouted Abby's mum from the bottom of the stairs.

"Well, I must say, I am quite relieved," said Abby's mother firmly. "This has all gone far enough. It's about time you concentrated on your studies. That's the main thing. It's time to look after *yourself*. All this injustice elsewhere ought not to take over your time and energy to the detriment of your own life."

Abby boiled. "Mum, how can you say that? That is the most selfish thing I've heard you say... ever!"

"Oh, I'm not thinking about myself – I'm thinking of you, Abby."

"It's the same thing. It's your interests, not the interests of those who haven't a chance in the world. It's we who should be thinking of those who never get a chance to protest for themselves."

"Abby, you're sounding like a reactionary! Your father and I will not stand by while you throw your life away like this. Look, Abby, we love you! We don't want to see you get hurt. You're too young to get involved in politics. If you want to change the world when you're twenty-five, then OK that's up to you, but until then, get your head down and pass your exams… And, while we're on the subject, I'm really not happy with you rushing off to see Bandi every five minutes. That's another distraction…"

"So you're one of them, too, are you, Mum? Not only have you joined the conspiracy to prevent me from having an opinion and expressing it, you are going to imprison me!"

"Dave, don't leave all this to me," pleaded his wife. "Speak to her!"

"I already have," said Dave quietly.

"Have you told her to get on with her studies?"

"I have. But I have also told her that I am proud of her. Lynn, just think how it could have been. We could have had a lying, cheating girl, or one chasing after worthless boys or worse. Instead we have a young woman with principles and a passion for helping the helpless. How can I criticise her if she appears to have caught on to what the teaching of Jesus is about?"

"Dave, you're impossible!"

"Lynn, you are right. Abby should not abandon her studies and I have told her I think this underpants thing is now finished, but I don't agree about Bandi. He is a keen student himself, with a good dose of common sense. He will only encourage her."

"And if I am not meant to see him, then all God has to do is take away the gate!" said Abby defiantly.

"Alright," said her mother more quietly, "but no more bonfires."

"Agreed?" said Dave, smiling at his daughter.

"Agreed," exhaled Abby with a deep sigh.

"Wisdom," said Dave, "is not just knowing what is right, but about when and how to proclaim it. Your time will come."

"But not before tea," declared Lynn.

★ ★ ★

It was remarkable how quickly the reporters abandoned the chase once they realised there was to be no bonfire. Abby consistently declined to speak to them and, since she was a minor, their lawyers were advising of the legal minefields. The election campaign continued along the lines the candidates and their parties determined. The issues were local and national, but nothing at all was said about international politics or exploitation.

"It's all so selfish," commented Abby to her friends. "They are talking about retaining the small hospital on the outskirts of the town, free nursery places for three-year-olds (or not), and the powers of the local council versus Westminster. No-one is considering the interests of people who don't live here. It's all about what benefits 'me, me, me' – irrespective of who might miss out somewhere else."

"Of course," said one, "democracy is about making sure you get as much as you can for your own community."

"Or even your own family…" added Abby.

"Nothing wrong with that," said a second. "My father says, 'Charity begins at home'."

"I've always taken that to mean that being charitable begins with you doing it first."

"What?"

"'Charity begins at home' means it's *you* that starts the giving away."

"That's not what my father means."

"No," came in a third, "what gets me is that most of what they want is just to get into parliament. It's about them and their career in politics. That's all they really believe in."

A month before, Abby would have thought that rather cynical, but the recent events had made her think there was a lot of that in it. The candidates of the main parties – the ones who thought they stood a chance – were mostly thinking of their own careers, she decided.

Since the school had abandoned the mock election, interest in the by-election among the students had largely waned. Attendance at the political societies had diminished. To the principal's satisfaction, things had quietened down, and it was business as usual at the half-term break in Abby's penultimate term before the onset of the dreaded GCSEs.

As for the by-election itself, the interest seemed to have come mainly from the Westminster Village. Persham was languishing under a long, wet winter that saw everything muddy and soggy. Parts of the country were suffering from protracted flooding, which was distracting national attention. In the end the Thursday of the election was dry, but it did not do any good for the turnout which was a sad forty-eight per cent. Some of this vote had been drummed up by the local churches who encouraged the people to appreciate the gift of a secret and free ballot, unlike those suffering under oppressive regimes elsewhere in the world. The Churches Together in Persham had even provided a hall for the candidates to come together and put their views across – but even that was poorly attended. Abby wondered whether Guy's bonfire, had it been allowed to go ahead, might have spurred on a few more people to vote. Abby was all for giving the vote to sixteen- and- seventeen-year-olds. So was her father who believed that the younger generation were much more likely to vote from the heart than from self-interest.

The same party had retained the seat – just – with a total of thirty-three per cent, or less than sixteen per cent of those eligible to vote. Abby had been studying the rise of Nazi Germany in her history course. She had written in one of her essays that the same could happen in Britain if people were not more outspoken. To her amazement the history teacher agreed with her, but explained that in an essay about the 1920s and 30s she had to remain "on task" and not "go off at a tangent" by getting onto a soapbox. The two things that were keeping Abby's frustration in check were her soothing visits to Woodglade – where Bandi agreed with everything she said, but intelligently – and her father's clear pride in her, along with his continued encouragement.

7

"Getting married?" marvelled Shaun. Kakko had just opened a letter of invitation to *The Marriage of Yuttia, the eldest daughter of Mr and Mrs Aston Klempt, to Mr Trim Gwaco, second son of Mr and Mrs Roya Splinda of Hill End, Joh City.* "But they're not even twenty."

Kakko nudged her brother in a *'meaningful'* way. "Some people," she said calmly, "are ready to marry young." She glanced towards the open door where their mother was engaged in making a cake. Shaun coloured up.

"Sorry," he whispered, "I didn't mean that it is always the wrong thing to do."

"Glad to hear it," called Jalli from the kitchen, who had not only heard Shaun's original reaction, but also his noisy whispers. "So who's this getting married?"

"It's Tam's cousin's brother-in-law, Trim Gwaco," said Kakko, coming into the kitchen. "I think – but don't quote me on this – his fiancée, Yuttia, is pregnant… Shaun's got a point, though. It's not their actual age that matters, it's just that Yuttia and Trim are not very mature. They're still kids in many ways."

"They haven't seen much of the universe?"

"Haven't seen much of Joh City, even. They have lived, went to school and worked in Hill End since they were born. They would be lost in most of the rest of the city. Trim does gardening – but he's only really good for clearing and cutting grass. He doesn't know one plant from another."

"It takes all sorts to make a world, we shouldn't judge."

"I know. But I also know when someone's a bit of a loafer. He could do much more with his life. Yuttia's not much better."

"They're probably getting married," suggested Shaun, who was now engaged in scraping the mixing bowl and licking the spoon, "because Mr and Mrs Klempt want to keep up appearances."

"And because getting married means that Yuttia feels more important than the rest of us unmarried girls her age," added Kakko.

"And is she more important?" asked Jalli.

"'Course not. I wouldn't swap with her in a million years. And, anyway, Tam is worth a million Trims."

Kakko and Tam replied that "they would be delighted" to attend the wedding of Yuttia and Trim.

★ ★ ★

The very next day, Trim rang Tam and announced a "stag do." Tam was reluctant to go along, but felt obliged to. In the end it was agreed that Tam should be the one to stay sober – something he was pleased to do. He had drunk a glass of beer on one occasion to oblige the likes of Trim and his friends, but he didn't like either the taste or the effect it had on him. Since then he just stayed clear of alcohol – and the young people who derided him for doing so. If they couldn't accept him for what he chose to do, then he would hang out with people who could. But Trim was his cousin's wife's brother – so, sort of family – and he couldn't not go.

The stag do got under way with drink from the outset in a local hostelry in Hill End before they set off in a hired people carrier (which Trim could ill-afford) driven by Tam. It headed off down the coast to where there was a beach, a hotel and nature walks in an attractive gorge. They began in the hotel, then went onto the beach where they almost threw Trim into the sea fully clothed – but they were just sober enough not to do it. They went back to the hotel and then, despite the fact it was now almost dark, decided to go on a ramble up the gorge. Tam, of course, remained sober. He tagged along, having a miserable time. The others were now far too intoxicated to listen to any reason, even if they had been in the first place, which they hadn't.

They whooped and screamed, disturbing all the wildlife whose home this was. They were supposed to keep to the paths, but Trim and his friends just roamed through habitats that had been carefully preserved by nature wardens throughout the previous year. Tam stayed on the path and watched as the group dared Trim to climb a tall tree – the tallest of a little copse where the ground ascended to the scree at the base of a cliff. Trim set to, climbing up the tree. Tam watched from his position on the path below. *He'll never get down*, he thought. Trim continued to climb. He just climbed, unable to think of the consequences. Ten metres, fifteen metres, twenty, and then after he had got near the top of the tree he became aware of the night breeze and the fact that his friends were now so far below him. They sounded to be in a different world. At twenty-five metres above the base of the tree and thirty-five above the path to which the others had retreated to be able to see him, he looked down. He froze for a minute, then began to feel for the branch below with his foot. He couldn't find it. He looked down at his feet, and was filled with a nauseous dizziness; he couldn't decide which of the half a dozen or more boots were his – and below them was a deepening darkness. His head spun.

"Hey, you lot," he slurred. "You gotta get me down."

Tam sprang into life. "Just hang on, Trim. Don't try to move." The others were just confused. One began to laugh; it sounded hollow and scary in the cool darkening world of the gorge. Then they fell silent, and the sounds of the night – the creatures that owned this place – gradually returned to their nightly life. It felt spooky.

Tam tried his mobile. No signal. The gorge was too narrow. He sent two people off back down the track to phone the emergency services from the hotel. When he saw them struggle to find the path, he dispatched two more. They hadn't got a torch with them. All they had was the starlight. Trim could fall long before anyone got there to rescue him. Tam wondered how he was going to help him. He decided he had to climb up to Trim, but even if he reached him in time, he could not hold him as well as cling to the tree himself. Once Trim lost the ability to hold on by himself, then Tam hadn't a hope. He decided he needed to tie him to the tree somehow.

Tam remembered the last time he was called upon to climb. That was the first time he had really prayed, and this evening was going to be another one of those in which he would be talking to his Creator step by step. Then the answer dawned on him; he gave thanks that he had been given long legs that needed long-legged trousers. To the amazement of his useless chums, having emptied his pockets, he took off his trousers and tied the legs around his waist. He put his phone into his shirt pocket – perhaps it would work from the top of the tree.

To someone trained on a climbing wall, climbing the tree was relatively easy. Fortunately, going up, the black bows stood out against the starlight that was remarkably bright in this dark corner of Planet Joh. Getting down, he knew, would be much harder.

Eventually he reached Trim, who was now moaning quietly – and shaking. It was evident that Trim could not hold on for much longer. "Alright mate," said Tam as he pulled himself up beside him. Trim began to relax. "No, not yet," ordered Tam, "hold on." Trim obeyed and tensed.

Leaning against the trunk, which was quite slim at this height, Tam undid the knot in his trousers' legs and pulled them free of his waist. Clutching the end of one trouser leg, he positioned himself close enough to Trim to get his arm around him. He reached round the trunk with the other. "Hold still," he said quietly. Trim wasn't about to do anything but shake. To his relief, Tam found that he could just reach and grasp both trouser legs with the same hand. He tried tugging the trousers around the trunk, but they snagged. He couldn't slip them past a stub of a branch on the other side. Tam breathed, thought and prayed. He had to get round the other side of the trunk while not letting go of the trousers. He tried one way, but he found himself leaning too far out as the trunk bent under his weight. He could not get a foot on another branch. He pulled himself back. Then, he transferred the trouser legs into his other hand and stepped across the back of Trim, but he still couldn't do it while holding the trousers.

"Look, Trim, you're going to have to help me. Can you find my hand around the other side of the trunk? Go on, I've got you," he spoke with a confidence he didn't feel. The cold night air on his bare legs made him shiver.

Reluctantly, as he clung to the trunk, Trim felt for Tam's hand holding the trouser legs. "Now," commanded Tam. "Take hold of the trousers." Trim did so. "Both legs... Use the other hand... Great. Now, hold onto them. Lean against the tree. That's it."

Trim was now shaking quite violently. With both hands free, Tam swung himself around the trunk and got a foot on a second branch. Secure, he took the trousers from Trim and tied the legs together, firmly. He felt Trim close up against the trunk. He tightened them further – just in time. Trim's legs buckled under him and he slid down, now supported solely by Tam's trousers. Tam couldn't have readjusted them now even if he needed to – but he didn't. He looked down into the darkness below him. He couldn't see a thing. He judged it best to wait with Trim anyway.

Tam checked his mobile. A signal! Brilliant. What he needed was a climber – with equipment. He thought of Coach Jim – but he didn't have his number in his phone. Instead, he phoned Kakko.

To his relief, Kakko picked up.

"Hi, Tam. Thought you would be in a party."

"Some party," said Tam. "Look, Trim is stuck up a tree. He's drunk and has just passed out. Can you get Coach Jim to come with his equipment?"

"Where are you?"

"You know the gorge behind the hotel on the beach?"

"In the nature reserve down the coast from Hill End?"

"Yes. We'll need some kind of rope chair to get him down."

"Where are you?"

"Up the track in the nature reserve – about a kilometre from the hotel. The stand of trees on the left – you can't miss them. There's a bunch of pissed lads on the path below."

"Right. So are you OK?"

"I'm great. I'm up the tree with Trim."

"Tam, what in the name –"

"Kakko, tell me off later! Just phone Coach Jim. I'm going to phone the emergency services." He rang off and dialled the three numbers he needed.

Kakko phoned the coach. His wife told her he was at the centre and he didn't have his mobile with him. She found the number for the centre and rang the centre office, but no-one picked up. Then she remembered that her erstwhile school friend, Kopal, took charge of the kit. Perhaps she could help. Kakko still had her mobile number in her phone. As it turned out, at that very moment, Kopal was with Coach Jim checking the equipment for the weekend. Very soon Kakko had explained everything, assuring him that she was certain Tam wasn't responsible but sounded desperate. Coach Jim didn't argue. He and Kopal filled his little car with ropes, pulleys, hard hats and everything else that went with such a challenge.

Kakko texted Tam, and told him Jim was on his way, then rang for a taxi.

When the taxi arrived, she, Shaun and Jalli piled into it, and they sped towards the beach hotel. They arrived to see a police car, a fire engine and an ambulance parked alongside Coach Jim's car and the hired people carrier.

They ran up the path to find a policeman interviewing half a dozen dishevelled young men, feeling pain and shame as the anaesthetic effects of the alcohol wore off in the cold air. Beyond were a cluster of paramedics and firefighters. Ladders had been placed at the base of a tall tree, but were useless beyond a few metres among the branches. Kakko saw four figures silhouetted against the sky towards the top of the tree. One of them, she shuddered at the thought, was her Tam. *What the hell was he doing up there? Wasn't it she who was supposed to be careless?*

Then, Mr and Mrs Klempt and Yuttia arrived. "Where's Trim?" she barked. Jalli gestured towards the tree. Yuttia squealed and went limp. Jalli caught her. Kakko was angry and thought, *Don't you dare freak out. Your stupid fiancé has put my Tam into danger. Shut your mouth.* But she said, "Don't worry, they're getting him. He'll be alright." But Yuttia was inconsolable.

Her parents took charge of her. You could see Mr Klempt was embarrassed. He tried to persuade her to leave them to it and go back down to the hotel – but his wife was having none of it. This was their future son-in-law, they should be there, so Yuttia was left to sit on the path and moan. Trim's parents were out on the town somewhere and wouldn't know about the escapade until the next morning.

Meanwhile up in the tree, Coach Jim was fixing a pulley and a boson's chair. With his help, Tam had climbed down a branch. Kopal was just below him and they were passing stuff up to Jim. One firefighter was clinging to the ladder, while two more were taking charge of a rope that Coach Jim had dropped down. Jim positioned the chair under Trim's bottom. Then, Tam pushed Trim's legs up and they slid him into it. Jim applied the straps and called down for the firefighters to take the strain. When he was certain they had control of Trim, he took out a knife and cut through one of the legs of Tam's trousers. They fell from Trim's waist but stayed snagged on the trunk. Tam manoeuvred Trim around a branch as the fire-fighters began to lower him. Kopal did the same as he passed her. He was now completely unconscious. As the chair descended, the man on the ladder helped to take control, and soon Trim was on the ground being tended to by paramedics. They wrapped him in foil and he was carried down the path, into the waiting ambulance.

Coach Jim and Kopal helped Tam down. He was also given a foil wrap, but declined a lift to the hospital. All he needed were the warm arms of his girlfriend.

★ ★ ★

Trim was lucky. Apart from a few scrapes, he only needed treating for exposure. But he grew up more on that night than he had done over the past three years. Kakko's belief that Yuttia was pregnant turned out to be a false rumour. Trim put off the wedding. He wasn't ready to be married, he explained. For a time, Yuttia was embarrassed in the company of her friends, and especially in front of Kakko and Tam, whom she avoided. Tam had been profuse in his apologies for bringing Coach Jim out.

"Nonsense, young man," he had said. "You saved that boy's life. The only right thing he did was take you along and expect you to remain sober. And you called the right people. When am I going to see you back at the centre?"

"Thanks," blushed Tam. "I might come back, but I am rather busy with my studies these days."

"Your choice," smiled the coach.

Kakko was proud of her boyfriend. She took him to town to buy him a new pair of trousers.

"Thanks," he said, as Kakko insisted on paying. "Why is it that the absence of trousers keeps coming up in my adventures?"

"You've got nice legs."

★ ★ ★

Tam's trousers were to fly as a flag from that tree for years. Looking up at them in the light of day, Tam wondered how he had ever dared to climb up there, and he hoped he wouldn't ever have to climb to rescue anyone again.

8

"Do that once more," said Shaun's teammate, Gollip, as he ran past him while the opposition goalie prepared to take a goal kick. "I promise I'll get on the end of it next time."

"No problem," smiled Shaun. "This lot are leaving so many gaps – just be ready and don't rush it!"

Two minutes later the ball was again at Shaun's feet in the middle of the park, five metres inside his own half. He looked up, spotted his teammate and knew exactly where he wanted it. The ball looped over the heads of the opposing midfield, split the defence and landed right in the space Shaun intended. It was too short for their goalkeeper to come to meet it, but it sat up nicely for Gollip to run on to. He hit it first time. Bang, top right-hand corner. The poor goalie didn't stand a chance. A small knot of away supporters jumped and cheered. They blew on a trumpet and waved their banners. The rest of the stadium stood in silent shock, seeing their team taken in so slickly.

When the game ended, the visitors were three to nil winners.

★ ★ ★

Shaun and his team were conveyed to a hotel for the night. It was already evening. They would return over the mountains to Joh City the next day. Some of their travelling supporters were there to cheer them into the hotel lobby. Among them

71

were two dedicated people Shaun recognised – a young man and a girl. He had gone to school with the muscle-bound young man dressed in a larger version of the red and yellow team shirt. Alongside him was his sister, slim and petite. How the two shared the same parents, Shaun couldn't imagine, but the big man watched over his sister attentively – caring for her almost as much as his trumpet, which he carried to every game. They were at nearly every match – a distinctive couple.

"Ho Shaun, brilliant," shouted the big guy and he gave a blast on his trumpet.

"Hey, Aril. Thanks." Aril's sister was less known to Shaun. She was two years younger and had not been in the same school year. "Better leave it off now," suggested Shaun. "You're rather outnumbered by annoyed local fans."

"Told you," smiled the girl, watching a gathering of passing disappointed opposition supporters. If looks could kill…

"Right," agreed Aril.

The rest of the team were already inside the glass doors.

"You coming in?" invited Shaun.

"I think we'd better for a bit." Aril was not intimidated, but he was aware of his sister and wanted her to be safe.

"Delighted," said the girl softly.

Shaun smiled. He liked the girl. She was quite different from Kakko, who probably wouldn't have had much patience with her. She was clearly someone who spent time on her appearance. Her hair had been carefully styled, and her fingernails manicured. Her face was tastefully made-up and her hair was controlled with a smoky blue ribbon, matching her belt and shoes and nail varnish. Not a team shirt for her, but a delicate blue and purple cotton print top, trimmed with lace around the generously cut square neck that revealed just a hint of powdered cleavage. Her pale blue trousers fitted tightly around her hips, and flared at her calves and ankles over casual, but stylish, blue suede lace-up shoes. And this was for a football game! Shaun guessed she would probably have an elegant change for the evening, too. But for all this attention to her appearance, Wennai, for that was her name, was not vain. Dressing like this seemed to come as naturally to her as Kakko's speedy simplicity. It was who she was. It suited her – and Shaun liked it. She was beautiful, but Shaun was no fool – he knew true beauty came from within. Putting a face on without a foundation of personal depth looked just false – beauty and integrity go together. But Wennai seemed genuine enough. If she had anything of the nature of her brother, she would not be trying to appear different from what she was.

Inside the hotel, the air was cool, and the sounds muted. Shaun took his guests into the bar and offered them a drink. To his amazement, Aril and Wennai both asked for a soft drink.

"You sure?"

"We don't drink alcohol," explained Wennai. "But don't let us stop you from drinking what you want."

"I generally avoid alcohol, too," said Shaun. "My family have seen too much suffering caused by drunken people. Besides, it affects the brain, and precision is part of my game!"

"That pass," whistled Aril, "the one that led to the first goal. It was superb."

"Thanks. After that they were a bit wiser to the danger, and I never got quite as clear-cut a chance again."

"But you were instrumental in the third goal, too. You drew two defenders off after you and opened it up. That was clever."

"You really know your game. Do you play?"

"No. I'm too slow."

"But he works out," explained Wennai. "He's a champion weightlifter."

"I wouldn't have guessed," joked Shaun, feeling his rock-solid biceps. "That takes time and effort."

"I'm down at the gym every day."

"I know. You have been going there for some time… but tell me, when did you become such a fervent football fan?"

"It's Wennai really," said Aril. "She's the one."

Wennai blushed. "I like watching football; I like the excitement – and the skill. At first Aril came with me because I needed someone with me, but now he is a big supporter, too – with a big trumpet!" she teased.

"And she has a favourite footballer," informed Aril.

"Aril! You mustn't say that. You embarrass me."

"But she does. He's called *Shaun Smith!*"

"Aril! Now you have said too much. I'm sorry, my brother's so… forward. But I do think you are our best player. A good midfielder is vital to a successful team."

"Thank you," said Shaun. "I agree… but I'm not sure that I am the best player. In fact, I know I'm not."

"But she likes *you!*" Wennai's brother was enjoying himself.

"Aril!"

"Don't worry. I know your brother," assured Shaun. "We have been in the same class at school for many years. He's laughing at me, not you,"

"So have you got a girlfriend, then?" asked Aril.

"No," replied Shaun. "Have you? Whatever happened to Sandi?"

"Who?"

"Sandi Froo. You know, the girl you've been chasing since primary school… Your brother was a terror to the girls there," Shaun explained to Wennai. "But when he got into secondary school, he got scared of them."

"I did *not!*"

"You did. I remember you hid from Fruma Chum in the

cloakroom behind the coats and you got me to say you had gone the other way."

"Well, Fruma Chum! What do you expect?"

"Fruma is a nice girl. I like her. She's honest and hard-working," remonstrated Wennai.

"She's certainly persistent, I'll grant you that. Anyway, I thought we were talking about you and Shaun," said Aril, trying to turn the focus back onto his sister.

"I'm not," laughed Shaun. "I still want to know about you and Sandi Froo."

"I can tell you," smiled Wennai. "He's still keen on her. He was heartbroken when she went on a date with Zim."

"I was not!" said the big lad forcefully.

"But you were!"

"Not!"

"Confirmed then. You like her."

"Do you want me to tell her? She might ditch Zim for all those muscles of yours," offered Shaun.

"Don't you dare."

"OK. Just kidding." Shaun pretended to be scared.

The conversation eventually moved on to school in general, and then to weightlifting again before they decided to call it an evening. Wennai took Shaun's hand and he kissed her on two cheeks as they parted.

Regaining the street, Wennai turned to her brother and told him off for telling Shaun how she felt about him.

"I thought he might as well know the truth. I wouldn't mind him as a brother-in-law!"

"Aril. You are so…"

"Come on, Wennai. I know Shaun. Even if he liked you, he would be too shy to make the first move. I was just paving the way for you."

"It's a good job he's such a gentleman. Deliberately

moving the conversation onto you and your love life like that was kind."

"Yeah. Nifty that."

"So, what about you and Sandi Froo? Do you like her? And did you hide from Fruma?"

Aril sighed. "There's me trying to help your love life, and I end up a laughing stock."

"So?"

"So what?"

"Sandi… and Fruma?"

"Yes, I did hide from Fruma. That was last year. She was getting too keen. I like her, but not like that. She was following me everywhere."

"And Sandi?"

"OK. She's… well, attractive… Zim is out of the picture – it was a one-off."

"So would you like me to tell her you fancy her?"

"Hell, no. That would be *so* embarrassing!"

"Right!" his sister said pointedly.

"OK, Wennai. I get it. I won't do it again."

"Good."

★ ★ ★

Back in Woodglade, Shaun was thinking of Wennai most of his waking hours, and some of his dream time, too. She was clearly embarrassed by her brother. It may be true that she liked him, but she was so different from his usual friends that he hadn't seen her as being in the same sphere as himself. She definitely liked football, though, so at least they had that in common.

★ ★ ★

The following week, Wennai and Aril were in the stand for a home game. The team were in good form. This time Shaun was on the scorecard with a swirling free kick over the wall. Between the satisfaction of seeing the net bulge and his teammates racing to embrace him, Shaun caught sight of Wennai leaping and cheering next to her brother blowing his trumpet. Something told him, as he retook his position for the kickoff, that if he didn't date the girl soon, someone might beat him to it. A good-looking unattached girl like Wennai would attract any number of offers and, since he had been clearly told by Aril in her presence that she was keen on him, if he didn't act, she might think her interest was not returned.

When he got home that evening, he looked up her home number. It was in the book – it wasn't difficult to find. Now what? He hadn't ever done this before.

He rang the number and her sister answered.

"Hello, can I speak to… is… er, Aril in? It's Shaun Smith."

"Sorry. He's out, I think… Wennai," she called. "It's Shaun Smith for Aril. Do you know when he's coming back?"

"Er. Will you put Wennai on?" asked Shaun.

"Sure… Wennai, he wants to speak to you."

"Hi. Sorry I don't know when Aril's coming in. He's with… a friend."

"Not Sandi Froo?"

"Well, actually he is. He rang her and, like, well…"

"Great!… Er… actually," said Shaun, feeling more awkward than he could remember, "I wondered… I mean, it was really you I wanted to talk to. I thought the other day… well, like, perhaps… if-I-asked-you-out-you-might-say-yes-and-so-I'm-ringing-you-to-ask-but-please-if-you-would-prefer–"

"Yes."

"What?"

"Yes, I am saying yes."

"Yes to what?"

"Yes to you asking me out."

"Er. Great! I mean… great!"

"Where? Where would you like to go?"

"Er… you choose. I hadn't thought…"

"Fitch's Coffee house, then, by the park?"

"Yeah, sure."

"When?"

"There's not a match next week. I mean, on Saturday. So what about then?"

"OK. I'll meet you at Fitch's at, say, two o'clock, Saturday."

"Great."

"Fine."

"Gr… I mean… er… thanks. OK. See you, then… er… Bye."

"Bye."

Aril was right, thought Wennai, *he is shy.* She stood for a moment still clutching the receiver.

"Hi, sister," called Aril as he bounced in through the front door. "You OK? You look like you've seen a ghost."

"A ghost? No… how did it go with Sandi?"

"Great. Fancied me for years, she said. She never guessed I fancied her."

"So Shaun has done you a favour embarrassing you."

"Yep. Pity he doesn't think the same about you."

"Doesn't he?"

"If he did, he would have asked you out after last week."

"Perhaps he has."

"Wow! He hasn't? Wow! That's great!"

"Do you boys have any other words in your vocabulary other than 'great!'?"

★ ★ ★

The coffee at Fitch's was followed by a walk in the park. Wennai had stuck to a carefully coordinated casual look. They spent all afternoon together and they found out they liked the same music – a balance of pop and classical. Shaun also discovered why Wennai and her family avoided alcohol. Their mother had been run down by a drunk on a motorcycle when Wennai was only thirteen. Mrs Fout had simply been walking back from the market when the bike had mounted the pavement. One moment she was a lively mother looking forward to cooking a meal for her family, the next she was a lifeless corpse lying in the gutter amid the fruit and vegetables she had bought. That was four years ago. Thinking back, Shaun remembered Aril saying about it, and him taking time off school. The oldest of the three, Patia, had been seventeen at the time, and she had held the siblings together in the family home which, they had all inherited. Some believed they shouldn't be allowed to do that, but Patia quickly showed her competence and the teenagers had clung successfully together.

As they walked, Wennai asked about the white gates that everyone associated with the Smith family. The whole school knew Bandi was dating a girl from another planet – how cool was that?!

Shaun saw Wennai back to her home. They agreed to meet up again after Shaun's training in five days' time.

9

Two more dates preceded Shaun's eighteenth birthday. The relationship was becoming known and was the subject of social media, and everyone expected to see Wennai as the leading guest among his friends at the coming-of-age party he was having at White Gates Cottage.

Shaun also invited Aril and Patia. He had already sent out invitations to the whole football squad, and asked them to bring a guest, (having a men's football team arrive in numbers without their girls, he felt, would not have been a party that would have properly graced White Gates Cottage.) Bandi had made sure Abby had had it in her diary weeks before. And Jack had seen to it that Matilda was not going to miss out, despite her being of a different generation. She had indicated that perhaps she would give Shaun a birthday kiss at breakfast and then disappear to Ada's out of the way, but Jack and Jalli were having none of it.

"Why don't you invite Ada?" suggested Jalli to Shaun. "Then Nan can't run away."

Shaun got his sister to design a really nice invitation to send her. Shaun's friends didn't get one, of course. Paper, as opposed to electronic, invitations were reserved for "the old folk". Ada loved it and wrote back saying she would look forward to coming. She hadn't been to a proper birthday party for years.

"She's no idea what she's in for," sighed Matilda. "Better warn her to bring earplugs. What about the neighbours?"

"Already invited," said Jack. "It'll be the biggest gathering White Gates Cottage has known since we've been here."

"So, that's why you asked everyone to bring something to eat."

"No real idea of the numbers or what people like to eat these days," replied Jalli. "Callan and Hatta are bringing their barbecue."

"Shaun has told them all, however, that we shall provide the drinks. He has deemed his birthday party alcohol-free, which is quite a thing with a football team. Says they are all coming, though. He puts the team's success down to fruit juice."

"I'll tell Ada to leave her bottle in the pantry, then," said Matilda. "We can't have the old folk in their cups while all the young ones are stone-cold sober, can we?"

"Are you suggesting Ada is often 'in her cups'?" laughed Jack.

"No. But I don't think she is averse to a drop of 'Irish' in her tea after I've left. Not that I'm supposed to know, of course."

"Shan't say a thing," laughed Jack. "I've forgotten it already!"

★ ★ ★

When Jack and Jalli first arrived on Joh a quarter of a century earlier, they had been a quiet couple of teenagers in love, known to only the immediate neighbours. Now, half the city seemed present. Shaun had invited everyone at the worship centre informally, and many had come. The barbecue was augmented by Jalli cooking burgers and sausages non-stop in the kitchen. Every table and chair from both White Gates Cottage and Callan and Hatta's next door had been set up in the garden.

Jalli reflected on the scene. "Jack, do you remember the first time I came into this garden? It was so quiet and lovely, and the grass so pristine."

"Yeah. It was magic."

"I wonder what the Owner thinks of all this?"

"I have no doubt He's having a ball, too. These are good people. Joy is from God – as is exuberance."

"Yeah…" Jalli stopped, sighed and dropped a tear.

"What's wrong?"

"All here, except…"

"I know," said Jack, holding his Jalli to him. "But just think how proud Grandma would be to see so many. For so long, there were just the two of you, but look how her love and devotion have borne fruit. And, Jalli, remember she is back home with her mum and dad and your father."

"Do you think she's looking down on us?"

"Love knows no bounds, nor does rejoicing. She taught me that."

"You're right. Got a tissue?"

"What's wrong, Mum?" Kakko and Tam came across with Pastor Ruk.

"Just the girl," said Jack. "Your mum's got something in her eye and I'm definitely not the one to deal with it."

"Got a message," said Ruk, coming over, "that the turnout was higher than expected."

"Didn't know the lad was so popular," said Jack. "What message?"

"The one about running short of drink."

"Ah, yes. I rang the store. They're going to deliver. I hope they don't take much longer."

"I've got it. I intercepted them just as they were carrying it out."

"But I haven't paid them."

"All sorted. A little bird…"

"Pastor Ruk! Let us put that right straightaway."

"I told you, a little bird…"

"Ruk. Pastors are not supposed to tell untruths."

"Well, then. Let's say that it is my pleasure. All I need is a little help getting it out of the car."

"But…"

"Hush!"

"OK. But…"

"No buts."

Jack pressed Ruk's hand. "Thank you. It's good to have so many friends."

"Tends to happen when you give so much to others as your family does."

"Tam," called Jack, "can you organise a couple of folk to get the drink out of Pastor Ruk's car?"

"It looks as if your Shaun has hit on someone special," said Ruk, looking across at Shaun with Wennai. "I can't imagine why all your kids want special friends so young."

"Goes in the family," smiled Jack. "Me and Jalli met when we were eighteen and seventeen."

"They are a nice family, the Fouts. You know the tragic history?"

"Yes. All three are here somewhere."

"I'm glad they have become friends with your family. You know they might value you and Jalli being around sometime…"

The party continued on through the evening. Everyone was having such a good time, but eventually the sun began to set, and parents and friends were beginning to arrive to collect the football team, and the church people gradually melted away in knots. As Daan's rays were just a glimmer on the western horizon, only the Smiths and Fouts were left with Ada and Abby.

"Goodness," Ada suddenly declared, "is that the time? I've missed my last bus!"

"So you must stay the night," said Matilda firmly.

"But you haven't any room?"

"Yes, we have. There's a spare bed in Yeka's room. They've taken her cot into her parents' room for the night because of all the coming and going."

"Well, if you think that's OK. I haven't brought any night things."

"You can use some of mine," said Matilda.

"Thank you. Perhaps we should ask Jalli, though."

Just at that juncture, they overheard Kakko calling excitedly, "Can the Fouts sleep over? Patia and Wennai could sleep in my room and Aril, Shaun's. They can use our sleeping bags. Bandi says we can have his."

"Can't see why not," said Jalli, "so long as they don't mind the floor."

"And I've invited Ada to stay in the spare bed in Yeka's room," broke in Matilda, "if that's OK."

"The more the merrier," replied Jalli. "What about you, Abby?"

"No. Sorry. I have to go. I've got an assignment due in on Monday. I must get it done. In fact, I really think I ought to go now, so that I'm not too tired tomorrow to start."

"We'll miss you," said Kakko.

"Thanks. I'd love to stay, but Shakespeare calls. 'Fairies, away! We shall chide downright, if I longer stay.'"

"Is that really Shakespeare?" wondered Bandi. "I thought he was all blood and battles."

"He is, mostly, but this is not a tragedy but a comedy: *Midsummer Night's Dream.*"

"I never did get that one," said Jack.

"Never too late," ventured Abby.

"Perhaps next year."

Bandi saw Abby through her gate and then a few minutes later returned, and quietly took himself to bed protesting that he wasn't feeling that well.

"It's the clearing up. He's trying to dodge it," protested Kakko.

"No. I've been concerned for a bit," said Jack. "I've been thinking he could do with an early night. You can have too much excitement when you're sixteen."

★★★

Matilda and Ada were 'up with the lark' as Matilda put it, but no-one else, not even Yeka. Daan made its lonely course up the sky and was well above the trees when they gradually began to appear.

Shaun stretched and dragged himself out of bed. He stood and opened the curtains.

"Is it time to get up?" asked Aril from inside the sleeping bag.

"No, stay there. No point in us all heading for the bathroom at the same time."

Shaun should have taken his opportunity when he could. Even Kakko found it difficult to access the bathroom and turned up to breakfast unwashed. No-one had anticipated just how much time Wennai would need. Shaun, still feeling the effects of the day before, found himself getting annoyed with her. But when she finally emerged looking so beautiful and bright, his irritation immediately subsided. Needless to say, Wennai's wonderful appearance did nothing to improve Kakko's discomfort. And all the stuff Wennai had applied made the bedroom smell. "Stink" was the word Kakko used.

Bandi, however, was feeling much better.

"Is Abby well?" asked Jalli. "She didn't look her usual bright self yesterday."

"Exams… and stuff."

"What sort of stuff?" asked Jack.

"Oh. Friends and family – the usual stuff… I can't talk about it. It's private."

"Nothing's private these days," observed Kakko, setting about another chunk of bread.

"But *she* wants it to be."

"Understood," said Jack. "We shall not ask more – but we'll say a prayer for her. I go cold remembering my teenage years in Persham… and, in those days, there was nothing like the social media she has to put up with."

"Did you have a rough time as a teenager?" asked Wennai.

Jack whispered to her, with mock confidentiality, "It was *bad*… real bad. I was a miserable grouch…but don't tell anyone. Like Abby, it's 'private'." He smiled.

"So life got better, then?" said Wennai, brightly.

"It certainly did. Thanks to the Creator and the wonderful person he planned for me to meet."

"I'd love to hear about all that. Your romance, I mean."

"It's a long story – too long to recount at breakfast time. We'll write a book about it one day."

"*Breakfast* time?" questioned Jalli, playfully. "It's now almost lunchtime."

10

After they'd eaten, Wennai and Shaun took their tea into the garden – the kitchen was rather crowded.

They lay on the grass in the shade and listened to the bees. Shaun could smell her perfume, even over the morning scents of the cottage garden. This girl was so different.

Wennai said, "It was a wonderful party last night. Not everyone has such a great family as you."

"I know. I'm grateful. I could do worse for a mum and dad."

"They're wonderful. I wish I had parents like you."

"I bet your parents were wonderful, too… are wonderful," he corrected.

"You were right first time. You know they are dead."

"Yeah. Of course. But being dead does not mean they no longer exist."

"That's because you believe in God. I know your dad does. He said God had a hand in bringing him and your mum together."

"He did. The Creator brought them to this place from across the universe. Without Him, he may still be unhappy on Planet Earth."

"I'm happy for them. It's just how it turns out. There could be any number of reasons for your white gates, you know."

"Mum and Dad both believe they are given by the Creator of the universe."

They lay silent for a while and then Wennai said, "I

don't believe there's a God. If God exists, He took my parents away."

"That's awful. But I don't believe God takes anything away like that."

"So, one minute my mum is there and the next, poof, she's gone. It's easy for you, you've got a whole family."

"Wennai. It isn't quite like that. Lots of things – horrible things – happen to people, but the Creator never abandons them. It's, like, God 'being there' that makes it bearable."

"But your life – it's not so hard. Whatever happens it's not as bad as losing both your parents, is it?"

"I guess not. But if a person knows the Creator was with them… loved them… and that those who have died are still there loving them, things would be much better, wouldn't they?"

"Yes. But it'd be a lie. Anyone can make up stories that make them feel better. All that's wishful thinking… Look, I could never believe in a God who would hurt people, like what happened to me and my brother and sister. Let's talk about something else."

Shaun felt awkward. His family had always taken the existence of God as a given – even when they found life hard. He would have liked to tell her that it had not been as plain sailing for his mum and dad as it might appear. They had come to believe, more than that, 'know' – in some special way deep down – that they were loved and valued. His parents believed that when people suffered, so did the Creator. They did not know why She did not intervene to stop it – perhaps She couldn't for some reason – yet She was definitely there. But Wennai had not met her creator as a child like he had. And she was right, he had both parents and a grandparent living with him, and he could not imagine how it would feel if they had all died when he was only thirteen. Losing Grandma was bad enough.

They lay quiet for a time, looking up at the sky. Neither of them spoke. Shaun felt it was for him to break the silence. He tried to imagine what Wennai was thinking, but couldn't. He had a good idea what went though the minds of each member of his family when they were not saying anything – but he did not know this girl. She was different.

Then, the bees caught his eye. They were buzzing around the garden, from flower to flower, collecting the nectar and, without knowing it, transferring pollen from bloom to bloom. "The bees are busy today," he said. "I like to watch them."

"Yes. Busy little creatures, aren't they? Life is one long work session for them."

"They work hard. But they rest at night – and stay inside all winter… My mum studies bees and other pollinators in the college. She's an expert. She loves them." *Oh dear*, he thought, *I've done it again – talking of mothers*. But Wennai didn't seem to have noticed.

"Have you ever been stung by a bee?"

"Yes. Once. When I was small. Apparently, I screamed the house down."

"I haven't… If they ganged up on you, they could kill you, couldn't they?"

"They wouldn't – not unless you attacked their hive."

"No-one would do that, would they?"

"It has happened."

"What? Bees killing someone?"

"It happened in my mum's world, before I was born. They weren't bees exactly, but their counterparts. 'Parmandas' Mum called them."

"What happened?"

"You don't want to know."

"Tell me," Wennai persisted.

"OK. This man," said Shaun, "raped a girl while she was

watching them. He kicked her boyfriend half to death and then destroyed the hive."

Wennai sat up, shocked.

"Shaun, I didn't know you thought about such things."

"I don't – mostly. But this actually happened. It's a true story… I told you you didn't want to know."

"And you can still believe in God after that? You must be crazy."

"I believe in God because those people – the ones that were attacked – said that the Creator screamed with them."

"That's… that's weird."

"But it's true."

"Have you met these people?"

"Yep."

"I'm glad I don't live on that planet…"

"Anyway, I like bees. Without them, many of the plants would die out. Without them and the other pollinators, there would be no flowers."

"How d'you mean?"

"I mean the flowers are for the bees. Their bright colours and their sweet smell is to attract them. We enjoy them, but they are really there for the bees. You know, you must have done it in biology. The bees transfer pollen (that contains the male gamete) to the pistils, the female parts of the flowers."

"Help them have sex." Wennai was leaning on one arm and looking down at Shaun.

"Er… yes. I suppose you could put it like that. Flowers can't move around like animals and… people, so…" he trailed off in embarrassment. Whatever he said now could be laden with unintended hidden meanings. Wennai leaned over him and kissed his cheek, her hair caressed his face and his nostrils were filled with her scent.

"What about the plants that don't have flowers?" she asked, playing with a strand of grass.

"Some are wind-pollinated. The wind blows the pollen around. That's why the wind is a…" Shaun hesitated. He was going to say "a sign of the Spirit of Life bringing new life to everything", but he couldn't speak of the Creator again.

"The wind is a what?" asked Wennai, when he didn't finish his sentence.

"The wind is a player in the creation of new life, too."

"So the wind is sexy, too?" Then she bounced to her feet, caught hold of his hand and pulled him up.

"Let's see what happened to my brother and sister."

Unbeknown to them, Aril and Patia were spying on them from Shaun's bedroom window. To them, it all appeared quite romantic – they were not aware of the confusion in Shaun's head.

★ ★ ★

Shaun and Wennai arranged a date for the following week. Shaun was glad it was no sooner, because he felt that he needed that time to sort himself out. They were, however, to meet after the midweek football match. He had arranged seats for Wennai and Aril in the players' stand which they had accepted, even though on this occasion Aril would have to leave his trumpet behind.

A minute into the match, Shaun forgot all about Wennai. There was nothing like a good, robust game of football to clear the mind. He was going for a ball that was clearly his, when an opposition player tackled him from behind, scything Shaun's legs into space. It was as if the pitch had come up and hit him hard on the shoulder. After that, he kept his wits about him and the next time the man came from the side, he leapt over the clumsy tackle and only just managed to avoid landing on the man's extended limb. The referee had had enough and produced a second yellow, and the man was off the pitch. That gave Shaun a clear run in midfield and the game was played almost entirely in the opposition's half – the final score was four-nil.

Shaun left the pitch in a state of euphoria. It took him by surprise when Wennai greeted him on the way to the dressing room with a cuddle and kiss. His teammates all jeered and hooted. To secure the affections of such an attractive female was quite a coup. Shaun lapped up the attention, but as he showered, he began to wonder whether Wennai was in love with him or the footballer.

Meanwhile, among her girlfriends, Wennai was being given points for landing such a man. It was well known that Shaun, for all his eligibility, had never had a proper girlfriend before. That evening, the girls went out to a hotel and her mates bought her soft drinks.

★ ★ ★

The next date was a trip to the beach and an informal meal in the beach hotel. They had fun in the surf and kicked a ball around. Wennai looked great in a swimsuit, but couldn't swim so well. In the water, she looked awkward – but that was fine. It was having a go that counted, although kicking a ball around on the beach like he did with Kakko was a non-starter. Wennai tried but couldn't stop the ball with her foot. Shaun didn't mind. She never pretended to be able to play football. The important thing, he told himself, was that he liked her. She was a genuine person.

The meal was OK. But the conversation didn't flow. Shaun found, with any mention of spiritual things off the agenda, he had to think about everything he said and the awkwardness came back.

In fact, it was Wennai who helped him realise how important the Creator was to him. Not talking about Her was like being in a room with people, and ignoring the most important person there. He didn't just *believe* in Her, he related to Her all the time; he knew he was loved – really loved. He could not find the words to express it – they all seemed so naff, even cheesy. The truth was that God was beyond words. She just *was*.

★ ★ ★

Over the next few days, Shaun felt increasingly bad. He felt almost sick. He really liked Wennai. She was a real person, and didn't put on airs or pretend to be who she was not. And he found her sexually attractive, too. He was like a bee delighting in a flower. He was excited by her. And, what's more, having her on his arm had elevated him in the hierarchy of male acclaim and he couldn't deny that meant something. But below the surface, they seemed so different. Did he love her? The truth was that he wasn't sure what that meant, so probably not. But did she get under his skin? Yes.

★ ★ ★

"What's wrong, Shaun?" asked his mum the next morning.
"Nothing. Nothing much."
"Why the long face? Bad dream?"
"No. Not much sleep, actually."
"Wennai?"
"Is it that obvious?"
"Yep. Mums are not daft. Want to talk about it?"

It was like uncorking a bottle of carbonated drink. Shaun talked and talked. He could talk freely to Jalli because they understood each other.

"Wennai needs a mum like you," he snivelled.

"She needs to find someone to talk to?"

"Yeah. But her mum's dead."

"But she's alive in the next world. I spend a huge amount of time talking to Grandma. I don't know if she can hear me. Perhaps not. She'll be far too busy. But I know one thing for certain, she loves me – all the time. If Wennai just knew how much her mum is loving her."

"But she says all that is 'poppy-cock' and wishful thinking. There isn't a life after this one. There isn't even a God. This is all there is."

"What do you think?"

"No, it's not poppycock. God is always there… She's there if only to be complained to. Which I do all the time." Shaun smiled. He was already feeling better. "So, what should I do about Wennai?"

"What is the Creator telling you?"

"The thing is, Wennai needs to get it. I mean – have some idea where I'm coming from with God – even if she doesn't feel it for herself. Otherwise, I can't be free to be myself with her."

"So, can you tell Wennai that? It would be the honest thing to do."

★ ★ ★

The next time they met, Shaun took courage and tried to explain. He told her that she was his dream girl, but that unless he could talk about God, it wouldn't work. "I can't be myself without Her," he explained.

"I don't know why you keep calling God 'Her'. It's weird," said Wennai. "It's, like, She's... like, She's your girlfriend or something."

"I don't always call God 'She'. Mum doesn't mostly. Kakko always does. But it's definitely not like God being a girlfriend. It's more that the Creator is the mother of everything. This planet and the whole, vast universe, dimension upon dimension, and, of course, heaven, too."

"You really believe in all that, don't you?"

"Yes. So you see that underneath the surface, I mean my surface, I'm free. It doesn't get narrower, but wider and wider... and it's all full of Her."

"While for me there's emptiness?"

"No, there isn't. You only feel it's like that. If you wanted to you could – just let go and explore it, too."

"So you don't think I'm telling the truth," she said with an air of annoyance. "I am being honest with you, Shaun."

"I know you are. I don't doubt it. That's why I like you so much. You're authentic. You're not skin-deep like so many girls. You never pretend."

"So you believe in God and I don't. We're both being honest then. So, what about *us*?"

"I really like you. You're the nicest girl I've met. We're not that far apart because we think about things. Nothing can stop us being friends. I want to be friends. We've got a lot in common."

"But you don't want to be my boyfriend unless I believe in God."

"No. It's not exactly like that. I just... I need to be able to talk about Her sometimes – "

"Look, Shaun, I like you. But we're worlds apart. You think that believing is normal – "

"It is."

"It isn't, Shaun. Normal is not believing in stuff you can't see, hear or touch. And, before you say it, don't tell me you can see, hear or touch Her because you can't."

"No. I can't in the usual meaning of those words but... She is just there, Wennai. It's like... breathing. It's, like, you don't think about it, but it gives you life."

"We live in different worlds, Shaun."

They stood together silently, apart. Then, Shaun spoke, "I... I'll see about getting you a special seat in the players box every game."

"Thanks. But Aril wants to take his trumpet."

"Tell you what. Let's make a date for the Sunday after the season. Dinner together."

"OK. Why not?"

That night, Shaun got angry with God.

Wennai wept. It was as if the life had been taken from her again. But life was like that. If God was really there, it was a cruel thing to do to introduce her to Shaun and then make him choose. He might not think of the Creator as his girlfriend, but She sure was a rival for his heart. And all this about being a mother of everything – it was as if Shaun had two mothers while she had none.

11

It was just before dawn with no moon – just a profusion of stars on one side of the sky. The other was dominated by a large spiral galaxy, its plane tilted at an angle of about thirty degrees. Kakko and Shaun had found themselves on the edge of what appeared to be a small village, not unlike the one they had seen on Planet Earth One. But, with that sky, it certainly wasn't Earth.

"We appear to be on a planet on the outer edge of its home galaxy," observed Shaun, "with another in relatively close proximity."

"A long way from home, then?"

"Definitely."

They may have been hundreds of thousands of light years away from Joh, but only a couple of steps through the hedge of the garden in White Gates Cottage, where the evening shadows were just beginning to encroach across the lawn. They could still see the cottage through the gate among the undergrowth on the side of the track onto which they had emerged. Kakko had been disappointed that Tam had not been invited. Shaun wondered how it would be to have Kakko all to himself, but as it happened, they were both free from commitments over a long weekend. The season had finished for football and they both had more free weekends. Shaun had indeed taken Wennai out for a meal, but it was quite clear that she was not going to accept any "God-talk", as she put it, and so nothing more had been arranged. They had agreed to be "just friends".

As brother and sister wandered down a lane in the direction of the village, they were passed by a long single-decker bus. It was sleek and built for speed but it was going no more than a few kilometres an hour. Walking past the first few houses, Kakko and Shaun saw the same vehicle drawn up beside what appeared to be a community building. Its occupants – nearly all young women of around Kakko's age, though there were two men, too – got off the bus and filed into the doorway.

Then more young people came up behind them, and greeted Kakko and Shaun.

"Hi. Come from far?" asked a young woman with her long hair gathered into a ponytail by an ornate scrunchy.

"Um… not so far," said Kakko hesitantly. She never knew how to answer that question.

"We're local, too – Banes. I'm Jullam, and this is Krinto." They gave a little bow.

"Kakko."

"And Shaun," said Shaun diffidently.

They attempted a similar bow, feeling rather awkward.

"We're not local – just haven't come far today," explained Kakko.

By this time they had reached the door, beside which stood a couple of ladies smiling, greeting and bowing. Kakko looked at Shaun, who gave a little smile of acquiescence. It felt like they were meant to be there. They entered a large hall that was full of chairs, three quarters of which were already occupied by young women and the occasional man.

One of the men approached Shaun.

"Welcome. I think perhaps we men can make a real difference. Men who believe in the freedom and equality of the female can have a meaningful impact."

"Certainly," said Shaun, who had never imagined girls to be anything other than equal. But he knew firsthand, of course, that this was not true in every society. Not only had this been particularly the case with the Sponron commanders on the *Tal*, but it had been so on Planet Earth One for much of human history. He recalled his nan saying that in Britain a hundred years ago, women were regarded as the 'second sex', and Abby had complained that some of the families in Persham were dominated by patriarchal husbands and fathers – especially among ethnicities originating in other parts of the planet. It appeared that the female sex were experiencing something of the same problem here.

Kakko picked it up at once. "I reckon this is part of a female emancipation meeting," she ventured to her brother. "I can't read those banners, but you can tell from the images."

"A backward society," whispered Shaun.

"Prehistoric… but that bus was pretty cool. I'd like to get a look at the engine. It's quiet and doesn't appear to be producing much heat – at least, not excessive heat. There is no radiator at the front and it is clearly built for speed."

"Rear engine?"

"Yes. But in a combustion engine you need an air intake upwind wherever the engine is situated. Did you see any exhaust?"

"No."

"Neither did I. I'd love to lift the lid."

"You might get a chance – but I think these women have more pressing problems."

"If the women were permitted to access technology, that would solve some of the problems."

"You mean engines could be a male preserve here?"

"Probably closely defended. The suggestion of an equal society may undermine the male's sense of purpose."

"Precisely so!" said a middle-aged woman in shirt and trousers, who had approached them to lead them to a seat, and had overheard. "I see you have grasped some of the psychological impact that all too often gets ignored." She wore a badge that probably indicated that she was among the organisers. Kakko and Shaun allowed themselves, with Jullam and Krinto, to be conducted to a row in the middle of the hall.

"You are partners?" asked the woman.

"Sister and brother," answered Kakko.

"You are most welcome. Can I give you an order of proceedings to share? The turnout has been heavier than anticipated." She thrust a folded leaflet into Kakko's hand and moved on to conduct a group of girls looking lost.

"I can't read this," said Kakko. "Can you?" She passed it to Shaun, who shook his head. He wasn't getting a translation either.

"It'll probably be obvious when it happens. There'll be a few speeches followed by questions."

Jullum and Krinto whispered that this was their first time at such a gathering, too.

The proceedings began. Several women in their thirties and forties took a row of chairs on a raised platform facing the audience. A robust-looking women got up and welcomed everyone. She seemed to be well known and was greatly applauded. She introduced herself as Mia Tong. She was delighted with the turnout and pleased to see so many young men. This was not just about "female liberation", but "gender liberation", she explained. It was about empowering both women and men to achieve the potential of the race. "When men realise that in an unequal society they are also trapped by the system, even if not to the same extent as we women, then we can look to a rapid revolution in all-round attitudes and cultural assumptions. It can happen within a generation.

"Fellow campaigners," she continued, "it can happen in our generation. I believe it is just around the corner. And so do some of the men who jealously guard the ways that have prevailed over our race since its inception. They are panicking." The hall applauded loudly. "They are on the retreat. They are eking out the time before ultimate defeat." More applause.

"So now is the time to push... and to push hard. Those trying to hold on to power are against us. They will resist, they will prevaricate, they will seek to discredit us. They will pull the strings of nostalgia among the old; they will even use physical force." The hall was alive with enthusiasm. "We must fight; we shall show them we have every bit as much mental muscle as they have, and..." she continued in a low voice, "we shall win!" The woman was a gifted public speaker; she held her audience in her thrall. Whether or not you agreed with all she said, you wanted to.

After an hour or so of addresses by speakers of a similar ilk, a break was called. People got up to stretch their legs and talk to those around them. Kakko got into conversation with Jullum and Krinto, and moved away with them as they filed out into the aisle. The girls next to Shaun chatted excitedly among themselves but completely ignored him. He felt embarrassed, and just sat down again, pretending he needed to check his shoelace.

At last, after some less inspiring speeches, they broke for lunch. Kakko was swept up by her two new companions, introduced to a group of others and was soon out of sight. Shaun just sat alone. He thought, *It's all right making the point that some worlds oppress their females. I don't doubt it, but when it comes to it, they can be ignorant, too.* No-one seemed to notice him on his own. He began to resent his sister's apparent insensitivity to him. *She's no idea what it's like to be a guy that doesn't fit in. Not all of us are gifted at pushing their way in as she does.* Shaun just sat where he was. He didn't feel like queuing to eat – he told himself he wasn't hungry. Still no-one spoke to him.

Having made loads of new friends, Kakko returned and took her seat. She was alive and animated. She hadn't even noticed Shaun hadn't eaten anything and was completely unaware of what he was suffering.

"We really have to do something to help these people," she declared. "They are totally bossed about by their menfolk. They don't even get to vote in their elections. What kind of democracy is that?"

"How can we help?" muttered Shaun.

"Not sure yet. Let's listen. But we just have to. That's why we're here, I reckon."

The chairperson was standing and addressing the company, and the conversations died away. There was to be one more short address and then the conference would be called on to divide up into action groups. Shaun felt the woman at the mic was too strident. He was already fed up, now he became disturbed. Kakko, however, seemed to be quite accepting of it. It occurred to Shaun that his role might simply have been to accompany his sister at the beginning of this visit. The thought of going home grew in his mind. The more he thought about it, the more he was sure he shouldn't be here.

At the break, the girls that had engaged Kakko invited her to accompany them in their group.

"Sure," she said. "Where are you going to go, Shaun?"

"You would rather I didn't tag along with you?"

"Yeah. Fine," she said, with an indifferent air.

"No, I shan't stay. I think I shall go back through the white gate now," he said, in as matter-of-fact a manner as he could muster.

"But, Shaun, we've only just got here. We can't go now."

"No. You stay. I don't really belong here."

"Shaun!"

"What?"

"These people need us."

"They need *you*. Look, sis, I'm one of very few blokes here. I'm like a fish out of water."

"Shaun, you have to stay. You just can't go running off."

"Why? Because *you* say so? Talk about oppression, you've been bossing me all my life… and besides, it's not 'running off'. It's knowing when to withdraw. It's about – "

"Shaun, this is not the place to have an argument. It's not about us…"

But Shaun's temper was stirred. His failed relationship with Wennai had left him vulnerable – his self-confidence was at a low ebb. Suppressed resentment from his pre-school days bubbled up to the surface – years of having Kakko dominate the house fuelled his rising anger. She had always been the first to act and speak. She had been bigger and quicker than him for most of his life.

"There may be a problem with gender bias here," he spat, "but in our house it's about being the elder sibling. You've bossed me about, pushed me aside when I got in the way, decided things for me – or simply ignored me in your rush to get what you want."

Kakko stood stunned. She knew Shaun could get angry. It had happened when Grandma had died, and at times it had erupted on the football pitch. Kakko was dismayed and didn't know what to do. The hall was rapidly emptying as the delegates found their way into meeting rooms. Jullam and Krinto had waited, but then decided to leave Kakko and Shaun to it, and had gone on without her. Kakko just looked at her brother and then, to her surprise as well as his, began to cry. Tears welled up in her eyes and ran quietly down her cheeks. Shaun's temper subsided.

"Do you really feel all that, Shaun?"

"Sometimes," he whispered. "I guess right now it's really about how uncomfortable all this is making me feel." He waved his arm at the retreating delegates.

"I had no idea."

"You hadn't noticed that no-one has spoken to me while you were making friends left, right and centre. I have been sitting here feeling like a… like a spare part."

"No… Sorry. Maybe we should go."

"I –"

"Come along, you two," commanded one of the organisers, coming upon them. "Why don't you join the group in Room 5? They're rather light in numbers. Down the corridor, second on the left."

She shooed them down a passage in the opposite direction to the exit. Shaun had missed his chance. To leave now, he was going to have to get past this rather daunting woman. He and Kakko were forced to move off in the direction indicated. He found a tissue for his sister.

"Unused," he pronounced.

"Thanks. You wouldn't really have left me, would you?"

"You're more than capable on your own. You even took on a prime minister, if I recall correctly."

"Of course, I *can* hack it alone… if I have to. But it's always nicer when I'm not."

"Even if it's your pesky younger brother?"

"You're not pesky… except when you're feeling sorry for yourself like now. Look, half of what you say is true. I have been a bossy sister, but –"

"Only half? Which half?" Kakko looked up at him. He was teasing her now. The storm had abated.

"But with the other half, I love you. Only half, mind… I don't want you to leave me and I don't want to leave here."

"OK. As long as you don't forget that I find a hall full of females a bit scary."

"Shaun, you're more than equal to it. Just go for it. Pick the prettiest one you can find and chat her up. Be bold!"

It's easier for you, he thought. *Some of us just aren't made that way.*

They had arrived at Room 5 and their conversation was at an end. They joined a dozen others. In front of them on a whiteboard were some words that they couldn't read. Kakko peered at them and tried to memorise the shapes of the letters, but they were quite complicated. The bespectacled woman next to her saw her looking hard and said, "Forgotten your glasses? I'm always doing that myself. It says, 'Ideas for Positive Action'."

"Thanks," said Kakko, resolving to remember that trick.

"We've been invited to write down any ideas and pass them up," said the woman.

"Ah, I see."

"Have you got any?"

"Nothing at the moment. Let's see what other people have to say."

The woman at the front wrote the suggestions on the whiteboard. They all sounded very militant. They ranged from a nude demonstration through the city centre to burning an effigy of the president, or even hijacking his plane. Eventually the facilitator threw in a remark that stoning the president's train with pebbles was going the rounds. The intention would not be to actually hurt him, but if he got hurt a little it wouldn't do their cause any harm.

"A large contingent of disenfranchised females throwing off the bonds of oppression to show they meant business would attract media attention," she said.

"The editors of the papers are all men, though. They won't be on our side," suggested a person at the back.

"That doesn't matter. Any attention at all is better than being ignored. What men want is that we females keep silent, meekly toeing the line –"

"Doing their washing, and being baby machines to satisfy their egos and male bloodlines…" put in a woman from the front. "I know. And I'm damned if that is going to be the lot of my daughters and their daughters after that!"

She was clapped and cheered.

Kakko and Shaun were alarmed. Shaun hated violence, even when riled he would never actually hit out. Kakko thought the whole idea naff and childish. It reminded her of her petulance as a little girl, stamping her feet and throwing down her toys in frustration at not getting her way.

12

When they all began to reconvene in the central hall, it turned out that five out of the six mini meetings had all come up with the same suggestion. They were all wanting to stone the president's train.

"They're being manipulated," whispered Shaun to Kakko. "Someone has had this planned all along."

"Yes," she said. "I agree they have to do something, but *this* isn't right."

"Apart from the violence, I can't see how it would make people more inclined to change things. It might even make matters worse."

"You're not a pacifist, though."

"No. But this isn't armed resistance. It's akin to terrorism," he asserted. "It could be counter-productive. I can imagine those in power saying that females should be more controlled, because left to their own devices they will become unruly."

"You're right. What do you think they should do, then?"

"Round up some men as well as women. It should be seen as the demands of the people, not just women, and then –"

"Ladies." Mia Tong had retaken the dais and was calling them to order.

"And gentlemen," murmured Shaun under his breath.

"Ladies. Let us get feedback from the groups."

It was quickly resolved that stoning the president's train was the order of the day.

"So, we are all happy that the committee here should

look into this kind of positive action?" asked the leader, in an almost rhetorical manner. She didn't expect what came. She hadn't reckoned on a young woman who had grown up an equal, and who had confidence to speak her mind in public. Kakko was on her feet.

"No!" she shouted. Shaun almost died of horror.

"Such an action," said Kakko with authority, and in a voice to be heard, "would almost certainly be counter-productive." The hall was all shocked into silence – you could have heard a pin drop. "I believe any kind of violence, such as what is proposed, will play directly into the hands of those we are most trying to overcome. They will use it against us. They will say, 'See how irresponsible they are,' and they will call us 'hysterical', like we've got our wombs in a twist. It'll be put down to our hormones and used as justification for not giving equal freedoms."

"So what do we do – sit down and 'behave' like countless generations before us?" shouted another woman from the floor. "Do nothing? I'm for positive action." There was a rising clamour.

"No," Kakko was shouting, "we *should* take positive action, but without violence."

"But then they won't listen!" shouted an exasperated woman.

"Yeah, it's time to give them something to think about – show them we aren't weak," called a woman behind Shaun. "The men need to hurt. I say, let's punish them!"

The passion in the hall rose. The ladies on the dais were conferring. Mia Tong called for order.

"Ladies… Ladies…" she held up a hand. "Let us hear this young woman out," she pleaded. "Tell us how *your* kind of positive action would work," she demanded.

Kakko stood and gripped Shaun's shoulder. "The first

thing you need to do is engage the men from your own families. You have to start with them. If you cannot get your husbands, boyfriends, brothers or your fathers to back your cause, then you don't stand a chance anywhere else. Tell them they will have to do more than just support you with words at home – they have to come out and be seen – speak up for you, carry your banners alongside you. That is why my brother is here with me. He believes in equal opportunities, not just for women, but everyone.

"Then, you have to demonstrate you can do things that have traditionally been done by men. Actions speak as loud as words. Then, after that –"

"What's your line of work? Tell us what *you* do then?" heckled a woman in a mocking tone. The idea of getting her menfolk involved had not appealed to her.

"I'm studying agricultural engineering. But I like engines of all types… Tell me, what kind of fuel does that bus run on? The one parked outside."

"It's electrical. It uses the latest in battery technology," called a young man from the back of the hall.

"I'd love to get a look at that engine," replied Kakko. "What kind of system does it employ? Is it magnetic or piezoelectric?"

"I'm not sure," said the lad. "Piezoelectric, I think."

"Linear or rotary?"

"Dunno. We'll ask the driver to let you have a look after the meeting," he laughed.

"I guess you've made your point," broke in the organiser, fearing the meeting might move into a discussion about motor engineering instead of women's rights. "You had another suggestion."

"And then you go out onto the streets," said Kakko, "and get onto the media, and make a fuss. It will probably take years – but you can't turn millennia of prejudice round in five minutes... You've got to be patient..." Kakko stopped. She couldn't believe she had said what she had just said. "And patience," she added, "is what I'm rubbish at – ask my brother – but there isn't a quick fix." Kakko stopped speaking, but stayed standing.

"She's right," said a voice on the other side of the room. "If we got our menfolk to actually come out with us, like that brave young fellow there," she pointed at Shaun, "that really would make a difference."

"I vote," said one, "that we come back here – say, in two weeks time – and bring as many men as we can. My Jo is fully on our side, but he doesn't get involved because he doesn't think it's up to him. But it is. I've got to try to get him out with me."

"He's going to have to be damn brave," muttered another.

"But that's the point, isn't it?" declared Kakko. "If things are going to be changed, they are going to have to be changed by men in the first instance, whether we like it or not. They have the power. Any man who takes up our cause, even if it's the president himself, is going to have to be brave. The more men we have on board, the more the bravery will be shared."

"Tell me, young lady," interjected the strident organiser, "what is your name and where are you from?"

Kakko was anticipating this. She was determined not to make the same mistake she thought she had made with the British Prime Minister.

"Some of you here have been praying to God about this issue... about this meeting today. You have asked God to help you. Well, She has. She has summoned us to be here – both of us, my brother as well as me, because," she looked down at Shaun, "I couldn't speak without him here."

"What was that you called God?" asked the leader.

"God called us here. She –"

"God is a 'She'?!"

"Well, yes. You can say 'He' or 'She' because God is neither male nor female really. But I often use 'She' because that's how She makes me feel."

"That is one of the most wonderful things I have ever heard," said Mia Tong. "It has never occurred to me to use a feminine pronoun for God."

"I dumped the idea of God a long time ago," said a young woman just in front of Kakko, "but if God isn't an old patriarch, I might reconsider Him – I mean – *Her*. Wait until I tell my priest we met an angel from God that called God 'She'!" she whooped.

The people on the platform were again conferring. "Alright," called the leader, "we will put this to the vote. Who is in favour of reconvening here in two weeks with as many men as we can persuade to come. Two weeks will still leave us all options so far discussed, including the president's train. Those in favour?" A forest of hands were raised. "That is overwhelmingly carried... And please keep any talk of positive action at this stage to a minimum – we don't want to be arrested before we act. Now, I expect everyone would like to speak to our young newcomers..." people were already converging on them, "but I would ask them if they would come up here for the moment while the rest of us avail ourselves of the fine tea our friends from the village have laid on for us."

The people around Kakko and Shaun ushered them to the front as the rest attacked the food tables for the second time.

Kakko and Shaun did the best they could to explain the white gates. They were used to it by now and had learned how to do it in a way that did not make them sound so odd. Kakko described how it was on Planet Joh, and how she and her friends, both male and female, had grown up just assuming that they were equal. Between mouthfuls of cake – he was hungry since he had not had any lunch – Shaun told the story of the *Tal*, and how shocked they all were to think they had different rules for men and women. Kakko said that her nan spoke of what it had been like on Planet Earth, and how quickly things were changing. But by "quickly" she meant over three or four generations, and that was only in the western world. There was still a long way to go.

Kakko and Shaun were relieved to discover that the connection with other planets through portals was not a huge surprise. Their biologists had long pointed out to the people of the planet, which they called Wjik, that they all must have arrived through some other means than evolving locally. They were an alien species.

"We are human, like you," explained Kakko. "We are not angels."

"You *are*, in so far as you believe you are sent by God. Human messengers."

Surrounded by curious delegates, Kakko never did get a chance to study the bus engine – but a large number of young women demanded the driver open it up to view, and quizzed him about it. He showed them where the batteries slid in and out from beneath the length of the bus. On longer trips, while the passengers were in the café, he told them how he took the bus into a bay at a service station where the batteries were replaced with fully charged ones. On short trips, this wasn't necessary. A small diesel-driven generator was employed to add charge, while the bus waited for the passengers. This was augmented on sunny days by photovoltaic panels built into the roof.

Jullam climbed a tree to look. "I've never thought about all this before," she said. "I'm going to study engineering when I leave school."

"They wouldn't have you," asserted Krinto.

"There are no laws about it. My best subject is maths. If I can persuade my father to let me stay on to advanced level, I will prove that I'm as good as any of the boys."

"That's it, isn't it? It's like Kakko said. We have to start with our own families."

★ ★ ★

By the time Kakko and Shaun stepped back into White Gates Cottage garden, they were exhausted. It was early morning, so they just lay back on the grass in the shade of the tree as Daan rose higher in the sky. A gentle breeze wafted across them as if God were saying well done, now rest. Blossom fell like little blessings, petal by petal around them. They looked up into the blue sky.

"This is such a beautiful place," sighed Kakko.

"So that was Planet Wjik. I can't get over that fantastic spiral galaxy against the black sky."

"Yeah. It was so close. You could see it, like, in 3D."

"Yes. It would have been several hundred light years away, but that's close in galactic terms. We were at exactly the right distance and angle to see it in all its vast glory. This universe is so beautiful. I will never forget that sight." They fell silent again.

"Shaun... I..."

"Yes."

"I'm sorry."

"What for?"

"Being such a pain. I don't want to be a bossy big sister."

"No. It's me that should be sorry. I shouldn't have said the things that I did. I have been rather mixed up recently. Sometimes, things just flare up."

"I know. We're both a bit... impassioned... but those things you said, they're all true! I *am* bossy."

"Look. You are two years older than I am. You can't help that. You've always been a live wire – that's part of your nature. You're an extrovert and I'm definitely not. And I'm slower to act than you, so that means I'm bound to come second sometimes… mostly, in fact. But that's how it is. It doesn't mean that it's wrong. You don't set out to be bossy."

"You forgive me?"

"You're forgiven… Did you mean what you said in that hall – about not being able to say what you did unless I were there?"

"Most certainly. You told me what to say."

"Did I?"

"Yes. You said they had to get their men involved."

"Yeah. That was me, wasn't it?"

"And you didn't only tell me what I needed to say, you were also there to prove the point – a 'brave young man' that girl said."

"Not that brave, I almost ran away. If we hadn't had those 'words', I would have already gone. I only stayed because I had been trapped."

"Whatever. You were there and you were meant to be there."

"Yeah… Thanks, Sis."

"It makes up for all the other stuff you said…"

"Forget that. That's about me, not you."

"Shaun, I want you to be happy. I really do."

"Thanks."

Kakko lay thinking a while. Then, she said, "Shaun…" But he was asleep. She lay back and drifted off herself.

Some minutes later Shaun awoke, propped himself up on his elbow and looked at his sleeping sister. She looked innocent and delicate, breathing gently as she lay on the soft grass. He was so proud of her. He was amazed at just how much she took on – and succeeded in. He knew she was always aware of the presence of God with her, but, still, she could act and speak out. He could never be like her. *I must give up comparing myself to her,* he thought. She was in trouble so often, though, and he knew she was as self-deprecating as he was. *And I haven't done much to improve that today, have I, Sis? What I have to do, is discover what I have to give this universe. And to affirm you, as you use what God has given you.* He recalled what Pastor Ruk had once said:

"We are each of us unique. Nowhere in the whole universe is there anyone like you or me. And every one of us is precious to God. Never forget that. There is something you have to give, every one of you. Don't judge yourself just on human measures – exams, looks, sporting achievements, wealth, respectability and the like. There is much more to being human than those superficial things – find out what wonders you have been given to give, not keep, and share them at every opportunity."

"Thanks God," prayed Shaun quietly, "for directing us to do what we can in your universe. I reckon we've achieved something for you today."

★ ★ ★

Kakko and Shaun were never to return to Planet Wjik. But the meeting reconvened with more than a handful of men. Peaceful, if vociferous, protest was made as the president arrived in his train. Mia Tong was arrested, accused of inciting violence, but it was not proven. She was released when hundreds of letters began pouring into the prosecutor's office, including many from men who did not just add their signatures to those of their womenfolk, but wrote on their own behalf.

And Jullam was not just allowed to continue her education, she was actually encouraged by a proud father. She was the first female in her school to study advanced level maths, physics and mechanics – things were indeed changing on Wjik.

13

"Goodness!" exclaimed Ada. "What in heaven's name is that?"

Ada had just entered the cottage garden and was staring at the hedge opposite.

She had loved to hear Matilda's tales of her adventures, but she never felt like travelling much herself – she had never been very far from Joh City. And, what Matilda told her about Planet Earth didn't make her feel like going there at all. But now, just as Ada had stepped through the gate that Matilda held open for her into the garden of the cottage, she was transfixed by the sight of the gate opposite, which seemed to glow. Above it, the world appeared to fold in upon itself. The frightening thing was that she knew what she was seeing – and the implications of it.

"Oh my!" was the whole of what Matilda could say for an entire minute.

Eventually she managed to ask, "What can you see, Ada?"

"That gate over there… tell me it's not… it's not one of your…"

"Ada Pippa, you and I are going on an adventure."

"Who says? No-one has asked me if I want to participate in anything… anything…"

"Exciting?"

"No. Well, yes. I don't do 'exciting', I never have, and I do not plan to now."

"Adventures are not always something we plan, Ada. They just happen."

"Not to me."

"They are now. You are being called."

"What if I say no?"

"No-one is forcing you, Ada. But you'll regret it if you don't accept the invitation. You're bound to be nervous, but, trust me, if you are doing the Creator's bidding, you will never regret it."

"What if I never come back?"

"Then you will have found a better place than you are in now. I could have stayed on Planet Earth, but I'm jolly glad I didn't."

"But Joh is much nicer than Planet Earth."

"Is it? It depends on where you are and who you're with."

"Does this gate lead to Earth?"

"No idea… Look, we'd better check to find out if anyone else can see it. It could be we're part of a larger party."

Matilda entered the house and called. "Jack, Jalli. We can see a new white gate. Can you?"

Jalli came to the door. "Mum, a white gate? Where?"

Matilda pointed in the direction upon which Ada's gaze was still fixed.

"No. Nothing."

Jack joined them. "Can't say I'm sensing anything either. It's pretty obvious when there is a gate for me."

One by one, the children followed them outside. Kakko walked up and down along the hedge while Matilda called out.

"Yes, there. Stop."

"Come away, Kakko," said Jalli. "You clearly can't see it. No, Mum, it seems that it is just for you and Ada."

"What in heaven's name am I going to do?" asked Ada.

"Ring your neighbour and tell them you're going on a trip with me. Then they won't be alarmed if no-one is at home tonight," suggested Matilda.

"Come in and I'll put the kettle on," said Jalli. And then added, "I don't think it will hurt if you put off your departure until after lunch... What do you think, Jack?"

"I say have lunch first. The Creator will not expect Ada to rush at her first opportunity!" said Jack.

"Not like me, you mean..." broke in Kakko.

"I doubt there is anyone on Planet Joh quite so keen as you were that first time," sighed Jalli. "Ada's brain doesn't work as fast as yours."

"It certainly doesn't," muttered Ada. "Lunch and that kettle sound lovely. I need time to decide whether I'm going or not."

"But you can't –" began Kakko.

"Yes, she can," interrupted Bandi gently.

"Thank you, young man," sighed Ada and followed Jalli into the cottage.

Matilda wandered over to the white gate and found two suitcases – the kind with wheels and a telescopic handle. She wondered why the idea of a handy case with its own wheels hadn't been dreamt up earlier in the history of humankind. She thought how neat they looked and wondered which was which. She bent down to examine them. They had labels attached with her and Ada's names and an address, 'Teapot Cottage, Trocklestone'. *Sounds nice,* thought Matilda. *This has the promise of a pleasant adventure.*

"Whatever am I going to wear?" worried Ada over lunch.

"You're probably alright as you are. I don't think we have to change. There are closed suitcases for both of us with our names on."

"The Creator thinks of everything," explained Kakko.

"So it seems," replied Ada. "I don't really have a choice in this, do I?"

"Yes, you do," answered Bandi again, quickly, before

Kakko could reply, "but as soon as you get through the gate you'll be pleased you went."

"You're sure?"

"It brought Jack and I together," smiled Jalli. "I'm glad I went through my first… not that I knew what I was doing at the time."

"I think I'm past finding a husband," stated Ada firmly.

"You never know –" began Kakko, determined to get a word in.

Matilda raised a finger. "What Kakko means is that something good will come out of every adventure, no matter how much of a challenge; and I say that God will never ask you to do anything that is not 'you'. And I doubt it'll be about finding a partner in life. There are all sorts of things He invites us to share."

"So what is this place going to be like?"

"No idea, except that the cases are labelled 'Teapot Cottage'. So, I expect we'll be greeted with a pot of tea."

"Well, alright," agreed Ada. "But you'd better fill up my cup before we go. You make nice tea, Jalli, and it will fortify me for the journey."

At this rate, I hope they have a handy loo, thought Kakko, but she didn't say it out loud.

★ ★ ★

The first thing Ada noticed when she opened the gate and entered the new world was the scent of sweet grass and the nectar of a richly stocked flower border. Wherever it was, this place was warm and lush with a myriad shades of green. Then they heard the sounds of children.

"Aunt Ula," said a little girl, "how long before we can see Mummy?"

"That depends on how she is, Sita," answered an older

woman about the same age as Matilda and Ada. "We will have to wait to see what the doctors say."

"We know she's poorly," said a boy a little older than the girl. "We promise we will be good."

"I know you will, Natu," answered his aunt, "but, you see, your mother has not woken up properly yet. When she's awake and stronger, then we can all go and see her in the hospital."

"What about Daddy?" asked the girl.

"Your daddy is with her, holding her hand. He hasn't forgotten you, but I promised him you could come and stay with me until your mother gets home. You see, he can't look after you and be with your mummy all at the same time."

"But we wouldn't need any looking after," answered the boy.

"Your daddy is in the hospital. He's staying there. He wouldn't leave you all by yourself at home, now, would he?"

"I don't suppose so," whined Natu.

"Don't you like being with your aunt Ula?"

"Yes. We just miss Mummy and Daddy."

"Of course you do. And so do I… now, why don't you go play for a bit while I get us something nice for tea –"

Ula looked up and saw Matilda and Ada at her gate.

"Oh, hello. Sorry, I didn't see you there… I'm sorry, I haven't time to talk at the moment. There were two people from your temple here only last week. You are from the temple, aren't you?"

"No," said Matilda warily, remembering how she used to deal with the pairs of people from different sects that had called at No. 68 Renson Park Road back on Earth One, "we are not. We are very sorry to trouble you, but is this 'Teapot Cottage', Trocklestone?"

"It is."

"Well, we have just been given this address, by er… we found these cases with our names on and our way led here. Er... um... have you asked anyone to call – asked anyone to help?"

"No," said the woman, "the only person I've talked to in the last two days, apart from these children and my brother-in-law on the phone, is the Almighty. So–"

"That'll be it," ventured Ada.

"What?"

"Well, I gather from my friend here, who is always telling me about her adventures, that they often happen as a result of prayer."

"You're from God?"

"Strange as it sounds to you and us, kind of, yes. It is the only explanation," said Matilda. "Invited by the Almighty – but very human and not very 'mighty' ourselves."

"You don't sound like Temple People."

"We aren't. We're just quiet folk who sometimes find ourselves... venturing."

"The cases? Are you staying?"

"We haven't arranged to do anything else. Perhaps, if you could tell us what you were asking the Creator for? –"

"You'd better come in. Do you drink tea?"

"I've just had –" began Ada, but Matilda nudged her gently in the side.

"That would be lovely. I'm Matilda and this is my friends Ada."

The children had taken to playing with a ball and some skittles on the lawn.

"Sorry, grass needs cutting," said Ula as they entered the house. "Haven't had a chance to get to it for over a week and it grows very fast this time of the year."

"I know the feeling," replied Matilda. "I used to be very bad at gardening indeed. It got on top of me. Perhaps we could run the mower over it for you."

"You will not!" said Ula. "I don't put jobs onto people I've only just met."

"That rather depends what you were asking God for," answered Matilda boldly.

"You really believe He sent you. You sound so sure. Are you ghosts or something?"

"We need to explain," said Matilda.

And so, over the cup of tea, Matilda explained all about the white gates and her family's experience. Ula didn't interrupt her once, except to offer them a second cup of tea. At the end of it, Matilda sat silent. Then, she said, "That's about it, really."

"And this is my first time," added Ada. "I must say I was very apprehensive –"

"Scared," interrupted Matilda.

"Apprehensive. But it's really wonderful here. You have such a beautiful home and two lovely children."

"They are my sister's," said Ula. "Let me explain."

Ula went on to tell them that three days before this, while the children were attending school on the last day before the holidays, her sister, Tani, the children's mother, and her brother-in-law, Billum, were driving together when a truck lost control down a steep hill. It had taken out two parked cars and sent one of them into the path of the car that her sister was driving.

"She has sustained damage to her spinal column just below her neck, concussion, broken ribs and collarbone, and one broken arm above the elbow," she elucidated. "She is currently in intensive care in the hospital. Her husband got away with just a few bruises and is at her bedside."

"What are the doctors saying?" asked Ada.

"She's stable, but they are keeping her sedated for the moment. They don't want her to aggravate her injuries.

Her spine is braced. When she comes round, they'll have a better idea of how much damage has happened to the spinal cord. The worst-case scenario is that she could be paralysed – although tests are showing that that might not be complete."

Ula told her new friends that she had taken the children to care for them until things changed.

"They often come here for a few days in the holidays," she said. "We get on fine… Billum cannot cope with them at the moment. He wants – needs – to give his whole attention to Tani. He's still in a state of shock."

"What about you?" asked Ada.

"Me? I wasn't there when it happened."

"No. But she is your sister."

"Well, since you mention it. Yes. You're the first people I've been able to talk to since it happened. There aren't any other relatives and my neighbours this way," Ula pointed up the hill, "are away. And Gus down below rarely comes up the valley. I don't think he has been past his own house more than half a dozen times in the twenty years I've lived here."

"A person needs to talk sometimes."

"Yes. I don't know why I've told you all this – you being perfect strangers and everything."

"Sometimes you can say things better to people you don't know. History can get in the way."

"You're right –"

"Hello. Have you come to stay?" asked a small voice from behind them. They turned and saw a rather grass-stained little boy standing in the doorway looking at Matilda and Ada's luggage.

Ula turned to him and said sternly, "We haven't talked about that yet, Natu… I'm afraid," she continued in a softer tone to her visitors, "I don't have any spare rooms – with the children here."

"You can have mine," stated Natu decisively. "I can share with Sita. She wants me to stay with her in her room anyway. She gets lonely at night."

"Natu," whispered his aunt forcefully, "these ladies haven't decided whether they want to stay yet."

Sita pushed her way in past Natu. "But they've got cases. It says 'Teapot Cottage' on them," she said. "I can read it 'cos it's written right. Daddy showed me how to write it when we sent you your birthday card."

"And this one said she would cut the grass," added Natu.

"Natu! That's rude. You have not even been properly introduced."

Matilda and Ada introduced themselves, and they all shook hands.

"Can I take the cases into the bedroom now?" asked Sita. She had been longing to wheel them.

"It looks as if you are staying, unless you'd rather go into town. It's a couple hours by car to get there I'm afraid."

"We'd be happy to stay," said Matilda, "unless we're in the way."

"We insist on helping," said Ada. "That's what we're here for."

"I'm hungry," droned Sita after the novelty of wheeling the cases into the downstairs bedroom had waned.

"We can eat. But first we need to get you two cleaned up. You both need a bath."

"Where's the kitchen?" asked Ada, already on her way. "Ah, I see." The dirty dishes from several meals were piled up on the side, and the draining board was also full.

"Got it. Leave this to us." Ada and Matilda were rolling up their sleeves before Ula could protest, while Sita dragged her aunt to the bathroom.

"Where's the hot water?" called Matilda.

"In the kettle on the range. I'll need the water in the tank for the bath," replied Ula from halfway up the stairs.

"I can see why this isn't a job for my grandchildren," laughed Matilda to Ada as she cleared a space for the clean pots from the draining board. "You see, Ada, adventures needn't necessarily involve climbing down cliffs, running from massive explosions or falling in love with a native of another planet."

"Each to their own. Kakko would despise this kind of adventure, I guess."

"Not half. But that's the way it works… I like these cups, they're so delicate and rather pretty."

"She brought out the best for us. I wonder when she last used them. I think the family use the mugs."

By the time the children were bright and shiny, so was the kitchen.

"We haven't put anything away," said Matilda. "Tell us where it all belongs."

"I'm hungry," repeated Sita.

"Me, too," said Natu.

"OK. We'll put these things away and then I can look for a tin of beans," said Ula. "That'll be quick. I know Aunt Ula usually has something special, but I haven't had time to get ready for you this time."

"We can cook," said Matilda. "Point us to the food."

"But –"

"No buts. This is what we're here for."

It was quite evident from the things in the cupboard that Ula cooked most things from scratch – bread, vegetables and meat. It was a country cottage where the owner was not used to nipping out to the shop everyday. So, most of the ingredients that Ada and Matilda needed to make the food were at hand, and in less than an hour they had assessed what they found and put it together in a kind of Earth-cum-Joh dish. It was a surprise to everyone, and delicious. The children, to Matilda's relief, thought it was great, too, and Natu declared that they had to show their mum how to make it.

"I can't say we could make it again," replied Matilda. "I don't even know what we put in it – we're not familiar with all your vegetables and powders."

"I don't know how you do it," said Ula. "I've been trying to make something good with the stuff I've known from childhood for years, and you just come in and invent the nicest dish the first time you enter my kitchen."

"Beginner's luck," stated Ada. "Still, it's a pity we didn't take a note of what we used."

The children ate ravenously. They were fascinated by Matilda and Ada, and asked so many impertinent questions that they soon ceased to be strangers. It appeared they adored their aunt Ula, who turned out to be a childless widow – losing her husband when she was still young.

"My husband, Jos, left me with a decent income and this cottage," explained Ula. "I let the land and that adds to my keep. But Jos didn't leave me any children, so I have borrowed my little sister's."

The children were silent. The mention of their mother brought the pain to the surface again.

"Let's pray," said Ada. "I think we have got lots to tell Him… or Her. What do you say? Him or Her?"

"We say 'God'," answered Sita. "God is sometimes a 'Him' and sometimes a 'Her'."

"It depends what we're praying for," explained Ula.

"Fine. So, thank you God," began Ada, "for –"

"We're in the kitchen," interrupted Natu. "We pray to God in the bedroom."

"Right," said Ada.

"I think," broke in Ula. "I think we should pray to God *all over* the house tonight."

"What a good idea," said Matilda brightly. "God is everywhere. God is here and with your mummy and daddy, strong, gentle – everything and everywhere all at the same time."

"Is God as far away as the stars?" asked Natu.

"He sure is," replied Matilda, "because, you know what, that's where we're from. From a star up there in the sky."

"Which one?"

"I don't know where to look from here," said Matilda, looking out the window. "They all look the same to me."

"But they aren't. Not if you look hard," said Natu. "Some are white, some yellow and some are red. Some of them are swirly galaxies."

"I guess Daan, our star, is a yellow one. My grandson, Bandi, knows all about them. I'm afraid I don't."

"You're a *kitchen* person," said Sita. "I know you like washing-up and you're good at cooking."

"Thank you. You're right. I am a kitchen person."

When they had said hello to God in every room of the house, and Sita and Natu were in their bedroom, Ula tried to say a final goodnight prayer with them. Matilda saw that Ula was upset and didn't want to show it, so she quickly intervened, asked God to help the children's mother to get better soon and bless their father. Then, she said a prayer she had learnt at school and the Lord's Prayer.

"That's an interesting prayer," said Ula. "Where does it come from?"

"Oh, the 'Our Father'? It's a prayer from Planet Earth."

"Say the prayer again!" demanded Sita.

"Yes. I will, but you must tell me the name of *your* world, *your* planet."

"Oh. Our ball is called Kroywen... the other one is called Sirap. Some people live on that one, too," answered Natu.

"Two planets to choose from! You are very lucky. OK. I'll say the Lord's Prayer and put in your planets' names instead of mine." Matilda prayed: "Your will be done on Kroywen and Sirap as it is in heaven."

"Tell us about heaven," demanded Natu.

Matilda explained that heaven was the dimension that was the home of God. It wasn't part of the universe, but held the universe within it. "Heaven is everywhere where God is. It is our homeland – the place where we all belong and where we go when we've done with this universe."

"We belong here on Kroywen," said Natu.

"You do – but your heart was created by God to be with him forever. You can't live on Kroywen, or any planet in the whole wide universe, forever, so you must move on to heaven when you die. Heaven is the best place of all – it is wall-to-wall love with no evil, no pain and no crying."

"Why do we cry when people die, then?"

"That is a good question, Natu. I think it's because we never like saying goodbye to someone we love – even for a short time. That's why mothers cry at weddings – their children have grown up and they are moving on. They know they will miss them."

"Is heaven a really, really nice place?" asked Sita.

"The best place – better than anywhere you could ever imagine. We can't know how nice it is until we get there."

"Will Mummy go there?"

"She will, one day. But we don't know when yet. Her body is very poorly, but the doctors say they don't think she is ready to go just yet."

"If it's such a nice place, I won't mind her being there... but I don't want her to go now... is that bad?" asked Natu.

Ada shed a tear. "It's never selfish to want to be as close as possible to the people you love," she said.

"Do you have people you love in heaven?" asked Sita.

"Lots of them. In my family, I'm the only one left in the universe," answered Ada.

"You must be very lonely."

"I am – but only sometimes. I have to be patient. But God is always cheering me up and giving me lots to do. He gave me Matilda here to be my friend – and now, it seems, He's sending me on adventures to meet lovely new people."

"Now, I think it is time to go to sleep," suggested Ula. "You know where my bedroom is. We're not far away. And if you leave the room, take care at the top of the stairs. I don't have a gate like you have at home."

"They scrambled into the same big bed together. Then, Sita said, "Story."

"Of course," whispered Aunt Ula. "A short one." She told them a little story about an angel who went around making the flowers grow.

"Thank you," said Sita

"Song," added Natu. Ula sang a song.

"Now it is definitely time for sleep. Aunt Ula is tired and is going to bed soon, too."

"And so am I," sighed Ada. It had been a tiring few hours. The children gave them all a goodnight hug.

Downstairs, Matilda and Ada decided to put the kettle on, and make another pot of tea.

"I can't thank you enough for coming," said Ula. "I don't want to admit it, but I wasn't coping."

"You're human," replied Matilda. "No human being can manage the shock of having someone special in hospital and then having to look after two lively children, too – all on their own – without needing someone to share it with."

"I should be able to. It's not as if I haven't had the children before. And they're not difficult. They're good kids."

"But lively…"

"You're right… And I can't get over how quickly I've taken two perfect strangers into my home. Why is it I can feel I can trust you?"

"The wise thing to do would be to remain suspicious of us," suggested Matilda. "Watch for any tell-tale things that don't add up."

"But they do. The whole situation is… surreal, but not odd or wrong. It's hard to explain. It was when you prayed that I really believed you were genuine. You let God in. People who want to deceive wouldn't want to risk that. What you did wasn't just words – I felt the breath of God in my heart… And, anyhow, I can't think what you would want out of me…" Then, she said quietly, "Whoever you are, and whatever you're here for, you have saved my sanity… You're people of my own heart," she smiled. "You know where to find the kettle!… Let's have that tea."

Over the next hour, Matilda and Ada told Ula all about themselves. Matilda explained how she had come to live on Joh, and the way the white gates had brought her son and her daughter-in-law together. She concluded, "Jack may have lost his sight, but he became a new boy. I shudder when I think of those dreadful years when he was a child. I was bitter a lot of the time… and he suffered." Ada put her arms around her friend.

"But he wasn't damaged beyond repair," she said. "You must have loved him."

"I did – but not as I should have done."

"No parenting is perfect," said Ada. "What's important is that the child needs to know he or she is wanted… you wanted Jack. And you prayed for him."

"I wasn't aware of that... and I didn't do much praying in those days – I was angry with God for most of the time."

"Well, I think He is big enough to take it," said Ula. "You know, I don't think people get angry with Him often enough. Sometimes, I reckon, He's there for people just so that they can get angry with Him. He wants us to get all the angst out there."

"I agree," said Ada. "God has very broad shoulders... Would anyone mind if I went to bed? I've had the most exhausting day. When I got up this morning, I had no idea I would be going on an adventure."

"I'll join you," said Matilda. "If our host doesn't mind..."

"Not at all. I'm ready myself."

"Tomorrow... do you have plans to visit your sister?" asked Matilda.

"Yes. I thought I might take the children in the car. I know they probably wouldn't be allowed in, but they could see their father in the car park."

"They would like that. Does the hospital have a café? That would be better."

"I don't know. It's all new since I last went. I expect they might these days... Billum is going to ring in the morning and we can make the arrangements then... Is there anything else you need?"

"No. Just a bed. I must say I'm shattered. I can't imagine how tired you must be. Goodnight."

14

They were awoken at six in the morning by the ringing of the phone. It was Billum. Tani had taken a turn for the worse – her temperature had shot up. An infection had set in in one of the wounds, and they were taking her into theatre again to try and clear it. That day was not the time to visit. Could she keep the children another day?

Sensing something was not right, Ada and Matilda had got up, and were next to Ula as she took in the news. "I think Billum fears the worst," she sighed, sinking into a chair. Matilda took the phone from her hand. Ada went into the kitchen to find the kettle and the teapot. Hearing things going on, the children bumped down the stairs.

"Was that Mummy? Is she coming to get us?" demanded Sita. Matilda replaced the receiver on its stand and took the children into the kitchen.

"Sit down at the table you two. That was your daddy. They are having to give your mummy another operation, so she's going to have to stay asleep for at least another day. That means Daddy is very busy looking after her in the hospital, and we are going to have to stay here and think of something very special to do, so that we can tell your mummy and daddy all about it when it's time for you to go and meet them."

"But we were going *today*," protested Natu.

"I know, but this new operation means that you and your aunt Ula are going to have to be rather patient. What we have to do is find something wonderful to do to tell your mummy when she wakes up. What do you like doing best?"

"There isn't anything to do here. All our toys are at home," sulked Natu.

"But you must do something when you are here. What do you usually do when you stay with Aunt Ula?"

Sita bounced. "We go to the woods. We explore up on the hill. Aunt Ula knows where all the creatures live – she shows us their holes and their nests," she explained.

"But we can't do that. You heard Aunt Ula – she must be where the telephone is in case Daddy rings," said Natu.

"Of course," replied Matilda. "Leave this to me. Do you know what is the first exciting thing we can do?"

"What's that?" mumbled Natu, becoming slightly intrigued.

"Make a special breakfast. What do you usually have for breakfast?"

It wasn't long before all the ingredients they ever had for breakfast were lined up on the table.

"But we don't eat all of them every time," laughed Sita. "We have to choose."

Ula was still in the same chair in the living room she had sunk into following the phone call. Now she sat with a cup and saucer in her hand, and Ada was contemplating getting her something warmer to put on. That was what you were supposed to do for someone in shock, wasn't it? Matilda put her head round the door to ask about breakfast, but Ula was clearly not in any frame of mind to think about breakfast. So Matilda came back to the row of things on the table.

"Are you sure that's all of them?" she asked.

"You need milk," said Natu, "on those. But not these."

"I think, as it's a special breakfast for me, that I want to taste a little of each of them. Let's mix them all up."

"But we never do that," explained Natu, horrified.

"Not on normal days when me and Aunt Ada aren't around. But I think I want to be greedy today."

Sita laughed and was soon absorbed with counting a few of each cereal, nuts, seeds, biscuits, pieces of fruit and other things that Matilda did not have a clue about into three bowls. She then began to spoon jam on top. Natu was about to protest again, but Matilda held her finger to her lips and winked at him. He had become an accomplice in caring for the spirit of his sister, and understood he had to be 'grown-up' and pretend. Sita looked around the table for other things to add and, to her delight, she found some chocolate chips on the baking shelf. Then she announced, "We are not going to put any milk on."

"Won't it be a bit dry to eat without?" wondered Matilda.

"No *milk. Ice cream!*"

"But –" began Natu and then looked up at Matilda as she said in a covert tone, "Natu, is there any ice cream?"

"Somewhere – in the freezer." He went hunting for it, and tugged a box from out among the 'snow' and began to try and prise off the lid. Matilda helped him. It came off all of a sudden, and the box shot onto the floor and skidded across the kitchen. Sita shrieked with delight. Matilda retrieved the box and soon Sita was heaping scoops of ice cream on top of her creations.

"Is it ready to eat now?" asked Matilda. Sita nodded and ordered, "Spoon!"

That breakfast was quite memorable. Matilda wondered why we don't allow children their heads more often. *Adults can make life so dull*, she thought. Ula and Ada declined the mixture in favour of a second cup of tea. But Matilda did her best with it and, actually, quite enjoyed it. Natu ate it all without further protest. His sister might have broken the conventions – but it was more than acceptable to enjoy it when it was there.

It soon became evident that Ula was not going to be able to concentrate on anything that morning. She gave permission for Matilda to take the children out into the woods, while Ada remained with her. She clearly couldn't be left. There are times when neighbours are important, but Ula had so few. The family up the valley were away and the man a kilometre below hadn't been near Ula's house for years.

Matilda and the children roamed the wood. Matilda was fascinated by the myriads of wonderful new living things she was being introduced to. They were quite like some of the things she knew from Earth or Joh, but different, too.

At the end of the wood, they emerged onto a path that overlooked the neighbour. Smoke was issuing from his chimney.

"He always has a fire in his house," said Natu, "even when the weather is hot."

"There he is," pointed Sita. "He is doing his garden again." She waved to him frantically and, at last, caught his eye. He waved back. They descended the path and walked up the lane to the house.

"Hello," he said. "Where's your aunt?"

"She's at home," Natu told him. "This is her friend, Aunt Matilda." The man extended his hand.

"Having a few days in the country?"

"Mummy is in hospital," explained Sita. "We have to stay with Aunt Ula until she is better, and Aunt Matilda and Aunt Ada are helping."

"Ah. Sorry to hear that. I mean about your mummy."

Matilda added some details, and told him that she and Ada were staying for the time being until they knew which way things were going.

"Give your Aunt Ula my regards," he said. He was not a man who said much.

"We will… we'd better let you get back to your garden,

you still have some weeding to do. Why is it that the weeds grow even if it's too dry for the vegetables?"

"That's because the weeds are natives here; the vegetables aren't. It'd be like asking my daughter to live here instead of the city where she feels at home."

"But you're different. I guess you have more in common with the weeds than your vegetables," suggested Matilda.

"You could say that. But at the moment I'm contemplating being like a vegetable and going to live near my daughter. It doesn't do to be on your own when you're getting on... I bet Ula is mighty glad you're here this week."

"She is..." said Matilda. "Well, it's been nice talking to you... Come on, kids, let's get back to your aunt Ula, and put the kettle on again."

★ ★ ★

By lunchtime, they had heard that Tani was back on the ward. Mercifully, her temperature was getting back to something like normal. The crisis was over – but the final outcomes were still unknown.

★ ★ ★

That evening, Ada and Matilda were encouraged by the children to cook again.

"I don't know if we can find something different" protested Ada. But they were told that exactly the same again would be just fine. Of course, it wasn't. When you are cooking something new without a recipe, it never is.

"Oh dear," pronounced Matilda when it was finished, "it looks as if we have way too much! We're eating you out of house and home, Ula."

"No worries. I have plenty in store – I never know when I will be in town and it seems silly to go there just to shop. The truth is that, in fact, I shop every time I go and visit these folk and it stacks up. I'm glad of the help to get it eaten."

"Well, I reckon we have enough for two days here," said Matilda.

Just then, there was a knock on the door. They all fell silent.

"More unexpected visitors?" asked Matilda.

Ula nodded. It was crossing her mind, as well as those of Ada and Matilda, that it could be bad news. Billum wouldn't want his sister-in-law to find out the worst on the phone.

Before they could stop him, Natu ran to the door and opened it. There stood neighbour Gus.

"Er, sorry ladies, I hope I haven't called at a difficult time… Oh dear, I have, haven't I? You're just about to eat… I'll call back –"

"No. Perfect timing! Absolutely perfect," said Matilda delightedly. "We have cooked way too much. Come in. Come and join us."

"You know each other?" asked Ula.

"We met today while were on our walk," explained Matilda.

"I just thought I would call. Matilda here told me of your… your problems."

"You are welcome, Gus. How long has it been since you were last here?"

"Far too long… I didn't want to be in the way."

"You're never in the way… Well, don't stand there with your hat in your hands looking like a freshly dug vegetable. Come in, sit down and eat."

Gus did. He definitely knew how to eat. Sita pronounced that that day's dish was even better than the one before, but it was Gus who had the most seconds. Ada moved from feeling relieved to being quite proud of herself. It was good being useful. She felt she hadn't been quite so useful in years. Adventures to new places where you could be useful were much better than being a tourist. She'd gone off holidays to resorts a long time ago.

They had just completed the washing-up, and were sitting down with another pot of tea, when there was a second knock on the door. This time, Sita beat her brother to it. She lifted the latch and yanked at it, but it was hard for her as the handle was above her head. The person on the other side pushed a little to help, the door swung open and there stood Billum.

"Daddy!" yelled Sita. Natu rushed at his father, and with barely one foot inside the door Billum was encompassed by arms, bodies, legs and faces. He held on, just managing to keep his balance.

Ula's face dropped. This was the thing she had been dreading. Matilda, Ada and Gus stood and watched.

"Mummy. Is Mummy better?" demanded Sita as she dragged her father into the sitting room.

"I'm glad to say she is much better. She is still being kept asleep… they think they might be able to wake her up tomorrow. The doctors sent me home, but all I could think about was you two… and your aunt, of course, so I drove out here instead…" Billum looked up and addressed Ula, "She has fought off the infection well. They have done a lot of scans and X-rays. They're hopeful that she could make a full recovery – but, of course, we won't know until she gains consciousness… I hope I haven't come at the wrong time," he added, noticing the company.

"Of course not… Let me introduce you to Ada and Matilda, who have… er, just dropped in in my hour of need, and I think you know Gus, my neighbour. Billum, my brother-in-law."

138

"Very pleased to meet you." Matilda took his hand. Ada did the same.

"I don't suppose you've eaten?" asked Ula rhetorically. "Come and sit down, there is plenty left… I don't think this is going to go round again tomorrow," she laughed with a nod to Ada and Matilda.

"Let me warm it up," said Ada quickly.

★ ★ ★

That evening ,the children wanted Matilda to tell them a story. Their daddy had to listen, too. "You are very good at stories," he observed, when she had finished. "At home, I leave that to my wife."

"Oh, you mustn't do that. Everyone should tell stories," said Ada. "You don't have to do it from memory. Read from a book."

"I'm not very good at reading aloud."

"Then you must practise."

"Yes," said Sita firmly. "Daddy read now!"

"It appears I have no choice," he smiled. "What shall I read?"

"I have just the book," said Ula. "Would you like some of the princess stories?" she asked Sita. Sita climbed on her daddy's lap and Ula passed him the book. Even Natu was pleased to hear his father read – even if it was from a little girls' book.

Bathtime and bedtime followed. Sita took control of the prayers. She prayed for her mother and then, one by one, everyone else including "Uncle Gus", which touched him. Then, Natu insisted that Matilda say the Lord's Prayer for all the planets.

After the children had gone to bed, Billum asked whether

Ula and the children would return with him to their city home. "I think the children would be easier to care for if they had their friends around them," he conjectured. "I don't expect it would have to be for very long. When Tani wakes up, she will want to see the children."

"Anything you want," said Ula. "But that makes sense. I think I could manage in your house."

"Thanks, Ula. You're a Godsend."

"That," she said, smiling towards Matilda and Ada, "is a description more fitting of my unexpected angels here." Billum smiled a tired smile. The day had been a hard one.

"Oh dear, we don't have any more beds," sighed Ula. "Gus, can you help? Have you got a spare room?"

"No," protested Matilda, "he must stay in the same house as his children… I think, Ada, that our job is done."

"I agree," said Ada. "I don't think Ula is in need of our company anymore. And tomorrow you're all going to the city. Time we were on our way."

"But it's nearly dark," said Billum. "You mustn't set off for the city tonight."

"Who says we are going to the city? Our gate is just over the road." But Billum was too tired to follow this up.

Matilda and Ada stuffed their things in the suitcases while Ula changed the sheets.

"Are you sure? Gus might help."

"Certain. I'm missing my little flat," said Ada, "and Matilda's family will wonder where she's got to, anyway."

"Say goodbye to the children for us," said Matilda. "It has been wonderful knowing you… and we shall continue to pray for your sister, Tani. God listens in every part of the universe."

"Thank you… I have no doubt you *are* angels."

"Human ones."

"You are welcome any time."

"Thanks," said Matilda, "but I hope and pray you don't need us. It's been good to have been here to help."

Billum was fast asleep in his chair, and Gus declared he was ready to leave, too. He believed the two ladies were telling a tale about a gate opposite. He knew no-one lived in the woods over the road and he thought they were just being gracious – so he was ready to rescue the ladies with the offer of his spare room. But Matilda and Ada took their leave of him, too, and, before he could catch up with them, they had crossed the road and simply vanished.

"Told you they were angels," stated Ula.

"I'll have to try this praying thing a bit more often, myself," said Gus, still staring at the hedge and scratching his head under his cap.

★ ★ ★

It was late afternoon on Joh. Ada was pleased to know she was in time for the last bus into town.

"These adventures take it out of you," she said. "I'm going to sleep very well tonight. There isn't time to come in."

"Shall I see you tomorrow?"

"What day is it tomorrow?"

"Sunday," said Kakko, as she swung through the conventional gate. "Glad to see you back."

"Sunday! I suppose it must be. See you at the worship centre then."

"If I manage to get up… better be off, the bus'll be coming soon." She gave them a wave. "Bye."

"So what have you been doing on your adventures, Nan? You look tired."

"I am."

"So, spill the beans. Where did you go? What did you do?"

Inside the cottage, Matilda sat down and ordered Kakko to make her a mug of tea. She then told her all about being there for Ula and the children.

"So, what did you *do*?" Kakko repeated.

Matilda went on and described the two days. Put like that, it didn't sound like they had done that much.

"So all you did was cook, wash up, tell stories, go for a walk in the woods and drink endless cups of tea?"

"But being there to listen, and help the woman mind the children were important things."

"I suppose so. But it wasn't much of an adventure, was it?"

"Kakko, some sorts of adventure don't involve exploding arms factories, broken limbs, getting yourself on TV and the like. I'll leave the daring deeds to you. Being there for someone in need is very important – just listening may be all that is required… but, believe me, listening can be very tiring."

"If you say so, Nan," said Kakko, unconvinced.

15

"How beautiful is that?!" marvelled Bandi as he and Abby stood gazing at a magnolia tree in full bloom. The smoky pink and white blossoms stood upright from the end of every twig, bright green leaves just emerging around them. Beneath the tree, which was more than three times Bandi's height, the grass was littered with its petals.

"Awesome," agreed Abby. "I marvel at this tree every year. And when this has finished, that may tree over there comes into bloom. I love the spring!"

It was just before Easter that Dave made the announcement. He had been interviewed for the parish of St Chad's, which boasted the largest membership, not to mention the largest church building in Persham, and had been offered the job!

Abby was stunned. A new job for her father meant moving from the vicarage. She could hardly remember the first house she had lived in, as she was only six when they had moved to St Augustine's. This was her home – and, of course, it was the location of the white gate that was her only way of seeing Bandi.

"Dad," whined Abby, "we can't leave. We just can't leave here! What about our white gate?"

"But surely," intervened her mother, "I remember you telling me once that the white gates are arranged by God. If it is God's will that your father take on this new parish, it follows that your white gate will follow you."

"That makes sense," said Dave. "*If* it is God's will."

"Of course it's God's will. You did not look for this appointment. God has arranged it," said Lynn.

"Or the archdeacon has conspired to get me it. I haven't accepted yet."

"What! After going through with this application and the interview, and leading me around the vicarage and the parish…"

"I haven't said no. I need time to pray about it… but whatever happens, Abby, your mother is right. The white gate is something that has been given you and Bandi. It is only there for you. Neither your mother nor I have ever seen it. It goes with you – not the house. It may be you're going to have to take a step of faith on this one – the same as me and your mum. At least you won't have to move your school – and it won't happen until the holidays after you have sat for your exams."

"I'm not sure I want to stay at that school," said Abby quietly. "Some of the kids are going to the Longmead Sixth Form College across the town. I could go there – or I could go to the FE college."

"What's wrong with your school?" asked her mother.

"What's right with it? OK, it turns out pupils with reasonable grades – but there should be more to a school than that."

"Like what?"

"What it feels like. Whether they care about you… treat people as people rather than learning machines to get the school a good rating."

"And your school doesn't do that?"

"No… well, some teachers do, but the same rules apply to them – results are what keeps them in a job. That's all that Silent Sam goes on about."

"And that makes a big difference when it comes to A

levels," put in her father. "Education should be about helping people to think critically – and that is required at A level – especially if you choose to do humanities subjects."

"I also thought I could do something vocational – and not do A levels…"

"Not do A levels!" Her mum spoke with force. "A bright child like you can't opt out of education at sixteen!"

"But, Mum, it's not opting out. Not everyone has to go to uni these days. I mean, if you want to be a lawyer or something, you could do it without going to university."

"But not without A levels. Do you want to be a lawyer?" asked her dad.

"No. I guess not. I have thought about nursing, though."

"If you want to go into medicine," said Dave, "with your predicted grades you should consider being a doctor."

"Do you think I could? I have thought about that, but it would mean studying all the sciences – and I don't want to drop history or literature…"

"… and those subjects are not 'vocational' ones," said Dave. "So it's back to A-levels."

"What do you want to do with yourself – apart from change the world?" asked Lynn.

"I do want to do something that will make a difference. It's not, like, I think I can 'change the whole world'. I'm not stupid!" said Abby, getting cross. Her mum was so annoying sometimes.

"You could always take after your father," suggested Dave quietly. Lynn let out an audible sigh. Two vicars in one family would be more than enough.

"No. I don't want to spend every other day visiting people in hospital or taking their funerals. And I don't want to be a social worker or a teacher – which is a lot of what you do. Not that I don't think that is important, Dad."

"A politician then?"

"Sometimes I think that." Abby glanced up at her mother, expecting another putdown, but Lynn had been called to take some buns out of the oven, so she continued quietly to her dad. "But that would mean joining a political party – and they're all naff."

"Well, for now I suggest you follow your nose and decide on your subjects for A level – and then choose the school or college that does them well. Your mum and I will not put pressure on you to stay at your present school if you don't want to, so long as you are making the most of yourself. Your mum loves you and she doesn't want you to waste your opportunities. It wasn't that long ago that many girls were forced to drop out because their parents and their grandparents didn't believe girls needed education. Your mother had to fight to stay on at school."

"Thanks, Dad. I understand… The Longmead Sixth Form College has a debating society and a dramsoc. They do plays – like those written by Harold Pinter."

"And getting to this college will be easier from St Chad's than from St Augustine's," added her father as Lynn rejoined them. "So what do you say, girl? Shall we agree to change both school *and* parish?"

"Well, if you think the white gate will follow me?"

"If it doesn't no-one will be living here for at least six months – probably nine – and after that you could always see if you can make arrangements with the new incumbent's family to visit the fairies at the bottom of their garden. But, somehow, I don't think it will come to that. If it does, I shall be as angry with the Almighty as you will be!"

"But you shouldn't get angry with God, should you?"

"I would, if God did not live up to his promises! I think even *He* would agree that we are entitled to get angry. God is not like your distant headmaster that only calls you to Him to tell you off when you've done something He doesn't like, you know."

"I know. 'God is Love' 1 John 4:7 – your favourite verse."

"One of them."

"OK. Let's go to St Chad's," said Abby decisively.

"I have told the archdeacon I will ring him tomorrow and until then I shall keep an open mind. But it does help to know you would not oppose the idea."

"It is promotion."

"Of sorts… but I do not see this job as a career. You know that. It's being where God wants me to be, so that I can be the most useful."

"And that's probably why the archdeacon thinks you're right for the job," said Lynn.

"The archdeacon, perhaps. But I'm not so sure that that is the thinking of the churchwardens – they think I might be sufficiently safe and not want to change things."

"And do you?"

"If I were to go to St Chad's an awful lot will be challenged. That's what the archdeacon wants… and the bishop. They know me. 'We are here,' he said, 'to comfort the disturbed, and to disturb the comfortable'. But I'm not sure yet if I'm the one to do that."

"How could you turn it down?" remonstrated Lynn. "It's a step up."

"It might be in the eyes of the world. But that means nothing to God. What I have to decide is if it is where God wants me to be. If it isn't, I'll be in the wrong place and it won't work."

★ ★ ★

The very next day, Abby sort out the careers teacher and made an appointment for the following lunchtime. She had spent the late evening, after finishing her assignment, on the internet researching the Longmead Sixth Form College pages – and she liked what she saw. She could take any combination of subjects she liked – even have her own choice of history and religious studies modules, which was not possible at her present school. And there was a full spectrum of societies to choose from. She didn't have to do games – but if she wanted to she could select the ones she liked. That would mean she could concentrate oh her cross-country! Yay! And what's more, there was no uniform! The place seemed tailor-made for the girl with the revolutionary spirit! For the first time since the by-election débâcle, Abby felt positive about her prospects.

★ ★ ★

Meanwhile, Dave had also stayed up late. After he got in from his evening meeting planning the future budget of St Augustine's, he and Lynn had debated the pros and cons of a move to St Chad's. They had agreed that it was time to move on – but neither of them had seen St Chad's as the remotest possibility. Dave again said he would sleep on it.

The parish of St Chad's was a wedge of territory that spread from the centre of town out towards some of the expensive 1930s detached houses in tree-lined streets. There were a few less salubrious establishments that had once been posh Victorian houses, but which had now been subdivided into small flats and bedsits and housed rent-paying low-income earners, young and old – but, over the years, these had gradually been overcome by the extension of town-centre facilities – stores, car parks and offices. St Chad's stood at the divide between the Victorian and the 1930s housing, and the rectory was a big Victorian detached property of three floors that had seven bedrooms – the top floor being for the servants in former days.

★ ★ ★

Dave didn't sleep much. He had looked at all the options – staying put, going to St Chad's, applying somewhere else, even giving up full-time ordained ministry and going into teaching or something. What did God want him to do? That was what mattered, of course. If he went to St Chad's, it would be to stir the place up.

After he had got up and showered, he emailed the archdeacon and said he would be honoured to accept the appointment.

16

Abby's time with the careers teacher went remarkably well. He listened to her. He noted that she had thought through her options well, and had researched into the sixth form college which gave her options her present school did not. To her surprise, he endorsed her plan and said that he thought she was making a wise decision.

"Aren't you the girl who wrote the columns in the student magazine?" he asked.

"Yeah. Before it was closed down by… before it closed down."

"Before it was closed down by the principal."

"Yes."

"Do you still believe in fighting for the underdog?"

"You mean, do I think people with no power are exploited? Of course. How many people really care for children made to work in sweatshops. I didn't even think about it much until Guy came up with his idea for an underwear bonfire."

"Would you have gone through with the burning if Mr. Whitecastle hadn't stopped you?"

"Of course!"

"Even if it made you unpopular with adults?"

"It did, anyway."

"Not everyone, Abby."

"It felt like it."

"Well, don't take it to heart. I think you have made the right decision here. Here are the necessary application papers for the Longmead Sixth Form College. I recommend you get them in as soon as you can to ensure your place. You can send them to the address at the bottom, but they have an open day next week, and I suggest you take advantage of it. If you like what you see, leave the application with them then."

As Abby left his office, she wasn't sure what to make of the conversation. He seemed very eager for her to go to the sixth form college – almost too eager. Was the careers teacher telling her she wouldn't be welcome to stay on at the school – that they didn't care for her type around? That seemed like the only explanation. He hadn't been so willing to agree to what some of the others said they wanted to do. He was actively encouraging her friend Becky to stay on, but Guy was also thinking about the Longmead Sixth Form College and he had not tried to talk him out of it either. Abby smelt a conspiracy. Why had she said what she had? Mr. Whitecastle had their names in a little black book somewhere! She only hoped it would not appear on her final report... Abby shuddered at the thought.

★ ★ ★

Abby and Guy and a few others travelled together to the Longmead Sixth Form College. Lynn had wanted to accompany her daughter, but none of the other parents were going and Abby was not going to be shown up. Her dad couldn't have gone anyway. He had already got an appointment that day with the churchwardens at St Chad's; but he was happy if Abby was. He knew quite a bit about the college. He was acquainted with families whose sons and daughters had been there, and he had even been once to talk about being ordained as a job – not that he had expected a large number of young people to show interest. Vocations didn't happen that way.

But it had given him an insight into the ethos of the place and he felt Abby would fit in well.

By the end of the day, Abby was excited. She had been recommended to choose four subjects at AS level, and had gone for English literature, history, French and P&B (philosophy and belief). This last option was taught by a woman belonging to a religious studies department in Oxford, who came down to Persham for the day. Dad had read one of her books. In history, Abby had put her name down for modern European history (1789-1919) with the possibility of doing post-Second World War international history in the second year.

★ ★ ★

Two weeks later, at the morning service on the third Sunday of Easter, the congregation at St Augustine's were told the news. At the same time, an announcement was made in St Chad's.

The folk at St Augustine's were sorry to hear of the departure of their beloved vicar. Many of them had joined the church after he had come and those who could remember former vicars were apprehensive. New vicars always meant change – and who knew when they would get a new one. Vicars were not ten-a-penny these days.

At St Chad's, the congregation were all asking questions about this man and his family. Was he married? Did he have children? A name like Dave Brook did not inspire much awe. What school and university had he attended? Some openly challenged the choice of the churchwardens when they discovered Dave had studied at Birmingham. All their previous incumbents had been Oxbridge men. One lady knew Dave well because she had once attended St Augustine's before coming to St Chad's. She had decided to move because she didn't like the vicar. So now here he was following her!

Needless to say, her opinions about her former vicar were not the most comforting to her new friends. But others were willing to give the new man a chance. After all, not everyone at St Chad's had been to Oxford or Cambridge – in fact, many hadn't. Perhaps this was what the church needed. Some felt some work should be done in the poorer end of the parish, which did not provide even one regular member of the congregation. The churchwardens invited Dave and his family to come and meet the St Chad's folk in a couple of weeks' time at their May Fair. Then, they could see what they were getting in the new rector and his family.

★ ★ ★

Abby did not have to wait till then to get a look at the St Chad's rectory and the church. Two days after the announcement, her mum and dad met her out of school and they went to meet a churchwarden who let them in. The church was huge. Built in the last half of the nineteenth century, it had been one of those inspired by the Oxford Movement. At the top of a series of steps and landings, the high altar was built into a vast apse that soared into the shadows above the dim lighting. Abby had never seen such tall candlesticks. How on earth did they get up that high to light the candles – let alone change them when they had burned down? In the centre was a tabernacle that contained the consecrated bread of the Eucharist. The churchwarden genuflected deeply in the centre of the aisle and Dave followed suit. Lynn did a little courtesy and Abby thought she had better do one, too – but they never did anything like that at St Augustine's where the reserved sacrament was kept in an aumbry in a corner of the Lady Chapel. The place smelt damp and the walls radiated cold. The nineteenth-century stained-glass windows, which the churchwarden never stopped talking about, let in cold air that streamed down to the tiled floor. Abby felt the cold air surround her ankles. In one spot, the draft was so strong it ran right up inside her school uniform skirt! Was it any warmer on Sundays? Abby was certain to wear trousers in this building all the time. The big iron radiators looked original, Abby thought, although they probably weren't. There were no pews, only wooden chairs that fastened together in rows. Imagine dusting this place.

In the vestry they spotted the first signs of the twenty-first century. A very large industrial-sized vacuum cleaner stood in the corner, together with some extremely long brushes with several extension poles. "For the cobwebs," the churchwarden explained when Abby took an interest in them. There was also a long pole with a snuffer and taper. That, at least, explained how the candles got lit. Abby could not see herself in this place. It spoke of an exalted and distant God. That didn't seem to fit with the one she had imagined – for her, God was someone beside you that knew you and lived in your personal world. In this place you felt small – even insignificant.

"It's creepy," she said to her dad as they followed the churchwarden into the noisy street outside, where he wouldn't be able to hear her.

"It's empty and cold," whispered her dad. It'll be different on a Sunday with the heating on, and 150 people in the chairs."

The rectory was of the same proportions. The Victorians did not do things by halves. The place had been designed for a large family with servants. There would have been at least a housekeeper, a cook and a general maid – and probably a nurse for the younger children. The first rector in this place moved out of a thatched house in what had been up until then a largely rural area. As Persham grew so did the population of the parish, and with it the standing of the rector. He and his wife quickly filled it with eight children, two of which were also to become clergymen. But the last incumbent was a bachelor and, of course, he had no servants. He could have employed a cleaner and someone to do the garden, but he didn't.

They soon discovered the rooms that had been used – one downstairs reception room, the large kitchen and one bedroom. The rest had grown mouldy from lack of heating. The top floor, which had been the servants' quarters, was derelict. The roof had leaked at some point, and the plaster was falling off the ceilings and the walls.

"Father Bright didn't use these rooms," declared the churchwarden, "and it took sometime to discover the roof was leaking. But it is all hunky-dory now. The diocese had it repaired five years ago. But they wouldn't have it re-plastered. Maybe if you insisted on it they might…"

"I don't think we'll bother. I can't see us ever having need of this – certainly not at this stage. Perhaps at some time in the future we could let out some rooms to students…" The churchwarden turned, wearing a stiff expression, and Dave decided to hold his tongue. Whoops, he'd made his first blunder.

The rest of the rooms were very high and they all needed decorating. There was no way that they could begin to think of doing it themselves. The diocese would give them a moving-in allowance that would pay for sanding and staining the floors, and perhaps buy a bit of carpeting, but not much more. They encouraged the parishes to help with the decorating and the churchwarden announced that the Parochial Church Council had voted £600 to help with this. That might just pay for the materials, Dave calculated, but not any labour. Many parishes – most parishes – came up with some volunteers who delighted in the opportunity of getting stuck in, and having fun slapping on paint while others made tea and cleaned. This had not occurred to the PCC at St Chad's.

"Perhaps if we were to ask for some volunteers," suggested Dave.

"You can do it when you come to the May Fair," replied the churchwarden. Permission was granted!

The garden was a jungle. It wasn't so very big, but there was an overgrown patio, a small patch of mowed grass and, beyond that, who knows what. The first thing Abby thought of was where in all this mass of brambles, bindweed and overgrown shrubs was the Creator going to site a white gate? On one side, there was a huge apple tree. Many apples were still rotting in the undergrowth, but someone had trodden a path round the base of it. From behind it, there was a low tunnel through the undergrowth. Abby pushed her way to the base of the tree, and then bent down to look at the tunnel. The smell was really strong.

"Phoah!" she exclaimed. "This pongs!"

"Don't get yourself caught in the brambles," called her mother.

Dave followed his daughter. "You're right – and I think I know what this is."

"What?"

"Foxes."

"Foxes. What here?"

"Ideal place for them. We'll have to get all this cleared out."

"There seems to be an awful lot of clearing out to do," sighed Abby.

"You're right – and not only in the house. I guess there are a lot of things in a mess here."

"You can still say no, Dad."

"Someone's got to do it, Abby. Why not me?"

"Are you two alright in there?" called Lynn. "Are you stuck?"

"No. Just examining the foxes' den," replied Dave over his shoulder.

"Foxes?"

"Perfect place for them," said Dave, extricating himself. "St Chad's has everything," he teased the churchwarden, who didn't seem to enjoy the joke.

Abby looked down the tunnel again and this time heard tiny squeals coming from a reddy-brown heap in a small hollow right under the mass of bramble stems. "Babies," she called. "Baby foxes! Still very tiny."

17

"Bandi," pleaded Abby, "please come back with me to Persham. I want to take you to see the new house."

"You should be concentrating on your revision."

"I know. But I have worked out a detailed revision programme. The teachers all say that you should take time off in between sessions and go to bed early. I'm doing that – but with the sun rising so early now it's May, I get up long before I need to study, and I go out for a run most mornings. If you came early, too, we could go to the garden before I need to start work…"

"OK. But I shall leave you to it from nine o'clock."

"Fine. So how about tomorrow – it's supposed to be fine. I'll be by the white gate at five. It'll be getting light by then."

Bandi arrived at the arranged time. Abby was dressed for running, with her long blonde hair tied up into a ponytail and bright white trainers on her feet. Bandi felt scruffy beside her, but she chided him for saying so.

"It's two-and-a-half miles. Can you manage to run that?" she teased.

"Jogging or sprinting?"

"A nice steady pace."

Bandi realised that he really ought to do more of this. Abby was fit compared to him, but he did his best not to show it. He soon got into the rhythm, however, and within twenty minutes they were pushing open the wooden gate with flaking black paint.

"You should paint this white," suggested Bandi.

"It would only remind me of where it didn't lead," sighed Abby. "I do hope our white gate follows me."

She led Bandi up the weedy drive that led round to the back of the house. The dew was still on the shaded parts of the overgrown garden.

"Wild!" said Bandi, a little surprised. "It's been let go."

"It's magic, though," smiled Abby. "Look round here." She took him along the little path to the base of the apple tree that was in full blossom and showed him the tunnel beneath the brambles. The little squeals were quite audible as they approached. The mother had probably not yet returned from her night-time foraging and they were getting hungry.

"What are they?"

"Baby foxes. A fox litter. They're called cubs."

"Can you pick them up?"

"I expect so. They might nip you. But it might not be good to leave your scent on them – the mother would know, and we wouldn't want her to reject them or anything… they're out of reach, anyway… look, did you see that? A robin. He and his wife have probably got a nest in here, too."

"Is it him who is making all the noise?"

"Yes. He's very territorial and probably doesn't like us too near the nest. Let's go back to that patch of grass."

Bandi and Abby sat on the rapidly drying tufts of grass that purported to be a lawn and absorbed this patch of wonder. There was so much life. Not only were there robins, but a blackbird, too, who, after a few minutes, abandoned his alarm call and resumed his melodic song. The air buzzed with bees delighting in the apple-blossom and the plethora of wildflowers that surrounded the brambles. Abby identified some she knew the names of. There was a patch of red campion and another of blue alkanet. On the margins of grass, where they were sitting, were stems of pale mauve cuckoo flowers.

"Some people call them maids of honour," explained Abby. "If ever I got married, I would like bridesmaids dressed in that colour."

"What if your husband wanted a different colour?" teased Bandi.

"He wouldn't. And if he insisted on it, I wouldn't marry him," Abby retorted.

"I'll bear that in mind," said Bandi with a cheeky grin.

"But, seriously, there is so much I want to do before I get married… I don't think I'll marry until I'm thirty…" she mused. "Look…" Abby had lifted a flat slab that had once belonged to the patio, but was now overlapping the grassed area. Beneath it was deep brown soil dissected with tunnels full of panicking ants and, in the centre, a disturbed pale, grey-brown snake-like creature about fifteen centimetres long. It began to wriggle.

"A snake?"

"Slow worm. It's really a lizard without any legs. This is a baby one. I've seen them much bigger. They like hiding under things that get warm." Abby picked it up. It was smooth and shiny, and seemed to settle in her warm hand. She passed it to Bandi.

"Do they bite?"

"No. They seem to like it if you are gentle… We'd better put it back. The ants definitely don't like being disturbed." Abby replaced the slow worm and then the small slab very gently.

"This is a very beautiful place you are coming to," said Bandi. "I like it here."

"Yes, it's a bit of the countryside in the town, isn't it? It's much the best part of the place. The house is far too big. The ceilings are high and the rooms dark – even when the sun shines." She indicated the tall French windows behind them.

"It was built in the days of big families and loads of servants, but there will only be the three of us... And the church is a *massive*, ugly red-brick building. I reckon it should, like, be demolished or sold off, or whatever you do with churches that no longer appeal to most people, but Dad says it's grade-two listed, which means it has a national preservation order on it and we have to keep it, whatever. It would be illegal to get rid of it."

"If it is so ugly why does it have to be preserved?"

"Because it is a historic building... and because not everyone thinks it's ugly. Dad says it reminds them that once Britain had an empire bigger than any other empire the world had ever known, and we should be proud of it."

"But you don't feel like that?"

"Of course not. The British Empire did some things to help other places, but mostly it exploited them. It was about trade and wealth, and didn't care about people. Some parts of the Church of England tried to change that. They said God would not like it and they did improve things a bit – like they abolished the slave trade."

"The slave trade? What's that about?"

"Up to the beginning of the1800s the British went off to Africa, mostly, and 'bought' some of the native people, packed them in ships with no room to turn round and shipped them off to America as slaves. People got very rich doing it. Dad has friends who went to Bristol University. They told me the city of Bristol was built on the profits of the slave trade."

"But that was a long time ago."

"Yeah. But the British Empire was still going on up until the second half of the twentieth century – although they outlawed slaves in the 1830s. My dad's great-granddad was a diplomat in East Africa when he was younger. Some people still like to think of Britain as 'great' like that. They can't think why Africans and Indians want to be independent from us, because we taught them civilisation and cricket. But we also kept most of them poor and we still do. We are still exploiting poor people – that's why I supported Guy and his bonfire. I mean, there are people who make money out of poor people making them poorer, and then say it is their fault for not working hard enough."

"But Pastor Ruk says the people who follow Jesus work for justice and to see what they can do for other people. Like, that's what he taught, right?"

"Bandi, I have come to learn that, on Planet Earth, whatever people say they believe, most of them are really only out for themselves."

"Most people? You are getting rather despondent about your people, Abby. Surely, there are many good people about."

> "…but who knows nothing, is once seen to smile;
> Where sighs and groans and shrieks that rend the air
> Are made, not mark'd; where violent sorrow seems
> A modern ecstasy; the dead man's knell
> Is there scarce ask'd for who; and good men's lives
> Expire before the flowers in their caps,
> Dying or ere they sicken."

Macbeth, Act Four, Scene Three," muttered Abby.

"Whoa! That's something. Sad thoughts – beautiful language…"

"I'm doing it as a set book for GCSE. It's a Shakespeare tragedy. It only ends when most of them get killed."

"Abby, there is so much really beautiful about your world – tragic but beautiful. What makes it so beautiful is that there are people like you – and your dad – who see the good, the wonder and the true. You *do* care. And nature spills in at every opportunity, too. Whatever bad people do, however selfish they are, there is so much that is beautiful. Just listen and smell this garden…" and Bandi reached out a hand and took Abbey's, "and… and you, you are lovely, too," he stammered, embarrassed.

"Ooh you are sooo romantic. Thanks for the compliment… but, seriously, Bandi, in the last few months I've seen so many people just looking after their own interests. It's bound to make you cynical. It goes with growing up, I suppose…"

Bandi said nothing. Abby needed loving and he just held her.

"Anyway," whispered Abby, "right this moment I'm with you, and I don't want to spoil that. You being here has blessed this place, Bandi. When I watch this jungle and its creatures, I will think of you wherever you are… Bandi, I don't ever want this to end…" Bandi put his arms around his friend as tears fell from her eyes.

"Look," he pointed, "there! See that tiny little bird."

"It's a wren," sniffed Abby through her tears. "She's so small, and so beautiful…"

They sat close together and listened. Bandi studied a cuckoo flower. It was tiny, yet perfect, and Bandi knew that the beauty of it, right down to the arrangement of its tiny molecules, was a wonderful construction of order and life. It might even have a scent all of its own to attract the bees. Bandi bent forward to smell it… but he was interrupted by an alien sound – a heavy engine that grew louder as it approached. It came to a halt outside the rectory gate.

"This is it," called a man.

"Right," said his colleague. "No problem. Should go in there easy. Room for the skip, too."

"A right palace if you ask me," said the first. "Bet they rattle around in this place. Can't imagine why anyone would want something so big."

"Goes with the job. Vicars and them like it… come on, we ain't got all day, let's get the digger down… ah, here's the man himself." Abby discerned the voice of the churchwarden she had met the day before.

"Thanks for coming so quickly lads. The garden is a right mess. I hadn't realised myself until yesterday. I was ashamed to show the family around. The girl even found a foxes' den in it!"

"We'll make short work of it with this. Let's take a butchers…"

Bandi and Abby heard a clank as a heavy ramp hit the road and then the sound of a mechanical digger starting up. The warden and a man in a high visibility jacket rounded the corner and stopped when they saw Abby and Bandi just getting up off the grass.

"What? Who… oh, you're the daughter, aren't you. I met you yesterday didn't I?"

"Er… yes," stammered Abby. "This is my friend… we were on a run and I thought I would bring him here to see where I was going to live."

"Pleased to meet you, young man… You will be glad to know that I am getting this garden into some sort of order, pronto. You can tell your father that when I saw this, I didn't hesitate to get it cleared – I'm only sorry you had to see it. Up to now, it had been the responsibility of my fellow warden."

"But it's lovely," smiled Bandi. "It is so beautiful."

"You don't have to be diplomatic," laughed the churchwarden. "I know a mess when I see it. Right," he said, turning to the workman who was directing his mate in with the digger, "know what you are doing?"

"One day'll easily do it. We've sent for a skip and will order another… OK, Rich, start this side. Still not sure about the tree?" he asked the warden. "It won't be any trouble."

"No, leave the tree, we can take it down later if we need to."

The mechanical digger advanced to the brambles in which the fox cubs were now letting up a more distinct noise, if you were attuned to it, which Abby and Bandi were, and the churchwarden wasn't.

"YOU CAN'T COME IN HERE WITH THAT!" yelled Abby. "There are fox cubs in there!"

"Don't worry. They won't hang around. They'll scarper as soon as we get anywhere near them."

"But they're not weaned yet!" screamed Abby.

"They're vermin. You're not standing up for them, are you? This town is overrun with them. Don't worry, they ain't going to be extinct in a hurry…"

The man in the digger raised the arm of the machine and advanced. Abby rushed out between it and the brambles.

"Abby," yelled Bandi, running after her. "Be careful. You'll get hurt!"

"If you want to make sure she doesn't," said the man in the vest, "get her out of here."

Abby sat down on the grass, her head in her hands. Bandi came up to her and knelt beside her.

"It's not fair!" sobbed Abby. "This is the only beautiful bit about the whole place and they want to destroy it. I don't want anything more to do with this horrible world. I hate people, all of them! You said I was over-cynical. If you want evidence I know what I'm talking about? Well, here it is!"

"Just give us a minute… please," begged Bandi to the three men. This was not part of their plans for that morning. The well-intentioned warden thought that he would never understand the way the young were turning out these days. *Why did young people have to be so bloody unreasonable?* He wanted the task finished in one day… and this was costing money.

Bandi stared at them until the men had retreated round the corner, and he and Abby were alone.

"I am sure they are only doing what they think is right," said Bandi.

"But they're not doing right. They're wrong. *Very* wrong!" Abby was seething. "I'm NOT LEAVING THIS SPOT until they go away."

Bandi didn't argue. There was no point – anyway, she was right. He agreed with her. He walked around the corner, and approached the men. "I'm sorry," he said, "but there is no way my friend's going to move."

"Can't you talk some sense into her?" demanded the warden. "This is costing us money. It's for her family, when all is said and done."

"If you mean, 'Can I persuade her to move', the answer is no."

"Look," said the man from the digger, the one they called Rich. "Why don't you call her father?" The warden nodded. Bandi went back to be with Abby. When he had gone, Rich put on a thoughtful expression.

"I tell you what, me and Fred'll go and have a cuppa tea," he said. "I have had teenage daughters myself. I know how stubborn they can be. You'll not budge her while the digger's around. We'll load it up and go and get another breakfast."

"Good idea," agreed Fred.

They loaded the digger back onto the trailer and drove away, and then the two teenagers were alone once more and the peace returned. As they sat, they saw the tail of the vixen as she slid back into the den, the blackbird resumed his melodic song and life in the jungle gradually regained its former intensity. Bandi took his arm away from Abby's shoulders.

"They've gone. They said they were going to call your dad… and we've a deal."

"A deal?"

"You have to get back to your desk. Remember? You have a revision timetable and you owe it to everyone who has got you this far, as well as to yourself, to do your best in the exams."

"I guess so. I'll tell Dad and he'll put a stop to this."

As they left to run back to St Augustine's vicarage, the warden who had been hiding behind a tree put his mobile to his ear.

"Hello, is that Mrs Brook?… the warden from St Chad's here. Look, me and my fellow warden wondered if you would like us to tidy up the garden a bit – at our expense, of course. I was ashamed to find it was so unkempt…you would? That's fine. No, no trouble… in the next day or two. Next time you come it will be spick-and-span… no, thank *you*. Cheerio for now."

Next, he called Fred and Rich. "They're gone."

Rich laughed with his mate as they sat, not a hundred metres from the rectory, in a fast-food café. "Told you! I know how to handle teenagers. You can't face them straight on – you've just got to be a bit clever," he said, tapping his forehead.

By the middle of the same afternoon, the garden was empty of all greenery except the apple tree and the small patch of grass that Abby and Bandi had sat on. The original ornamental shrubs had gone, too – all that remained was an expanse of brown earth. Even the small slab that had harboured the slow worm and the ants had been thrown into the skip. Only God knew how many creatures had been made homeless that day.

★ ★ ★

Abby elected not to go to the May Fair. She didn't fancy being exhibited and used the excuse that she was now less than two weeks away from her first GCSE exam. Her father said that it was a good decision. If he had been in her place, he wouldn't have gone either. Instead, Abby went to White Gates Cottage. Bandi insisted that she kept her visits very short while she was sitting her exams. Her mum and dad were delighted with him.

18

Abby and her family pulled into the vicarage drive after a week's holiday. Dave had been determined to have a proper holiday. Abby would rather not have been away, dreading as she was the leaving of the white gate. Her exam results were due the next morning. She had elected to get them by email rather than go into the school, because, she reasoned, she was finished there, and didn't fancy going back. She thought of the teachers, who only wanted to know the results so that they could take the credit. She couldn't have stood either their tutting or their rejoicing. And the thought of meeting her classmates as they bounced or cried depending what was in the envelopes, and demanding to see what she had achieved (or not!) was unbearable. It meant waiting a few more hours – but it was worth it. She knew where she was going. Her place at the Longmead Sixth Form College only depended on her getting a C in maths and English, and another in history if she wanted to take that subject. Her predicted grades were all Bs – and, besides, a few days did not make any difference either way. It was her mother who was the most impatient. She feared that her daughter's troubled life was going to affect her scores.

★ ★ ★

During the morning, Abby kept her Facebook account open and watched her friends report on their progress. Nothing surprised her. It was all going as expected. Most were staying on to do the regular subjects. Some, of course, had already got jobs. Those were mostly the ones who were not predicted to get Cs or who had chosen to do apprenticeships. Guy was like her – waiting to get his results by email.

When they came in, she was astounded. Despite all the trauma of recent weeks, she had managed twelve GCSEs, six of them A-stars and five As. Geography was a B. This didn't surprise her as the geography teacher couldn't teach that well, and she had relied almost entirely on course books that did not give her a proper grasp of the subject. Anyway, the way was open for her to go to the sixth form college. She emailed Guy, who replied immediately that he had done well, too – not as well as her, but well enough for his own satisfaction. Abby deliberately did not post anything on her Facebook page – let them keep guessing. Despite these wonderful results, Abby was not elated. In three weeks' time, the same time as starting her new college, she would be moving into a new home across the town. She lay on the bed, thinking.

Eventually, Lynn came up the stairs. "You OK, Abby?"

"Yeah."

"Can I come in?" she said, putting her head around the door. "The school are taking a long time to let you know."

"I've got an email."

"You didn't say. Abby, tell me –"

"One B, five As and six A-stars."

"You passed?"

"I passed."

"Wonderful. Come and tell your dad. He's just come in."

★ ★ ★

"Still happy about Longmead?" asked Dave, when he had heard the news.

"Yeah." The idea of being able to concentrate on the subjects she most enjoyed, to start doing philosophy properly and to be free from Silent Sam's regime for ever, at last, finally showed on her face. Dave grinned. "I'm delighted for you, my girl. You're going to go far!" And he took her up and gave her a big cuddle.

★ ★ ★

The move was a miserable day. It rained heavily all day. As soon as they had pulled into their new drive, Abby leapt from the car and splashed around the back. This was the first time she had been aware of the chopping down of the jungle. The bare brown earth had sprouted all sorts of new weeds over the summer, but the bushes, brambles and all that they had given a home to had gone. Her hair damp against her face, Abby stalked back round the house, and straight down the drive, passing her parents without a word. Tears flooded from her eyes. She knew exactly where she was going and no-one was going to stop her. She covered the two-and-a-half miles by going a roundabout way. She didn't want her parents to follow her and bring her back. Dave went round the back to see what had upset his daughter. He was devastated. He had no idea what the warden had intended to do and knew what all this was about – and he also knew exactly where Abby was going. He drove back to St Augustine's and, from the end of the street, he waited and watched as she went back into the garden of the vicarage. He followed her round just in time to see her disappear through the hedge. At least he knew she was safe. This was the first time he really began to think that moving to St Chad's was a mistake. If it was God's will, He was demanding a big sacrifice – and it was not Dave who was going to suffer the most. He and Lynn could manage whatever situation they found themselves in –

as he had told himself many times, it was not about him, but about the task and he was the best person for it. But Abby. He felt ashamed. She had never wanted to go. She had been brave – very brave – and she had succeeded in her exams despite everything. She was a remarkable young person. If only St Chad's had come up two years later when she had moved onto a university or a job somewhere. But it was too late for regrets. Thank God she had Bandi and his family. He wouldn't blame her if she decided to emigrate to Planet Joh on a permanent basis – but how he and Lynn would miss her!

"God Almighty!" he yelled out loud. "You had better move Abby's gate or I'll chuck the lot in – whatever your damned will may be! In fact, You and I will not be on speaking terms until it happens. Do you know what, sometimes I wonder whether all this faith bit is only a figment of human imagination like the secularists tell us. Perhaps we, who seek to follow you, are all fools. Maybe the people who just want to get as much out of the world for themselves as they can are right!"

Dave was hurting. He phoned Lynn to say he had seen Abby disappear through the hedge. She was safe. Lynn screamed at him. "Didn't you try to stop her?"

"No," he said. "She's better with the Smiths."

"Dave. She's our daughter!"

"She's safe. That's what matters."

On his way back to the car at the end of the street, Dave passed Abby's career teacher.

"Good morning, Reverend."

"Good morning." Dave didn't feel like talking, but Mr Beckingsale looked, as if he wanted to.

"You might not remember me. I'm – I was – Abigail's teacher contact in the career department at the school. Congratulate her for me on her results, will you. She didn't come back into the school in person."

"I will. No, she didn't. We had only just got back from a holiday. Thank you."

"She's going on to Longmead."

"Yes. She liked the course options."

"And the freedom of being a young person with initiative that was being stifled where she was. I am certain she has made the right decision."

"Abby did feel a bit… put upon, a few months back."

"Put upon! She was downright squashed. Deliberately silenced and intimidated."

"Those are strong words, Mr…?"

"Beckingsale. I would like to tell you something, Reverend Brook – but it has to be in confidence."

"Anything you tell me will remain with me, Mr. Beckingsale. Look, let's not stop here in the street. We have just left the vicarage there – it's now empty of every stick of furniture save for one broken chair! Do you want to come with me to my car?"

"Sure."

Sitting in the car, the rain running down the windscreen, Mr. Beckingsale explained that he would have loved to have encouraged Abby, but his professional loyalties had prevented him from doing it. He didn't want Abby to think that his ready agreement to her decision to go to Longmead meant that he didn't care. He had now left the school himself and was, temporarily he hoped, without a job. During the time of the bonfire affair he had openly stuck up for Guy and Abby and the others, and in a staff meeting had objected to the principal's strategy. He had called it manipulative and deliberately intimidating, and had then been, himself, called to Mr Whitecastle's office and told that he had overstepped the mark – he had put the interest of the pupil before the interest of the school.

"I'm afraid I spoke out at that moment. I blurted something about 'education being to enable children to think for themselves' and was told that the purpose of a comprehensive school was not to breed subversives. The reputation of the school was paramount. When Abby came to me before her exams to tell me what she wanted to do, it helped me make up my mind. I immediately sat down and composed a letter of resignation."

"Before you had a new job?"

"Unwise? Maybe. But your Abby had integrity – everything I lacked. I couldn't have lived with myself a moment longer… will you do something for me, Reverend?"

"Call me Dave."

"Dave. Thanks. Will you pray for me that I will get another job? I have an interview tomorrow. You see I have a wife, two kids and a mortgage. The latter is the most demanding. I am very fortunate that I have the full backing of my family."

"Certainly, Mr. Beckingsale."

"Tom."

"Can I ask where the interview is?"

"Longmead Sixth Form College, actually."

Dave smiled. "This is good news. Very good news. I shan't tell anyone."

"But, please. Do tell Abby that I think she has made a very good decision… and I wish her all the best for her future. What courses is she taking?"

"She's going to do history, English literature, French, and philosophy and belief – that includes ethics."

"Ethics. That's a subject that should figure on Mr. Whitecastle's curriculum – but he doesn't rate it. The suggestion was squashed in favour of business studies. Tell Abby I shall watch her progress with interest. And now I must let you get on. I've taken up too much of your time already."

"Before you go, Tom. Let me say a prayer with you." Dave prayed for Tom, his family and the forthcoming interview.

"Amen," said Tom. "Thank you." He shook Dave's hand, smiled, opened the door, stepped out, pulled up his hood, and walked away down the street.

Dave sat behind the wheel for several minutes. He recalled that before he had met Tom Beckingsale he had had a one-sided row with God! And now here God was – he had witnessed the courage and integrity of a man brought to see what was good and right through the actions of his Abby.

"God, you are so wonderful! Just when I think this world stinks, you break in with roses! You can't keep a good God down. God, I'm sorry for what I said just now. Bless Abby and Lynn, bless Tom and bless those folk at St Chad's, who are scared about what is going to happen… and me!"

★ ★ ★

Matilda was the first to see Abby as she ran across the lawn of White Gates Cottage. "Goodness me, my child, what on earth is the matter? You look like Alice in pursuit of a white rabbit."

"Alice?" said Abby, catching her breath. "Oh. Alice in Wonderland!" She breathed in the soft air of Woodglade. "I *am* in Wonderland. And this time I am not going back to grotty, horrid Planet Earth! Is Bandi in?"

"He's at the Institute today. He started last week if you remember. He has important exams in three months' time. But come on in; Jalli and Yeka are about somewhere."

Within half an hour Abby had poured out her heart, while Jalli and Matilda plied her with Johian sodas and listening ears. She concluded, "… and I don't know what I would do without you and Bandi. This could be my very last chance to visit. If they wreck the garden in St Augustine's vicarage the same way as they have in St Chad's!"

"The gate can be anywhere," reassured Jalli. "It doesn't have to be anywhere beautiful. It often isn't. One of the places Kakko went to on Planet Earth was right in the middle of a city by the TV people."

"Yes, London. The BBC. She told me."

"Don't worry about the gate, Abby. There is nothing either you or anyone else can do to put them in place or move them."

"No. I know that really. It's this whole business. It's getting to me. I hate it."

"It's all new, Abby. It might not turn out to be quite as bad as you imagine. Nothing can stay the same for ever. It has to change. You have to change. And by all accounts you are pretty pleased with the idea of the new school – col-lege."

"I am. That's true."

"I know what Persham can be like," ventured Matilda. "I've lived there most of my life. It's improving. St Augustine's has been transformed. St Chad's is probably headed the same way with your father there. Britain is probably better now than it was, believe me. You must be proud of your father."

"I… I guess I am… really. I've been so caught up in myself… so terribly selfish."

"Not terribly selfish," said Jalli. "No-one can just give. We all need building up and affirming, as well as sacrificing."

"I never thought of it, like, sacrificing. But I suppose it is."

"Vicarage families do it all the time," said Matilda.

"I suppose so."

"Now," said Jalli, "you've been here long enough."

"But what about Bandi?"

"Bandi won't be in for hours. And your family need to know you're safe. You did not tell them where you were going."

"No. But they'll have guessed."

"Maybe. But they don't know. If you don't show soon, they may be worried."

"You're right, I'd better go. Not that I want to."

"Don't worry about the gates. The Creator will have that in hand."

Abby stepped through the white gate that had stood in the hedge of White Gates Cottage almost as long as she had known Bandi and this family. And, to her amazement, she emerged, not in the garden of St Augustine's Vicarage, but in that of St Chad's Rectory – almost on the same spot that the foxes' den had once been.

"Abby!" screamed her mum from somewhere inside the house. There followed a lot of thumping and banging as she tried to open the French windows that led onto the lawn. Eventually they did open with a harsh squeal and lots of black dust and cobwebs. This was probably the first time they had been opened in some years. Lynn leapt out into the garden.

"Oh, Abby. We've been so worried about you!"

"I'm OK. I've been to Woodglade."

"I know. Your father saw you disappear."

"So you needn't have worried then."

"No. We knew you were safe. But that's not it. You were beside yourself. I've never seen you so upset."

"No. Mum, I'll be OK. I know, my job is to study for my A levels – and Longmead is much nearer here."

"Yes. But exams are not everything."

"Say that again, Mum!"

"Exams are not everything. I never believed that. As long as you have things balanced. Life is not passing exams – it's about making the most of your time, both for now and the future."

"Thanks, Mum. I do intend to do that – make the most of my time. I shall get involved in some of the social things at

Longmead as well as the study… and now – yay! – the gate, my white gate, is right here – over there!"

"I thought I didn't see you come up the drive."

"No. I thought I was going to be in the old vicarage. But instead I found myself standing over there behind those weeds… I mean, wildflowers."

Lynn laughed. "We'll get a jungle back next year – just for you! Dad will do nothing to stop it. He'll be pleased to oblige…"

"Abby!" Her father came bounding through the door. "I didn't expect you so soon!"

"Jalli said you would be worried. She wouldn't let me wait for Bandi."

"She's a very wise woman. Come here. Give me a hug."

★ ★ ★

"Phone's ringing!" It was Dave calling from behind the doors of the cavern-like downstairs loo. "Can you answer it, Abby? I'm in the bathroom!"

"Sounds like you're in an echo chamber!" replied Abby finding her own voice resonate in the tiled hallway. It would take a bit of getting used to this living in such a big house.

Abby answered the phone, which was still on the floor of the room designated as her father's office – or "study" as the churchwardens called it. The decorators had been through the house, and everything was bright and new. At the expense of a combination of parish, diocese and family. The archdeacon had been brilliant in this regard, and, pleading special circumstances, had got the bishop and diocesan machinery to find some extra help.

"Hello," said Abby in her best vicar receptionist voice, "St Aug … I mean, St Chad's vic… rectory."

"Hello is that you, Abigail? This is Mr. Beckingsale."

"Er.. hi," replied Abby, surprised to hear her erstwhile teacher on the phone. *What on earth did he want?*

"Did your father relay my congratulations and best wishes for Longmead?"

"Yes. Thank you."

"I am very happy for you, Abby. You have made the right choice... Is your father there? Can I speak to him?"

"Yeah... er... somewhere. DAD!" Dave appeared at the door.

"Thanks, Abby. Who is it?"

"Mr Beckingsale," mouthed Abby, "from Renny Park High."

"Did he say what he wanted?"

Abby shrugged. "Just wanted to talk to you."

Dave took the phone.

"Hello, Mr. Beckingsale... Tom. What can I do for you?"

"Sorry to bother you. You know I told you about my interview."

"Yes, have you got news?"

"No. Not exactly. It's just that I am applying to be a teacher in the creative arts department, and they have asked me to come up with an art project that will get the students involved in the community – something that can be seen publicly, and promote the students' work. I've been giving this a lot of thought, and I wondered... I hope you don't mind me asking this... I was wondering whether... how you would feel about the students making large plaster sculptures... representations of the nativity – and erecting them outside St Chad's before Christmas?"

"Go on, tell me more..."

"Well, it would involve some kind of shelter to act as a 'stable' and these figures would be life-size... not too many of them – Mary, Joseph and a couple of shepherds... and the baby in a manger, of course."

"Sounds brilliant, Tom. You would want these figures to connect with present-day young people, rather than pre-Raphaelite models. I guess?"

"Well, yes. I wouldn't expect them to be dressed in jeans and T-shirts – but maybe the sort of stuff they would actually have worn in Bethlehem in those days. They would also be artistic interpretations, rather than life-like. The figures would have to be designed by the students and the idea would be to get them to be properly creative – their concepts."

"I can think of just the place, Tom. I love this idea. It would have to go through the PCC – Parochial Church Council – of course, but *I* think this would be great for the church as well as the young people in the college. It would get them to think about what the birth of Jesus meant for the people of Judaea in the first century AD – and what it might mean today... for young people, I mean."

"So I can get on with drawing up a proposal to present at the interview? I will send it to you first, of course."

"When's your interview?"

"Four days' time! I know it's short notice, but it was only meeting you today that sparked this off. I'd been thinking of other things, but trying to draw them together just wasn't working. This excites me."

"Go for it, Tom. Send me your proposals and I'll get back to you by return."

★ ★ ★

The following morning, Dave discovered a detailed project proposal in his inbox, which included everything from recruiting the students to a timetable for each of the design stages, and then the final execution of the project with materials, workshop requirements and some preliminary costings. It was carefully – artistically – laid out over six pages and entitled, "Nativity of Jesus: Baby, It's Cold Outside: Proposed sculptures for display in front of St Chad's Church." Dave marvelled at the quality of the work. How had he done it so quickly? He must have been working all night.

Dave read it through immediately. If Tom had burned the midnight oil, it was only fair for him to prioritise this work. Sorting out the office would have to wait. After examining the details of the proposal, Dave could see no problem. There was plenty of room between the front wall – the west side – of the church and the perimeter wall. He thought that a plan of this area would be useful to Tom, so he took his tape measure and iPhone outside to measure and photograph the space.

When he got there, he realised his tape measure was too short and he had no way of fixing it. He wished he had brought Abby. He often got Abby to help him do bits like this. But just then, one of the churchwardens drew up.

"Good morning," sang Dave. "Thank you so much for all your help in moving in. The decorators have done an excellent job... I know it is two weeks before the induction day, and I'm supposed to be settling into the rectory, but as you see the phone has already rung, and people are setting me on."

"So it seems. Why the tape measure?"

"Well, I wanted to get some simple measurements of this area here in front of the church. It may be that Longmead Sixth Form College will send something for Christmas – some Christian artwork."

"Isn't that where your daughter is going to be going?"

"Yes. But it won't involve her. She is not going to be doing art. A prospective teacher has approached me." Dave noticed the alarm creeping into the eyes of the churchwarden. He would have to tread carefully.

"I wonder, would you lend me a hand? The tape measure

isn't quite long enough." Before the man could object, Dave held out the tape for him and instructed him where to stand. He did as he was asked. This was happening too fast for him to object.

Dave took note of the measurements as he kept talking about the real opportunity of involving young people, when so many of them these days just ignored the church.

"It's all about breaking down barriers. Sometimes they think about God, but not about the Church. We are seen to be irrelevant – but if we can just attract their attention, they might see we have something positive to contribute. Not that I expect them all to troop into church on a Sunday... I am a realist..." Dave kept talking. "But we have so much good news to offer, don't we? I mean, if they really understood the significance of the incarnation..." Dave thought that the more 'churchy' words he used with this man the better. "I mean the concept of Emmanuel, 'God with us', is so central to the Tractarian movement. God in the midst – the transcendent in the immanent... that is what excites me about the long tradition of St Chad's. This would be developing on from its Victorian foundation..."

Dave had no idea whether or not the churchwarden understood, but he seemed to be 'thawing'. Perhaps the words 'Tractarian' and 'Victorian' sounded reassuring – he probably hadn't registered that Dave was referring to the 'Oxford Movement', which was, in the 1840s, a revolutionary one – and that Dave was going to adopt some of their revolutionary spirit. Dave knew what he was doing – he was deliberately fooling the man. Was this a sin? Was this double speak allowed? And getting him to help, too. Was this like getting him to dig his own grave? Dave wasn't sure – he would have to consult his books on ethics (still at the bottom of a pile of unpacked boxes!). Anyway, whatever its rights and wrongs, the man had gone off happily enough and would not be galvanizing any opposition. He resolved he would share the project proposals with him the moment Tom told him it was a "goer" – and emphasise that it was just as important for today as Pugin was for the mid-nineteenth century. After all, wasn't this what the archdeacon had sent him to do? But he would do so with respect for the genuine faith of those who felt so threatened by the changing culture of the country. Not only was he here to change things, but to reassure and comfort those who lived in fear.

Dave returned to the rectory and emailed his delight at Tom's project design, attaching the measurements and the photos. He added that he would be praying for him on the day of his interview, saying, "May the best person win!"

When it came to it, Tom found that he and one other were the only ones shortlisted. That evening, he was offered the job – and they particularly liked his project proposal because, "it gave the students scope". Tom immediately called Dave.

"OK," said Dave. "I'll have to get this through the PCC, which is meeting in two weeks' time. If they oppose it, then you can do it in my front garden!"

The churchwarden appreciated Dave calling on him to discuss the proposals. The previous incumbent had never consulted anyone. He saw the point of "leaving the designs to the young people." After all, this was an art project and art meant self-expression. Dave explained that it might be a bit of a risk, but he was sure the gains would outnumber the negatives. He trusted that what Tom was going to allow would be thoroughly compatible with the biblical record.

★ ★ ★

Meanwhile, Abby and her mother were struggling to fit into the new congregation. There was not one other teenager – or, indeed, young family of any description. The youngest appeared to be in their forties. Lynn felt so young and inexperienced compared with the overwhelming numbers of octogenarians who exercised the social power. Lynn and Abby were made to sit in the "rectory pew" right at the front.

"This is going to take some time," said Lynn, hoping to encourage patience in her daughter.

Abby said nothing.

★ ★ ★

Dave (Father David, as he was to be known here at St Chad's) was still in his "honeymoon" period and the PCC approved Tom's proposals. At least, thought Abby, there would be some young people about when the project got underway.

19

Kakko and Tam found themselves surrounded by giant trees and thick undergrowth. The atmosphere was hot and sticky. Before stepping through the white gate that had appeared in the hedge across the grass from the cottage, they had found two rucksacks containing clothes and basic toiletries. They could not get through before they had changed – Kakko into a loose calf-length skirt and Tam into long cotton trousers and a colourful but smart short-sleeve shirt.

"Tropical," breathed Tam.

"A proper jungle! Do you think it's safe? I mean it's probably thick with snakes and scorpions and other horrid things."

"Spiders. Giant ones."

"Don't tease, Tam. You know I don't like spiders."

"I thought *I* was meant to be the wimp…"

"But spiders are diff… Tam, stop teasing me. You know I don't think you are a wimp… So, what is it we have to do here? There doesn't seem to be anywhere to go. We are surrounded by undergrowth."

But before Tam could answer her, Kakko was aware of a short semi-naked figure pushing through the bush towards her."

"Tam…"

"Yeah?"

"Tam…"

"Ooh…" Tam saw her as the figure approached. She came

up to them cautiously and eyed them quizzically. "You are from God?" she asked.

"Erm, no!" replied Kakko instinctively.

"Yes," Tam overruled. "We are because God has led us to your land."

"We prayed. You have come. You are from God. Please, you follow, I will take you to our village elders." And the small, bare-breasted teenager gave them a broad white-toothed smile.

Kakko and Tam followed. Not far through the trees they came across a clearing, in the centre of which were a collection of square wooden huts roofed with large dried leaves. Each hut stood on wooden stilts that kept it safe above ground away from jungle floor insects and other small creatures. Outside each group of huts, sitting beside cooking fires, were women intent on preparing food – tubers and greens and what looked like beans of some kind. As Kakko and Tam passed, the women looked up, then followed behind until they were all standing before a large, central long-house, on the steps of which sat a small elderly man.

"They have come," stated the girl.

A few women began to ululate. The elder raised his hand and they were silent. He addressed Tam. "White man, you have come from God?"

Tam explained about the white gates and how the Creator led them to different places, but it wasn't until they got there that they found out what it was God wanted them to do.

"The brown girl," the elder continued, indicating Kakko. "She is your servant girl?"

"She is my partner. She does not serve me – only God."

"So you are her servant?"

Kakko spoke. "We come together. We work together for God." Kakko put up her two index fingers and moved them together.

"A oneness!" announced the elder. "I have heard of this. Two people, one spirit."

Kakko looked at Tam and they smiled. A "oneness" sounded good.

"Two people under God," explained Tam.

By this time the elder was joined by other men in front of them, while the whole village crowded around behind. Kakko saw the bright little faces of children peering from beneath the house posts. One enterprising one had even shinned up a tree to enjoy the spectacle. Kakko smiled at him.

Half a dozen elders led the way up the steps into the house. The floor was made of rolls of bark rendered smooth with use. It was well swept. A kind of straw matting was produced and laid on the floor in a semi-circle. Kakko and Tam were given one long mat between them. They sat before the elders.

A woman appeared with a wooden bowl and a jug. She approached Tam and held the bowl out in front of him. Tam went to take the bowl.

"They want to wash our hands," whispered Kakko. Tam took the bowl from the girl, who looked confused, and gave it to Kakko, who whispered, "Put your hands over it!" Tam got the idea and the girl gave Kakko the jug. She poured water over Tam's hands. Then Tam took the bowl and jug, and did the same for Kakko. The elders began to slap the floor with their hands.

"A true oneness!" declared the chief elder. "See, they are a oneness. Each serves the other. This is a sign. They are from God!"

The elders brought cups containing some kind of drink. Two cups had been brought, one for Tam and one for Kakko, but the elder barked an order, and they were taken away and quickly replaced by a single small bowl.

"We give to each other," smiled Tam. "We are a oneness."

He took the bowl and offered it to Kakko. Kakko took and drank.

"Wow. This is so nice!" she exclaimed and gave the bowl to Tam. They had neither of them tasted anything like it before. It was sweet and fruity and so different.

"Nectar," smiled Kakko. "Food of the gods!"

"Don't get too into this," whispered Tam. "Remember, we may be from God, but we still don't know what is expected of us."

"Thank you," said Kakko, bowing to the elders. "This is good. Why have you prayed? What have you asked the Creator for?"

"Tonight, we will show you. You cannot see in the day. Tonight, when Tiwan has gone down, you will see. But now we eat and you must rest. You have come on a long journey."

Tam and Kakko were led out of the long-house to a guesthouse opposite. The room was Spartan. On one side there were two sleeping mats rolled against the wall, and floor mats for sitting on in the centre. Bowls with jugs stood against a third wall – bathroom on one side, bedroom on the other, sitting room in the middle.

A girl rearranged the sitting mats to be close together, and then picked up one bowl and both jugs, balancing the second on her head. With her free hand she gestured to the sitting mats, and Kakko and Tam sat down.

"Not so easy on the bum," grimaced Tam.

"You have to sit cross-legged," said Kakko.

"I can't," replied her boyfriend. "My legs don't go that way."

"Nah, you never were very supple. I recall the climbing wall."

"Don't talk about it… but I make up for it in other ways, don't I?"

"At the risk of giving you a big head, yes," smiled Kakko. "But your lack of flexibility is to keep you from thinking you can do everything."

"Got you… oof, this floor is hard!"

Kakko laughed. "You need practice."

As they were getting settled, they became aware of lots of faces peeking through windows and around the doorframe. Interested children. A woman shooed them away, and then brought water in the jug, which was placed before Kakko and Tam with ceremony. They repeated the ritual of pouring water for each other. Then bowls of food were brought and placed on the floor in front of them as the washing things were removed. It was clear that one ate with one's fingers.

"Am I supposed to feed you, and you me?" mused Kakko. "I don't fancy that much."

"Let's compromise. You choose something for me and I for you. Then the rest we feed ourselves. It smells good."

"OK. Together…"

Kakko took a small piece of what looked like bread and Tam followed. They looked at each other and put the morsels to each other's mouths. They bit in synchrony. The act was almost as intimate as a kiss – perhaps more so as they could look into one another's eyes. A oneness, indeed.

"I hope God knows what He's doing," said Tam.

"She does! Don't you feel it?"

"I do."

They tucked into a meal of fruit, honey and what could only be described as pancakes made with eggs and cream. It was delicious. Another woman came and removed the bedrolls, replacing them with one large one. The oneness was to be extended to the bed.

"How far then is this oneness expected to go?" wondered Tam aloud.

"Down boy!" smiled Kakko gently. "Only as far as a teeny kiss. There are eyes at every crack!"

The woman indicated the bedroll. "You rest. Long journey," she said. She left the house and shooed the children away again. Kakko took Tam in her arms and kissed him, then led him to the mat.

"Oof," said Tam again, "this floor is so hard. And this pillow is – a log of wood!"

"Stop complaining," whispered Kakko. "At least you can stretch out… and give thanks that our journey has been so short. I'm not tired at all." She lay down beside Tam. "But I can't imagine how they make love in these parts – it's so hot."

"But they do, though – often. There are many children… and they are back in numbers."

Remarkably, the floor became less hard as an hour, then two, passed. Kakko and Tam lay side by side listening to the sounds of the village. After twenty minutes or so, the children had grown bored and departed. They could hear the elders talking in deep male voices in the house opposite, but they could not make out anything that was said. It was muffled and not translated.

"They're taking stock of the situation," suggested Tam. "They are satisfied their prayer has been answered."

"I hope they don't have too high expectations of us."

"The highest, I would think. They have prayed that God would send someone and they believe He has. Now we must pray that we can do what is required."

"Whatever it is, we have to do it together, O Oneness."

"Do you imagine," said Tam, "that I would ever think of going it alone? It should not be a surprise they perceive us as a united entity. In many ways, we are – in most ways, actually."

"Tam… Tam? What would your parents say if we were to live together… I mean, like, some of the time?"

"What would yours say?"

"I don't know. I guess Nan would say we should be married first, but I don't think Mum and Dad would be uncomfortable with it… not nowadays."

"Most young people live together – then get married later. That's how it has worked for most of human history."

"Yes. But in a way they were, kind of, getting married then. They meant it for life, even though they didn't have a legal thing."

"I don't approve of living together just to see how it goes; going into it ready to call it off if it doesn't work. If you are not properly committed, it won't work for sure."

"They just want fun together, I guess… live for now."

"Yeah. But it'd be no fun for me if I thought it might not last. If *we* began living together, Kakko, I would want it to be for ever. It will mean giving you everything – and I'm not going to do that if one morning I wake up and you are gone."

"That's nice. I feel the same. That's what I would expect, too. So, if we say it *would* be for ever, would you set up home with me?"

"Yes. I would. Kakko, there is not much of my heart you do not already possess… but *I* would have to be dead certain that *you* were dead certain."

"So… if I were?" They were silent for a moment and then Kakko said quietly, "What you are actually saying is that, before we share a home, we should make an irrevocable promise to each other that we would be a oneness for life. Isn't that, like, the same as getting married?"

"I suppose it is. It would be making that promise public."

"I will think about this and pray… Tam… have I asked you to marry me?"

"Yep. And the answer is yes. Of that I am certain… But exactly *when* is not so easy. I'm not sure I'm ready for what setting up a new home entails just yet."

"Yeah, getting married depends on so many other things – like study and work, and an income."

"Moving out of our parents' homes would be a big thing for them, too."

"Tam, if you love me, I can wait. In the meantime, I am glad we are an undisputed oneness on this planet, in this whole universe, now… listen to the birds, they have changed their song."

"It's getting dark."

As Tiwan set and the night-time insects began their serenade, the elders left their house, and came across the open area towards the guesthouse.

"It is time," called the old man they had first met.

Kakko and Tam pulled themselves up stiffly, and descended the steps.

"You come."

The elders led them out to the edge of the village to the centre of the clearing where they could see a magnificent array of stars shining brightly in the night sky. The constellations were entirely different to those they knew from their viewpoint on Joh. So many were visible.

"So beautiful!" marvelled Kakko

"You wait," said the old man.

"I can never really take in the wonder of the night sky," whispered Tam. "So vast, so beautiful, so… wow! Look at that cluster over there."

"You can see that the whole expanse is far more than just an assortment of stars," said Kakko.

"Yeah. With a telescope you can see more detail of a particular area, but the whole sky together is so special."

"I wonder which one is Daan."

"That you will probably never know. It will be a small yellow star. But beyond that it might take a lot of calculation.

And that assumes that we are in the same galaxy and on the same side of it."

"Look," said the elder, "it rises."

On the eastern horizon, Kakko and Tam saw a large silver blob emerge above the trees. It was by far the brightest thing in the sky.

"A moon?" suggested Kakko.

"No. I don't think so. It is reflecting a huge amount of light, but probably isn't so very big. I would guess it's an interplanetary craft in low orbit."

"A spaceship."

"Exactly. And we are the ones to deal with it – or at least its occupants if they decide to land."

"They may already have done so."

"This thing. Has it sent any messengers?" asked Kakko of the old man. He nodded his ascent.

"Wait. They come again – perhaps tonight."

"This doesn't sound good news for these people," said Tam to Kakko. Then he asked the elder, "When they come what do they do? Can you understand them?"

"We don't know. We fall down – asleep. When we wake, one of us is missing."

"Abductions," said Kakko.

"Or hostages?" suggested Tam. He looked into the face of the elder. "Why do they do this?"

The man appeared awkward and looked towards his fellow elders. They nodded.

"They want to know what was written on the stone. But we do not tell them. This is only for the elders to know. The stone – it is destroyed."

"Who destroyed it?" asked Tam.

"Our ancestors. So many people came like this from the sky. They came seeking the stone. Our ancestors do not tell them where it is. Then one day after a big fight and many of us are killed, our ancestors decide to smash the stone – spoil the writing. Next time people from the sky come, we show them the stone all broken. They are angry but they go away. But this time – these people – they don't leave. They took one of the young people and tortured him, and they find out that the elders remember what was on the stone. Now they try to make us tell. First they torture the elders – we do not tell. Then do this to us. They take our sons and daughters – one more each night."

"And so you prayed?" concluded Kakko.

"We pray for a long time and then you come…"

"But are you not afraid that we are not from God but from that?" Tam gestured to the ship.

The old man looked sheepish. "We thought, maybe. Then we decide to trust you. You are different. You are soft. You show love. You are a oneness. We hear you laugh together. These people, they do not do these things… And you do not demand to know about the stone."

"We shall not ask you to tell us what was on that stone. Do *not* share that with us. That is not why we are here," stated Tam.

There was an audible collective sigh from the leaders. "You do not want to know?"

"No. We are here to help you. We do not need to know."

The old man smiled. "You are indeed from God! Praise be to God!"

Then, the women on the edge of the village began to let up a howl. "They are coming, they are coming!"

Kakko and Tam spotted a shuttle craft, lights blazing, low down coming over the hills. The people ran to their houses – the women gathering their children as they went. They tugged Kakko and Tam after them. The old man stood firm as the craft approached the clearing, hovered and dropped in a vertical landing.

20

Tam and Kakko stood inside the guesthouse. They watched through the window as several dark-clad, apparently human, figures approached the village.

"Kakko," hissed Tam. "I have just realised something. There are some numbers jotted down in the corner of the bottom of my bag. I hadn't given them a thought until now. I reckon they could be some kind of co-ordinates. Maybe this is what these people are after."

"Why? Why should we have these writings?"

"I don't know. But we're sure to find out."

They watched as a child ran out and hurled a stone, but it glanced off an invisible force field around one of the figures.

"Deflector shield," whispered Tam.

The figure retaliated with a stun weapon. The child was lifted from the ground and landed with a thud. His mother screamed, but her husband held her from running to him.

The figures approached the old man who stood his ground.

"So, old man. Are you ready to tell us?"

An icy shiver went up Kakko's spine. What she heard was not the usual translator that intervened in most communications with foreign speakers. She did not hear him in English but Wanulkan. They were speaking her mother's language.

The old man shook his head. "You know the answer to that."

"You will tell us one day, old man. We have room for many more slaves." He signalled to an aggressive-looking man to his right who lifted his hand up. In his palm rested a small device that began to emit a high-pitched wine. For a split second Tam, felt his body shudder and his head reel. Then he slumped to the floor at Kakko's feet. Kakko gasped. She ducked down to him but he was quite unconscious. She felt his pulse, which was thankfully still strong. And then she began to notice the silence. The whole forest was silent. The insects had stopped their trilling, the dogs no longer barked and the sound of children was stilled. Kakko looked up above the window ledge. Three of the assailants had selected the young woman who had first encountered Kakko and Tam, and they lifted her over one of their shoulders. All the while, the man with the device emitting the noise kept it held aloft.

Everyone but the assailants and Kakko seemed to be affected by whatever the box was sending out. Then Kakko remembered her mother telling her the same thing. A device belonging to some Wanulkan pirates had not affected Jalli on a spacecraft. It was one of their white gates adventures before Kakko was born. It had not affected Jalli because she was from Planet Raika. These people spoke Wanulkan and so probably had the same Raikan immunity. And Kakko clearly had inherited it from her mother.

Kakko kept low but observant. She watched as they carried the girl towards the shuttlecraft. As they moved away from the village, and the device became more distant, the people began to stir. They came to in time to witness the captive, still unconscious, being taken aboard. Then the door to the craft closed, the engines started up and in a roar of sound that was in stark contrast to the erstwhile dead silence, they lifted off.

Kakko bent down to Tam who was now trying to get back on his feet. "What happened there?" he asked as Kakko took him into her arms.

Kakko quickly explained about the device. "But I guess I

am immune because I have Raikan blood," she concluded. "So it is for me to do something... but I don't know what."

"Kakko. I think I know what was on that stone. Co-ordinates for Planet Rweennaalla. It means 'Planet of Wonder'. Do you remember the legend of the lost planet? It's the place we all grew up to revere. Some people think it is not just a fairy story, but there is a real 'Planet of Wonder' out there. It is renowned for its beauty and wonders – including great wealth. It was supposed that, hundreds of years ago, the inhabitants had to abandon it because of a radiation scare, but before they left, they prepared co-ordinates for people of new generations to find the planet again when the radiation had diminished. The story goes that two of the three co-ordinates have been known for generations, but the last has been lost. Legend has it that they were written on a standing stone on a small hot planet in 'the Tiwan system' – but nobody knows which star is meant by Tiwan. The elder, he called the sun here Tiwan. My guess is that these Wanulkans, and others before them, have worked this out. They have evidence that the co-ordinates were here on such a stone, that the stone might be destroyed, but that the villagers here remember the numbers."

The elders had now gathered outside the guesthouse and were waiting.

Tam and Kakko came out and stood at the top of the steps.

"I think we understand this thing," stated Tam.

"I have seen it all. I have not been asleep," confirmed Kakko. "We will get your people back!"

The people began to slap their hands on the posts of their houses in appreciation.

"I admire your confidence," whispered Tam, but with a smile. Then he said, "We need to return to where we came from to gather the things and the information we need. Then we will come back... we promise."

"Keep praying to your God," called Kakko. "We cannot do this without Her."

"You can be sure of that," said the elders as one.

★ ★ ★

An hour later, back in the cottage, Kakko was telling her mother what she had witnessed.

"It's probably the same people – or their children," said Jalli. "They do not give Planet Raika a good name. You can bet all they want to do is ransack Rweennaalla."

"I think we can find out exactly where it is," said Kakko

"How do you mean? You have the final co-ordinates?" asked Jalli, puzzled.

"They are written on the inside of my bag," said Tam. "They are very small but they are there."

"So, what does this mean?" asked Kakko. "Are we meant to give them to the Wanulkans? I'd hate to do that. It doesn't seem right after all the sacrifices of the Tiwan people."

"If they have them they will leave the people alone," said Jalli.

"They will, but they already have a number of them aboard their ship. Can't we get them back to their families?" wondered Kakko.

"We need a plan," said Tam.

"But we have not got much time," said Kakko impatiently.

"This time I agree with my daughter," said Jalli. "We have to act quickly before these pirates do any more harm."

"A plan," said Shaun, "you need a cunning plan? Then ask the expert at strategy."

"This is not a football match!" said Kakko, exasperated. "Don't forget it was me who said you would be good in midfield."

"Because you recognised my natural ability."

"OK. So if you're so clever, what would you do?"

Shaun looked thoughtful, then said, "This is like, having to score a goal with your first attempt. You don't get a second chance."

"Exactly. It is not like football!"

"Well, what I think is that you *pretend* to the Wanulkans that you are their allies…"

"Go on," said Tam. "How?"

"Well, you speak Wanulkan, don't you, Kakko? You speak to them in their own language – that will make you sound, like, on their side."

"But I'm not good at Wanulkan. They would know immediately that I don't live on Planet Raika."

"Perhaps. But when were they last on Raika themselves? How did you feel when you heard them speak?"

"My spine tingled."

"Exactly. And if you speak with authority – and in a way that gives them what they want – they might let all the hostages free."

"This sounds good," said Tam. "I like it."

"But what do we say… with authority?"

"Tell them," said Shaun, "that you will give them the co-ordinates if they let the people go."

"They wouldn't buy it," said Kakko. "We could tell them anything – and they know it… Hi Bandi."

Bandi came into the kitchen, having heard his sister, and asked, "Tell who what?"

"Tell the people with long ears not to be so curious!" said Kakko.

"Bandi," intervened Jalli, "you could be useful here."

"How?"

"Maths. Tam, you say you have the last co-ordinates. Where can we find the known ones?"

"I don't know. We could ask at the space centre."

"The co-ordinates for where?" asked Bandi.

"For Planet Rweennaalla, the Planet of Wonders."

"No problem, I have them in one of my textbooks. It is a standard maths problem. Calculate the possible location of Rweennalla (or the Beautiful Planet) given the co-ordinates in circulation. The planet could be anywhere on a line 'x, y' but this line stretches into infinity. In order to locate the planet's exact position, a third set of co-ordinates is needed. But these have not been discovered. Probably never will –"

"Until now," said Shaun. "Tam has them."

"Where?"

"Written on the inside of the bottom of the bag given me by the white gate."

"Let me see…"

Bandi took down the numbers and disappeared to his room. Ten minutes later, he returned.

"There must be some mistake. By my calculations, this puts Rweennaalla only four light years from the location of the planet with the standing stone. You see, these first numbers confirm your present position – assuming that you are reading them in situ. They refer to a small planet in the Sinusi system."

"This would be what the locals call Tiwan," said Tam.

"That makes sense because, according to the legend, the third set of co-ordinates are on a planet in a system called Tiwan."

"Exactly. Just what I remembered," said Tam triumphantly.

"The second set," continued Bandi, "indicate the position of Rweennaalla on the line 'x, y' that we already have: the position of the planet in relation to the two planets of the other co-ordinates. But this is where it doesn't make so much sense, because, by my reckoning, this would be a planet only four light years away from Sinusi, or Tiwan, in the adjacent

Forma system. Forma is a medium-sized star that will have a Goldilocks zone similar to ours. But four light years away… This doesn't sound right."

"Why not? The co-ordinates do work for a real star system. When you think of the amount of open space, the fact that it refers you to somewhere at all is significant," observed Tam.

"True," said Bandi.

"And it means that you won't have so far to go," added Kakko.

"Let *me* look," said Shaun. He took Bandi's calculations and perused them. "Can you plot these on a 3D model?"

"Of course. It is simple. It doesn't require a high-spec program. Wait on."

Bandi disappeared and came back with his computer. On the screen appeared three points (the planets) and dotted lines connecting them. Bandi rotated the image. In the middle of the lines, but right next to Tiwan, was a dot representing Rweennaalla – in the Forma system. He got Shaun to read the co-ordinates and typed them in again carefully. It produced the same pattern.

"Definitely Forma," said Bandi.

"Can we trust your textbook?" asked Kakko.

"I can't see why not. Hundreds of them have been printed. If there was a mistake, someone would have spotted it."

"Right," said Tam. "Here is our strategy. When the pirates come again tonight, we approach them before they can use their zap machine. Kakko tingles their spines by addressing them in Wanulkan – with authority. She tells them that I have the co-ordinates up here," he tapped his head. "We promise them we will give them what they need in exchange for their captives. They will want to buy it, because they are already pretty convinced the elders on the Tiwan planet will never tell them. They understand that this is a sacred trust that comes even before the capture and destruction of their whole community. The pirates are desperate."

"But we already agreed that they would probably suspect we would tell them an untruth. Do you want them to go to Rweennaalla?"

"Yes, I do. I don't believe Rweennaalla has what they want. They think it is full of gold and precious things – I believe the wonders are different – proper wonders like love, joy and peace. And, if we wanted to deceive them, why would we give them somewhere that is so close? Four light years would only take them a matter of weeks. If we were going to send them somewhere that is wrong, we would think of somewhere so far away that they would not be in a position to come back with a vengeance."

"That makes sense," said Jalli. "But I still don't see how they will believe you."

"This is the cunning bit," smiled Tam. "We tell them that we will *take* them. We will attempt to go with them. We, too, want to go to Rweennaalla."

"But we don't want to," protested Kakko.

"No. We don't. Don't worry, they wouldn't want us to either. They will stop us. So they will take me and threaten me, and force me to tell them. Of course, I'll do this quite quickly because I am a wimp. Kakko, you will be screaming at me not to tell – all the time telling me to be strong. And then, when I have told, she will beat me up – with words(!) – and make it look as if I have betrayed her. Our real motives must appear to be that all we actually want is a free trip to the Planet of Wonders. Then they zoom off leaving all the hostages and they will never come back. When they find that there are no material riches on Rweennaalla, either they will leave everyone alone – unless, of course, they are detained in Rweennaalla and their ship is impounded – strong possibility."

"Can we contact Rweennaalla and warn them?"

"We could try. But it is more likely that a new civilisation doesn't yet have the technology to pick up our signals. If they were engaged in interplanetary communications, we would know about them already."

"Sounds a good plan," said Shaun. "Just as long as Kakko doesn't get too carried away."

"But I can't act!" declared Kakko.

"Don't have to. Be yourself on a bad day," said Bandi in a matter-of-fact mocking tone. Kakko made to hit him with a cushion. "See what I mean," he laughed, ducking. Kakko spluttered – then saw the funny side of it herself.

"OK. I fell for that one. But I need to work out what I have to say – in Wanulkan."

They were agreed. Jalli took Kakko off into the sitting room and coached her in the necessary Wanulkan. Tam asked for the boys to pray for them, which they did. If the Creator had provided the white gate, there was a way. They prayed to God to bless their strategy, and if it wasn't the right one to direct them anew. Tam felt at peace, and he and Kakko took their leave and disappeared through the gate.

Jalli sighed. There was always danger to their adventures, and it bothered her more as a mother than for herself. She was anxious to have Jack home and fill him in on the situation. "OK, you two," she said to Shaun and Bandi. "You have two hours to catch up on your studies and I'll call you for dinner when your father comes home."

Just then, Matilda came into the garden with Yeka in her pushchair. She reached out for her mother as soon as she saw her. Jalli bent down, picked her up from the chair, cuddled her and whispered into her ear. "There you go, little lady. Listen to your mummy – don't you go growing up too fast!"

The people of Tiwan were relieved to see Tam and Kakko back so soon. The elders summoned a meeting and, without revealing to them that she knew their closely guarded secret, Kakko outlined the plan to get the hostages back.

"We will approach them and speak to them in their own language," she explained.

"You speak their language?" marvelled the old man.

"I am ashamed to say they come from my mother's planet." She gestured to the sky. "It is a long way from here. They are bad men, and not representative of their people. My mother and father have already battled with them once. I believe God has sent us to you because of this. We can defeat them again."

21

That evening, the two intrepid young people stood with the old man as the shuttlecraft landed.

A tough-looking pirate ignored them and approached the old man, who resolutely shook his head.

"I am running out of patience, old man," he said. "Tonight we will take three, then four and then five. You have no choice but to reveal to us this small piece of information. When you do, we shall go and not return."

Then, Kakko spoke in her best belligerent Wanulkan. "You shall bring back your captives. Then, we go!"

The Wanulkans were taken aback. This was the last thing they expected. The pirate spokesman stared at her – at a loss of what to say. If Kakko spoke Wanulkan, he dare not, of course, say anything aside to his companions without expecting it to be understood.

"Speak," berated Kakko. "Acknowledge your mistake in coming here. Bring back the hostages. Then, take us aboard." She smiled a knowing smile and added more quietly, "My friend has the co-ordinates for Rweennaalla. We can take you."

"You… you know about Rweennaalla," stuttered the pirate.

"We know everything. We know about you, your ship and your lust for wealth –"

"*Spoolk*," ordered the leader. "Let me consult with my crew… *Spoolk,*" he repeated.

'*Spoolk*' was a Wanulkan word that Kakko was very familiar with. It was not one she liked. It meant 'wait'. Hearing it from this man genuinely annoyed her. "I do not like to wait," she spoke with controlled vehemence. "Do not say *spoolk* to me."

"What do they want?" Tam asked in a low voice.

"They have asked me to wait," said Kakko sharply.

"Ah. And that is why you are angry. You, who spoke up. My friend does not wait kindly. Do you accept our offer?"

"How did you get here?" asked one of the pirate band.

"In our own space cruiser," replied Tam.

"Where is this cruiser."

"Orbiting this planet."

"We have detected no other craft."

"That is because it is cloaked."

"That technology is primitive. It will not evade our instruments."

"Your detectors, like your ship, are last generation. Our technology can detect and deflect all electromagnetic waves at all frequencies, then return them to their original course. You do not even see any distortions. We have the, how shall I put it, 'state-of-the-art' technology. Your ship would have an interhelical engine. Ours has an intrahelical power source that is half as fast again and uses a fraction of the fuel."

Wow, thought Kakko, *when my Tam lies, he does it with panache. If I didn't know otherwise, that would have convinced me. Over to you, Mr Spoolk…*

"What do you want of us?" asked the leader.

Kakko demanded in Wanulkan: "The return of the hostages you have seized. We do not want you on Rweennaalla, but we are willing to acknowledge that, since you have got this far, we will share the planet with you… Now go and bring out these innocent people's loved ones. I trust they are unharmed?" declared Kakko.

"They are unharmed... How can we trust you? You're Wanulkan – it is artificially generated, is it not – although it doesn't sound like it?"

"It is not. I am half Wanulkan."

"Then, if you are Wanulkan, tell me something about Planet Raika. What happened to Zonga, for example."

"Zonga was mother's village. It is no more. It was washed into the sea. My mother and my great-grandmother were the only ones to survive."

"Not so," said the man quietly, "my grandfather survived in the ocean for many days. He was rescued and taken in by a family not his. He was among those who stole our first craft and committed ourselves to a life of opportunity."

"Your grandfather? He is aboard your ship?"

"No. He passed away many years ago. I am the third generation. Many of us are fourth generation."

"So. Now you know that we are not completely against you. But we will be unless you bring back your hostages... Now... tonight," said Kakko authoritatively.

The pirate leader indicated to his crew to return to their vessel. It started up and took off as the old man stepped forward to Kakko and Tam.

"They have gone to get your children," said Tam.

A broad grin spread across the old man's face. "How? Why have they changed?"

"We have agreed to go with them in the place of them."

"But," protested the old man. "They are evil."

"Not evil," said Tam. "Lost. They have no world of their own."

"But where will they take you?"

"The Creator will protect us," said Kakko, trying not to let the doubt sound in her voice. Believing took so much faith. It wasn't that she doubted that she belonged to God into eternity, but she was not ready to let Her take her out of this universe yet.

"God will protect us all wherever we may be for ever... I thought that God sent us to help you – but now I am wondering if he has sent us to help these lost people of that cruiser, too."

As they walked back to the village to wait, Tam said to Kakko, confidentially, "You meant that about helping those pirates, didn't you?"

"Yeah. I was wondering whether they might settle permanently on Rweennaalla. Everyone deserves a home. At least one of their ancestors was left with nothing. That is probably what made him do what he did. I, kind of, want his children to be happy. I might be wrong, but I don't think they really want to be cruel, deep down. And, as it turns out, I am sort of related to them. That's a funny feeling."

★ ★ ★

Later that evening, a lookout shouted that the shuttlecraft was returning. The villagers came out to the edge of the forest. The steps to the shuttle descended and a group of bewildered natives – traumatised but otherwise unharmed – left the craft. Kakko and Tam strode out to meet them. They greeted them.

"Are you all here?" they asked.

"We are all present," said the girl whom they had first encountered. "You are indeed from God."

"So now return to your people."

They began to walk, slowly at first, then more quickly, and then ran to the arms of the villagers.

Kakko turned to the pirates now assembled at the foot of the steps.

"Thank you. You have been true to your word. Now we will conduct you to Rweennaalla."

"No!" said the leader. "You will not come into our ship. You are too hot."

"Too hot!" remonstrated Kakko, proving the point. The plan was working.

"Too feisty. You will disturb us. We will not be able to speak. If you came, we would have to kill you! And we do not want to do that with a daughter of Planet Raika."

"But you still want the co-ordinates?" said Kakko, acting out the plan.

"We do. So we will take your quiet friend. He has them in his head."

This was not part of the plan. It had never occurred to Kakko that Tam and she could be parted. They had been treated everywhere they went as a united couple.

"He does not go without me!" affirmed Kakko.

"He comes. You stay."

With that, he nodded to a tough-looking pirate who turned on a stunning device. Almost immediately, Tam collapsed. Two burly pirates restrained the angry, pleading Kakko as Tam was hoisted up onto shoulders and carried up the stairs. The leader ordered Kakko to be frogmarched back to the villagers. He informed the old man: "You have your people. We will not return. If anyone else comes seeking the stone or the numbers on it, you will not tell them any more than you have told us!"

Then they threw Kakko forward into the arms of some wailing ladies, turned on their heels and marched back to the shuttle.

Kakko wept uncontrollably as the craft lifted off and disappeared over the horizon. The plan had only partly succeeded. How could God let this happen? Kakko was in a state of shock. The villagers stood around her and stroked her.

An old lady wept, "They have sacrificed their oneness for us. This shows the greatest love of all. Our God loves us so much he has sent these people to sacrifice their oneness to rescue our people!" The people wailed.

The old man conducted his elders back to the village, while the women almost carried the distraught Kakko to the guesthouse.

They stayed with Kakko, washing her hands, her feet, her face and fanning her as they laid her on the bed mat. They stayed and sang songs all the rest of the night until she slept.

★ ★ ★

Morning came and Tiwan rose. The elders called the people together. Kakko was brought and as she sat cross-legged in their midst, they sang songs of praise to God.

"God has come to us in these his servants who have sacrificed their holy oneness for us. God is great," declared a woman. She was spokesperson for the people. The elders ordered Kakko be garlanded and given precious things. A necklace was placed around her neck, a bracelet put on her arm and a bangle on her ankle. They covered her in their finest cloth and put a crown of flowers on her head. Kakko said nothing while all this was happening. Finally, aware that they wanted her to speak, she found herself saying words of thanks. These lovely people understood her grief.

"Thank you for your kindness and your gifts," she said. "I am happy you are altogether again. I am trusting in the Creator that She will bring me and Tam into a oneness once more soon."

They slapped their hands on whatever they could find. Kakko smiled at the love of these people.

"I must leave you now and return to my own people,"

said Kakko, wanting her mother more than anything in the universe – except for getting Tam back of course.

Food was brought to her. She must eat for the journey. She took it. Eating something of the sweet things they gave her restored her strength a little. Then the villagers followed her as she traced her way back to where the white gate had brought her. It was there, shining white in the darkness of the forest. The same young woman who had first greeted her, came up to her and enveloped her in her arms. Then, Kakko said, "I am very happy for you. May your life be blessed." Then she turned and waved as she stepped through the gate, and disappeared from their sight.

"Wow, sis!" laughed Shaun playfully as Kakko crossed the lawn. "My, you look fab in all that gear!" Indeed, it was the most 'feminine' he had ever seen his sister look. Then, the others came out to greet her.

"Where's Tam?" asked Jalli.

Kakko let out an eerie sound that came from somewhere deep within, and Jalli caught her and held her.

★ ★ ★

It was half an hour before they got even the main gist of what had transpired.

"So," said Jack, "Tam is on his way to Rweennaalla in an interhelical-powered craft. Bandi, you do the maths. How long will that take them?"

"Not long. What does an interhelical engine produce?" Kakko explained that if the engines were going full power, they should get up to a light year a week.

"At maximum speed then, we're looking at, say, four or five weeks at the most. Even with some inefficiency, I reckon they'll be there in six…"

"But, of course, that is from Tiwan," Shaun reminded them, "but *we* are not in the Tiwan system."

"And even if I were to get back there, I have no ship," sobbed Kakko.

"So we are looking for another miracle," said Matilda. "If you ask me, this was always too risky."

"You didn't say so at the time," wailed Kakko.

"Would it have made any difference if I had?"

Kakko bristled, but in her heart she knew her grandmother was right.

"The people of the Tiwan planet prayed for a miracle and got one," stated Jalli firmly. "So shall we!"

Jalli's phone rang when Kakko was in the shower. She drew it out of her pocket. It was Tam's parents. Tam wasn't answering. Did they know where he was? Jalli tried to tell them as easily as she could.

"Explain that again!" said Tam's mother, Mey.

"Can we come round to you, or you come to us? It's so complicated on the phone."

"What's so complicated? Do you know where he is?"

"Yes."

"So, where?"

"In a space cruiser between the Sinusi system and a planet called Rweennaalla."

"I don't understand."

"We're on our way!"

Jalli, Jack and Kakko made their way up the lane to where Tam's people lived. Fifteen minutes later, they were sitting in their house. Kakko explained as best she could the mission they had been on and how they had come to be separated.

"Our plan didn't work," she concluded. "They made him temporarily unconscious with a radio device, which affects the brains of everyone except those from Planet Raika, and they carried him aboard. They want him to show them the way to Rweennaalla."

"You're telling us that our son has been kidnapped as a result of a very risky and harebrained plan to rescue some complete strangers when their own elders wouldn't do it, even though they could?"

"It would have totally wrecked their integrity," explained Kakko.

"So are you telling us that our son," roared Tam's father, "has been sacrificed for the sake of the integrity of some complete strangers. It seems that *you* came back to consult with your family. Did it ever occur to you to come and consult with *us*?"

"I came to ask my mother because these pirates were speaking my mother's language."

"And that is the only reason?"

"Yeah. Normally, I don't ask for my parents' advice."

"That is true," nodded Jalli.

At that, Tam's dad launched into a heated monologue. "If you ask me, young lady, you have been leading my son astray long enough. He has been bewitched by you to the point of acting recklessly more than once. When you ended up in hospital after it appeared he had rescued you from some foolhardy mission down a cliff-face, we said nothing. I wanted to, but my wife said that you had learned your lesson – or so it seemed. But, instead of recognising you as a danger to his well-being, he became even thicker with you. I do not know what kind of hold you have over him, but I have long believed it is not a healthy one. Behaving the way you have, is selfish in the extreme."

"But," protested Kakko, "this was not selfish. It was about helping poor people who had been taken hostage."

"And not considering, for one moment, your own families!

213

Look what you have done to his mother. I believe you to be a highly irresponsible child and I hold your parents partly responsible."

Jack cleared his throat. "Can I say something?"

"If you have anything to reassure us?"

"I'm not sure I can do that... Look, I grant you Kakko can be headstrong at times." He reached over and squeezed her hand. He didn't want her to explode. "That is the way she is made, but in this instance I believe they planned what they were going to do carefully. When you set out to help someone in trouble, there is always a risk. I'm afraid it runs in the family. I was made blind trying to rescue Jalli. Before that, Jalli and I had other risky adventures. Once I, also, was kidnapped, albeit in a truck with soldiers and not a space cruiser. We did what we did – we do what we do – because we believe we are called to act... called by the Creator. Kakko and Tam feel the same. They can travel between planets only at the behest of God."

"The Tiwan people had been praying," said Kakko. "They saw us as an answer to their prayers... and so do I... so do we."

"The 'we' being Tam and you?" asked Tam's dad.

"Yes," replied Kakko. "Tam believed it, too."

"I don't mind people praying to their God, but when it starts to interfere with the way you live your life like this, then that is taking religion too far," stated Tam's dad.

"But if you believe God made you, lives in your heart, loves you, gave Herself for you and cares, not just for you, but the whole universe, then you have to do what She wants – live your life for Her and others, not yourself."

"And Tam was doing that? It seems to me he was just following *you*."

"No. He believes, too."

"Well he didn't learn that extremist stuff from us..."

"It's not extremist!" said Kakko, her vehemence building.

"OK, Kakko," intervened Jalli. Jack squeezed her hand hard. "I do not believe my daughter has behaved irresponsibly... but that is beside the point. However, it has happened, we have a situation that is causing us all much distress..."

"I... I love him," blurted Kakko. "I..." and she threw her arms up and stood, turned and sobbed, then paced the room. "I don't know what to say... it hurts so much. They – the natives there on the Tiwan planet – called us a 'oneness'. They wept much for me."

Mey stood and took her hand. "I know you didn't do this on purpose, lass. But we love him, too, you know."

"I know," sighed Kakko.

"Can I put the kettle on?" asked Jalli.

"No. I will," said Mey. "Come, let us put it on together." Mey and Jalli left for the kitchen.

"So, young lady. You are the one with ideas. What are you going to do about this, eh?" inquired Tam's dad. He was still angry but had calmed down.

"Pray," replied Kakko.

"And what else?"

"There is nothing else until God gives us something. A way to act."

"That is hardly a practical suggestion, is it? You mean you're stumped for ideas."

"Actually," said Jack, "I've always found praying works. It only seems like a dead end when I haven't asked God. Which, I'm ashamed to say, is far too often."

Without invitation, Kakko's heart overflowed to God. "O God, this hurts so much. We want Tam back. We want him to be safe. And God, please, *please* don't ask us to wait. His mum and dad love him very much, and I do, too. Show us a way to get him back. Show *him* a way of getting back… and make him strong. We know you are everywhere in the universe – light years mean nothing to you. So, God, we want a miracle – we demand a miracle!"

"I don't think God is getting off lightly," said Jack quietly to Tam's dad, who was silent. He had never come across that way of praying before. Kakko was definitely serious about the God thing – She was in her heart. And then something deep down in his own heart began to experience a peace. He quickly dismissed it. This was all emotional claptrap that he must pull himself out of.

"Your God better get my son back or there will be hell to pay," he declared with some volume, "I mean it, girl. This is not stopping here."

"Darling," said Mey, appearing at the door with a tray, "getting cross will not help. Clear a space for my tray, will you?"

Her husband lifted a pile of magazines from the coffee table and slumped into his chair.

★ ★ ★

Jack and Jalli agreed to stay in touch with Tam's people everyday, and report on any developments immediately. "Tam will probably arrive at Planet Rweennaalla in around six weeks' time," explained Jack. "That is significant. I hope… God may provide a white gate to help then, if not before."

22

When the seventh week came and went, and still there was no sign of either Tam or a new white gate that might take Kakko, or anyone to meet him, Kakko began to panic inside. She had told herself that this would require the most supreme patience and mentally noted Bandi's worst-case scenario of six weeks. Short of a white gate, there was absolutely nothing that anyone could do to reach Tam. Bandi had calculated that even if they had the most up-to-date intrahelical-powered ship, they would still need over ten years to reach Rweennaalla, but no such ship was stationed anywhere near Joh. The next craft of any kind was not due for another five years – Joh wasn't exactly on the superhighway of intergalactic travel.

However, despite her inner panic, Kakko schooled herself in being the epitome of selfless endurance. She visited Tam's parents daily – sometimes just to say "Hi", others to take tea. She took upon herself all the responsibility for Tam's plight – even though Mey was prepared to credit her son with some responsibility in what had happened. Tam was not unintelligent and he had been a positive influence on his girlfriend. The changes in them were not all one way. Mey was also ready to believe that her son was alive and bright enough to stay ahead of the game, and take every opportunity to escape.

In the Smith household, Kakko tried to make sure Tam's absence was not the only concern. Bandi was so distressed about Abby that he was behaving negatively at times. He had been rather surly and dismissive, for example, when Jalli had spoken well of one of Pastor Ruk's sermons. This was unlike Bandi. The strain all round was telling.

Now the eighth week had begun – was she not meant to see the boy again? Surely God could not do that to her! She had always found that God looked after them – perhaps this time it was not possible, even for God. Kakko took to praying hard. She had never minced her words in the way she said things to Her. Now, she was almost sweating blood. Did God not hear her? She was making no sign of having heard. In fact, Kakko realised, God had begun to feel distant – more distant than ever before. When she most needed Her, why was She not there?

It was in the ninth week that Kakko flipped out. On Sunday morning, she opted out of going to church, she couldn't face anyone. She couldn't – just couldn't – listen to any more sympathy. Her mother was unhappy about her staying at home, but understood. Bandi had gone to Persham. Shaun was coming back from an away match that meant he would be out for the weekend. For three hours, Kakko had the house to herself.

She began by yelling at God and then said at the top of her lungs: "Claptrap! Its all f… f… frigging claptrap! Why I ever believed in You, I don't know! I guess I've been praying to a figment of my imagination all this time!" She went on in a terse tone to herself, "Bandi knows. Abby knows – although they're not quite admitting it yet. The whole concept of a God just doesn't add up. OK. Maybe there are magic gates. They aren't miracles – there is bound to be some scientific explanation for them. The physics of cosmology has thrown up some remarkable things. Cosmologists find explanations for things that don't require the existence of God. OK, so these don't *disprove* the existence of a Creator, but the 'first cause' argument and the 'argument from design' have long since been shown to be only useful if you already believe. *Even you, Pastor Ruk,*" she continued to herself, "*say you cannot prove the existence of God through logical argument.* Nor does the 'argument from beauty' signify. Things may be beautiful, but then they fade or get destroyed – and why is there so much ugliness and evil, too?!"

Kakko threw herself on her bed. She had done it. She had converted to atheism. There was no future for her in a community of faith. Why should she believe? It was a waste of time. And perhaps Tam's dad was right. All this looking after others before yourself and your own came from the faith stuff. Sacrifice! What a stupid idiotic thing to do! *Start thinking about yourself, Kakko,* she hissed.

But then she thought of those people on the Tiwan planet who had wept so much for her. Had they not done what they had, who knows what would have happened to those poor people. It wasn't as if Tam had been killed even. Could it be that their parting was worth the reuniting of dozens of others? The words of love, and the love that she and Tam had shown, were celebrated in that Tiwan village.

Kakko recalled the love that surrounded her there. She liked that Kakko – the Kakko that hurt. The Kakko that gave so much. She remembered the time she risked her life to save a child she had only just met – two of them, in fact. But she did not like the Kakko she had just resolved to become – self-preserving, independent and opting out of self-giving… but she had no choice, loving like that hurt too much. And with God, it seemed possible, but without Her it was too much for anyone. Giving like that would destroy her, as it might already have destroyed Tam. The strong people were those who did not go there – down the self-giving road. Strong people knew when to draw the line. They were the ones that stood firm and resolute and unmoved. It was alright to be more like them – it was normal. Surely she didn't have to love so much? It was like Tam's dad had said – it was extreme.

She got up to go into the kitchen. She was not going to have a breakdown – she had to be calm and maintain control. It was strange to be the only one in the cottage – she must find something positive to do. On the kitchen table, she saw the copy of the Bible from Earth One that Abby's dad had given Bandi. He had used it to practice reading English. She picked it up and it fell open at Isaiah, chapter fifty-eight. She read:

When you pray, I will answer you. When you call out to me, I will listen and will reply to you. If you stop oppressing and abusing people, and cease saying evil things; if you feed the hungry and tend to the needs of those who are desperate, then the darkness that surrounds you now will become like the brightness of midday. And I will always show you the way to go and what to do, and give you good things too. I will keep you strong and full of life. You will be like a garden that is well watered, like a fountain that never dries up.

"Is that a promise?" she heard herself say, "do You mean that?… O God, why am I still talking to You? I have just decided you don't exist!" she said aloud, annoyed with herself.

Kakko looked up from the book – somehow, she knew she had been spoken to. Apparently, God was not going to be dismissed.

"Why haven't you said anything for so long?" asked Kakko. But even as she asked the question, she knew the answer. Pastor Ruk loved the Scriptures. God spoke to him through them. Had he not been calling upon his congregation to read them – week after week? And had Kakko done that? No, she hadn't. She had always been so sure of God. She knew Her in her heart. But since Tam's abduction, her heart had been so full of pain that she couldn't feel God there anymore. But here, in these words written so long ago on Planet Earth One to people who had been traumatised and exiled from their land by enemies, God had broken through.

Oh what an idiot I am! thought Kakko. She read again: *"You will be like a garden that is well watered, like a fountain that never dries up…"*

Kakko glanced out of the kitchen window to the garden that surrounded the cottage – always well watered and green. Then, her heart did a somersault. There it was! A white gate! A beautiful, shiny, white gate, right beside the greenhouse! Was she imagining this? Was it a phantom? She rushed out the front door, around the house and laid her hand on it. It was real enough. She wanted to open it and go through it, but thought about her family. No, if there was one thing she had learned in the last few weeks, it was to think more carefully and not act under impulse. She should wait until her mum and dad and nan got back from the church. But that might be hours. They would stop behind for the fellowship after worship. She decided to text Jalli.

"Hi Mum. White gate! Am waiting for you. Love K x"

Jalli had not turned off her phone but, concerned for Kakko alone in the cottage, had put it on silent. She felt it vibrate in her pocket and saw Kakko's name. In the middle of the sermon, she quietly read Kakko's message and nudged Jack. He bent towards her and she whispered, "White gate" into his ear.

They left quietly. Jalli read Kakko's message out to Jack. "Better get back," she said. "Kakko is going to be bursting with impatience."

★ ★ ★

They found Kakko in the kitchen, reading Bandi's Bible. "Mum, Dad, I didn't expect you home so soon!"

"We came straightaway. Didn't want to make you wait too long."

"Thanks Mum. Do you think the gate is going to help get Tam back?"

"Well, whatever it is, it's going to lead you to where the Creator wants you to be. Where do you see it?"

"There, beside the greenhouse." Kakko pointed through the kitchen window.

"Jack, I see it, too!... What about you?"

"Hm. Nothing. No. Not me."

"What about Nan?"

"We left her sitting with Ada. We'd better ring her. The worship will be over by now. But I doubt it will be there for her. Look, if it is, she can join you two later."

"OK. Let's look around the gate."

There were two sets of clothes – a blouse and a long skirt for each of them.

"That settles it," said Jalli. "Clothes for two... I rather like this skirt."

"Not bad," said Kakko, "but this one is definitely more 'me'."

"Of course," smiled Jack, "God is going to give you things to wear that will enhance his creation."

Kakko had already stripped off her things and was pulling on the skirt. Jalli followed her daughter's lead.

"Right, I'm ready," said Jalli, looking colourful in her new outfit. Jack encircled her in his arms.

"See you soon." Yeka was pressing in, too. "Kiss Mummy goodbye," he said. "And Kakko." Yeka did as she was bid. Then stated, "Dwink!"

"Of course," said Jack. "Straightaway!" He kissed Jalli one last time, and he and Yeka waved.

★ ★ ★

Jalli and Kakko stood on a strip of dusty, yellow grass that divided the beach from a busy road and a bustling city. Jalli's first impressions were that this was Wanulka, but then she knew it wasn't. The people did not dress the same and it smelt different. They sought some shade, and Jalli saw there were two suns rather than the three above Raika. But this place definitely reminded her of the home in which she had grown up.

"This isn't Rweennaalla," said Kakko with a sigh. "That place is supposed to be beautiful – and unpopulated."

"It depends on what kind of beauty you mean," answered Jalli, smiling at a woman as she bustled by. "Look at these people, they are happy. Their eyes are bright. Aren't they radiant with some kind of beauty?"

Kakko looked at the people walking along, or sitting on the benches under the trees that lined the road chatting with each other. They were indeed beautiful, dressed in colourful clothes like themselves, happy and friendly. Several of them spoke to Jalli and Kakko as they passed. One old man stopped and smiled and shook their hands, and then continued on shaking the hands of others as he went. Despite the heat and the dust, there was a gentle breeze from the sea.

"What next?" wondered Kakko.

"Let's just sit here a bit and see what happens," suggested Jalli.

★ ★ ★

Two hours later, they were still sitting on the bench as the first sun had already reached the horizon.

"That's beautiful!" remarked Jalli. "It reminds me of home."

"Home?"

"Wanulka: to watch one sun chase her sister over the horizon."

"Wow!" said Kakko. "I've never seen a sunset like this. The colours. Perhaps this is Rweennaalla after all."

Just then, a young man came and sat on the same bench. He spoke.

"You are not from Rweennaalla?" he asked. So they were on Rweennaalla.

"No," replied Jalli, "we are just visiting. Is it obvious we are strangers?"

"You bear the look that all new immigrants have when they first arrive, and see Forma and her sister set beyond the horizon. You are from the space cruiser?"

"There is a space cruiser?" said Kakko excitedly.

"Yes. The one that is in high orbit."

"We are not from the space cruiser," explained Jalli. "But we have come to welcome them."

"You are good people?"

"We come in peace," said Jalli. "We have come to ensure those on the space cruiser also come peaceably."

"All are welcome here," said the young man. "You are welcome. I am Manere." He extended a hand.

"Jalli."

"Kakko."

"Welcome to Rweennaalla. We have much empty land. Many years ago, there was a radiation spike from the small sun. Our ancestors had to leave. Now the radiation has cleared and the planet is being repopulated from many places. We have so much love in this place because all the people who have come here have known what it is to suffer, but have learned peace. Our young people know love, too. They know it is God who has brought them here. Rweennaalla has always been famed for its beauty. We have discovered that this beauty is chiefly in the hearts of God's people."

"Some people say that beauty lies in the things of Nature – the sky, the sea, the rocks, the plants – but not in the hearts of people," said Jalli.

"I know. There is darkness there. But the darkness is only because those hearts are empty. We have learned to open them to each other. People come here from different places. Sometimes they are broken inside but there is healing in love. Do you understand? Perhaps you have not known this brokenness?"

"I know it," said Jalli. "I thought I would drown in the darkness – but then a good man came to me and told me that there was hope and love. I didn't believe him at first. But then I acted on his advice and discovered he was telling the truth."

"I, too, now. In a very small way," added Kakko. "But not like my mother."

"She is your mother! You are so young."

"Thank you," smiled Jalli.

"You say your pain is small, but it is not old. It is hot… I can see you are from God. You have love born from darkness. Come, I will take you to our councillors."

23

As the final rays of the second sun dimmed beyond the horizon, Kakko was telling her story to a cheerful-looking official.

"We are aware of the cruiser's arrival," he informed them. "We are waiting for them to send a shuttle. This has happened before. On one occasion, people came with guns. We denied them permission to land."

"They went away?" asked Jalli.

"They went. One year later, they came back; this time without the guns. We dismantled their ship. Now they have completely assimilated."

"I have met the people on this cruiser," explained Kakko. "If they come with guns, let it be me to send them away. They will do what I tell them."

"They will obey you? You are only young."

"I… we speak their language. When they see me here, they will believe I am more powerful than they." She explained about their former encounter.

The official asked the young man to take them to his home. He would call them if a shuttle was spotted.

Manere introduced them to his family and they were showered with all the hospitality they could wish for.

★ ★ ★

The following morning, the twin suns having risen over the hills behind the city, the young man took them on a tour.

They discovered that the urban area was really quite small. In the foothills were large arrays of solar panels. The first ones had originated from spacecraft that had come to repopulate the planet in the early days. Now they had developed the technology to make them themselves.

"It is useful that many of us come from a scientific background," explained Manere. "So many were engineers, physicists, chemists and biologists on the ships. We had the 'know-how' and have built on it. Now we have many things. Microchips were hard at first but, see there?" Manere pointed to a low building below them. That is where we make our integrated circuits. Over there," he added, indicating a large factory, "is the metalworks. That was the hardest thing of all, because first we had to find the raw material. So much of what we have comes from the space vehicles we came in."

Manere's phone rang. He put it to his ear, then looked up into the sky.

"A shuttle craft is approaching. Look. There."

They followed his arm and sure enough a craft was approaching from above the sea.

"Now, where will they land? If it is like the others, it won't be far from here. There is a level place just over this rise."

I wonder if Tam is on board, thought Kakko. Her heart was thumping. But she didn't say anything – she didn't need to, she was visibly shaking with anticipation. It reminded Jalli of her and Jack when she was Kakko's age.

The shuttle did a double take of the area and, as predicted, stopped over the place beyond the rise. By the time it had begun to descend, Manere, Kakko and Jalli were already on the lip of the rise, and they watched the craft hover and set down. A few minutes passed as they waited, then the steps came down.

"It's definitely the same shuttle craft," said Kakko excitedly. "It's them."

A small group of Wanulkans dressed in black emerged, armed with weapons and the stunning device. Kakko scrambled down the rise and walked boldly towards them, quickly followed by Jalli and Manere. The pirates saw them and instantly recognised the jaunty stride of Kakko. Without a hint of fear, and without any hesitation, Kakko went right up to them.

"Put those things down!" she barked in Wanulkan. "You will not need them here."

They stared back at her. The leader raised his hand as if to speak.

"Down!" ordered Kakko. "On the ground. All of them! If you don't, I can't protect you!"

The man with the device hesitated.

"And I suggest you don't even attempt to use that thing here," said Jalli, firmly, in her native Wanulkan. "It will not work here."

"Do as she says," said Kakko. "Now!"

The man glanced at his leader who nodded. They put their weapons and the stunner on the ground. "Now, step away from them," ordered Jalli softly. "Right away from them!" They did as they were bid.

"Good," said Jalli. "Now we can talk."

"Haven't I seen you somewhere before?" asked the leader. "A long time ago."

"You might have."

"Many years ago. On the big emigration village ship."

"So it was you who attacked the *MEV Great Marton*," exclaimed Jalli.

"You! It was *you* who damaged our ship. You were not affected by the stunner."

"I was not. And I didn't damage your ship. It was the consequences of your own belligerence."

"It took us two decades of drifting until we managed to get power back into the vessel. Even now it only works at half power."

"Which is why it took you more than eight weeks to cover a mere four light years," observed Kakko.

"You have angered my daughter," said Jalli firmly. "It doesn't do to anger her. She loves peace, but hates anything evil. I recommend that you clean up your motives right now. Where is Tam?"

"He is still on the cruiser."

"Then one of you had better return, and bring him and all your people here. I gather you want to come to live here?"

"We thought it abandoned."

"So did many," said Manere. "On behalf of the Rweennaalla governing council, I welcome you. There is much empty land on this planet. If you come in peace, you can make this your home."

"We have been aboard our cruiser for two generations," declared the leader. "It is getting old and tired, and we are tired of it."

"Why did you leave your planet?"

"An old man – he has now died – was the only one who survived a disaster to his village. He was empty of love and found others likewise empty on the streets at night. One day, they stole the space cruiser when its crew were on shore leave."

"Zonga," said Jalli. "But he was not the only one to survive. My grandmother and I were outside the village when it happened. She never gave up loving. She loved me, she loved God."

"Perhaps if old Thanda had had a granddaughter left to love, he might not have felt so empty."

"Maybe not," agreed Jalli.

"Here on Rweennaalla your story is common," said Manere. "We have trauma care and places where you can learn to forgive, both others and yourselves. We see ourselves as the place to come if you are lost and broken. You are welcome."

Just then, members of the official planet welcoming committee appeared over the rise. They hesitated when they saw the pile of weapons on the ground. Manere beckoned them forth. Two trucks approached stealthily. They were solar-powered like everything else. Manere directed the leader to get into the first truck, but before he did, Kakko asked, "Who is going back to your mothership?"

The leader spoke up the steps to a man who had remained aboard, giving him orders.

"Take me with you," insisted Kakko and mounted the steps before anyone could stop her.

The steps were retracted as the first five Wanulkan pirates were driven away, and the crew of the second truck loaded up the weaponry and stun box. This truck headed straight for the metalworks where the precious metals would be recycled into useful items. Soon the whole cruiser would be stripped and demolished as it orbited the planet. Each item or piece being carefully returned to the appropriate factory.

★ ★ ★

As soon as the shuttle craft docked with the cruiser, Kakko filled the ship with her presence. She delivered the news to the men in the dock. The shuttle captain then headed for the bridge while Kakko demanded to see Tam. She had only gone the length of one corridor, when Tam came running towards her.

"Kakko, Kakko," he called.

She caught him up in her arms. Their 'oneness' was restored. Then Tam looked down at her, a concern on his face.

"It's alright. Everyone's getting off. They are going to live on the planet. Mum is down there organising them."

"How did you get here? No, don't tell me…"

"A white gate!" they chorused together. "Only the Wanulkans think that I have come in your imaginary state-of-the-art invisible cruiser!"

"I knew it would be like this," said Tam.

"I wish I had been as good as you. I'm afraid I got very cross with God over the past few weeks. Bandi estimated only four weeks."

"It would have been, except the ship is damaged. Happened about twenty-five years ago, I believe."

"I know. Mum did it."

"Your mum?! Jalli?"

"Yeah. Long story. Tell you later. Now we have to make sure everyone gets off this cruiser."

It took three journeys, but at last everyone was off. Most of the crew were men, but there were a few women and children. "You will be welcomed," declared Kakko.

She and Tam boarded the last shuttle, and soon they were reunited with Jalli at Manere's house.

★ ★ ★

The next day, they were summoned to the council officer's.

"You have not requested to stay," he said.

"No. We must return to our own planet. We have love and peace in our family. Tam's parents are missing him dearly."

"You are sure you are not in need of trauma care?" he asked Tam.

"I am, but Kakko is the best counsellor for me. What I really need is to get home."

"Being reunited with your loved one is better than

anything. You give thanks, young man. Not everyone has a loved one to care for them."

"I do understand," said Tam. "Living with those pirates – former pirates, I should say – for nearly nine weeks has taught me that."

"When will you leave?"

"Today. If we can," said Jalli. "Our people will be anxious until we return."

"Of course. But before you go, your Wanulkan 'friends' want to thank you."

★ ★ ★

Kakko, Tam and Jalli were conveyed to a reception hostel on the edge of the town near the hospital. They entered a large lounge and the whole company of the cruiser came in to greet them.

They are already being healed, thought Tam. *Their eyes are less sunken. The happiness of this beautiful place is already sinking in.*

The leader came forward and stood before Kakko. He spoke in Wanulkan. "You are the strongest female I have ever known," he declared. "But you also have the biggest heart. You take after your mother," he turned to Jalli. "You fight for good and you fight well. Thanda was my father. He felt abandoned by Wanulka and Planet Raika. And now it is Wanulkans who have ensured we come to this place."

"And Tam, too," insisted Kakko.

"Yes. I am coming to this boy. He could have hated us for parting him from you and forcibly taking him aboard, but he did not. He tried to understand us. He promised to bring us here and he did. He did everything he said he would. He said he believed Rweennaalla would be good for us. Our children love him. He is good with children, this boy."

The little ones were all crowding round him.

"I told them the stories like you tell them, Kakko," he explained. "They love the one about Goldilocks…"

"Goldilocks!" squeaked the children, "tell us the story again!"

"Perhaps one day," smiled Manere, who had just joined them. "But now these people have to go home to their own families."

"May God bless you all here in this wonderful place," said Jalli as they took their leave.

"You will be welcome any time," said Manere as he conducted his three new friends to the place by the sea where he had first met them.

"Thank you," said Jalli.

"I understand beauty better for having come here," Kakko said carefully. "It is not just about sunsets and stunning views and things, but people."

"Love," agreed Manere, "is the most wonderful thing our Creator has given us. Like the wind, no-one knows where it comes from or where it will go to next. It is the spirit, it is the breath of God."

"*Love – the winds of wonder*," whispered Kakko into her beloved's ear.

Then, they were back on Joh. The first thing Kakko did was to trip on a paving slab and nearly fall against the greenhouse.

"Kakko," called her mother instinctively, "when will you learn to be more careful?"

"So much for the 'winds of wonder'!" laughed Tam. Then, as he rounded the corner of the cottage, he was engulfed by his mother.

"Tam!" screamed Mey. She had been taking tea with Matilda – seeking strength in being together.

"Mum!"

"What took you so long?"

"It was my mum's fault," put in Kakko in a matter-of-fact kind of voice. "She had, like, wrecked the cruiser years before and it could only go half-speed."

"Your fault?" Mey said, looking at Jalli.

"So it seems – over twenty years ago," laughed Jalli. "It's generally my fault around here. It's complicated. I'll explain."

"Complicated? I've heard that before –"

"Mummy, Mummy!" Yeka tumbled across the grass, as she and Jack came through the usual gate.

"How's my little lady?" asked Jalli, grabbing her to her.

"I been good. I been good like Daddy said!"

"I'm sure you have," said Jalli.

"Well," interrupted Matilda from the doorway, "the kettle is on!"

"Thanks, Nan," said Kakko, kissing her.

"And I have rung your father," added Matilda to Tam. "He's on his way. Says he fancies a cup of tea, too."

24

The morning was bright and lovely, and Jalli decided to walk the long way round from the cottage through the woods and fields to the hives at the back of the agricultural college. She wanted to inspect them, but there was no urgency, as she wasn't expected in the lab until the afternoon. The principal had called a meeting of departmental heads for eleven o'clock, and she decided to spend the first part of the morning updating herself on the state of the orchards and the general development of the area her bees regarded as home.

The meeting was some sort of consultation regarding staffing for the following term. Such a meeting of all the departmental heads was unusual, but it made sense as they were coming up to the time of the term when the interviews for new members of staff took place. Jalli's department, however, would not be affected. No-one was leaving the entomology lab that year. In fact, they had a very small turnover – although Jalli had been working on pollinators at the college ever since she arrived on Joh, she was not the longest-serving member of her team.

Jalli stepped over the stile and entered the wood. It was wonderful to see the new leaf growth and listen to the birds defending their territories so melodically. Some people walked their dogs down this path, but Jalli knew that a dog nosing through the undergrowth was the quickest way to ensure many of the other creatures either went to ground or flew high into the trees issuing their alarm calls, and dog owners never experienced the wood as those who came alone. As the sylvan world became aware of Jalli's presence, so the birdsong changed. Jalli had no dog with her, but she knew she would have to stand still and silently for upwards of ten minutes for life to begin again. This, she did. But before long, someone else entered the wood – with dogs – and nature scuttled away and hid itself once more. Jalli continued on the path to the far side of the wood, climbed the style and set off across the field. This land belonged to the agricultural college. She was delighted to see the meadow had wildflowers and her bees were busy at work. Except for one experimental field at around the time Jalli had arrived, artificial fertilisers had not been used at the college since it was founded. They discovered they had a lot of nutritious muck from the animals, and spreading it was by far the best way of keeping the grass lush and green. Johian farmers were naturally suspicious of chemicals and the college had conducted a scientific experiment. The animals did not thrive any better on the grass that might have looked richer, but was empty of the self-set wild things that provided a variety of vitamins and minerals. And, of course, from the point of view of her bees, Jalli opposed the use of any herbicides. They needed the wildflowers, she felt, like humans need greens with their tubers. That, she had to concede, was not yet scientifically proven – it was a gut feeling. She was keen to establish it properly, but very few regions on Joh had farmers who wanted to use chemicals and it was hard to find anywhere suitable for a quantifiable comparative study.

The krallens, Joh's equivalent for cattle, were at the other side of the field leaving for the milking parlour. Jalli followed them out, carefully avoiding the splodges of steaming dung.

"It won't kill you," laughed Greta, the livestock-hand overseeing the procession. Jalli was leaping from side to side as the dung became more difficult to avoid around the gate.

Jalli knew the woman well; they had served the college for many years together. Greta was now only part-time, spending most of the day managing a sizeable family.

"What you don't get on your boots, you don't have to wash off," replied Jalli, taking the gate. "I'm calling in at the lab, then to the principal's office and I don't have anything to change into. We have a departmental heads' meeting – new appointments or something."

"Ah, yeah. Nat's leaving. We'll need a new head livestock-hand. I expect that's what this'll be about. We'll miss Nat. He's been here almost as long as the college."

"You applying?"

"Me? Nah. I don't want full-time. Anyway, they're looking for someone with managerial experience as well as stock experience."

"That'll be a tall order."

"It certainly will be."

Jalli left Greta and the herd, and turned the corner of a small enclosure with an outcrop of rock in the centre. It had been deliberately excluded from the adjoining field because of the outcrop. For the past several years it had been the home of Jed, an old krallen bull that had long since passed his sell-by date. Among others, he owed his continued existence to Jalli, who had held out for his retention despite his retirement. In his day, he had been quite something – he had sired many a krallen calf up and down the country – albeit mostly by artificial insemination. Nat had become very fond of him and could not stomach him being shipped off to the abattoir to become pet meat. Jalli had backed him up, despite the principal declaring that she thought she was head of a training institution that taught economic discipline in farming, not a pets' zoo. It was in the departmental heads' meeting that Jalli had argued that there was more to keeping animals than pure economics – the students needed to respect and appreciate them. The principal was not going to engage in a fight over one bull and she knew some of the students were ready to cause a fuss, too. So Jed had survived. Whether or not he knew how much he owed Jalli, he recognised her as a friend and came over to the fence as she passed. Jalli spent a few moments stroking and patting him, and talking to him. Seeing them together, no-one would ever imagine how dangerous a krallen bull could be if he or his herd were attacked. The college dogs still gave him a wary eye.

Jalli left the enclosure and rounded the corner only to be greeted by one of them. These animals weren't pets – the college kept them as working dogs for herding. It was good seeing them properly trained and doing only what their handlers required of them.

At last, Jalli pushed open the doors to her laboratory. At the far end, two of the hives had been constructed to be attached to the outside wall. A window had been formed so you could look right inside the hives through glass. The bees' comings and goings and, above all, the health of the little creatures could be constantly monitored. In fact, the feature was so fascinating that Jalli had had to put up curtains, not just to help the bees feel more at home, but to ensure that the students and herself were not permanently distracted from the other activities of the lab.

Jalli checked in with the staff. All was running smoothly. The pollen, honey and range experiments and surveys were progressing, but there would be nothing to report for a few weeks yet. Jalli sorted through the post. The internal memos included one from the principal reminding departmental heads of the meeting at eleven. The reason the meeting had been called was to be kept confidential – as Greta had guessed, it involved the applications for Nat's post.

★ ★ ★

Just before eleven, Jalli entered the small, but light, seminar room in which Mrs Trenz, the principal, was already sat at one end of a long table arranging piles of papers. Jalli took her seat as other departmental heads arrived. It was a beautiful day and the atmosphere was convivial. The course teaching had all been concluded and the students were currently hard at it revising for their exams. The immediate pressure was off – at least until the papers for marking started arriving. Most of the staff had been out and about inspecting their animals, fields, greenhouses and experimental plots. Mrs Trenz was stern-faced – but there was nothing unusual in that. She called the meeting to order.

"Thank you all for coming," she began, "I'll cut straight to the chase. As you know, there are a number of impending vacancies in our staff. You have all been involved in those concerning your own departments. There is one, however, for which I need to consult you all. It involves the animal husbandry department. You are aware that Nat, our senior livestock-hand, is leaving us at the end of the term. We need someone to oversee and administer the stock belonging to the department – chiefly krallens and morves, but also the poultry. There are five full-time livestock-hands and four part-time. The post-holder is also responsible, in partnership with the academic staff, for monitoring students working with the stock. We have had four applicants – three are, in my opinion, non-starters. Two have only been basic stock-hands, and the third has had some administrative experience but is not *au fait* with the most recent methods of animal care. We are an agricultural institute – not a farm. We have to offer the best and set the standards. Our fourth candidate, however, has all the right qualities – he has completed a recent upgrade at this college, and his former job was as a farm manager of a farm with twice as many livestock-hands and twice as many animals as we have."

"So what is the problem?" asked one of the assembled company.

"The problem is that he has just been discharged from prison."

"Why, what has he done?"

"He has served nine months of an eighteen-month sentence for embezzlement. He was responsible for the buying, and administered the funds on his farm. Over a period of years, he took thousands."

"I remember it well," said Jalli, "if it's Lumg Yulli – he had two children at this college, one in my department. He stole the money to pay their fees –"

"It *is* he and you are correct," affirmed the principal. "Among other things, he apparently used the money to fund his daughters' education."

"And when he went to prison, they were sent down because they couldn't pay. Gail Yulli was one of my best students. She loved the bees and worked really hard."

"…and we gave her an excellent report," added the principal, "but that is beside the point. The problem we have is: do we or do we not employ Mr Yulli? The chair of the board fears that the college should have nothing to do with anyone with a criminal record. I have agreed with him in principle. But it does leave us with an important hole in our staff provision. Any suggestions?"

"I am of the same opinion. No way can we have a felon on our staff," stated one of the group strongly.

"I agree," said another, "how could we trust him?"

"He wouldn't have access to any funds here, though," observed a third. "It's not like he could do it again here."

"In this case, I think we could disregard his criminal record," said Jalli. "I have met the man. He seemed to me to be a good father. He was desperate to keep his daughters in education. I say, give the man a chance. He did what he did for his family. He wanted his kids to have a better chance in life than he had… And will have no access to money here, in any case."

"I totally disagree. Should we employ a jail-bird? Absolutely not!" It was Follig, a beefy woman that headed up the engineering department – the one that Kakko attended. "Once a criminal, always a criminal. We have to take into consideration the example we set our students."

"What about the example of compassion and forgiveness?" asked Jalli. "After all, he has served his time. He was contrite from the start."

"Oh, no. No more of your sentimental claptrap!" blurted a man who had so far kept silent. "You and your precious bees with feelings, sticking up for an old bull that should have been carted off years ago, and now," he added with a sneer, "*forgiving and forgetting* the disgusting crimes of a man who has cheated and defrauded his employer! If you ask me, he got off lightly with eighteen months, and now has been let out after only nine… I think we are far too soft on crime on this planet."

"But, Mr Salma, we know why he did it –" began Jalli in self-defence.

"Don't give me that!" Salma's voice was raised. "You shouldn't try and do what you can't pay for. He was aiming above his station – what his children never saw, they would never want."

Jalli began to shake. She was too upset to say anything in reply. She hated it when people wanted to deny people opportunities. But the man continued: "You came here from God knows where. You don't really belong on Joh at all. You may have been fawning over your bees for the past twenty years, but that doesn't give you the right to tell us true Johians what's right and what's wrong-"

"Mr Salma, that is out of order!" interjected the principal. "Please withdraw that personal remark."

The room was silent. Then, Mr Salma muttered some apology, but added, "I don't retract what I said about employing Lumg Yulli."

The discussion continued, but Jalli didn't hear any of it. After several minutes she excused herself, and walked out into the open air. She decided to return home; she was too upset to stay. As she made her way past the little enclosure, the old bull rolled over and snorted.

"Well, you're still my friend, aren't you?" said Jalli, leaning against the rails. The huge animal dragged himself up – you could see it was an effort – and stomped over to her. Jalli enclosed the giant head in her arms. She stopped weeping inside and was filled with a new surge of strength. In a way she was glad that Salma had gone over the top – it showed him up for exactly what he was – a racist and a bully. But, at the same time, that made her incredibly sad. This beautiful planet was being spoiled and sullied by a selfish lack of compassion. Was this the start of a lurch away from the inclusiveness that she and her family had experienced when they first arrived? She hoped not – but this event had been a devastating eye-opener.

★ ★ ★

"Hello Jalli, you're home early today. Had your lunch?" called Matilda from her chair. She was reading.

"Oh, hi. No. I'll get something. What about you?"

"Already had some salad. I didn't expect you. Come on, I'll get it… What's wrong?"

"Nothing. There are no lectures today – the students are all revising."

"Maybe. But there's still something wrong. You have that look about you."

"I never could keep a secret, could I?"

"Nope."

"It's nothing serious… just something on my mind… to do with work. Actually, it's confidential – I'm not supposed to talk about it."

"If it will help, you can talk to me. You know it will go no further."

"I know, Nan. It's not that serious." And Jalli added under her breath, "Walls have ears in this house," nodding towards Kakko's downstairs bedroom. "She of the long ears is bound to overhear."

"But I wouldn't tell anyone, would I?" came a voice from behind the door that had been left ajar. Kakko emerged, revision book in hand. "Come on, Mum. What's up?"

"As I said," said Jalli firmly, "it's confidential college business. Which means I cannot discuss it – especially with students of the college present."

"But I'm your daughter."

"Makes no difference. Would you want me to talk about you with your friends listening in?"

"Well, no. But that's different."

"Is it?"

"Yeah… so it's about a student then?"

"Kakko!"

"But…"

"Concern yourself with what's important for you – revision… Now!" added Jalli, as Kakko continued to hesitate. The exchange made Jalli feel a lot better – it had given her a chance to assert herself and feel more confident again. She had no doubt that Salma had overstepped the line. He had been personal, rude and racist. Jalli toyed with the thought of making a formal complaint, then dismissed it – he wasn't worth it. She would not mention it unless it was repeated either to herself or elsewhere. If he reflected on his words, he would probably feel sufficient remorse anyway. She resolved on behaving towards him as if it had not happened. After all, he had apologised – if only peremptorily.

That evening, Jack asked Jalli what had transpired at work. Matilda had told him quietly that Jalli was a little upset when she got in at lunchtime – which was unusual because, even if she had no lectures, she generally worked at her desk in the lab.

"And she still had her packed lunch with her," explained her detective mother-in-law.

Jalli sighed. "Your mother reads too many detective novels than is good for her."

"Is it confidential from me?"

"Nah. But it isn't something I can talk about in front of Kakko… Remember me telling you about a student called Gail Yulli last year."

"Yeah, the bright one who had to leave after her dad screwed up."

"Right. Well her father was sent down for embezzlement, served nine months of an eighteen-month sentence and has been released on parole."

"So how does that affect you?"

"I'm coming to that."

Jalli recounted the discussion in the principal's meeting, concluding with: "I left before it had finished. I just couldn't concentrate, and I was afraid of disgracing myself with tears or saying something out of place. So, I don't know the outcome. I should probably have stayed and fought his corner, but I was too emotional. To tell you the truth, I'm angry with myself for being cowed by Salma. Kakko would have given him 'what for' – might even have laid him out – but me, I just evaporated."

Jack began to snigger.

"Jack. What's funny?"

"The thought of Kakko landing one on Salma… and you 'evaporating' – impossible. The bloke's probably feeling an idiot being made to apologise."

"Maybe. I hope so."

"Do you think Yulli should be taken on? I mean, before Salma got so worked up, you sound as if you were only putting the other side for the sake of the argument."

"You're right. I was only thinking it out. But the more I ask myself about it, the more he deserves a second chance. After all, I'm giving a second chance to Salma who overstepped the mark. If anything, Yulli's motives – to see his girls through school – are much more laudable than Salma's self-serving narrow-mindedness. Still wrong, of course, but I would find it much easier to forgive Yulli. He defrauded the company – what he did was wrong, but it wasn't so… so personal."

"Well, if you want my view, he deserves a shot at it – at least for his family's sake. He's not going to have to handle money. He'll probably be so grateful for the chance that he will give more than is asked of him. And you're right, students need to learn compassion every bit as much as the economics of keeping livestock… And I know I might sound emotional, for want of a better word, but krallen cows who are happy will probably produce more milk. It's mind over matter. Krallens have brains."

"Psychosomatic."

"I defer to the lady with the big word."

"It's the same with bees."

"Each one might not have much of a brain, but the hive works together. It has a collective consciousness. Each bee is like a brain cell in the colony."

"Correct," affirmed Jalli. "And in this regard, 'happy' is almost a scientific word…"

"And for some reason, sadly, Salma is not a happy bunny."

"While I am – even if I am upset today."

Jalli resolved again to put the incident behind her. She was not going to let a small thing like this get her down.

25

A new day dawned and Daan rose above the trees. Jalli took the direct route to the college – she hadn't left time to walk the long way through the woods this time and, anyway, she was keen to get back to the lab and her research.

She hadn't got far through the main gates, however, before she was met by a member of her team. "Mrs Trenz was looking for you yesterday afternoon. You'd better go in and see what she wants."

Jalli smiled. She was not going to get upset by being told off for bunking off before the end of the meeting. She reasoned that she had had good cause. She would take it on the chin.

When Jalli arrived at the principal's suit of offices, however, her secretary explained that Mrs Trenz was due in a meeting and began looking at the diary to see when it would be convenient for Jalli to return. But before she had finished, the principal herself came through, saw Jalli and beckoned her inside.

"Coffee?" she asked.

"Er… thank you. But haven't you got a meeting…?"

"They'll wait. Sit down. As a matter-of-fact I want you at this meeting."

"Me?"

"Let me explain. I apologise for Salma's outburst yesterday. You needn't worry, it won't happen again."

"I wasn't…"

"It won't happen again because he has been dismissed for

conduct unbecoming. What he did yesterday wasn't the first time. It was, however, exactly what I needed. He has been intimidating and bullying his secretary – and worse – for months. But until yesterday, I only had her word against his. He denied everything – denied he was capable of bullying, racism and sexism. Yesterday, after the meeting, I had it out with him. The stupid man then tried it on me… no brains… so I had him clear his desk there and then."

"Wow. I don't know what to say. I… I left because I didn't trust myself to say something rash… What about Mr Julli?"

"After some discussion, we agreed, subject to a satisfactory interview, to take him on for a probationary period."

"So you are going to give him a chance?"

"As you said, he has paid his debt to society, he cannot repeat his crime in this job and he has all the necessary qualifications. He deserves an interview at least."

"But the chair of the board –"

"Has agreed that this is a special case."

Jalli sipped her coffee.

"I want you in on the interview. That OK?"

"Er… yes. Of course," said a very surprised Jalli.

"The interviewers are meeting in Seminar Room One. Come when you're ready." She gave Jalli a copy of Lumg Yulli's application and references. "Confidential."

"Of course," she said again.

"Oh, and I just want to say that I know the difference between a happy bee and an angry one, and I don't have to be a scientist to prove it. And I saw you yesterday through the window with Jed. He has by no means finished serving his purpose here. You're not the only one he consoles. You would be surprised who I see from up here giving him a pat."

★ ★ ★

Jalli took her place behind the long table beside the principal, the head of the animal husbandry department and representatives of the board of governors. Mrs Trenz circulated the agreed list of questions marked as to which member of the panel should ask them. Jalli's wasn't quite a question: "In your own words, tell us why you left your previous employment."

Jalli prayed. She was so nervous for this man. But when he came in, the principal immediately put him at his ease by congratulating him on being invited for an interview. She explained that the college was very selective with those they invited, and praised him on his full and honest application. You could see Yulli begin to relax.

Questions followed about his experience, what he knew about the college (which was a great deal since his daughter had attended) and why he wanted the job.

"Working with staff on a farm is one thing," stated the principal, "working with unqualified students, some of whom come here not knowing the difference between a cow and bull, is another. How do you feel about working with students?"

Yulli smiled. He replied that what mattered was a student's enthusiasm and readiness to learn. If they liked animals, all the rest would follow. He would enjoy helping them to learn.

Then, it was Jalli's turn. She felt bad about asking her question. Then, she understood why the principal had asked *her* to do it. Of all those present, Jalli was probably the least intimidating. And he knew that she had been his daughter's teacher. Gail had spoken highly of her.

Yulli lowered his eyes. He repeated what he had written on his application, adding that he had done it for his children.

"Would you do it again? For them?" Jalli asked.

"No. No way. They suffered much more than me. I was stupid."

"But if you cannot pay for your children's tuition fees. What would you do?"

"Get another job. Get a loan from the bank –"

"Ask about bursaries?" put in Mrs Trenz.

"Yes… I hadn't bothered to look into it properly. It was all too easy, I didn't *think*… I would never, ever, do anything like that again. I've learned something about myself. I would never apply for anything that involved being responsible for someone else's money…"

"Well, this post doesn't involve being responsible for money, so we're alright on that one," said Mrs Trenz. "Mr Yulli, have you got any questions for us?" she asked brightly.

"Only one. If I were to be offered this job and took it, would it prohibit my Gail from resuming her course here – with the bees and things?"

"By no means. She would be welcome," said Mrs Trenz.

"Thank you."

"Well, if there is nothing else?" The principal looked left and right. "Then you may go, Mr Yulli. We'll contact you one way or another within the next few days… Mrs Smith, would you like to show Mr Yulli out?"

Jalli walked with Lumg Yulli to the main doors.

"I really am sorry I did those things," he said again.

"I know. I believe you."

"When I get a job, Gail can come back."

"Where's she working?"

"On Floss's farm… milking."

"Look, we'll get her an application form for a bursary. Now's the time to apply. Don't wait."

"You don't think they'll give me the job, then?"

"Mr Yulli, I have no idea. You'll have to wait and see… but I can tell you that you would not have been invited for an interview if the college was not prepared to employ you."

"So –"

"Wait, Mr Yulli… Come this way." She led him to a reception desk in the entrance lobby.

"Have you got a copy of a bursary application form for a student to enter the entomology department?" she asked the receptionist.

The girl opened a filing cabinet drawer and found a form. She gave it to Yulli. He glanced at it.

"It says here she needs a reference from her school. She's been left some time."

"That's fine. I'll do that. After all she was with us. We know all about her."

Yulli was ecstatic. Whether or not he had got the job, Gail stood a chance of getting back into the college. That meant everything. Jalli could see that his family came first. She could see why he had been tempted to steal. *And* why he would never do it again.

"If I remember rightly, you have three children, Mr Yulli."

"Four. The youngest was born only a few months ago… while I was inside. You see, the wife, she just adores children. We had three – three girls – then one day Gail came home from college and told us that her teacher – you – was pregnant. You see, you and my wife, you're the same age. So my wife got to thinking that she wanted another child – before she was too old. If *you* could then, perhaps… Well, it worked. We've now got a little boy. If only I hadn't mucked it up, I would have been there for her. As it was, she had the three girls, the pregnancy and the birth all on her own."

"Didn't they let you go to the hospital… for the birth?"

"You must be kidding. My wife would have had to be dying before they would let that happen…"

"But you're home now."

"Yes. The little mite is getting used to me being around.

For a bit, he thought he was the only male in the herd. But he's getting a bit fond of me now. Took a couple of weeks, though."

Jalli led Yulli out to the bus stop. On the way, they passed Jed's enclosure. He immediately made a friend of him. You could see his experience – he loved animals. Prison would have been harder for him than many others because, not only did he miss his family, but his animals, too.

★ ★ ★

Three days later, Lung Yulli received a letter to say that he had been appointed to the temporary post of assistant senior livestock-hand with a view to him taking over from Nat. The employment would commence the week after next and would be reviewed after six months, when upon good reports, it would be made permanent.

Gail got her bursary. She had already proved herself.

★ ★ ★

"You'll never guess," said Kakko, "Gail Yulli's going to resume her studies." They were sitting around the table for lunch after they had got back from church.

"I did know about it," smiled Jalli.

"Course you would. She's going to be in your department… but I bet you didn't know her father's going to be taking over from old Nat. You'd not credit it. He was, like, you know, impounded for ever for stealing all the profits from the farm he worked on. But they let him out and now he's going to work at the college. Some people have all the luck."

"I don't think being in prison is very lucky."

"No. Well, he did it. He admitted to it. But he's got out for

252

being a good boy. The winds have changed for him. Perhaps he's on the up from now on."

"Perhaps he is. He's certainly open to them. In his case, they didn't have to blow so very hard."

"You know him? You *knew* he was going to take over from Jed all along. You never said."

"Didn't I?"

26

"Wherever this one's taking us to," said Kakko determinedly, "we're going to stay together – all the time! No way am I going to lose you like last time."

"Last time, if I recall correctly, you didn't want to let me go either," commented Tam.

"Don't remind me! Tam, I can't say I'm not scared about this… this time. I mean, if it was just me, then I wouldn't be half as nervous."

"Didn't I prove last time I could look after myself? It turned out OK, didn't it? We have to trust Her."

"I know. 'All things will be well, all manner of things will be well.'"

"What's that?"

"Something Abby said her father keeps saying. Comes from something a woman on Earth One wrote years ago. Joan, I think she said… or was it Julian… Julian, that's it, Julian of No Ridge, or somewhere that sounds like that."

"That's a weird name. You don't usually call a place by something that isn't there."

"Although my father is from the same country on Earth One, I have to admit that my ancestors *are* weird… mostly."

"Do you believe it?"

"What?"

"That everything will be well, come what may?"

"Well, in the end. It's the journey that's kind of hard

sometimes. We're so lucky you know; billions of people around the universe suffer, like, all their lives."

"Come on, let's see where this gate takes us. It might mean someone's life might get better. Billions minus one – or even minus a few."

"Yeah. That's wonderful, isn't it? I mean: being the source of blessings to people. I shouldn't complain."

As they came through the gate, Kakko declared, "I know where this is! It's Planet Earth One and we've been here before. Look, there's the YWCA we stayed in with Da'yelni. Come on, let's go and see."

They crossed the road and pushed open the door to the YWCA in New London, Connecticut. They hadn't got more than a step inside before they met none other than Zoe, who had made such an impression the last time they were there.

"Well, look who it is! Don't rain but it pours… you lot got an interstellar convention or something?" she drawled.

"Hi, Zoe," said Kakko. "Great to see you again… you know how it is with us, we've no idea why we go places until we arrive."

"Hi Tam… still love her then?" joked Zoe, nodding towards Kakko. Tam smiled his ascent.

"Just checking… So, you staying? One bed or two these days?"

Kakko blushed. "You haven't changed then, Zoe? No beating around the bush with you."

"Nah. Come on in. I'll get you some tea… Oh, let me introduce you to Dev – he's here as a student… from India…"

"Hi, pleased to meet you," Tam took the hand of a large swarthy man that had just entered the room. "I'm afraid you missed Dah," continued Zoe. "She's gone off for a week. Won't be back until the day after tomorrow."

"Dah? Da'yelni is here? I mean, on Earth One?"

"Yeah. That news to you?"

"Let me get you the tea," Dev interrupted, "while you talk."

"Thanks," said Zoe.

"Yes," continued Kakko. "We didn't even know where we were headed a minute ago. Where is she?"

"Went to a gig in New York with John. Then, it seems, they met up with some folk and headed off to Nashville for a bash with them. John has to be back for work next week, so they can't stay beyond Sunday. You'd never see anyone so happy as he was when Dah walked in... Come in... Oh, this is my nephew, Buck."

"Hi," said Buck.

"Hi," answered Kakko. "You visiting your auntie Zoe?"

"Oh, forgot the 'auntie'. Makes me sound old. He is supposed to called me Zoe –"

"Except most of the time, I call her Zo-lo," said Buck. "You know, she's something to say about everything. That makes her old."

"I haven't and I'm not," she protested.

"You have. Tell them what you were telling me about your 'philosophy of love and life'."

"I'm sure they don't want to hear it, Buck. So button it..."

"I'd love to hear it," said Kakko. "Go on. You do have a wise take on things."

"Well..."

"We're all ears," said Kakko.

"Come on Zo-lo. Tell them!" exhorted Buck.

"Well, OK. It goes like this: I reckon, there are four sorts of people in this world – apart from those that muck up their lives by having multiple relationships and leaving children all over the place, of course."

"Here we go," interrupted Buck. "Zo-lo's got a 'theory of everything'."

"Everything?" mused Tam.

"Not actually, like, *everything* – but most things. She's very wise…" There was a touch of sarcasm in his tone.

"Oh, ignore him. He can be so rude. You'd do well to listen to my wisdom, sonny. The first sort of people are like me. I don't want to ever settle down and get married like Mom whines on at me. I'm not that sort. Not that I don't like men, you understand – if they're cute. But I'm not the domestic kind – there're too many things I want to do in the world that I couldn't do if I had a man in tow all the time… and I can't stand kids. So, my sort, we're content."

"So we all have to be like Auntie Zo-lo," mocked Buck.

"No, we don't. Just shut up and listen."

Dev returned with the tea. He had searched out some old china cups and a teapot, which he had arranged on a tray. Putting the tray down with a flourish, he began to distribute the cups and saucers, and placed the pot on the table. "We must let it draw for three minutes," he declared.

Zoe looked a little surprised. "Not the tea I had in mind, Dev. I was thinking of the iced sort. There is a jug in the fridge." Dev looked disappointed.

"This is wonderful," said Kakko, quickly. It was clear the young man was trying to make an effort. "I see this man is an expert. I am going to enjoy this tea. Thanks Dev." Dev's smile returned.

"Yeah, fine, Dev," agreed Zoe. She went on with her theory "Then, there's people like you two, and Beth with her Joseph, that do everything as a pair. You get the right partner and life is good – risky, of course, because love hurts as much as it delights. Thirdly –"

"How many sorts are there? We'll be here until Christmas… *Auntie* Zo-lo!" Zoe put her hand over her nephew's mouth and continued.

"Thirdly, there are those who would like to have a partner but never seem to meet Mr Right – or Miss Right. They're always hoping, but they are the ones that are great at giving. They are fantastic when it comes to looking after kids – other people's kids – loving those who get left out. They can not only *sympathise* but *empathise* – know what I mean? They are the ones that make the saints – the ones that take this world forward with their big hearts."

"Or you find them a partner like you did, Beth," said Kakko.

"Oh. That was just obvious… to everyone but her, that is. But, yeah, sometimes that happens."

"And the fourth type?" asked Tam.

"Yeah. They are the Johns of this world." She was coming to her point. "Romantic types who have met someone that they fancy, but it just doesn't work out. They are heartbroken for so much of the time, they ain't good for anything. I told John to pull himself together and be reasonable. Falling in love with an alien was just stupid. Surely this world contains someone he could fall for. But no, if it wasn't Dah, then he wouldn't even look at them. Last year we had two really nice girls who liked him. I told him, but he just wasn't interested. Affected his work, too."

"But he'd only met Dah for a couple of days."

"Two days too many. But then, last week, in walked Dah – just like you. When John saw her, I thought he was going to faint. Anyway, it was like the tear-jerky bit of a Hollywood movie. Everyone went quiet, then John stood up and scraped his chair back. We just stared as he pushed his way across the room."

"Dah, what did she say?"

"'Hi', just 'hi' and put down her guitar. They, like, just stared at each other for ages."

"Awesome."

"So, you know me, I couldn't stand it any longer. I shouted, 'John, just cuddle her, kiss her if you dare and let the rest of us get on with our dinner.' I know it was bad, but who knows how long they would have stood there gawping at one another. So John then grabs her and they both start to cry – straight out of those stupid Hollywood rom coms – and then everyone started to clap. Anyway, the next day they were, thank the Lord, off to Grand Central Station with a couple of others to some country music gig somewhere in Queens… but now you've arrived, too. I guess the Lord has some other motive than just reconnecting a couple of lovers, if He has brought you onto the scene."

"Yeah," grunted Kakko. "How many days before you expect them back? It would be nice to see them again."

"Don't know. Sometime before Sunday – unless John has forgotten he has a job."

They didn't have to wait long. That evening, Zoe rang John and told him of Tam and Kakko's arrival. As soon as Dah heard, she was anxious to meet them. They were enjoying Nashville, but the attraction of meeting her old friends put the music into second place.

★ ★ ★

"That didn't take you long!" said Zoe, when John and Da'yelni walked in the following morning.

"We flew!" exclaimed Dah.

"Her first experience on an airplane," explained John. "She was worried she would miss her friends."

Kakko came down and was amazed to see the couple so soon among them. They hugged. Tam took John's hand.

"Great to see you," said John. "Wow, so we're all here again!"

"Like a cat who's found the cream," sighed Zoe. "I suggest we eat. At this rate it'll be dinnertime before we start."

"You hungry?" smiled Jack.

"You bet. Always am first thing."

Insisting on taking breakfast turned out to be a wise move – especially from Zoe's point of view. Returning her dirty dishes to the kitchen, Kakko glanced out of the window and saw a white gate.

"Tam," she called, "there's a white gate in the yard." Tam went to the window.

"Yeah. So we're off again."

"So soon," sighed Zoe. "I was just enjoying myself."

"God's time. We let Her make the decisions," said Kakko. "Well, mostly – in my case," she added. Tam laughed. John looked as though the bottom had dropped out of his world. Dah was already going to the window to see if she could see the gate.

"Me, too," she said. "More adventures with you!" She jumped up and down delightedly. But then looked at John and a little tear appeared in the corner of her eye.

"It was good while it lasted," said John, struggling to control his anguish.

"Too bloody cruel if you ask me!" remonstrated Zoe. "God, I hate You sometimes. You give them romantic hearts and then you go breaking them!"

"The gates?" asked John, "are they, like, waist-high with white ornate bars on top?"

"Yes. So you can see it, too!" declared Kakko. "You are coming with us, it seems."

John's mood changed like the sun coming out from behind a deep black cloud. "It seems I'm invited on your adventure, too!"

"Whoops," uttered Zoe, "sorry God. Telling you off too qui... Ruddy rabbits! My aunt's got blue ears with green spots on them –"

"Your aunt's got what?" blurted Kakko.

"I think it might be that Zoe has just seen the gate herself," said Tam quietly. "It's probably what she says when she's in a state of shock."

"So her aunt hasn't really got blue ears?" asked Dah.

"Doubt it," said John. "You up for an adventure, Zoe?"

"Do I have a choice?"

"Yes," said Kakko, "of course. You can turn the Creator down, but –"

"But I'd be a dumb-ass if I did?"

"Quite."

"Well then, aren't you all pleased I made sure you ate your breakfast?"

"Sure are," said John.

They emerged in what appeared to be a cave with a high roof. The air was breathable and the rocks glowed a bit – enough for them to see one another. The place had a pungent smell – a smell you could almost taste.

"I'm not sure I care for this at all," said Kakko.

"It's not like stepping into a garden with grass and trees like New England," agreed Dah.

"I found myself in a cave once before," said Kakko. "It was the only place to be, because outside they were dropping bombs. I have a bad feeling."

But then they heard something that made them feel much better – singing. Several voices, definitely not human, were singing in chorus.

"Duh-de, duh-de... hey-de, hey-de... duh-de, duh-dide, bum. Duh-de, duh-de... hey-de, hey-de... duh-de, duh-dide... dide... BUM!"

The rhythm was infectious. After two or three repetitions, Dah found herself joining in with the final "BUM!"

But the singing was growing nearer. Should they hide? Zoe was looking terrified.

"Those singers don't appear to be out looking for trouble," suggested Tam. "No point in hiding – we are here to meet someone, sometime."

The singing grew nearer. There were a lot of voices – it was impossible to say how many. The friends stood and faced the music.

What they saw was totally unexpected. The creatures had legs, black spindly ones, many of them. Above the legs were flat bodies, the leading edge of which contained bright beads – eyes? The singing was emanating from a long tube structure that sprang from the centre of the flat bodies. It opened up into a kind of horn shape that had the subtle movements of a human mouth.

Who was more frightened of whom was difficult to say. The leading creature stopped singing, his tube mouth retracted towards his body and his legs vibrated. Others did the same, but the rearmost of the creatures, not yet having seen the alarming shapes of alien creatures, continued to sing. But the sudden realisation that he was singing alone caused him to stutter and trail off.

"Oh, my giddy aunt," uttered Zoe, terrified.

Then, suddenly, everything was complete silence. The only thing that either local or alien heard was the slow, regular drip of water somewhere further down the cave system.

Seeing the terror they were inflicting, Tam decided to break the silence. "Hello. We come in peace," he said in his best Johian.

There was a ripple of alarm among the locals. Tam

spread his arms, palms outwards. Getting the message, his companions did the same.

"We mean you no harm," said Kakko, as softly as she could. Did they understand her? She couldn't be sure. Then, Dah struck up. She began to sing. She began with a slow ballad of her own composing, then moved into a gentle humming of the song the creatures had been so gaily chanting before the encounter. It seemed to do the trick. The creatures stopped shaking so much and their speaking tubes grew upwards a little as they relaxed.

Kakko realised she and her friends must seem like giants as they stood upright on two legs. The locals were barely half her height. She bent down, bowing.

It was the right thing to do, because one of the leading locals bent his spindly forelegs and tipped his body forward too. Tam bowed and the other humans did likewise. All the locals – there must have been a dozen of them – followed. So far, so good.

Zoe was relieved to see they only had six legs. One thing she couldn't cope with were scorpions – which definitely have eight. These creatures did have two other limbs – short ones on top of the body that protruded each side of the speaking tube. But they didn't have pincers and, as far as Zoe could see, no tails either – which probably meant no sting. Then, to her amazement, the leading creature extended his or her speaking tube and spoke, and she understood every word. The sound was light and lyrical, but clear American English. For a moment, she tried to work out where in the US the creature came from. But then she remembered that her friends were from alien worlds, too. They already spoke different languages. The Creator was actively translating, then. *Nothing to fear, God is here*, she reminded herself. It helped – a bit. *So, what next? Take us to your leader?*

"You have come from above?" asked the creature.

"From another planet," explained Kakko. "Someone may have been asking the Creator for something..."

"Planet? Beyond the surface?"

"Yes. Among the stars."

"We know little of the stars. What is your intention? Why do you come? How many?"

"Don't be concerned," assured Kakko. "We are just here as visitors to help. You see us all here. There's no-one else."

"You came through... from the surface?"

"No. We entered through a white gate. Just here. It is the Creator's... Her gift. Most cannot see it."

"You have come to help us. How?"

"What is it you need?"

The creatures rustled among themselves.

"You come with us."

Yeah. Take us to your leader, thought Zoe. *Let's hope they haven't been praying for meat due to a shortage of food... God, sometimes trusting You gets a bit extreme. I know I asked to be called to San Diego when that blizzard set in last winter – but I didn't really want to leave Connecticut.*

"You wait here," commanded the leader.

They brought forward a kind of cart that hovered. It was loaded with equipment. Three of the creatures began to take pieces from the cart and assemble them together. At first, even Kakko thought they were weapons, but it was soon evident that whatever it was, was going to be far too long and flimsy for a gun. Four or five of the creatures then began to lift it up and point it towards the roof of the cavern. Others scrutinised a screen with an image and columns of figures. It reminded Zoe of the machine the men from the honey wagon used when they cleared a blockage in the New London sewers. The screen crew shouted instructions to the scanning rod.

Another noted the figures. Two more had their backs to this process – these had all their eyes on the newcomers.

"The atmospheric loss here is within acceptable limits," said one of those studying the screen.

"Are you sure we are in the right place?"

"There is no abnormal air movement, now."

"Then it must be related to the arrival of these intruders. For a moment, I thought we had a problem."

"We do. But not an atmospheric one," stated the leader looking directly at the humans. "Security is on their way. Meanwhile, we are to escort our new friends to the 'main arterial'."

They ushered the humans forward. Kakko bowed again and they all followed. Half the locals followed them, pulling the hover cart.

At the 'main arterial' – a high, wide passageway – they encountered a stream of hover vehicles, all moving silently at a fare speed.

"They drive on the left," observed Tam.

"I would love to reverse engineer one of those," whistled Kakko.

John was trying to be protective of Dah – but she was less fazed than her boyfriend. With Tam and Kakko, she had become accustomed to the unexpected. Zoe was finding her confidence return – and her nephew was in his science fiction element. For Buck, it was as if he had stepped straight onto a set for a new and, as yet, unreleased Hollywood movie. Brilliant!

Two brightly coloured vehicles pulled off the 'main arterial' and two creatures clothed in dark blue stepped from them.

"Police," suggested Dah. "They look the same no matter where you are."

The leader of the party spoke as they both eyed the

humans. Their presence was certainly attracting attention because vehicles were slowing down as their occupants gawked at them. One of the police officers stood on his hind legs and waved his front ones from right to left, urging the traffic on.

"Come with us!" commanded one of the officers. No courtesy then. "Get inside."

They were bundled into the back of the vehicles, which were hardly big enough to sit up in. Tam, Kakko, Zoe and Buck in one, and John and Dah in the other. They were soon speeding down the road while one of the police officers talked on his radio. How would their reception with the authorities be? *Hope the leader turns out to be pleasant,* thought Zoe.

27

They travelled for less than fifteen minutes and pulled up in front of, what appeared to be, a magnificent palace. The wall stood back from the highway behind a large plaza. The rock glow here was augmented by some kind of artificial light. They were still underground, but the ceiling at this point was high and remote.

As they crossed the plaza, Tam whispered. "This is probably some kind of government headquarters. Look, that wall seems to have been carved right out of the rock face."

The red-brown rock, streaked with yellow, was beautiful. It shone with jewels that looked as if they had been formed in situ – just exposed with the carving. On Joh, this would have been a tourist Mecca. A high arch, flanked by uniformed locals and carrying what looked like rods or blunt spears formed up in front of them as they approached.

Inside was a huge staircase which was hewn out of the same rock. From it, they saw low doorways leading onto several levels. At the bottom of the staircase, there was a reception desk – made of what on Planet Earth One would be described as jade. There were colourful hangings and embroidered cushions. Everything else was made of stone or metal – there was no wood to be seen anywhere. They stood before the desk on a marble floor that felt warm – underfloor heating? The air was stuffy. John felt a growing desire to throw open a window, but, of course, there were none. The roof was very high – but they were still enclosed.

They were shown through a doorway into a large room. More locals stood before them. Kakko bowed again and they all followed suit.

"We have met your kind once before – many years ago," stated a central figure – the chief? "He lived here some weeks before he expired. He taught us many things. He taught us your kind need to fold in two and rest your top parts. I have sent for cushions. For us they are for decoration, but you may rest on them if you choose."

Embroidered cushions, made of some kind of coarse wool or hair, were placed on the floor beside each of them.

"We are to sit on them, I guess," said Kakko quietly. They sat on the low cushions, politely. Some of the locals made sounds through their tubes, as the humans bent themselves at the waist. Tam and Zoe struggled with sitting cross-legged, but the others did it naturally.

"So we talk. Why have you come?" asked the chief.

The friends all turned to Kakko. She was not slow at putting things into words.

"You have a need – somewhere – that we may be able to help you with. The Creator organises us to go to places…"

"What might that need be?"

"We do not know. We have a lot to learn. We must start with listening… to you," explained Kakko, trying to sound as polite as she could.

"Too many altogether," said the chief. "We take you, two, two, two."

"Agreed," said Kakko quickly and, then, turning to the others, "It'll be OK. Go with the flow."

The chief looked towards a gentle, nervous-looking pair of locals. They came forward, and Kakko motioned Zoe and Buck go with them. "Trust the Creator," whispered Kakko assuringly. "Pray."

"I *am*," smiled Zoe, weakly.

John and Dah stood, and walked behind another group of locals who could not seem to stop talking. Kakko and Tam faced the chief.

★ ★ ★

Two hours later, the leader called everyone together. The group were reunited. "Now you eat and you rest."

They were led to a small room that had been filled with embroidered cushions. The 'food' that was placed before them was nothing they recognised. There was water that smelled slightly sulphurous, but otherwise drinkable.

They compared notes. It transpired that the locals called the planet Zilaka. The Zilakans lived completely underground. None of them had ever been to the surface, which was airless and covered in super-cold ice. The 'air' in the underground world came from below. Apparently, the planet had a molten core and chemical reactions released a breathable gas – but they weren't quite sure what it consisted of. It must, however, contain at least eighteen per cent oxygen or they wouldn't be able to think straight. All the heat was gathered from the thermal activity. Metals were being smelted, and fashioned into tools and machines. They were using electricity generated by steam turbines powered through a vent at some distance from the populated caves.

There were three main settlements. Altogether there were only 800,000 Zilakans, but even this was a problem. Newly discovered technology had led to a rapid population growth. New tunnels were being excavated in the hope of discovering new habitable caves. In addition to the 'people', the Zilikans farmed a variety of 'animals'. These they described as dumb creatures – not because they were silent, but because they couldn't speak intelligently. They were used for meat and their hair was spun for cloth. Both people and animals ate a variety of moulds that grew in shallow heated pools, and fungi. John and Dah had been taken to what they described as a 'fungus farm out the back'.

"We saw huge toadstools," declared John. "Actually, they smelt better than the air. They were proud of them."

"Our hosts were scared for the future," contributed Zoe. "They feared that they could experience some kind of catastrophic event. The ground shakes all the time – sometimes, it produced landslides. One day, they might experience something much bigger than hitherto recorded. They were especially nervous that a fissure of uncontrollable proportions could appear and allow all the atmosphere to escape. Air leaked all the time. That was normal, and also important so there could be an exchange of air. These fissures were always temporary, however, because the escaping warm air melted the ice, liquid water blocked the outflow and the water refroze making a new seal. The occasional dangerously large fissure could be artificially treated. They squirted water just above freezing point upwards, encouraging a new seal. That was what the party they met had been doing. They were investigating a reported air-leak.

"We have been hearing about the latest developments," explained Kakko. "They have invented the telescope."

"It's not very powerful," went on Tam, "it only magnifies about three times from what we can make out. But the significant thing is that they are looking at the sky."

"They have this thing inserted into a fissure. They have seen stars. There does not appear to be one as near as our sun, but what *is* close, is a giant planet. We are probably on a moon that is circling an outer planet. The geothermal activity may be caused by the gravitational effects of the giant planet."

"The telescope doesn't work well because of the cold," explained Tam. "They have to send up blasts of hot water to keep clearing the lens of ice. After a few hours, it is so covered in ice that it is useless and they have to withdraw it – which is quite a business."

"But the fact is: they have learned about 'out there'. They had so many questions about the universe. They wanted to know about other beings. We think the human that came must have been stranded here... landed from a passing ship and, somehow, got below the surface."

"The Zilakans say that he seemed to die of madness... they say his 'brain broke'... he only lived for a few weeks breathing this air, and eating the food and water they gave him."

"I can imagine it," shuddered Zoe. "I mean, being stuck here on your own... for ever. Enough to kill anyone."

"Anyway, back to the telescope. I asked them if they had discovered the reflecting variety which wouldn't require a lens on the surface, or anything except a tube above ground. All the works could be kept down here in the warm."

"And had they?" asked John.

"No," said Kakko.

"What's a reflecting telescope?" asked Buck.

"The sort that I told them about is one that uses a concave mirror at the base of a tube, a small angled mirror in the centre and an eyepiece in the side."

"Like the Hubble space-telescope?"

"Something like that," said Zoe, "except I don't reckon it's got an eyepiece on the side."

"I wonder why that would be?" teased Buck. Zoe ignored him.

"So you're going to build them a reflecting telescope?" she asked Kakko.

"Well, I can show them the principle... draw a diagram."

"*Our* group wanted to know all about us," said Dah, "but I told them what you said. We had come to listen... but I think we should tell them a few things about where we come from."

"Yeah," agreed Zoe. "They wanted to know if we were here because our own planets were at risk."

"What did you tell them?" asked Kakko.

"Oh. I said, Planet Earth was a very fragile planet, but that I had no intention of jumping ship."

"People say my planet could end any time," said Dah. "It'll happen one day – but we've no idea when."

"What'll happen?" asked John with concern.

"Oh. We'll be hit by a giant bit of space rock... but we've survived at least ten million years, so I'll take my chances that it wont happen in my lifetime. If it does... well, we all have to die sometime."

"We get that one on Planet Earth," said John. "Some random asteroid appears and blam! Curtains... Then, on the East Coast – the east coast of the States – they say it'll be an explosion on an island near Africa that will cause the biggest tidal wave you've ever seen and it will wash away every coastal city as far as Washington DC..."

"On The West Coast, it's the San Andreas Fault. They're waiting for the 'big one'... any time," added Buck.

"What about in the middle?" asked Dah, "Is that safe?"

"Not much luck either," said John. "Yellowstone National Park is a caldera. If – when – that blows, we're *all* dead from coast to coast."

"What about Britain?" asked Kakko, "where my dad comes from."

"Global warming – rising sea level will drown London," said Zoe in a deadpan voice.

"From what I hear your dad say," said Tam, "the biggest

risk is that the people on Earth One will blow themselves up with a nuclear war. There are enough nuclear warheads to destroy the planet many times over," he said. "It only has to get into the wrong hands…"

"I can well believe it," agreed Kakko. "If they can do what they do in the Africa I visited – everything on Planet Earth is very fragile."

"It *is*," said Dah, "… and it *isn't*."

"How do you mean?" asked John.

"Kakko, Tam. You remember the first time we met," she explained. "On the bridge. You persuaded me to step through a white gate. Step off the bridge – over the river."

"Yeah. I think you were more scared of the cops."

"True. But the thing is, I trusted you."

"Yes. So, what are you saying?"

"I'm saying we all live in a fragile universe, right. But we ain't alone. We're all in this dimension temporarily. Just a few years and then we're history – if we're lucky. But suppose we matter… to Her – the Creator. Then, whatever happens, whenever it happens, She has got us safe."

"You're right," agreed Zoe. "It all comes down to trust. If God is good, then we're fine. If He made us out of love. We have to trust Him."

"And if He didn't make us out of love, then why send Jesus?" added Buck.

"Quite," agreed Zoe.

"Dad and Nan talk about Jesus… and Pastor Ruk," said Kakko. "But whether or not you live on Planet Earth One, the principle is the same all over the universe. The Creator created out of love and teaches us to love. And love and trust go together."

"So if you lived here, what would you do?" asked Dah.

"Go about my daily life, love and live… and explore."

"And try to make someone else happy," suggested John.

"Sing," said Dah. She began to hum the song they heard the leak repair party singing. "Duh-de, duh-de… hey-de, hey-de… duh-de, duh-dide, bum. Duh-de, duh-de… hey-de, hey-de… duh-de, duh-dide… dide… BUM!"

They laughed.

"Zo-lo can sing," volunteered Buck.

"Can *not!*" said Zoe.

"You can," smiled Dah, "I saw you singing with everyone else at the concert last time I visited your place."

"We can all sing," said Tam. "I suggest we practise something together. Then, go to sleep or we will not have rested before they come back for us."

Dah taught them a lullaby. They all sang in unison.

"You sure can sing lovely, Dah," complimented Buck.

"Thanks."

"Let's sleep now," suggested Tam.

It was amazing just how soft the woolly cushions were.

28

Sleep comes easily to the young. They were underground in an alien world, breathing some unknown, stuffy concoction of gases, and laid out on strange-smelling cushions – but still they slept soundly. They were woken by the sound of Zilakan footsteps, skittering across the marble.

Soon Kakko and Tam were working with engineers, drawing up a sketch of the workings of a reflecting telescope. The Zilakans were nodding and cackling excitedly.

"It's so simple," said one. "Why did we not come up with this before? We have had mirrors for a hundred years."

"Some civilisations were using concave mirrors for far longer than that before their best brains came up with the idea of making a machine to look at stars," said Kakko.

"And if they lived on the surface they would have known about the existence of stars all along. It was only recently that we came up with a system to examine what lay beyond the roof of our world... Having you here has enabled a huge leap forwards. With this design we can have ten times the aperture, and far less of the icing problem."

"Tell us," asked a second scientist who had begun, "how many stars are there?"

"Trillions upon trillions upon trillions – far more than you can ever see. There are thousands of known galaxies – and many beyond those we can see with even the most powerful telescopes."

The questions piled on. What's a galaxy? How far away are

275

the stars and galaxies? Why are stars different colours? Then, what is your world like? If you live on the surface, why doesn't your air escape? How is it not too cold? – and many, many more. Kakko and Tam spent all day enthralling the scientists. In some ways, they felt inadequate to the task because they were not the most learned on Joh by any means. They thought of their professors and university research scientists, and the depths of their knowledge that far surpassed their own – but this was not what the experts of Zilaka needed. The locals were still on the basics, and what Kakko and Tam could share was enough. It was only the year before that they had agreed it was they that orbited the large planet world rather than the other way round. It would have only complicated matters to explain that, even if the bodies were of vastly different sizes, they technically orbited each other. The wobble in the huge planet, however, would have been barely discernible. One of the scientists had also discovered in a hard and painful way they should not look directly through the telescope at the home star.

Meanwhile, Dah and John were testing the acoustics of a large theatre built out of the rock wall. They exchanged songs and tried out the Zilakan instruments. The Zilakans were fascinated by the wood from which Dah's guitar was made. All their instruments were either made from metal or stone. The quality of sound from the acoustic guitar mesmerised them. It was obvious from the start how much music meant in Zilakan culture.

Zoe and Buck were into politics with the chief's high command. It had stemmed from a chance question of Buck in which he asked how they elected their president. The US presidential elections seemed to be a constant feature of his nation. Within months of a new president taking up office, they seemed to be campaigning for the mid-term elections of Congress. Then, they were into the primaries for the next presidential election. It hadn't occurred to him that other nations did it differently. But the Zilakans were interested. They started by posing questions relating to the democratic process. The president of Zilika, because that was who the chief, in effect, was, explained they had a pure democracy. There were no political parties, and anyone could stand for election and many did. He had been one of sixty. Every adult had a vote and each week for six weeks, ten candidates had been eliminated. Then, the final ten were questioned in the great hall for two days when the populace could ascertain the various qualities that each candidate offered. The third day was given over to the elections. The people numbered each candidate in order of preference and the votes were reallocated as many times as it took. At each vote the least popular candidate dropped out, until one candidate had a clear majority. It was then up to the new president to appoint people to help him or her – and it was politic to invite people from among those who had been eliminated on the way.

"I don't think that would work in the States," Zoe had commented. "We have too many people."

It was difficult for the Zilakans to get their minds around a world with seven billion people and counting. In fact, scale was something they were only just discovering. The universe was much, much bigger than they had ever imagined.

"That," Zoe had said, "is not just your problem. There are many people from my world who don't think much beyond their own small town or even their block." She thought of one old lady in her neighbourhood who had been born, lived, shopped, worshipped and died all in the same few streets. There, the light pollution had meant few stars could be seen, and Zoe wondered if the lady had ever even bothered to look up and contemplate the scale of the universe. If she were honest, it had taken Kakko and Tam to stir her, herself, into doing more of it.

And, finally, it was fortunate that Zoe had applied herself

in religious studies, because, after describing the way society seemed to work on Earth, they had gotten into God-talk. Her father had told her that if she wanted to get on with folk, she had to avoid religion and politics. Now here she was in a completely alien world, goodness knows how many light years from her own, discussing just those. But, somehow, she felt that she had been sent here to do it.

★ ★ ★

"I have learned so much today, I think my brain'll burst," stated Zoe when they were altogether in their little cushioned room. "How much longer do we need to stay here?"

"I don't know," said Tam. "But my insides are telling me that we mustn't stay much longer. This food is OK –"

"But it ain't steak and fries," interjected Zoe.

"I could just murder a burger and a coke," added Buck.

"I told you you were addicted to that stuff," said Zoe. "It isn't good for you. All that caffeine and sugar rots your brains – not to mention your teeth." Buck wanted to object but, being made aware of his teeth, which he hadn't cleaned for two days, he kept his mouth shut.

"I'm more concerned with the air," said Tam. "There is definitely sulphur in it, which is poisonous to us. We can only take so much of it. To be honest, I think we should try to head back tomorrow."

"If the air is poisonous, why don't the Zilakans die?" asked Buck.

"They are not made of the same stuff as us," replied Tam. "I wouldn't be surprised if they were not, at least partially, silicon-based."

"How do you mean?" asked John. "Silicon is what they make computer chips of."

"It is. But it is also the eighth most common element in the universe. On this moon, it is probably the most common element of all in its various compound forms. The point about silicon is that, like carbon, it is tetravalent."

"Go on, blind us with big scientific words," said Zoe.

"I know what he means," said John. "He means it is stuff that could form large molecular chains like carbon DNA."

"Right," said Tam. "Life molecules."

"But not life as we know it," said Kakko.

"Clearly," said Zoe, "they've got eight eyes each – all except that one astronomer who looked at their sun; he's only got seven."

"Yes. But it means they are different from us – all carbon-based life – on the deepest, most fundamental level," said Tam.

"Whatever they're made of, they are not endangered by sulphur gases," said Buck. "How long can we survive here?"

But, feeling grotty or otherwise, it did not feel the right time to leave. They seemed to be making so many new friends and Kakko in particular was keen to learn, and share, all she could with the engineers. They decided to try and tough it out a bit longer.

Unbeknown to the humans, it was Kakko's enthusiasm and willingness to impart new knowledge, as well as Dah's real interest in Zilakan music, and Zoe's straightforward openness that was the subject of a high-level conference in the Zilakan high command.

★ ★ ★

They were preparing to spend another day with their Zilakan contacts, when a delegate arrived from the chief ordering them to attend him forthwith. The delegate was accompanied by a couple of large Zilakans in police uniform and the group sensed something was up.

"Whoops," muttered Zoe, "methinks there has been a mood change overnight."

John looked scared, Buck apprehensive, Tam wary and Kakko defiant.

"No choice but to go with the flow," said Tam quietly.

"Well, there ain't no way out of these caves except the way we came in," commented Dah.

"And that's back up way along the highway," reminded Zoe.

"Bring your guitar," said Tam to Dah, "it could be that they want us to sing."

They sat on cushions before the chief, who was flanked by his high command and advisers. They all looked stern.

"Greetings on this new day…" He seemed friendly enough. He continued, "We have not been transparent with you. We have observed you and have seen that you are a different race from the man also calling himself human. You have not sought to take from us – you have technology and knowledge in advance of ours, and you have been willing to share it without restraint. You have given more than you have received. Above all, you have respected us and valued what little part of our culture you have seen. There is an honesty about you and a readiness to trust.

"Yesterday, I told you that we had experienced the arrival of another human who had expired. You did not seem to know this man, you did not ask about him or inquire of his purpose here on Zilaka. You did not question us when we said he had expired… I must now tell you that he is not dead. He came equipped with a special suit to shield him against cold and provide his own atmosphere. He entered through a fissure that he had apparently created and dropped through the roof of Hall Four in the south-west quadrant. This hole would have been large enough to cause a major catastrophe in that sector had not the emergency repair teams acted as efficiently as they did. The man resisted with violence, but we overpowered him and apprehended him. We had to forcibly remove him from his suit. Unlike you, his speech is not clear and he does not appear to understand us... I have to ask you, is this man associated with you?"

"No," said Kakko, firmly. "Wherever he is from, he is not from our party. We have no wish to make holes in your world. As your team reported, there were no problems in the place we entered through our portal. What is this man's name? Did he say where he is from?"

"No. He is not soft-spoken like you," said a commander who wore the uniform of a security chief, "He is defiant and abrasive. He shows no respect. He fought hard when we made to remove his suit."

"He might have feared he could not survive without it," suggested Tam. "Has he eaten anything?"

"Very little."

"I wonder what his business is?" said Kakko with some curiosity.

"Do you want us to sort him out?" volunteered Zoe.

"Sort him out?"

"Yeah, get to the bottom of his story. Work out whether he eats straightforward food or lives on stuff with loads of strange ingredients."

"What's straightforward food?" asked Dah.

"Oh, I guess she means burgers, fries, PBJ – that sort of thing," suggested Buck.

"Somehow, I hope he is *not* American," said John gently. "He sounds like one of those sort of men who doesn't give us a good reputation."

The chief was able, in part, to follow all this conversation, and get its gist. He looked towards his advisers, who nodded. "Bring the human in," he ordered.

A white man around thirty years old with a grubby appearance was half cajoled and half dragged into the hall. He had a dark beard and unkempt hair. He spotted the human party and his eyes almost popped out of his head.

"Great. Human beings," he shouted. "What the bloody hell's going on?"

"You speak English?" demanded Kakko.

"Yes. So, where are you from? You have a strange accent."

"So do you," affirmed Zoe.

"Earth Two?" suggested Kakko.

"Too right. I don't know where you're from, but I'm bloody darn glad to meet human beings here."

"Don't get too excited," retorted Zoe, "How much we'll be on your side depends on your story. What brings you here?"

"I might as well ask what brings a ragtag of a group like you here. You backpackers of some kind?"

"We ask the questions first," said Kakko with authority. "What's your name?"

"Bruce Salanger."

"And how did you get here?"

"We have a space cruiser. We came by shuttle."

"We?"

"Six of us. Landed on the surface ice. Set up a test drill to take a core sample. Next thing I knew, the ground gave way and I fell through into a bloody tunnel."

"What happened to the others?"

"How the heck would I know? The radio link in my helmet didn't work in the tunnel and then these blighters ripped the thing off me."

"What is your business here?" demanded Tam.

"I might as well ask what's yours, matie…"

"You might. My guess is that we have been brought here because you have landed."

"How did you know we were coming? And how the hell did you get here? It took us five years in a state-of-the-art space cruiser."

"It's miraculous," replied Buck. "One minute we were in New London and the next, wham – we were here."

"Christ!" swore Bruce.

"Precisely," replied Zoe. "A magic white gate provided by the Almighty."

"You really reckon *God* sent you here?" the man sneered.

"So who sent you?" demanded Tam.

"Well, it won't hurt to tell you, as I doubt you're in the same business. The Rare Edge Mining Company have obtained approval to come to Europa to explore under the ice for precious minerals and stuff. Our task was to land, collect samples and return to our space cruiser within a few hours. We had no idea that the area underneath the ice is riddled with tunnels, and populated by these creatures." He gestured to the Zilakans.

"I suggest you address them with respect," demanded Kakko. "Imagine what you would feel if some gross-looking stranger just appeared in the streets of Earth Two…"

"Europa? So the planet out there is Jupiter?" asked John tentatively.

"Too right, mate. Now you're getting it."

"You see," explained John with more confidence, "the humans you see here are not all from Earth. Kakko and Tam are from a planet called Joh. Dah isn't even from this galaxy… So, I'm John, and this here is Zoe and Buck, and we live in Connecticut, USA."

"OK. I think, I'm –"

But Bruce was not to finish his sentence. There was

a sudden screaming of alarms. The Zilakans all stood with concern on their faces. Another breach.

An important-looking official checked a device strapped to his upper tentacle. "Send as many as you can get hold of... Hall Four, south-west," he trumpeted. "This is the big one – scale fifteen! This is not an exercise! Repeat: this is *not* an exercise!"

There was an audible collective gasp before Zilakans skittered in all directions – each to their allotted posts. The chief rose up and approached Bruce Salanger. Although the Zilakan was not as tall, somehow he looked bigger. Kakko wondered if he were about to eat him like a giant beetle attacking its prey.

"Your friends?"

"I... guess they've come to rescue me..."

"By destroying our whole civilisation?"

"They... they don't mean to. They've no idea there's anyone else on this moon."

The chief addressed a general that remained by his side. "The section seals are in order?"

"They will be deployed if necessary. We are evacuating the whole south-west quadrant."

"Can I... can I suggest," intervened Kakko. "Can I suggest we get this man down to the place and get him to call off his friends. He has a communication device in his suit."

"Take him to Hall Four. Do what you must!"

All the humans fell in behind as Bruce Salanger was led back to his suit. Tam and John helped him into it, then they all boarded a transport trailer and were speeding towards the south-west quadrant.

"If the air is venting, it's OK for him," protested Buck, "He's suited up."

"Correct," said Tam authoritatively. "So when we arrive, you stick with the Zilakans. When they scuttle, so do you."

"Right," said Buck thoughtfully.

They soon encountered hundreds of Zilakans moving in the opposite direction. They were being hurried on by police, who were keeping a lane clear for the emergency vehicles heading towards the damage. They were following a truck packed with fissure-mending equipment, and Zilakans like the ones they first saw – only they were not singing this time. You did not need a detector to be aware of air moving gently down the tunnel. The atmosphere was leaking – the life-giving gases draining away.

As they progressed, the numbers of people moving in the opposite direction thinned out, until there were only ones and twos, and finally the police themselves, having done their job, were going, too. Now, except for the swoosh of the transport, the tunnel was eerily silent. They became aware the air was moving faster still. The fissure must be large.

Eventually, they came to a halt and the fissure repair crew in front of them dashed through an opening.

"Hall Four," shouted one of the police officers. They all bundled out and headed for the opening. The hall was full of Zilakans staring at the turning end of a half-metre diameter drill bit. Air hissed out through its grooves – the sound of the whistles of rushing atmosphere almost deafening. Zilakan fissure repairers were holding up their repair rods – puny in comparison with the slow-turning bit.

"Get your people to stop drilling," yelled Tam to Bruce.

"I'm trying," he replied. "They're not picking up... Red One, red one," he yelled, "this is green one. Stop drilling. Cease operation. Are you receiving me?"

All he could hear was static. "Nothing." Bruce raised his arms to indicate his frustration.

Then, the bit stopped turning. The humans breathed a sigh of relief. But only for a moment before it recommenced – this time in reverse.

"They're withdrawing the bit," yelled Tam.

"The atmosphere on Europa is too thin to maintain life, even discounting the cold," declared John. "If they pull that drill out –"

"Everybody out," bawled Kakko. Gathering Tam and yanking Dah by the hand, she made for the entrance to the hall. The Zilakans followed, abandoning their equipment and skittering after them. In the rush, Zoe and Buck were pushed aside.

"Don't mind me," asserted Zoe. But no-one heard her.

"Seal the tunnel!" commanded an officer. The last of the Zilakans made it through. Zoe, with Buck in tow, reached the gap, but at that moment an inflatable balloon-type device hissed full and into place, making a complete seal of the tunnel entrance. Zoe would have become part of the wall if Buck hadn't pulled her back. The seal missed her left foot by centimetres. The hall was empty apart from Bruce still trying to get through on his radio, a prostrate Zoe, and Buck looking over his shoulder at the roof of the cavern. The bit was slowly being withdrawn.

29

Why Buck did it, he couldn't have said. Upon reflection, it seemed like a stupid, useless thing to do. He took hold of a Zilakan sealing rod and whacked it against the drill bit. Zoe picked one up, too, and did the same. She said she had done it because she was angry. Bruce found a pick and hurled it at the bit, which made a hefty ting. He did it again. Then, they all started to throw things. There was something satisfying in the noise it made. Then, remarkably, the drill stopped. All was silent.

Clearly they had made some kind of contact with the crew above. But the danger wasn't over. If they were to pull the drill out, that would be the end of Zoe and Buck, and perhaps others. Whether the seal balloon was sufficient to withstand the violent virtual vacuum and cold that would follow the opening up of a half-metre hole was something that only occurred to Bruce. The seal looked flimsy to him – effective for now, yes, but not built for a sudden loss of pressure on a grand scale. It was not designed to endure such a sudden catastrophic event. But he needn't have worried. The Zilakans had already sealed off the whole of the evacuated area with a series of heavy-duty airtight metal doors. Those in danger were only a few remaining enforcement officers, together with Kakko, Tam, Dah and John who remained outside – just the other side of the inflatable seal.

Bruce persisted with his radio, but something was preventing his signals from penetrating to the surface. He had no idea how much rock and ice lay above them.

They continued to throw something at the bit. Then, it occurred to Buck. *Morse code.*

"Can your people read Morse code?" questioned Buck.

"That went out with the ark."

"Sure. But not in the Scouts. We use it to signal with our torches in the dark – between the tents when we're supposed to be asleep. Morse code is fun."

"But not useful in an electronic age–" began Bruce.

"Unless your stupid electro whatsits ain't working," rounded Zoe.

"We need to tap Morse on the bit to send the message. Tell them to leave it in place."

"We ain't got much time," answered Zoe. "The air is still leaking and I'm not feeling that bright."

"You seal up the gaps around the bit as much as you can," Buck ordered Bruce, "while I tap out a message. Perhaps one of your team has been in the Scouts."

Buck picked up a pick, but couldn't reach the bit end. "Zo-lo, I need your shoulders."

"It's a good job you ain't got a slip of a girl for your aunt, ain't it? And don't call me Zo-lo!"

Zoe hoisted Buck beneath the bit. He began tapping dots and dashes. *Dash dot dot – dash dash dash – dash dot – dash dash dash – dash – dash dash – dash dash dash – dash dash dash dot – dot – dash dot dot – dot dash dot – dot dot – dot dash dot dot – dot dash dot dot. 'Do not move drill.'* Then, Buck repeated the message, before adding, *'Maintain pressure below. Vital. Keep sealed.'*

After what seemed an age, the bit began to ring a reply. Someone outside had belonged to the Scouts, or else used the code as a child. *Dash dot dot dot – dot dash dot – dot dot dash – dash dot dash dot – dot.* Buck translated, "'*Bruce*'. They want to know you're OK."

"Tell them I'm fine. Tell them to leave the bit where it is.

We'll seal around it. Tell them I'm not alone and there is vital air down here that mustn't be allowed to escape."

Buck went about it, then told the people on the surface to wait. They sealed up around the now stationery bit, and the last of the hissing stopped.

"Right. Now we need to get out of here," declared Zoe. "The air is thin and pretty much used up. Do you reckon we could pop that balloon?"

But they needn't have worried. The Zilakans had been aware of all that was going on – the balloon was not soundproof. A new hissing began – this time from around the seal as new air rushed in to restore the pressure in Hall Four. The balloon deflated. Kakko was the first in and grabbed her friend.

"You did it! Brilliant."

"When I get my ruddy breath back, all I want is a glass of hot, sweet tea," Zoe declared. "It's freezing in here."

The Zilakans could not offer tea – hot, iced or sweet – but they did give Zoe and Buck a huge amount of acclaim and all the luxuries they could muster. Even Bruce was treated with a little respect.

An hour later, John had prepared a written statement in English at the dictation of the Zilakan high command, incorporating suggestions from Kakko and Tam. It explained exactly what had happened as a result of their drilling tests. If the Earthlings had thought that the moon they called Europa had been populated by intelligent creatures, they had been mistaken. Greater care should have been taken (this was Kakko's addition) in view of the fact that life on Europa had not been discounted by Earth scientists. According to John, they had long suspected that the moon was capable of it. They knew it was warmed by tectonic forces, and suggestions had been made that perhaps its water was not frozen all the way through. Anyway, now they were in no doubt, mining on Europa/Zilaka should not be contemplated. Any further invasive procedures would result in a report to the Galactic Council and also to the authorities on Earth One.

This last was a threat that the cruiser crew would be keen to avoid, since most people had been unaware of the technology introduced by external space travellers to certain scientific institutions on Earth. Had more been known by governments elected and, in particular, non-elected, then restrictive regulation and taxes would be sure to have followed. They saw secrecy as key. After all, they were not intending to colonise any of the places they visited, merely bring back the occasional ship full of goodies that could be sold at a good profit, but not in any significant quantities to draw attention. It was not so much about money-making, but sustaining the research and the communications programmes with worlds beyond their own.

Buck was dispatched to Hall Four to signal that Bruce would be left in a tunnel open to the outside above the spoil heap ravine. The Zilakans had discovered a cave that led to the top of a very deep cleft in the surface. They had built a very sturdy exterior door, and then several metres back, another door to provide an airlock. The spoil from new tunnel excavations was brought and placed against the exterior door, the inner door closed and sealed, and then the outer one reopened. A mechanical ram ejected the spoil into the rift. Bruce Salanger would be left in this tunnel, suited up, with the outer door open. Buck tapped out its approximate location. He received an acknowledgement.

Bruce had been given a copy of the order written out neatly by John. But it was to be his testimony that convinced the cruiser crew that the threat in the report was entirely credible. "These were just kids," he explained, "but they knew what they were about." They were not trained space travellers, they wore what they would have done on Earth. He fully believed that if he looked up the YWCA in New London, he would find them – or some of them.

Within the hour, more tapping was heard on the drill bit. Bruce was reported safe and seemed grateful for the care he had been given. There was an apology and a promise that the Zilakans would not be further threatened or disturbed. But would it be alright to collect the rubble in the spoil heap in the ravine that appeared to contain things precious on Earth Two? They would collect it without using any drills or explosives, just use a probe to melt the ice and a heavy mechanical bucket.

A short period of debate saw the Zilakans give their consent. The removal of the spoil heap actually solved a long-term problem, because it was not something they could easily have undertaken themselves.

Buck was delighted at the fuss that was being made over his ability with Morse code. "Just shows that kids can make all the difference," he gloated.

"Sure can," said Zoe. "But that doesn't allow you to call me Zo-lo."

★ ★ ★

"Right, so we leave tomorrow," said Kakko when they were alone to take stock.

"I ain't arguing," said Zoe. "I've never been one for long vacations."

"Actually, I ought to be getting back home, too," said Dah. "People will be getting concerned about me on my planet."

John stayed quiet, studying the beautiful designs of the embroidered cushions. Leaving Zilaka was one thing – parting from Dah, quite another.

★ ★ ★

The following morning, they were not feeling at all well. The Zilakan environment was getting to them. Kakko would have liked to have gone back to talk to the engineers, but it was clear that sometimes you have to put your health before your passion. They explained their decision to the chief, who came to breakfast with them in the beautiful hall. He did not need any persuading – he could see they were struggling. It was time to return them to their natural habitat.

They stayed long enough for representatives from all the interested groups to come and meet with them one last time. The scientists begged something from them that they could keep and research. Kakko cut a lock of her hair, Zoe gave them her jacket, and Tam took his stuff out of his leather wallet and gave them the wallet. Dah could feel her musician friends staring at her guitar. It was dear to her – she had had it a long time – it was almost part of her. But, suddenly, she felt a breath of joy in her heart that said, "Generosity is my gift to you. Give and you will receive – many times over." Dah took the guitar and handed it to the group of musicians. There was a rustle among them, first of delight, then of discussion. Two of them left looking purposeful.

The chief presented them with three of the most ornate and intricately embroidered cushions, and made a short speech. "The breath of the Creator," he said, "has come upon us. He has sent us the blessings of these humans with their knowledge and their beauty. They have filled us with wonder about what lies beyond our world and also given us hope. They have saved us from possible destruction from ignorant beings. We know that there are many living things outside our tunnels – many more than we can possibly imagine. We are not alone, neither are we forgotten. Our Maker has sent us His angels to bless us."

"It has been an honour and privilege to have been welcomed by you," said Kakko.

Then the two musicians returned with a wonderful trumpet made from some form of metallic silicon alloy, etched with the most intricate and beautiful designs. Its burnished surface reflected the soft cave lights with all the colours of the rainbow. Before presenting it to Dah, the leading trumpeter put it to his tube mouth and produced one of the most enchanting sounds she had ever heard.

"Th… Thank you," she stuttered. The instrument was so balanced and smooth in her hand – she had never held anything like it.

"Time to go!" ordered Tam.

The same group who had first encountered them was detailed to lead them back to the tunnel in which they found them. They were escorted to the lay-by as they travelled together in an open-top vehicle along the highway. They took their leave of what seemed a huge percentage of the populace and entered the tunnels with their guides. As they rounded the bend out of sight and away from the sounds of the people, Dah began to sing: "Duh-de, duh-de… hey-de, hey-de… duh-de, duh-dide, bum. Duh-de, duh-de… hey-de, hey-de… duh-de, duh-dide… dide… BUM!"

The locals joined in with enthusiasm. This was their song. Humble fissure inspectors and repairers they may have been – people that would never have qualified as scientists or been selected for the leadership – but now these humans were showing them they were special, too. Their song was not a patch on those of the musicians – but that hadn't seemed to bother Dah, the beautiful human bearing a very special trumpet.

"Duh-de, duh-de… hey-de, hey-de… duh-de, duh-dide, bum. Duh-de, duh-de… hey-de, hey-de… duh-de, duh-dide... dide... BUM!" They all laughed as they shouted "BUM" as loudly as they could.

Buck was the first to spot the glowing white gate. They took their leave of the Zilakans.

"Thank you. May the Creator bless your journey," said one of the group.

"Thanks," said Tam.

Buck pushed open the gate and Zoe followed. The Zilakans sang as one by one the humans stepped through. Kakko was the last to leave. She waved and then was gone.

The Zilakans danced; they would go down in history as the people who had welcomed the aliens from God.

The air in New London was cool and so fresh, it was such a treat to suck it in.

"Never thought New London air so good," said Zoe. "I'll not take it for granted again."

"Well, that was something," said Tam. "We've been to a place or two, but that is among the strangest."

But teenage Buck was not thinking of the air or the adventure. "Zo-lo. I reckon it's meal time. Can we go to the burger joint – or Hannah's Diner?"

"Why not... Better tell folk we're here, though. I left a message, but didn't say when we'd be back."

"What day is it?" asked John.

"I reckon... I reckon it'll be... Sunday. Hannah's will be shut – but the burger joint'll be open till eleven."

"Sunday. I have to go to work tomorrow," sighed John. "I don't want to lose this job, but–"

"No buts," said Zoe. "Leave it in the hands of the Almighty. *She,*" Zoe emphasised the feminine pronoun, "has got it all worked out... Right now, I think She is definitely pointing us in the direction of the burger joint."

"Yay!" exclaimed Buck.

Zoe put her head inside the door and called. "Hi, anyone at home?" Dev appeared.

"Good to see you, Zoe. You have been gone a long time."

"Not that long – but we've definitely had an adventure to beat all others. Don't say y'all missed me?"

"We missed you, I–"

"Tell 'em we're going to the burger joint. We'll be back later."

"Sure."

★ ★ ★

Kakko and Tam had rather expected to see a white gate to Joh that same evening. Tam was anxious to get back because he knew that his mother would be getting distressed. She had not recovered from his last ordeal. If only he could call her – but there was no way of getting a message across so many light years.

"I reckon we still have work to do," reflected Kakko as they prepared to sleep. "But right now, all I want is this bed." She lay her head on the pillow and slept like a baby.

★ ★ ★

Tam had just woken when Dev appeared with a cup of tea. "Oh hi, Dev. Thanks. That is very welcome."

"I heard you moving. Look, before you go down to breakfast, can I ask you something? While we are alone."

Tam was intrigued. "Sure."

"You… you know Zoe? You met her last year and have just spent time with her in this strange world."

"I'm not sure what you're getting at."

"If I tell you something, will you promise me that it will go no further – at least in this world?"

"Of course."

"I think I like Zoe. I would like to ask her… how do they put it in the West?… 'on a date'."

"Oh. You would like to ask her out. Make her your girlfriend."

"Yes, yes. Exactly… how do you think she will… would you think? I… I don't want to make mistake."

"Oh, I see. You think that if she said no, she won't want you around?"

"You understand… you are a wise man."

"I wouldn't say that… look, Dev, I don't think she would be angry with you. But to be honest, I don't think she'd be interested. Don't take it personally. It's not you in particular. She just isn't interested in having a boyfriend. She only said the other day that she prefers to be independent… likes the freedom… You could ask her, but I don't think you would get anywhere."

"Thank you… Then, I must stop thinking of her like that. You are very wise. I am happy to have talked to you," said Dev quietly, his head lowered.

"Try not to be too disappointed, Dev."

"No. I must not. Two months and I return to India. There, my parents will find a wife for me."

"What? Someone you don't know?"

"Of course. It is the custom. If I don't like her, I can say. But my parents will do a good job. They will be happy."

"But you are attracted to Zoe?"

"Yes. She is a very special woman. I like a strong woman. Everyday the same with Zoe. But she is American and don't look for a husband. I must accept that door shut."

"Oh, Dev. I'm sure you will like the girl your parents find for you."

"Yes. I will like her. Learn to love her, perhaps."

★ ★ ★

Breakfast was fun. Kakko and Tam laughed as Zoe held forth about her adventures. They met Beth, Lucy, Jane and Amy, too.

"It looks like you kidnapped our Zoe," laughed Amy.

"Kidnapped! We'd never kidnap anyone... not ever!" stated Kakko fervently.

Tam saw the alarm on Amy Merton's features and explained, "On the last adventure, I was actually kidnapped. Kakko's still sore."

"Oh, I see. Sorry. I didn't mean to imply–"

"Of course you didn't," said Zoe, "After all, who would ever want *me*?"

"I couldn't imagine," laughed Amy, playfully.

★ ★ ★

In the middle of the morning, after most had gone off to work, and Kakko and Tam were left just with Dah, Tam spotted a white gate.

"Our gate, Kakko."

"Mine, too," said Dah. "If the gate lets me back, I'm going to tell my parents that I like the USA and I am choosing to stay here, with John."

"Wouldn't you miss your own world?"

"I guess. But I would miss John much, much more. I think the Creator understands. She understands love. I'm praying She lets me back."

"So am I," said John quietly.

"My parents," said Tam, "would find it incredibly hard if I

297

did not return. My mother will already be worried, especially after last time. I think we should be getting back, Kakko."

"You're right. And I have a pile of college stuff I ought to be doing anyway."

"I think we shall meet again," said Dah positively, as they cuddled each other. "I have hope that we shall meet again."

"There will be a next time," agreed Tam.

"Thanks for the adventure," said Dah.

"'Til next time. Bye."

Dah's parting from John was painful, but the agony didn't last long because within twenty-four hours she was back, this time with a rucksack full of her own precious things and her second guitar. She had come to stay.

30

A bby was doing her best to get used to St Chad's vicarage, but it just didn't feel like home at all. She tried to support her father in encouraging the sixth form art department with the crib project.

As it turned out, nearly all the work was done in the school. After a short visit to the site to measure and take pictures, a team of budding artists worked to design and produce the sculptures. They were finally brought to St Chad's during the college day, and Abby didn't see them. Abby liked the figures. Set under a rudimentary roof of straw, they were tall and thin with elongated faces – more 'alien'-looking than life-like human beings. They wore representations of Middle Eastern workaday clothes of the period, which were not at all like the Pre-Raphaelite paintings inside the church. They looked cold – which was the idea. The manger was roughly constructed of well-used hand-hewn timber, and the baby in Mary's arms against her breast was tiny and well wrapped in coarse grey linen. What Abby liked most about the crib scene was that it expressed something different about the birth of Jesus from the standard church sort with their warm, Christmassy feel. She liked the fact that Mary and Joseph were exposed, and there was nothing cosy about anything. Placed, as it was, in front of the church rather than inside, it spoke a lot about Jesus the 'outsider' – the child born outside that was eventually to be rejected and killed on a cross on a hill outside the city walls.

Sadly, there were few of the 'insiders' at St Chad's who thought much of it. Dave's 'honeymoon period' was not going to be a long one. The churchwarden was charged with saying something to him about how the congregation would put up with this this year, but the link with Longmead should be limited to just this one occasion. He did it kindly and Dave thanked him for the feedback, and tried not to let his disappointment show.

Sunday by Sunday, Abby sat in the rectory pew with her mother. There were no other young people in the church. Dave had thought that perhaps she could robe occasionally, and serve at the altar as she and the other young people had done at St Augustine's – at least she would be involved. But it wasn't to be. That job was done by two elderly men who had been appointed several decades before. It would have been difficult enough to get a *boy* to help them, but a *girl* was completely out of the question. Abby began to dread Sundays. Dave was sympathetic and suggested she just concentrate on God like he did – but even he was feeling the pressure of the tacit disapproval from many and the more explicit dislike from a few. It was going to take a lot of patient work to win these people over.

Dave had invited the students from the sixth form college to come to a blessing of their work. On a December Sunday morning before the service, they and Mr Beckingsale came and stood with some of the hardier members of the congregation in a strong north wind as Dave said a few prayers. Sadly, no-one from the regular congregation spoke to the artists and when the blessing was done, and they moved inside for the rest of the service, the young people didn't follow. *It feels like they don't feel as if there is any room in the inn for them*, Dave reflected. That day, Abby stayed outside, too. She went off with them to the café with Mr Beckingsale and really enjoyed it. She told them how much she liked their work, and that it was probably much more like that in Bethlehem in 6 BC when Jesus was born than the usual crib scene – but it appeared that none of these young artists believed in the story at all.

* * *

Abby braved out Christmas at St Chad's. The one new good thing in her life was that she was so pleased she had made the move to the sixth form college. The atmosphere was brilliant. They treated the students as young adults and, for the first time, Abby was only doing her favourite subjects. Dropping maths and the sciences was a release. Calculating moles in chemistry had been a real chore for her and she found logarithms really difficult to get her head round. But studying French with students who enjoyed the subject and were good at it was *'formidable'* and she made huge strides in the first term – especially in her speaking skills. Among her set French literature books was one by Albert Camus – *La Peste* – which fitted well with her philosophy syllabus that included twentieth-century existentialism.

The end of the Autumn term and the holidays were tough days. Christmas didn't feel right for Abby in her new home.

For St Chad's, the big service was at midnight – but like the Sundays, there were no young people. After he had dedicated the traditional crib with its large early twentieth-century painted figures, Dave spent most of the service way above the congregation at the high altar.

On Christmas Day, Dave was out at church most of the morning. He came in for a cup of tea after the eight o'clock service, and then he and Lynn went back for the nine-thirty Eucharist. Abby elected not to go; she spent all of Christmas morning on her own in bed in the vast Victorian house, reading *La Peste*. She wanted to go to see Bandi but felt that wasn't fair on her mum and dad. On Boxing Day, they would go to see her grandparents.

She missed the college, too, and most of the Christmas holidays Abby spent studying. Dave had a few days off and he joined them relaxing in front of the fire in the high-ceilinged sitting room to read a novel set in the fourth century AD that he had got as a present from Abby for Christmas, while Abby curled up with *La Peste* in an armchair. She was determined to finish it before college restarted. She had been given a new smartphone for Christmas and she was enjoying using it to look up the French words she didn't know.

★ ★ ★

The New Year came and, for the first time in her life, Abby was glad Christmas was over. She and Bandi visited each other, and she told him all about Albert Camus and his existentialism.

"So he doesn't believe in God, then," observed Bandi.

"No, not at all. He thinks that if God existed, He would be a tormentor. The priest in the story has nothing to contribute, only saying that the plague was visited on the people because of their sins. The whole idea of God, and *any* reason behind existence, is what he calls 'absurd'."

"That's harsh. God is the one who created us and loves us," said Bandi.

"But, if He loves us, why does He allow things like the plague to ravage innocent people? Many Christians believe that disease and suffering is a punishment from God, but I can't see why a child should suffer and die just because someone else has sinned."

"And none of us are perfect, so–"

"So we all deserve to be punished with a horrible plague?"

302

"Well, no… I don't know. Isn't that where Jesus comes in in Christianity?"

"Yeah, He died for our sins. But that still doesn't work. Why should an innocent man take the punishment for the guilty? That's totally not fair."

"But, Jesus – isn't He supposed to be God, Himself?"

"Yes. But if God comes to Earth and dies, then He does so for Himself, because he is not innocent, not really when He makes a world in which so many people suffer."

"That's like saying God is responsible for everything anyone does, just because He has dared to give us free will. God has to give us free will because if we don't have it, then we can't love, because love has to be given and received freely."

"Well, I suppose that's true… But, the thing is, most of the people who follow Christ on Earth think they are better than other people. Most Christians think they are different from the rest. You should listen to what some of them at St Chad's say about people. A tramp came into the midnight service on Christmas Eve – he only wanted to sit quietly at the back. Sure, he had been drinking, but he wasn't really drunk… lots of people at St Chad's smelt of drink – sherry and the like. But they threw him out anyway. Dad went out after him and gave him something to eat. Dad said the tramp sat down beside the figures in the outside crib scene to eat it and swore he heard the baby say to him, "Never mind, George, I've been trying to get in there for years!""

Bandi laughed. "I don't think that's true of all Christians. I mean, from what I have seen on Earth – which I admit is not much – there's a lot of loving God followers – like your dad."

"I know, but most of the people I meet in the church aren't."

"Maybe… maybe it just feels like that because you don't get on at St Chad's… Look, why don't you try and join in with some young Christians somewhere else? Aren't there any Christians at Longmead?"

"Not many. There is a Christian soc, but most of them go to the Christian House Fellowship on a Sunday."

"So what's wrong with that?"

"Nothing. Except it doesn't feel right to be with people away from Dad and Mum."

"You don't have to go to their church on Sundays – just give the Christian soc a go."

"Perhaps."

★ ★ ★

On the first Sunday of the New Year, Lynn suggested Abby put on a skirt instead of the jeans she always wore.

"Why, Mum?"

"Well… because it would come over better in church."

"No-one dresses up for church these days, Mum."

"I do."

"Yeah, I mean no-one my age. I've been going to church in jeans for years, you know I have, and you've never said anything before. All the kids at St Augustine's wear them."

"Yes, but we're not at St Augustine's, are we?"

"No, we're not! Have people been complaining about me?"

"No, not actually complaining. But if you made an effort, and put on a skirt or something, I know that would be appreciated."

"No way! That's selling out to reactionary forces. It's like Renny High – all about appearances and their so-called 'standards'!"

"Abby, that's not called for!"

"Isn't it? Dad and you, you've been trying your best not

to upset people ever since we came here. I knew it would be like this. They're not going to change! It's *you* who are being changed by *them* – but they're not going to change *me*!"

Abby resolved to go along to Christian soc.

★ ★ ★

"You are very welcome," gushed Josie, one of the leaders of Longmead Christian soc. "Are you a Christian?"

"Well, yes," replied Abby doubtfully. She wasn't entirely sure what Josie meant by 'being a Christian'.

Josie read the doubt in Abby's voice and went on, "Have you accepted Jesus Christ as your Lord and Saviour?"

"Yes," said Abby, more decisively. Now wasn't the time to engage in theological nuances.

"Great!" continued Josie. "When?"

"When what?"

"When did you invite Jesus into your life?"

"Oh, He's always been there. I can't remember when he wasn't. I've been saying prayers with my parents as long as I can remember…" Abby tailed off, losing confidence. Judging from Josie's expression, this was not what was expected.

"You have to make a personal commitment. You must own your faith and declare it."

"Oh, I did that when I was confirmed."

That clearly didn't seem to satisfy either.

"But did you really really mean it?"

"Of course," said Abby firmly. "You don't say things like, 'I turn to Christ', 'I submit to Christ' and 'I walk with Christ' in front of a church full of people and the bishop lightly."

Josie seemed satisfied, at least for the moment. "Come and meet some of our members."

It turned out that all the members of the Longmead Christian soc attended the Christian House Fellowship, which met in the college hall on Sundays. Some had gone elsewhere before, but when they joined the society, they had also transferred their church allegiance. This was what they would expect of Abby, too. *But why not? s*he thought. *I don't think I'll be going to St Chad's again.* By the end of the meeting, Abby was feeling pretty good. She readily agreed to attend the college hall on Sunday morning and see what the Christian House Fellowship had to offer.

At 10.30 am on the Sunday morning, the hall was pretty full. There was hardly anyone there over the age of forty. And *everyone* was wearing jeans – even the suave-looking man on the stage that looked set to lead the service. He was a large man – tall and broad – with floppy hair, which he kept sweeping back with his hand. Confident and in control, he was definitely what some women would call a 'hunk'. The stage also boasted a band with drums, two guitars, a keyboard and a female lead singer with long, brown hair who jumped up and down when she wasn't singing. They were really loud – the loudest thing Abby had heard on the college hall stage.

There appeared to be around a hundred or more people present, but it was difficult to say as so many of them were children who weren't in the same place more than a minute at a time. The leader greeted the people and they went immediately into a song projected on the large screen at the back of the stage. As they sang, people raised their hands, clapped and danced. There was no shortage of enthusiasm. This was a world away from anything Abby had ever experienced – not at St Augustine's and certainly not at St Chad's. Faced with a choice of high-quality contemporary surround-sound, energy and performance, there was no way the traditional churches could compete with this for young hearts and minds. Abby had been sucked up into a group of young people she already knew, and made to feel really welcome. After the initial impact it was as if she had belonged there for weeks, because it was so easy to get into the swing of it. The words were all displayed, the tunes repetitive and the rhythms predictable if you listened to the charts – they, kind of, went where the young people expected them to.

After the worship, the families and young folk all queued up for burgers and hot dogs. What a difference to coffee after the Eucharist at St Augustine's when the kids thought mere biscuits were a treat! Abby wanted to resist the temptation to indulge because she knew her mother was preparing a good Sunday lunch for them, but it was all too much for her. She wondered whether the preacher ever got round to the evils of gluttony.

By the time she got home, Abby had decided most definitely that she was going to go again the following week – and she was going to see if Bandi wanted to go with her.

★ ★ ★

But it was at the second Christian soc meeting that Abby first started to be aware of a sense of discomfort. The speaker brought with him an old tattered Bible. He told a story of a new Church of England curate fresh from theological college, who came full of his critical university studies, which he began to spread around the unsuspecting congregation.

"First," said the middle-aged man, who was introduced as a pastor of a congregation in a nearby town, "he questioned the literal truth of the creation stories, calling them 'aetiological legends'. They weren't really the word of God, but human inventions; there really wasn't anyone called Adam and Eve." Then, the pastor took hold of his old Bible and ripped a section out of the front of it as the students all gasped.

"Quite right to be horrified," went on the pastor. "You wouldn't want to mistreat the word of God, but this young curate didn't believe it was God's word. The next week he preached on the Book of Revelation, explaining to his confused congregation that the world was not actually going to end as it described. Oh, no, this was only picture language. What the writer was doing was writing in code to encourage the congregation. They weren't to take St John's vision literally... really?" He tore out the Book of Revelation from the back of the old Bible. "What were the poor folk to believe?" he continued.

Abby felt there was something really wrong about this. Did he really believe that what she had always thought of as picture language was literally true? And if so, it spoke of a different Christianity from the one she had always believed in. This God was rigid, vindictive and violent. Not a friend at all.

By the time the preacher had finished, pages were flying about all over the place. "So then, what are we to believe about the resurrection?" he concluded. "You might think this was safe from criticism. But, no, on Easter Sunday, the people learned from this curate that Jesus probably didn't rise literally – it was a spiritual affair!" And the pastor finally flung the rest of the book in the air and lowered his voice for dramatic effect. "Once you begin to question the word of God, the Devil takes a hold of you and leads you into dark and dangerous ways. My brothers and sisters, every single word in the Scriptures is inspired by God. It is quite literally the Word of God. Are you going to criticise *Him*? Dare you subject the scripture to textual analysis, form criticism or whatever else the professors dream up to debunk it?"

It was a most powerful presentation. The pastor sat down and the room was silent, in awe of this preacher's power and conviction. Tearing a Bible apart definitely made an impression.

Abby was decidedly uncomfortable. It made some sort of sense but… it just couldn't be right. As they milled about afterwards over coffee, Abby voiced her concern.

"How does a real Adam and Eve square with evolution?" she asked some of her friends. "I mean if we evolved over millennia, there wouldn't be an actual first man and first woman, would there?"

Her friends shifted uncomfortably and one of the senior boys said, "That's why the theory of evolution is bunkum."

"Bunkum!" proclaimed Abby, rather too loudly. "How do you explain all the fossils of early … early … human …oids?" Abby tailed off. *Of course,* she said to herself, *these people don't believe in evolution, either, do they? Oops.* But it was too late. The visiting speaker had been invited across and was explaining to her the scientific conspiracy and deception concerning evolution. "The world was created – indeed, the whole universe – exactly as it is now, just six thousand years ago. You have to accept that or reject the inspired, inerrant word of God as it is in the *Bible*."

Abby felt all this was an assault on common sense. Could all those scientists be wrong? Cosmologists had agreed on the age of the universe – fourteen billion years. And whatever the man had to say about the dinosaur bones, she wouldn't know. But she had no doubt that the geologists, who located them in a period around a hundred million years ago, were right.

"But," said Abby, gaining confidence, "there are two different creation stories from different sources, aren't there? How can they both be factually true?"

"Abby's father is a vicar," explained her friend apologetically.

"Ah, I see. That is the problem. You see, Annie–"

"Abby, my name's Abby…"

"Er… Abby. You may have heard that some people believe there are different sources. But to analyse the Bible like this is to totally mishandle the word of God. Once you start taking it apart you can never get it to go back as it should. I'm not blaming your father – he and most Church of England clergy have been trained by deceived academics."

Abby could not ever believe her father was deceived by anyone. He was clever enough to think for himself – but Abby realised this was not the place to take on this man – even if she had the knowledge to do it, which she hadn't. So she just smiled. He seemed satisfied that he had won the argument and moved on.

"Are you coming again on Sunday?" asked her friend.

"I think so," said Abby. "I told my parents I would… can I bring a friend?"

"Of course."

"He's not from Persham. He might be here on Sunday, though."

Abby desperately wanted Bandi. She was lost and confused, and wanted his help and support. She hadn't asked him on a Sunday before – he had never come to church with her since she had been living at St Chad's.

★ ★ ★

Bandi understood her need and readily agreed.

"The people are kind enough and welcoming, and the music is great – but they have a take on things that is very different from Dad," she explained.

31

"Hey, Charlie," called Guy. "Great to see you. So you decided to come back after all?"

"Yeah. Couldn't let Old Man Gubbins and his English lit down, could I? Not after he said how great it was to see me at the end of last term, when half the class decided to bunk off. He went: 'Nice of you to rock up to my lessons, Charlie.' So I thought I might just show my face at Longie's after Christmas. What about you? You've been away?"

"Longbeach, California for a couple of weeks."

"Wow! Bet that was cool."

"Kind of. Got bored after the first week. Just sunshine, sea and sand – oh, and sex, booze and pot. It's a rip-off really."

"Whereas at Longmead Sixth Form College, we just have the last three..."

Guy laughed. "Chance would be a fine thing... Oh, hi Abby, nice to see you." Abby led Bandi into the group.

"Chance for what?" asked Abby.

Charlie went a little beetroot-coloured and Guy explained, "Sex, booze and pot."

"Right. Sounds just like you, Charlie – not... Let me introduce you to Bandi. Bandi, this is Guy and Charlie. Don't believe half what they tell you about their exploits. Guy, here, is the one who had the idea of the underwear bonfire."

"Hi," said Bandi, who was still trying to catch up on some of what they were talking about. "Abby told me about the bonfire. Sorry it didn't work out."

311

"He's waiting for the General Election," said Charlie, in a sly tone that Bandi had difficulty interpreting.

"Actually, that's not a bad idea," said Abby, with a serious expression.

"You weren't living in Persham then?" asked Guy.

"No. I'm just visiting. I'm living with Abby at the moment."

"He means," explained Abby hastily, "he's staying with us – with me and my parents – in the vicarage."

"Ooh…" said Guy. "I've heard about you. You live… abroad somewhere and you're Abby's boyfriend. Actually, to tell you the truth, we were wondering if you actually existed, I mean… actually… er… existed…" Guy tailed off and looked for someone to rescue him.

"What he's intimating–" began Charlie,

"Wow! Big word!" exclaimed Guy. "You can tell he's doing English…"

Charlie ignored him. "What we thought – since nobody had actually seen you – was that Abby was making you up… to stop boys pestering her."

"Thanks!" said Abby in a disgusted tone. Although, she had to acknowledge to herself that telling people that she was in a relationship did prevent a bit of hassle. She *had* used the mention of a boyfriend to deflect approaches from urgent young men often enough that it wouldn't have been a surprise to her friends if he had only been invented as some sort of cover. After all, Abby hadn't told them anything about where he lived or which college he went to – all they had gathered was that he was foreign. Some said they had seen him in the park once – but where he had got to after that, they had no idea.

Bandi extended a hand in greeting to each of the young people in turn as they joined the group – it was always the established custom on Joh to shake hands and bow. Abby's friends thought it was quite cute. "Thank you for your welcome," Bandi smiled. It was good to be greeted so warmly. Abby, however, was aware that her friends were more curious than anything else, and quickly suggested they go and find a seat in the assembly hall to which they were all being summoned.

"They're dying to find out about you," she whispered. "They keep asking me about you and I don't tell them much."

"You haven't told them about the white gate?"

"No way! They wouldn't understand – and they'd gossip it all over town and I'd be pursued by reporters again. No, I've just told them you're from Joh. They think it's somewhere in Eastern Europe or Asia, or somewhere."

A young women leaned over to say hi. "Love your accent."

"Thanks," smiled Bandi. "I am trying to learn English – Abby is a good teacher."

"Where are you from? Where do your parents come from?"

"My father is from here – from Persham – but they have lived… away… from before I was born, and so I have only spoken English at home. Where do you come from?"

"Oh, me? Persham – boring old Persham… but I'm to go somewhere cool for university, though."

Bandi had successfully got her off the subject of him and she went on to tell them of her applications to study English. Then, the band struck up and any further conversation was impossible. They sang, swung and gyrated on the stage until the congregation had all been gathered in and everyone had found a place to sit. Not that anyone was actually sitting until the band ceased and the suave pastor, his muscles rippling under a tight, checked shirt, strode up to a microphone stand, and welcomed everybody in a low but powerful voice. The band broke into another song and the words on the screen flitted in front of Bandi's eyes between the swaying arms of the worshippers. He might have been able to speak and understand English, but it took him a song or two to read the words and join in. Abby looked up at him and smiled.

The address was about the importance of the Virgin Birth. This was the doctrine that Jesus was not the natural son of Joseph (or any human father) but that Mary conceived him while remaining a virgin. The Holy Spirit of God had put him directly into her womb. Abby had always thought that this happened so that Jesus was truly God Himself, come to Earth in human form. But the preacher didn't mention that. Instead, he spent twenty minutes on the virtues of virginity – he kept on about intact hymens and purity.

As they queued for the burgers in the after-service mêlée with Abby and her friends, the preacher came across and introduced himself.

"Hi, you're the girl with the golden hair I saw last week. So pleased to see you here again today. They tell me you haven't been baptised yet."

"Oh. Hi. Yes, I have been baptised – when I was a baby."

"But not as an adult – as a believer."

"No. But I have been confirmed – I mean, when I confirmed the baptismal vows. I was thirteen then."

"Confirmation is not biblical. If you believe, you must be born again of water and the Spirit – totally immersed in a believers' baptism. You will need to be properly baptised. As it happens, next month we are travelling to the seaside for a baptism in the sea. Some of your friends are being baptised then. Perhaps you might like to join them… think about it." The preacher was about to walk away when he noticed Bandi, whom he had totally ignored up to that point.

"Er, is this your friend?"

"Yes," said Abby. "This is Bandi."

"Unusual name. You're not from these parts?"

"No," replied Bandi, "I don't live here."

"Are you a Christian?"

"No. There are no Christians where I come from."

"That is very bad news. But you are here today! You have been sent by God to learn that there is no salvation outside of Jesus Christ. No-one can be saved in this life or the next except through faith in Jesus Christ. While you are here, you might like to attend one of our enquirers' sessions."

"Thanks," said Bandi politely, "but I'm not staying."

"That's a pity. Don't forget, though – take this opportunity. This is God's calling. You don't want to end up in perpetual damnation in the fires of hell. Jesus is the only Way to life."

"Thanks," replied Bandi. "I won't forget."

They ate their burgers in the presence of a few of Abby's college friends and talked about all sorts of things, but none pertaining to religion. As soon as she could, Abby made their excuses and led her boyfriend to the door.

Outside Abby breathed a heavy sigh, then, despite herself, she began to cry. "Let's go somewhere… somewhere private," she sobbed.

They took a short cut across the town and found a tree-lined avenue with benches down the middle. It was dry if not warm, and Abby plonked herself down on the nearest bench. She had given up crying now – her tears had turned into anger.

"How dare he?" she declared. "He has not the right to imply – to say – you were going to go to hell! How could you have been a Christian on Joh?"

"Well, I suppose I could. My nan and dad are from Earth, and know a lot about it. Nan would say she was a Christian. And, since I have been to that meeting, I have had a direct invitation, haven't I? So, now there is no excuse. He would say the ball was in my court."

"But God would never send you to hell and yet let in a person like that pastor. He makes my skin crawl. He spent half his long sermon going on about purity – just like he did last week – and the second half slagging off Christians like my father."

"I noticed that – he probably wouldn't say your dad has been… how did he put it?"

"Saved."

"Yeah, that was the word – 'saved'… presumably from the fires of hell."

"Where the Devil reigns with his great big toasting fork."

"Ouch!" Bandi laughed.

"You don't think he's right, then?"

"Do you? The God I know wouldn't just look after a few people from one of the planets in the whole universe. I think God in Christ is true. What your dad talks about has a ring of truth. But I would say that lots of the rest of the stuff is all made up by people – it's about belonging to the club."

"The club he runs."

"Exactly. When you listen to it, it's not really about letting God in. Did you notice that in all his long sermon he hardly ever referred to God? God got very few mentions compared to the Devil… or the Virgin Mary's 'intact hymen'. What exactly is one of those, by the way?"

Abby giggled. "Is this an English problem or a lack of biological knowledge?"

"The first – I guess."

"Let us say that *you* haven't got a hymen, being a boy. All girls are born with them and mostly keep them intact until they… have sex or something, then…"

"OK. I understand! It was an English problem."

And they laughed and laughed as the tension of the morning fell away from them.

"That man has a problem," concluded Bandi. "I think he is obsessed with sex... girls. He was all over *you,* but hardly noticed me until he had made sure of getting you into the seaside. I was an afterthought. I bet he can't wait to get you and other 'virgins' in the seaside. What happens in 'total immersion'?"

"Into the *sea,*" corrected Abby. "Jade – the friend you met – she explained it to me. She's going to do it. She has to wear nothing but a dark-coloured cloak that comes up to the neck. She says they have to walk into the sea and the pastor dunks them three times right under the water – then they take off the dark cloak and put on a white one someone gives them."

"So basically you get naked in the sea with this man!"

"Well, I suppose so. Now you put it like that, it sounds quite... quite–"

"Lewd?"

"Creepy. But it's supposed to be about God and-"

"Purity?"

"Exactly."

"If you ask me, I don't think this pastor has much to do with God at all. Are you going to go back next week?"

"No. The music's great, but you ought not just go for the music – it's hypocritical."

"St Chad's, then?"

"No. I can't stand them. I won't go anywhere." They sat together, thinking their own thoughts. Bandi put his arm around his friend and pulled her towards him, gazing into the dull clouds. Then, it suddenly changed. The sun broke through.

"Look!" pointed Bandi. "The sun's shining." Then, from nowhere, large raindrops began to fall, too, and the stub of a rainbow appeared at the end of the street. It lasted only a few seconds before the sun went in again.

"Spring's on its way," declared Abby, feeling a little bit happier.

★ ★ ★

When it was time for Bandi to return to Joh, Abby accompanied him to the white gate.

"Can I come with you?" she asked. "Just to say hi to your parents." She was reluctant to let him go.

"They won't be at home yet," smiled Bandi. "Look, we've had a good day and we're both tired. Come and see me tomorrow – we can go to the seaside on the bus."

"I didn't know you were on holiday."

"Study leave. I have to write an essay for geography, and I have chosen the development of the coastline, so this can be my research."

"A date with a boy with a clipboard?"

"Camera."

"OK. Bandi… and thanks."

"What for?"

"You know – everything."

They parted with a kiss and when Bandi had gone, Abby was tempted to spread her coat, lay down on the damp grass and listen to the sounds of the spring evening. The wild things – the weeds – were beginning to grow again. Her father was true to his word and was going to allow the jungle to grow back for his daughter, despite Lynn's urging him to keep everything tidy. Her parents both loved her, but not in the same way. Dave indulged her. Lynn was more strict – Abby had never managed to get round her like she did her father. Her mother provided the rock that allowed her father to encourage her to explore. She needed them both – she valued them both. She stared up into the darkening sky and watched as the stars came out. As the sun's rays died away she could see more and more, and deeper and deeper into the heavens. The brightest stars were mostly the nearest, but even they were tens of light years away. Most of the light from the stars she saw had left them well before she had been born – even been thought about. The light from the furthest ones was older than the Earth and beyond them, she knew, were galaxies upon galaxies whose light had left them not long after the universe began. Wow! *What,* she thought, *is the greatest miracle – the vastness of the universe, the new life of the spring where living things were so wonderfully growing or the fact that, in the middle of it all, were tiny human beings with the ability to be aware of them? And there were bound to be dimensions upon dimensions she couldn't even contemplate. Was the supernatural really so absurd like the existentialists claimed? Their doctrine was so one-dimensional – here and now – while the universe spoke so strongly of past, present and future interweaving and inter-penetrating each other.*

'He was, and is, and is to come' – the words of the last book of the New Testament resonated in Abby's mind. Abby rejoiced in her father's ability to perceive God through the picture language of the Scriptures – something he had passed on to her. The Christian soc speaker, in requiring the universe to be a mere six thousand years old, had missed the wonder entirely. And poor Camus had seen only a tiny part of the picture. The bit he saw was indeed absurd, if that was all that there was to it, but the vastness of the creation spoke of so much yet to discover – about God, about freedom to be and become, and about love. That was the problem – both for the Christian House Fellowship people and for Albert Camus – they were too narrow; they missed so much in trying to keep it so strictly logical. Love in creation defies definition and limitation.

★ ★ ★

The following Sunday, Abby sat quietly in the designated pew at St Chad's and listened to her father talk of God's love. Her heart warmed as he smiled at her – God was on the move, even if it would take many a long year to break down the hardness of some people's defences against Him.

★ ★ ★

As the Easter holidays approached, Abby became aware of trouble in the Christian House Fellowship. Apparently, the band and a few others had decided to found a new fellowship somewhere else in Persham. The pastor's wife had left him and had decided to worship with them, taking her children with her. There was some talk that the pastor had made a pass at the lead singer – others said it was more than a pass. Abby's friends in Christian soc were confused and didn't know where their loyalties lay. People couldn't agree on where God wanted them to be. Abby was glad to be out of it and suggested that God probably didn't want either faction. To her surprise, her friends didn't argue with that.

★ ★ ★

On Good Friday afternoon, Abby decided to go and sit at the back at St Chad's. She wasn't alone. Josie came with her and another friend from Christian soc who wanted to go somewhere else. This service wasn't a liturgy – that had happened in the morning – but mainly preaching and singing old hymns. Her dad was brilliant – he just spoke about God and His self-giving in Christ. There was no slick rhetoric, no appeal to repentance or anything deliberately aimed at making the congregation feel guilty, or anything against other denominations or anybody. Abby was proud of him.

"Authentic," commented Josie afterwards. "He's for real."

"Thanks," said Abby.

★ ★ ★

On the Friday after Easter – the day they got back from a few days in a country cottage that belonged to a family friend – Dave picked up a heap of letters and took them to his desk. After a few minutes he walked into the kitchen holding out a letter for Lynn to read. Then, they called Abby away from her computer. Abby sensed something was up, so she selected 'sleep mode' and went downstairs. Dave told her he had received a letter from the bishop. He had been invited to take up a job in the diocese as a youth chaplain. It would mean leaving St Chad's.

"But, Dad, you haven't been at St Chad's a year yet?"

"I know, but I couldn't resist applying. The bishop is delighted it seems. I told him I would apply because I needed to do something for you."

"But the archdeacon—"

"Is also happy. I have, apparently, done such a good job in a few months that he doesn't doubt he would get the right kind of applicant for St Chad's next time. We have got a new PCC with a few people who are ready to change. And I won't be taking up this post until August – so they will have had me for almost a year."

"So this means leaving this house?"

"I'm afraid so. We won't have a vicarage, but an ordinary house. I would be based at the Diocesan Youth Adventure Centre in the valley. We can live in town somewhere convenient to Longmead."

"Where will you be on Sundays?"

"I'll be at the Adventure Centre most of the time. Your mum is happy to make that her base. So, what do you say?"

"Cool, Dad. Real cool. You know, my friend Josie said you should be doing things with young people. She says you're 'authentic'."

"Wow. Now, that's a compliment. So, you think I could do this, then?"

"Dad, if you really want my frank opinion–"

"Don't I always get it?"

"Well, yes. In my opinion, you are wasted here at St Chad's. You're better with teenagers than nearly anyone else in the church I've met."

"Authentic?"

"Precisely… Dad?"

"Yes."

"I… I was going to ask you. About Bandi–"

"Look, I wouldn't worry about the gate – it belongs to *you*, not the house."

"I know. It's not that. It's, well, Bandi would like to attend college here. I mean at Longmead, so he can go on to study philosophy at uni. They don't have Earth philosophy on his planet. So, I was wondering, if we had a big enough house, could he come and stay with us? I mean, permanently."

32

Kakko, Tam and Shaun stepped through into a world of falling leaves. A strong wind was blowing across what appeared to be a park with large deciduous trees of a variety of species, which had been carefully planted, in years gone by, to flank a gravel drive, which curled its way up a slight incline.

"You did well, sis," said Shaun.

"How do you mean?" Kakko was wondering why the compliments all of a sudden.

"You had to wait patiently for me to come back from the match."

"We had no choice. For some reason, you don't take your phone on the pitch. But it was clear you were expected. There were three sets of clothing and they weren't for anyone else."

"She's not in quite so much of a hurry these days," said Tam firmly. "And we've never seemed to miss anything by accepting your mum's entreaties to make sure you're ready."

Kakko decided to ignore them. Not even she would abandon playing in a football match for a white gate. Imagine, in the middle of a half, just going up to the captain and saying, "Sorry, I have to go now."

Unthinkable. As it was, Shaun had torn himself away from the post-match celebrations. Having lost the previous two, the win was particularly welcome, and the club were in high spirits. The party had been tempting, but Shaun knew the call of the white gates. He was needed somewhere else, somewhere that could be anywhere in the universe the

Creator wanted him to be. The adventures could be fun at times, but they were always hard work and sometimes painfully dangerous. Shaun tried to shake himself out of the post-match euphoria that continued to engulf his brain – he could still feel the sweetness of his connecting with the ball, and the way it swerved from low left to the top right-hand corner just beneath the bar, and the delectable bulge of the net…

"We needed these heavy coats," said Tam with a shiver. "Which way?"

"Let's go up – round that bend. We might be able to see something from there," suggested Kakko.

Tam picked up two large stones and placed them carefully on the side of the path in front of the white gate. "We might need to know exactly where we came in. This road could go on like this for a long way."

"Good idea, Tam," agreed Shaun, adding a third stone.

Kakko put a small one on the top. "Perfect," she smiled.

They all laughed as they made their way upwards. They need not have worried about getting lost. As they rounded the bend, they came in sight of a large stone mansion. It had a terrace and statues positioned around the lawn below it.

"Wow! Posh or what?" said Kakko, impressed.

They approached the house, but there didn't appear to be any signs of life. There were chimneys, but no smoke. It wasn't exactly cold, yet the wind meant you would need something to keep things a little cosy inside – especially in a large place such as this. They went up to the front door and knocked. They weren't surprised when no-one answered.

"Let's go round the back," suggested Shaun.

They followed the gravel round to what looked like stables, or garages. The door to one of them stood open, but the place was empty of any mode of transport. They continued on around to where they expected to find a back door. Just as they came through a hedge, they heard the sound of a vehicle approaching. It stopped in front of the house and then they heard the slamming of doors. The car moved again and came around the drive towards the garages. The three young people abandoned their search for a back door to walk towards the car. Shaun was still just by the hedge when a piece of gravel slid into his shoe and brought him up suddenly. It had gone right beneath his instep. He would have to take the shoe right off.

Kakko and Tam approached the car. A young man got out, and they began talking to him. As Shaun struggled with a knot in his laces – he had not taken enough care in the changing room as he had hurried to get back to White Gates Cottage – his companions accompanied the young man around the front of the house. He was just getting his shoe back on, when a second vehicle – a much heavier one this time and driven fast – smashed through the chippings and skidded to a halt.

"Don't move!" said a man in a loud, ugly voice. "Stay right where you are, unless you want to die now!"

"Don't... don't shoot," squeaked a young woman. "We're unarmed!"

"Get in! Get in the back! All of you!" commanded the gruff voice.

Shaun peered carefully around the corner and saw a large, black people carrier (oddly shaped compared to those on Joh) with a driver and, beside it, a man with a substantial pistol. He watched as the driver got out, opened the back door and lowered a seat in the middle row of seats. With their hands in the air, the young woman, an older man and the young driver he had already seen put his car into the garage were pushed roughly by the armed man towards the people carrier.

"And you! Whoever you are," he directed at Tam and Kakko.

"We… we just… we were just walking this way. We don't know where we are…" protested Kakko.

"You're in the wrong place at the wrong time. Now, get in!" He took Kakko by the arm and pulled her forward. *Oh no!* thought Shaun, *Kakko, don't retaliate. That man's not going to argue.*

Kakko turned and gave the man a dignified stare, but refrained from getting into a fight. Shaun breathed again. He kept himself hidden behind a bush where he could watch without being seen.

The gunman ordered his accomplice to search them. "Two. Empty their pockets."

Two searched them in turn, manhandling them in a way that made Kakko wince. But she was conscious of the large pistol aimed at her head as her pockets were emptied and her bag was confiscated. As he came across them, Two threw their phones, combs and wallets on the gravel, and then, one by one, they were forced into the vehicle.

It was clear that they had arrived at exactly the right time – or *wrong* time, depending on one's point of view. Kakko and Tam were having to go with the flow.

"Cuff them!" the gunman commanded the driver as he went around the car to keep them covered with his pistol. The occupants made no resistance.

The gunman then went inside the house. After several minutes, he re-emerged and nodded to the other. "All clear." Then, he took out what looked like a phone. "All clear, sir. We've got them… all three of them… plus a couple of others who were snooping around… I don't know, but I'm bringing them in."

When the people carrier had left, Shaun stepped out and stood where it had been. He thought, *What now?* He suddenly felt very alone in this strange place. The wind was getting up even more strongly and he shivered. "OK, God. *You* tell me. What do I do now? Do I stay here or follow?"

Shaun retrieved the personal items that Two had cast on the ground, stuffing them into the pockets of his heavy coat. Then, he noticed that the door of the house was open – moving in the wind. He decided to go inside and see if he could find any clues about what was going on.

As he entered, Shaun was amazed. Instead of the richly furnished hallway and polished staircase he expected in a house like this, he encountered a bank of screens and multicoloured wires leading up the stairs. To the left was a room with machinery – to the right what looked like a giant photocopier stood in the centre of the room with a thick umbilical cord connected to the centre of one side. He examined it. It could be a generator he decided. Whatever it was, it was turned off.

Shaun followed the wires up the stairs. They led to a rear bedroom where he saw a dish two metres in diameter, like those associated with satellite communications on Joh. It was pointing towards one of the windows.

He had been inside the house less that ten minutes, when Shaun heard another vehicle approaching. Instinctively, he looked for somewhere to hide. He found a bathroom just as two men stepped through the front door. He prayed that they didn't want to use the toilet – at least not the one he was hiding in. He needn't have worried; they were more interested in the machinery.

"Look at this?" said one. "Who would have thought that they had got this far?"

"We would not have known if they hadn't tried to test it," replied the second.

Like Shaun, they traced the wires up to the back bedroom.

"If they'd been allowed to operate this, it might have been enough to disrupt the cleansing."

"Depending on the power, it could have done more than that. An accurate enough counter beam to the cleansing blast could have caused it to backfire. Do you think they knew what they were doing?"

"Who knows. We'll get it out of them."

"All they needed to do with this stuff was to activate it at the right time. But they would have to have inside information to know that."

"They couldn't know that, could they? I mean, no-one but those on the vessel know that. Unless they can mind-read."

"There is no evidence for that on this planet. If you ask me, though, the quicker we get this planet cleansed of all the 'chemical scum', the better. If this small crew has worked on this, there might well be others. Too many of them know what we did last time. News of our activities on Planet Xochon leaked out. Our superiors failed to register that some individuals from this place were in radio contact with them and were able to pick up our communications. I can't think how else they would have known."

"But this stuff shows that they do... and they have the technology to foil us."

"Pity we can't cleanse the place today."

"No, we have to wait for the alignment. It won't work properly otherwise. One thing we can't afford is a botched job."

"Do we take all this down?"

"No point. We'll mark the co-ordinates and destroy it as and when. In the meantime, anyone that comes near here will 'just disappear'. We can detect any intelligent being from this planet with the life-tracker."

"Better turn it on now. We don't want to be caught here."

"Thought you had it on already!"

"Er… ah, yes. You're right. I have. There is no intelligent being within two kilometres of this place."

"Good. You had me worried then. Suppose someone was listening into what we were saying."

"No. They weren't. This device can detect brain activity for up to two kilometres. I have never heard of any intelligent being that has ears that sensitive. And, besides, even in these bodies, there is the language barrier."

"Radio?"

"Easy. Any radio signal of any frequency is also picked up. There is nothing. This place doesn't even have an electrical connection. That's one reason they need that generator."

"One reason?"

"The other is to generate sufficient power to counter the cleansing signal."

"Dangerous, then?"

"Yup. But the alignment is due in three days. The scum won't be to able to use *this* array. Let's leave."

"I hate these bodies we have to put on."

"I know. But we can't travel uncovered. When we get back, you can divest yourself of it."

The men left the bedroom and then the house. The vehicle parked out the front roared into life, wheels crunched the gravel and silence was restored.

Shaun stepped out of the bathroom. One thing he was sure of was that, according to their definition, he was an intelligent being. He had heard and he had understood – but their device had failed to detect him. He was beginning to understand why he was here. Could it be that he, Kakko and Tam were here to operate against these people under their radar, so to speak? He had no doubt whose side he was on – anyone who spoke about 'cleansing a planet of chemical scum' were not the kind of people you wanted to be friends with.

Shaun decided to check out the machinery and then see if he could find the others. He examined everything carefully, but exactly how it worked, he couldn't decide. It was clear that the generator was at one end and a powerful beam was emitted from the other, but exactly what happened in the middle he wasn't sure. One thing he was certain of, however – Kakko was the person to do it. She would know; she was a whiz with machines. She loved them and they loved her. His task was now to find her and free her. According to the enemy, they had three days.

He went into the kitchen, and found a bottle of water. He drank some, and took another in a plastic bag. There was no telling how long it would be before he found any more.

★ ★ ★

The people carrier bumped down the drive for a couple of kilometres and then purred along a tarmac road for what felt like half an hour. Then they struggled up a steep track where the driver had to engage the four-wheel drive. Eventually, they came to a halt beside a rudimentary log cabin. A roughly dressed man approached.

"Yuk," he said in a disgusted tone. "Five of the scum. Good job you had room."

"Two of them apparently 'were just passing through'. We'll find out soon enough."

"Fine. I hate this scum, but it's fascinating to see them squirm!"

"Yeah. But first we must contact the cruiser. We can't do that until it comes around. It'll take another twenty hours, because they are adjusting velocity and position ready for the alignment."

"Can't we just torture them now? I mean they're all going to be wiped out anyway."

"Not without orders. If you want away assignments in the future, you have to be disciplined."

"Right. I don't want three more unbroken years cooped up on that engine deck. Getting to the planets is interesting and—"

"Don't worry, you'll get to torture them soon enough…"

Tam and Kakko took all this in. They were conducted to a windowless room beneath the house and their handcuffs removed. The only light and air were through a slit high up near the ceiling. The door was made of thick wooden planks. Tam was grateful for the wind: it prevented the place from becoming unduly stuffy. Sounds from outside were muffled, and Kakko and Tam felt around in the gloom for anything electronic that might be listening devices, but there were none. This was just a hole in the ground – the place had an air of temporariness – but it was certainly secure.

"I think we're safe to talk," said Kakko quietly.

"Who says we want to talk to you?" said the young woman. "We don't know anything about you or your situation—"

"We have just arrived," said Kakko, a little crossly.

"What my sister means is: how do we know that you are not one of them?" The young man nodded towards the door.

"You have a point," sighed Tam. "But, honestly, we literally stepped though into your drive only moments before you drew up. Kakko, you'd better explain."

Kakko explained about the white gates, and how they never knew where they were bound or what they were going to have to face. "The only clue we have," she concluded, "is in the stuff laid out for us to bring. This time it was warm clothing and a little bag of toiletries – which has been confiscated," she sighed.

The middle-aged man contributed his thoughts. "Your story is too unbelievable to be untrue," he smiled. "If the enemy had gone to the trouble of staging this, they would have come up with a more convincing story. Besides, it was a case of them following us, I'm sure. You arrived before we did and that would require them to have had prior knowledge of where we were going – and I don't believe they did… but, tell me, what do you know of Xochon?"

"Xochon?" queried Kakko. "We know nothing about him – or her. We've never met them."

"That confirms my belief in you," replied the man. "My name is Dr Seppa, these are my children, Moot and Hapla. Xochon is not a person, it is a planet – four light years from here."

"Where are we then? What is *this* planet?" asked Tam.

"You're on Planet Yuht. We call our suns, Bat and Mat. They are sister suns that dance in the daytime sky. We love our planet. What are your names and where is your home?"

"I'm Kakko. This is Tam. We are from Planet Joh. We have only one sun. We call her Daan. Our planet is very beautiful, too. We are human beings – our ancestors originally came from Planet Earth One."

"We, too, are human. Your appearance – is this your true shape?"

"Of course," said Kakko. "Why should we change it? Even if we could."

"Our captors do not possess a human shape," stated Moot. "What you see is a mask. They do not have carbon-based bodies."

"What do they really look like?" asked Tam.

"You can hardly see them. The Fogs, that's what we call them, are eight-tenths energy – only twenty per cent mass," explained Hapla. "We think that that mass is unlikely to contain carbon-based molecules."

"So, what are they doing here?" asked Kakko.

"They have come to possess our world," answered Dr Seppe. "We know this because, for some years, we have been able to communicate with the people of Xochon. The Fogs went there first. Their aim seems to be to bring habitable planets into their empire. Their motives we cannot guess at – they seem to be quite amoral. They can sense intelligent carbon-based life and then want to destroy it."

Dr Seppe went on to explain how they intended to rid the planet of all intelligent carbon life. "Plant life and lower forms of fauna," he said, "seem to be unaffected." All higher forms, including human beings, were destroyed – atomised. Their method was to position a craft in stationary orbit above a planet. For some reason, they needed an alignment of two outer systems and the parent sun – or, in this case, one of the parent suns – and then release a beam of radiation, the nature of which they did not understand. However, their attack on Xochon was in two phases. The destruction was not completed before the alignment was lost. In the intervening period – a year and two months before a new alignment was possible – the Xochons learned a great deal about their enemies.

"They were working on a disruptor," continued Seppe. "They had discovered that radio waves at a certain frequency masked the beam. There were patches of territory that had survived where that particular frequency was being used. They devised a machine to head off their beams at source. Perhaps, if the Fogs thought the business was too much trouble they might move on. The problem was, however, knowing when the attack would come. They couldn't generate the counter-beam constantly because that would simply reveal themselves. They conveyed all their research – all their discoveries about these beings – to us. Ten years ago, their communications ceased. Xochon now seems to possess no intelligent life forms – at least none that can communicate with us.

"We – I – believed it was only a matter of time before the Fogs turned their attention to us," went on Dr Seppe. "But I do not hold a position of influence with the government. Planetary governments," he remarked, "are too preoccupied with their immediate interests. They don't think of the medium term, let alone the long term. Those of us who were communicating with the Xochons were seen as a novelty. When the communications ceased, the interest waned. The threat was seen as nothing… I was accused of being delusional…" Dr Seppe sighed.

"*I've* been accused by a politician of being delusional," stated Kakko. "He just didn't want to know when I told him about children being bombed."

"I expect he had too many other pressing concerns," remarked Dr Seppe. "The same was the case here. However, *this* mad scientist," he said, tapping his chest, "decided that it was not impossible for him to build a disruptor. It did not need a huge amount of hardware. If the smallest of radio signals at the right frequency had affected the Fogs' beam during their attack on Xochon, then it would not take a massive installation. It was about accuracy and timing, rather than force."

"And so we bought The Mansion," broke in Hapla. "I was only ten and my brother twelve then. Dad moved us from the city after Mum died."

"It was a good life for them – the country – but they missed out on the stuff other kids had," added Dr Seppe.

"But we believed in Dad," broke in Moot. "One day, he was going to save the planet."

"Right. But we made a mistake – right at the start. We tested our system the other day. We didn't know the Fogs had already arrived in orbit. It flushed them out though. Two days ago, we went to the capital to tell the president. We spent a long time being pushed from official to official, but in the end we got nowhere."

"What about the media?" suggested Kakko.

"We tried them. But there has been a major rail accident – and it is the final of the open championships – so there was no room for 'zany stories'," said Hapla.

"We decided the only thing to do was return to The Mansion and see if we could work out when the Fogs were likely to attack. The rest, you know."

"We need a plan," stated Kakko.

"We do indeed," answered Tam. "We don't know when the attack is to take place, the one weapon we have is in the hands of the enemy, and we are their captives."

"There must be a reason the Creator sent *us*," said Kakko firmly. "The solution must be to do with us."

"Right," said Tam. "But please forgive my girlfriend for sounding arrogant."

"Arrogant? No, it just stands to reason."

"She's right," put in Hapla. "If the Creator has given you a white gate, then He must have a role for you. Isn't that right, Daddy?"

"Don't apologise for your friend," affirmed Dr Seppe, "it doesn't hurt to be positive. Our task is to discern your Creator's plan. What we didn't tell you was that, as well as constructing a disruptor, we have prayed. If God exists – something I cannot prove, of course – I do not believe it would be the will of a creator that His intelligent creatures are obliterated for no apparent reason."

"*I* believe in God," affirmed Hapla, "I am not a fatalist. We cannot know all that is in the mind of God, only that which He chooses to reveal to us. Why the Fogs behave the way they do, we cannot even guess at. They must exist for good somewhere. It may be that they have a higher purpose, which we, and they, still have to discover."

"We have to discover *right now* what we can do from inside this locked room," said her father.

"What we ought to tell you," said Tam in a very low voice, "is that there are three of us. These Fogs did not see the third. He was still around the back of The Mansion."

"Hope, indeed," smiled the doctor.

"Let's pray for him," said Hapla.

33

Shaun decided that his best plan was to try and follow the two whom he had overheard. They may well lead him to Kakko and Tam. He thought about the car in the garage. He was not a regular driver, even of Johian cars, but it was his only hope. He opened the front door of the car. There was what appeared to be a steering bar and several foot pedals. Was there a gear shift? He pulled at a handle on the dashboard. It resisted any movement. Shaun depressed one of the pedals. Nothing. He tried another and the handle came out in steps – one, two, three, four, five, six. There was also a red button. Red buttons are designed to be pressed. Shaun pressed it. The car burst into life and shot backwards. Instinctively, Shaun put both feet down. The engine roared in neutral, but the car continued to roll. He had found the clutch and the accelerator – and reverse gear. By deduction, he thought a third peddle had to be the brake. Shaun gingerly lifted his left foot. The engine ceased to roar. He kept his right foot on what, then, must be the clutch and transferred his left to the brake. The car stopped rolling. Good.

After several attempts, Shaun got the car moving forward and he drove down the drive. When he reached the T-junction he was lost for a moment, but all the marks in the mud seemed to be going one way. He turned left. He had no idea where he was going – and he was so far behind the men by now, he was never going to catch them up.

But Shaun didn't reckon on the inevitable consequences

of taking on 'chemical scum'. The Fogs' bodies were telling the men they had to relieve themselves.

"Ruddy carbon life," grunted one to the other. "I'll have to stop. Pull up."

"Me, too. However do these humans manage these terrible bodies? We're doing them a favour cleansing them." He pulled over to the roadside and they climbed the small bank.

Shaun was getting the hang of things and was pleased with the speed he was managing to control. There had been no turnings off to right or left – the road seemed to wind its way through woods for kilometres. Then, he saw a car parked on the verge. It was the only other car he had seen. As he passed it, he knew for sure it was the one he was looking for. He continued another couple of hundred metres and pulled off the road. He watched in the mirror as the two men got back into the car and drove off, passing him, but not going too fast. *Perhaps these aliens were as unfamiliar with the local cars as he was,* thought Shaun. He followed at a reasonable distance.

Shaun's gamble paid off. As the car in front turned onto the rough road and slowly mounted the hill, Shaun proceeded around a bend, parked the car, turned off the engine and listened. He heard his quarry labour up the incline and then stop. Shaun decided that from here he was best going on foot. He didn't want to alert anyone to his presence.

After half an hour, he stationed himself in the woods overlooking the log cabin. He was sure he had found his friends. *I must bide my time for the right moment*, he thought. *We have three days, there is no rush. These men are bound to go out sooner or later.* With luck they all would, but even if only some of them went, it narrowed the heavy odds against him. Getting caught himself was the last thing Kakko and Tam needed. He took a sip from his bottle of water. He was getting hungry, but he knew that he could cope with that for the time being.

★ ★ ★

Darkness fell, but no-one had made a move to leave the house. There were no artificial lights around it, but the starlight was enough for him to see by now his eyes had got used to it. There were lights on inside, but the windows were shut and the curtains drawn. He crept up to the wall of one side of the house, keeping below the level of the windows. He could hear the men talking – but he couldn't make out what they were saying. He moved to a corner and then around the back. The rooms here were not lit, although he could make out light coming through from the front – possibly through an open door. There was also a glimmer from a low slit at ground level. As he approached this, his heart leapt as he heard Kakko's voice. She was speaking softly, but distinctly.

"It's completely dark outside now, I can see stars though the gap. Do they intend just to leave us here, do you think? Leave us to rot?"

"I don't know. I could do with the loo." It was Tam. "Perhaps I should call and see what happens."

Shaun didn't hesitate. He did *not* want any of the men coming into the room. They were clearly together and the men elsewhere. He put his face to the slit.

"Hi," he whispered as loudly as he dare. "It's me."

"Shaun!" exclaimed Kakko in a similar whisper, only a couple of metres from the other side. "Fantastic to hear you!"

"I guess you're prisoners. Are you all together?"

"Yes. Five of us."

"How many men are there?"

"At least five. The two that brought us here, one already in the cabin and then perhaps two more later."

"That's definitely five then. I followed the second two. You know what all this is about?"

"Yes. These men are not human. They are invaders who intend to destroy this planet."

"I know. I heard everything the last two said. Something about waiting for an alignment… in three days' time."

"Ah! Three days," said Dr Seppe. "You sure."

"Absolutely. We've got three days."

"What else did you learn?"

"Lots–"

Just then, the bolt on the wooden door was suddenly slid back. A gruff voice called into the dimly lit chamber. Shaun stood up quickly and flattened himself against the wall next to the slit. "What's going on in here?"

The five stood in silence. They had been grouped around the slit listening to Shaun. They had been caught.

"I love the stars," rejoiced Kakko. "I adore the stars, and through this little slit we can see only five of them. Only five out of the whole panoply of the sky! You are cruel to us."

"Looking at stars? You don't know your luck. Just spend years in the engine room of a space cruiser. You might be out among the stars, but you never get a glimpse."

Kakko almost felt sorry for him as he pushed his way in among them to look through the slit himself. "What do you scum know about stars?" he mocked.

"Don't call me scum!" retorted Kakko.

"You are! Putrid scum – all humans are. You stink!" and he hit the back of her head with his palm.

That was it. Kakko could take no more. She clasped her hands together as she straightened her arms, and then swung them up as fast and hard as she could beneath the Fog peering out of the slit. She caught him a hefty blow under his raised chin, sending his head back and knocking him off balance. Hapla jumped to her left as the well-built Fog fell to the ground, grazing her sleeve as he passed. Thud! His back hit the hard, dirt floor. The Fog lay silent for a few seconds and then let out a loud groan.

"That's done it," said Tam. The other Fogs rushed in, one with pistol raised.

"Back up! Against the wall. What have you done to him?"

"He… he fell," said Moot in a shocked voice. He *was* shocked – he did not know Kakko. Tam wasn't. He had been wondering when it was going to happen from the start.

"I can see that. Why?"

"He was looking at the stars – his head went back and he toppled over," stated Dr Seppe firmly. "He was reflecting on the question of intelligent, carbon life. 'Chemical scum', he called us… if I recall it correctly. The comment seemed to cause him a problem–"

"Shut it!"

"Two. You alright?"

"Yeah, boss," said the Fog, who was now sitting up.

"What's the problem?" Not being used to human flesh, he didn't rightly know. It had all happened so fast that he hadn't realised that Kakko had hit him.

"This bloody body I have to wear. I was just looking at the stars and next thing I knew I was down here."

"Get up and get out… As for you," he turned to the group, "I don't want any more trouble. Right. If it was up to me, I'd kill you right here and now. But my orders are to wait… for the proper cleansing." He laughed. "You'll enjoy that – or at least *I* will!"

What he didn't realise was that the Fog high command had no intention of sending a shuttle to bring him and his three colleagues back before the cleansing. It was safer to keep them engaged on a task, it delayed the question of the shuttle. In human form, they would be vaporised the same as the rest. There was no love lost between the Fogs. Love was unknown among them.

When the prisoners were alone again, Tam whistled, "That was a close one."

"It felt good, though," hissed Kakko, "rubbing the back of her right hand. I felt his teeth clamp together."

"You nearly took his head off!" said Tam.

"Well, we seem to have survived your outburst," said Dr Seppe calmly. "Now we know we can rely on you if it comes to the need for fast, violent reaction. But let's wait for the right opportunity. I don't like the look of that one with the pistol – the one that seems to be in charge."

"*I* think what you did was cool," said Hapla, with quiet enthusiasm. "Just like Sara the Android... er... on the digital game," she explained.

"Yeah! Girls like her. One up for the so-called weaker sex," said Moot.

Tam sighed to himself. Oh, how he loved this girl!

"Pisst!" It was Shaun.

"Shaun," whispered Kakko. "Sorry. I'd forgotten about you."

"Obviously."

"You guys OK?"

"Yeah. Just clobbered an enemy alien."

"I heard... Look, I've picked up your stuff. The things they took out of your pockets before forcing you into their car. Shall I post them through?"

"Yes *please*, why didn't you say?" said Kakko, with a hint of irritation in her voice.

"I was going to – but you had a fight, remember? Coming

through." Item by item, Shaun emptied his pockets. Soon, everyone was reunited with their phones and wallets.

"Shaun. You're a marvel," said Tam.

"And one other thing, they haven't damaged your machine, sir – inside your big house… Now, how am I going to get you out?"

"Leave that to us," said Dr Seppe. "Now we have our phones, we can summon help. You just stay out of harm's way."

"The place is surrounded by woods. It's easy to hide. I'll leave you for the moment – but I'll be in earshot."

"Brilliant, Shaun. Don't I have a wonderful brother?" said Kakko, feeling guilty for telling him off.

"You do. Think of me out here in this wind."

"We will. Keep safe. Now, off you go," commanded Kakko. "Bye."

★ ★ ★

Less than fifteen minutes passed before the silence and the darkness was disturbed by the distant sounds of vehicles on the track. The noise stopped, however, some way from the house. Shaun felt prickles on the back of his neck as footsteps – many of them – approached. It sounded like an army trying to be quiet – which was almost what it was. Suddenly, a twig snapped behind him and Shaun turned to see a helmeted figure pointing an assault rifle at him. The soldier put his finger to his lips. Shaun had no intention of saying anything.

The house was surrounded by men in identical uniforms, each with their guns trained on it, as one of them approached the front door and tapped. It was opened slightly and, before the Fog had time to realise what was afoot, the soldier forced the door wide open, knocking him aside, seized him by the arm, leaving passage for four more soldiers to storm in. A pistol was raised, but the gunman stood no chance as he went down under a hail of automatic fire. The two others made for the back room but they were tackled and handcuffed before they had time to grasp what had hit them.

Shaun watched all this silhouetted against the curtains, hardly daring to breathe.

"M... my friends," he stuttered, "in the cellar!"

"We know," said the soldier. "Keep still!"

Instinctively, Tam, Kakko, Dr Seppe, Moot and Hapla had thrown themselves flat on the dirt floor of their prison. They had known it was coming. Dr Seppe had called on his mobile, and explained where they were and what they were up against. The thick wooden door was unbolted and a soldier ordered them to stand.

"Professor Seppe, I presume?" he said, staring at Dr Seppe.

"Yes... plus my son and my daughter – and two friends. There is another in the woods. We must get back to The Mansion and activate the disruptor or we'll all be dead – and I mean *all*! Perhaps now your commanders will listen..."

"Save your arguments for them," stated the soldier. "We're just doing our job."

★ ★ ★

Brother and sister sat together in the back of Moot's car. Shaun was relieved he didn't have to drive – but it didn't prevent him from bragging to his sister. She had to be proud of him, he said. Kakko was, she replied, but added that if it had been her that had remained uncaught she would have done the same.

"Of course," laughed Shaun, before he produced his bottle of water. "But would you have thought to make provisions?"

"Water!" said Kakko, not a little annoyed. "All this time you've had water and you haven't shared it!"

"Think about it, sis. When have I had the chance? Here." And he gave her the bottle.

"Sorry," said Kakko, genuinely contrite. "I wasn't thinking. I'm just so thirsty!" But she passed it on to the others without drinking.

Shaun smiled. "I do love you, sis. I was scared for you. I kept thinking you were going to act, and I knew that man was trigger-happy."

"So did I. Do you know what I was thinking?"

"No."

"Shaun has this covered. No need for desperate measures."

"Thanks."

They arrived at The Mansion and found everything still in place. This time, the whole estate was to be heavily guarded. Dr Seppe started up the generator and turned on the computers.

"So, we have a rough idea when they are going to fire the beam – but we still have to guess the exact moment. A moment too late and the beam will have done its work – too early, and they will take evasive action… even shut us down with a blast of a conventional weapon."

It was still dark, but the sky was lightening in the east. Daylight was on its way. The space cruiser was, however, clearly visible – a bright star, stationary in the northern sky. From its elevation, Tam deduced that they were in the temperate latitudes of the southern hemisphere.

"How can they attack the whole planet?" asked Tam. "From there a single beam would affect only a small area and nothing on the other side of the planet."

"I'm afraid they are more sophisticated than that," explained Dr Seppe. "Their beam can be spread widely – it is not a narrow one. It is designed to drench the whole surface of the planet. As soon as it commences – as the alignment is achieved – the cruiser will fire its retro engines, and slow its orbit to allow the planet to revolve beneath it. The beam is designed to continue for a full day and night, until the whole planet is, to use their terminology, 'washed clean'. That is why they need the alignment. According to Xochon, the alignment sustains the power required. In our case, if they manage the alignment better than on Xochon, the last survivors will have less than twenty hours after it has begun."

"As we can see it, we'll be among the first, won't we?" observed his son.

"Yes. But it also gives us the advantage of disrupting it from the start."

They stood staring up at the cruiser. From this distance, on this pleasant morning – the overnight wind had calmed to a gentle breeze – it didn't seem possible that such a comprehensive destruction was so imminent. But as they gazed, Moot's sharp eyes spotted a sudden darkening beneath the cruiser blip.

"Dad. Did you see that?"

"I can now!" A dark patch was enveloping the cruiser. "They've fired the beam! Quick, the machine!"

"No time, Daddy. It's already too near!" cried Hapla, grabbing her brother.

"It can't be the main attack. They're not lined up. This is a single blast directed at us – The Mansion. They are aiming to disable us!" surmised Dr Seppe.

"It seems as if they have succeeded," said Moot. "Dad, I love you."

"I love you, too, Moot, Hapla. We're on our way to the place of the dead. Think of Mummy." He put two big broad arms around his children.

The brightness of the dawn was increasing, but it was overcome by a fast approaching darkness that now obliterated a third of the sky. A dog whimpered and pressed against the leg of one of the soldiers, all of whom were now transfixed, staring at the sky. Instinctively, the soldier squatted down beside the dog and enveloped it in his arms. Tam grabbed Kakko who was already clutching Shaun. Kakko thought of her mother – would she blame her for endangering Shaun, too? As the radiation filled the sky, they could no longer look – the weight of the darkness was overwhelming. Kakko pictured her parents sitting in Tam's house with Tam's distraught parents wishing, once again, that their beloved son had never met her.

"Wham!" The trio staggered as the beam struck them like a violent blast of wind. It wasn't hot, just strong... and then it passed. Kakko opened her eyes, expecting to find herself in heaven... or somewhere, but she was still standing on the gravel drive clutching her brother and boyfriend. The dawn had returned. The beam had passed and they were still standing there, apparently unscathed.

"It didn't work!" exclaimed Dr Seppe. "We survived!"

"Daddy," shouted Hapla. "We're alive! Kakko, Tam?"

"We're OK. What, then, was all that about?"

But as their eyes became accustomed once more to the pale dawn, Tam spotted a soldier hunched over a pile of clothes. Then, they saw them. All the soldiers, except for one, were lying on the ground, their weapons beside them... except they were not bodies. All that was left were clothes laid out as they would have been on a body, but they were empty, from helmets to shoes.

"Vaporised," stated Dr Seppe. "So the beam does work."

"But why have *we* survived and not *them*?" asked Shaun.

"Soldier," said Seppe to the one man who had come

through the ordeal, "what were you doing when the beam struck?"

"I was squatting down, stroking the dog," he said. "I was comforting it." The dog looked up at him and wagged its tail, happy that he had found a new friend.

"I know what it is… or I think I do," said Kakko. "Those of us who were comforting another, loving each other, we survived. Those poor soldiers had no-one to cuddle."

"Not very scientific–" said Dr Seppe.

"Find a better explanation," challenged Kakko.

"I was going to say, not very scientific, but impeccable logic."

"Sorry."

"What for?"

"Interrupting you."

Tam smiled. "I agree," he said.

Hapla was moving from one set of empty clothes to another. "Each of these has a family," she sobbed. Moot had his arm around her shoulders.

"They needn't have died for nothing. What we need to do is get the word out. The alignment is in three days from now. No-one should be on their own when the blast occurs. Everyone should be prepared and in someone else's arms."

"The machine–" began Dr Seppe.

"Has done its job," stated Moot firmly. It has caused the Fogs to show their hand. Even if it works, the timing would have to be spot on. There's too much luck involved."

"You're right. But we must warn the world to leave no-one out, no-one unattended, no-one uncomforted. We must all be in a huddle."

Hapla was squatting over a dog collar. "Mini. She didn't make it. Instead of looking for comfort, she just barked. Her brother was a wimp, he'd never bark at anyone. Not much of a guard dog, we used to say. Daddy, can I phone my friends?"

"Go for it, Hapla." And he took out his own phone and called the ministry.

★ ★ ★

The word spread quickly. The social media buzzed. Hapla and Moot were followed by hundreds of thousands within hours. Young people around the world were sharing the news.

The media were showing pictures of The Mansion and ran interviews with Dr Seppe. The president was wholeheartedly endorsing the message. "Find somebody. Don't be alone. Comfort the elderly and the very young," he commanded. He explained the news they had had from Xochon, and regretted the inaction of his and the previous government. "But now is not the time to enter the blame game. We can defeat this!" he declared. "Find somebody to love!"

"What about our pets?" asked someone. Hapla posted the need to care for them, too. Anything with the remotest bit of intelligence, her father had said. Kakko added, "Anyone or anything capable of love."

"Of course, that's it," said Tam. "The Fogs see our intelligence as nothing more than a disgusting chemical scum. But they don't know or understand *love*. To something that is more energy than mass, even the use of machines might be challenging. The sight and thought of *carbon-based* life might sound revolting. But love is different. Love is not just physical – it is beyond both matter and energy. Love is from a completely different dimension, it is spiritual, it is of the very essence of God, Herself. These beings simply can't counter love."

The newspapers the following morning gave a blow-by-blow description of the events surrounding The Mansion and the log cabin. They had a testimony from the soldier of how a dog had saved him – and he had saved it. "LOVE WINS!" was the headline in one of them. They launched a column for people seeking partners with which to 'brave the storm'. Children were urged to abandon their individual digital pastimes in their bedrooms and remain in the same room as their friends and families. Travel should be avoided, better to stay with others. No-one was to sleep alone.

Neighbourhoods were on alert to seek out elderly people living by themselves, while social workers and religious institutions worked together to get in touch with those who might otherwise be missed.

The remoter regions of Planet Yuht were the greatest challenge. Three days was a very short time to get the message to those who did not share the same social networks – especially those isolated by local conflicts.

Inevitably, there were detractors. Sadly, there were those who thought the whole business of getting into a huddle was some kind of gigantic ruse to get soldiers to lay down their arms when an attack was launched. One dictator laughed at 'the pathetic attempt to weaken his magnificent forces' and he cancelled all home leave, and put his army on high alert. The president urged him, and those like him, to take the threat seriously, but the dictator replied that he was not going to be insulted by a 'colonial son'.

"Some people are so pigheaded and full of their self-importance that they jeopardise whole nations," sighed Dr Seppe.

"It's like that all over the universe," observed Kakko. "It appears to be part of the human psyche. If you had seen what I witnessed in one world where they were manufacturing weapons to bomb children, you would be horrified."

"I would be horrified, but not surprised," replied Dr Seppe. "The more you think about it, in the end, the only weapon we have against evil is–"

"Love!" blurted Kakko.

"Love," nodded Dr Seppe. "Until this moment, I had wondered about the possibilities of the existence of God. Now, I don't doubt His existence – at least, I don't doubt the power of *love,* which is beyond any dimension accessible to science."

"God is Love," said Kakko. "My father tells me that is in the Scriptures of Earth One."

"Have you read it?"

"No. Not yet. But I will when I get home. Bandi has a copy of the Earth One Scriptures."

★ ★ ★

When it came, Kakko, Tam, Shaun, Dr Seppe, Hapla and Moot were ready for it. They were sleeping in one room in The Mansion, keeping two of them on the lookout at all times. The beam came exactly as they had predicted – just as the sky was lighting in the east. The emission from the space cruiser was sustained and it broadened quickly to engulf a large area of the planet. The deep darkness seemed to continue for hours – although it was really only minutes – during which time they were buffeted by gusts of particles that felt like a strange sort of wind, although the air was quite still inside the house. They clung to each other and the dog, conscious of each other's presence and their powerful fellowship. At the end of it all, they were unscathed. Love had triumphed once again.

Across the planet, it was amazing just how many people were prepared to comfort someone – even complete strangers.

The beam arrived when predicted and they were prepared. Even in the countries where the dictators commanded that the warning be ignored, the majority of the people had decided that to avoid being alone was a wise course of action. The worst of the detractors had sat defiantly in his dictatorial palace – while his guards held hands! After the beam had struck, they survived – he didn't. Seeing their master's clothes lying empty beneath his desk, they understood how vacuous all his power really was. Without love, a person is, ultimately, nothing.

After the beam had passed, Dr Seppe immediately rang his contact at the ministry. All in his office had made it through, too. They were overjoyed and poured their praises on the professor. But Dr Seppe warned them that there may well be another attack at the next alignment, but he had no intelligence of when that would be.

"If only we could take out that cruiser," he sighed.

"No," said Moot, "that would be far too risky. The most we could do would be to cause damage. All that that would achieve would be to stimulate them into defence mode and work on outmanoeuvring us. Our best defence is to keep cuddling. If they aren't making any impact, they may move on."

"I agree," said Tam. "To defeat an enemy with little mass is a tall order."

"They are evil, right?" said Hapla. "The only defence against evil is love. Love can never be overcome by evil, because evil is, itself, empty."

"Darkness has no power over light, no matter how dim; evil is powerless against the light of love," muttered Kakko.

"Wow!" said Tam. "That says it all."

★ ★ ★

There was no second attempt at cleansing Planet Yuht. After the attack, a scan of the planet revealed, to the Fogs' amazement, that the beam didn't seem to be effective against the chemical scum on Yuht. The game lost its appeal – it would take several weeks and some complicated manoeuvring for a second attempt, and it wasn't worth it. They were stung and they didn't enjoy it. They moved on. The residents of Planet Yuht woke up the next morning and the cruiser had vanished.

★ ★ ★

The people of Yuht were never the same. Such a revelation of the power of love would never be forgotten. There were, of course, detractors from the outset. Some, for reasons best known to them, even circulated a conspiracy theory that the events had never happened. They were known as the 'beam deniers' and said some terrible things. Evil always sought a way. But many people experienced love and care at a level they had not known before. New friendships grew in many streets and communities. In some cases, new romances blossomed – people who had not known of each other before or who had not been aware of the potential for love.

★ ★ ★

The emergency over, it was time for Kakko, Tam and Shaun to return to Joh. Dr Seppe, Moot, Hapla and their dog walked with them to the white gate, which had now become visible again.

"You realise you have saved our race?" said Dr Seppe as they took their leave.

"No," replied Kakko, "*you* have. You already knew how to love."

"But it was *you* who showed us that love was the answer."

"You're welcome," said Kakko lightly. Tam and Shaun gave each other a knowing smile. Kakko was going to be difficult to live with for months. This time, it actually *was* millions that owed their lives to her.

34

Jalli went in to check on Yeka. The night had been a long and troubled one – she hadn't settled at all. There was no doubt that she missed her brothers and sister when they went off on their adventures – especially Shaun, who, for some reason, was her favourite. But now, as the first rays of morning sunlight streamed through the window, she had eventually started to sleep peacefully. But Jalli had given up on any more sleep for herself and had decided she might as well get up.

She looked out on the early morning light of the garden she had known as home for so long and recalled the first time she had ventured into it, fearing to leave a mark on the soft lawn. The grass had not changed since then. First thing in the morning, before the family was up and had invaded it, it was pristine. Except this morning, there was a distinct line of footsteps that had disturbed the morning dew. They appeared to begin at exactly the same spot that Jalli had first come in from Wanulka, although, of course, her white gate to that world had long since vanished. It was probably those footmarks that had started her reminiscing.

As Jalli made herself a mug of tea, she got to thinking what could have made the prints. They were not made by anything with four feet – and why did they begin at the hedge? Jalli slipped into her dressing gown and put on her gardening shoes. Taking her mug of tea, she ventured out to examine the marks further. They came from the hedge, extended a couple of metres where the owner of the feet had stood for a few minutes and then returned to the hedge. Weird. Was someone coming in through a white gate that Jalli could not see?

Jalli took her tea to the bench and sat for a while, listening to the birds and the lowing of the krallens in the neighbouring fields – they were looking forward to being called for milking. Jack, missing his wife, came to the door and called.

"Over here," replied Jalli, "on the bench."

Jack came across and felt Jalli's dressing gown. "What is my girl doing outside in the damp of the morning before she has dressed?" He joined her on the bench. She invited him to take a sip from her mug and told him about the footprints, and her reminiscing.

The sun came up and soon burnt off the dew. The footmarks disappeared. The day brought its own concerns. Shaun, Kakko and Tam had not returned, the incident at the college still preyed upon Jalli's mind, and Bandi was worried about Abby. Jalli didn't know where this was all going and wondered, for once, whether her son had got himself too deeply embroiled in this relationship. As much as she liked Abby, there were times when a teenager needed to concentrate on his schoolwork. Still, it was the Creator who was enabling things to happen through the provision of their apparently permanent white gate and she reminded herself she needed to trust Him.

★ ★ ★

Daan went to bed behind the trees and that night Yeka slept better, and so did Jalli, but she was up early. Still no Kakko, Shaun or Tam. But the footmarks were there again. Someone had crossed the grass. Jalli traced the dints to the bench beneath the tree and there sat a girl of about sixteen, with long brown hair and dusky-coloured skin like herself. The teenager, clad in jeans and a T-shirt, held her trainers in her hand – just like Jalli had done when she had first encountered the garden. It was such a weird feeling. Was Jalli looking back at herself? Had there been some kind of time loop? Nothing had ever happened like that before. But when she looked more closely at the girl, Jalli realised that it was not herself. She had a longer face and Jalli had never owned a T-shirt like the one the girl was wearing. But there was something about her that was familiar. The girl stood up and Jalli could see the T-shirt more clearly. It bore a sunflower and the words, *Everything Grows with Love* – in Wanulkan! It had been some time since Jalli had seen Wanulkan characters – not since she and Jack had visited and stayed with the Bandis.

Jalli scooped up her dressing gown, descended the stairs and opened the front door. She didn't bother with her shoes, but stepped out on the grass barefoot.

"Hi," she said in Wanulkan.

The girl took fright.

"S – sorry," she spluttered. "I shouldn't be here."

"Yes, you should," said Jalli.

"But this isn't the Municipal Gardens... I thought it was, but it can't be."

"No. You are not in the gardens, but you are very welcome here. I've been here nearly twenty-five years. I found this place just as you have done."

"Are you... are you... *trapped*... here?" she asked, with some alarm.

"No, not trapped. But I can't come and go from the Municipal Gardens anymore... Tell me, have you come here through a white gate?"

"Sure, that one over there."

"Has anyone else seen your white gate?"

"*My* white gate? They must do – it's pretty obvious in the wall of the gardens."

"But no-one else comes in here? No-one else uses your gate?"

"No. It doesn't seem like it. I don't know why."

"It's because only you can see it or use it. What is your name?"

"Dzeffanda. Dzeffanda Pinda."

"And you live in Wanulka. Are you at school?"

"Yeah. Wanulka High."

"What are you studying?"

"Most subjects – Wanulkan, maths, sciences, humanities… I'm doing my basics levels next summer."

"Working hard, then?"

"Sort of. I get stuck sometimes."

"With what?"

"Well, I've this biology thing at the moment. I have to do a project on some living creature. It has to include its physical features, its habitat, its food and its life cycle, and I don't know where to start."

"So, what creature?"

"I don't know. That's the trouble – I can choose anything… anything at all. I hate making those kind of choices because I never know where to begin. I wish the biology teacher would just tell me what to do – but she won't. She goes, 'I'm not going to tell you what to do, Dzeffi, because I don't know what will intrigue you. You have to decide that…' So, I saw this gate and thought I would come in here and see if there was anything that 'intrigued me'."

"And is there?"

"Yes. Everything! I see this tree, those flowers, the birds… everything. But I wouldn't know what to do – where I could find out about their life cycle and things. Could you–"

"I did the same sort of biology study when I was your age."

"Did you? What did you study?"

"Parmandas."

"Parmandas. They're so small. I never thought of them. Where did you find out about them?"

"Well, there are books – in the school library or the municipal library, but the best place would be Parmanda Park. You can look at their exhibition, and even go and stalk the hives… I guess they're still there."

"Yes. Parmanda Park. I never thought about that. I don't live on that side of the city."

"Where do you live?"

"Just off the Zonga Road. Do you know it?"

"I used to live right on the Zonga Road when I was your age… the same bus used to go all through the city as far as the park."

"Yeah, I think it still does… Do you think I should choose to study parmandas?"

"Like your biology teacher says, it has to be your choice… but you can always take a trip to Parmanda Park to see how it goes. Follow the guidelines when you get there… and look after yourself," added Jalli, with a frown.

"Why? Are the parmandas dangerous?"

"No. Not at all. It's just that… you should always take care when going anywhere on your own… Look, when you get there, ask to see Mr Paadi Bandi. He might still be working there as a part-time volunteer. He used to be my biology teacher when I went to your school… Tell him I sent you."

"I will. Oh, I will! But… what is your name?"

"Jallaxanya Rarga – Rarga's my maiden name."

"Rarga? But my aunt's name's Rarga. Finti Rarga. Are you related?"

"Could be. I don't know her. I was born in Zonga… before the earthquake."

"Her family came from there, too, originally. They had left Zonga a few generations before the earthquake. She lost relatives when that happened. Of course, you must have moved away, too. No-one survived."

"No, I hadn't moved away. I just happened to be visiting Wanulka City at the time. It was a chance thing. I was only three."

"You must meet her."

"I would like to, but there is no gate for me. I cannot go to Planet Raika."

"I don't understand. This is Raika. It's Wanulka."

"No, Dzeffi, it's not Wanulka and it's not Raika. Tell me, how many suns can you see?"

"I can see Jallaxa, but not the others."

"That's not Jallaxa. It is Daan, the single sun we enjoy on this planet. Here you are on Planet Joh."

Jalli explained to Dzeffi about how the white gates worked and about herself when she had first found the new white gate in the wall of the Municipal Gardens. She also explained that wherever she was in the universe, the Creator was with her.

"He never abandons us, Dzeffi. Sometimes hard things happen, very hard things, and not just on some other planet. I have experienced them on all the worlds I have been to, including Raika – and very recently even here… We just have to learn to trust God."

"You're right. I think He answers my prayers… kind of. I mean, not in the way I have in mind. Like, the other day I got out the biology textbook and I went, 'OK, God. You tell me what I should choose.' I looked at lots of pages, but nothing came to me. Then I thought, *You shouldn't talk to God like that, Dzeffi, you should be polite.* So I said, 'Please, almighty God, you're really great. Could you possibly, kind of, help me here,' then I read the book again. I still got nothing. But then, as I walked through the Municipal Gardens, I got to looking around. There was so much that was so fantastic, when you thought about it. So many wonders! But I still couldn't choose. Then, I saw this gate and it felt, kind of, different. The smells are different here… and this garden, it's really great. So I thought to myself, *The Creator is leading you to find something in the garden.* So I came again today… and met you. Are you from the Creator? Are you real? I mean… human? Is this a dream?"

"Dzeffi, this is not a dream. And yes, I am human. I am not a heavenly creature or anything. But the white gates are always there for us for a reason."

"I think… I believe… God has brought me here to meet you. I am going to explore the parmandas!"

"Good… but keep an open mind when you go to the park. You never know – but it won't hurt to begin with the little creatures. I have to say that they have shaped my life – I still work with their cousins here on Joh."

"Work with them?"

"Yes… I still study pollinators and I teach in an agricultural college."

"Wow! OK. I shall go to the park this weekend!"

"You want to come in and have some breakfast? I think I can hear my youngest. She will be looking for her mum."

"Thanks… but I think I should be getting back. I don't want to get stuck."

"Don't worry. No-one using white gates has ever got stranded anywhere… Two of my older children – almost grown up now – are off to somewhere else through a white gate at this moment and I have no idea where they are, or when they will be back."

"Don't you ever worry about them?"

"All the time when they are away – especially Kakko

the eldest because she dives into things rather – but she is learning."

"I would like to meet them sometime… but now… can I come again?"

"As long as the gate is there, that is what the Creator wants. Drop in any time. Next time you come, we'll put on a meal for you… We don't need days of warning in our house – just take us as you find us."

Dzeffi tiptoed across the turf back to her gate. Jalli walked with her.

"Don't worry about your shoes. I took mine off the first time I came. We don't worry about it now."

"But you have bare feet."

"Just because I'm not dressed," Jalli laughed. "I didn't want to risk missing you."

Dzeffi raised her hand to the invisible latch.

"Bye."

"Bye, Dzeffi. Good luck with the parmandas."

"Thanks." Then, she had gone. Jalli waved at the hedge. She could imagine Dzeffi looking back, although she could no longer see her.

★ ★ ★

"What have you been up to?" asked Jack as Jalli spooned cereal into Yeka's mouth. She could feed herself, but it was a messy affair and was taking too long. "Been following footmarks in the grass again?"

"Oh. More than that – talking to the person who made them."

"I thought you were out there a long time. Without your shoes, too."

"How did you know that?"

"When you weren't inside, I checked for them. I knew

you hadn't dressed. They were there – but you weren't. Then I heard you in the garden, talking Wanulkan. I thought you might be talking to yourself."

"No. I met this very nice young lady who lives very near where I used to live as a child. She had been asking God about what she should study for her biology project."

"So He has provided her a white gate to meet you. A bit extreme, wouldn't you say?"

"Maybe. But why should we assume the Creator only gives people white gates for exotic adventures? We began quite gently. And this Dzeffanda is quite a different character from our Kakko… I wonder what *she's* getting up to… Anyway, we probably haven't seen the last of this girl. Who knows what God has in mind… I think if she comes again, I might send something back with her for Mr Bandi and his family. What do you think?"

"I think that sounds a very good idea indeed. What about a copy of your dissertation for your Doctorate of Science. He would be very proud to think that a prodigy of his has gone on to great things."

"Isn't that rather showing off? And, besides, he wouldn't be able to read it – its not in Wanulkan."

"No, I don't think it's showing off – not to Mr Bandi. If a former student does well, the glory falls on the teacher for starting her going in the right way. And I don't think the fact that it is written in Johian matters – the diagrams and drawings explain what it's about."

"Well, if you think so… I'll look one out and write out the title page in Wanulkan… It's strange using that language again with a native speaker after so long."

"You miss Raika?"

"Yes, in a way. I miss my childhood there. Although I missed having a mum and dad like other children, life was good with Grandma. Home was where she was… I can't say

I was that happy as a teenager, though. I grew away from the others – I just wasn't into the things they were… and I couldn't stand all the competitive element – appearance, clothes, trying to be cool. I opted out."

"You dared to be different… as your T-shirt said."

"And paid for it! I was bullied – not physically, but socially. Girls can be really nasty. They are all looking for someone to look down on – and if you don't join in and fight back, you're, like, an easy target… And if you're good in school, get your assignments in and please the teachers, well, you're a swat, a creep or worse."

"It was just the same on Planet Earth… I didn't really bully anyone, but I'm afraid I would have been pretty mean to anyone who had tried it on me. They didn't bother. I wasn't teacher's pet anyway. I did enough to keep them off my back, but not enough so they would embarrass me by telling everyone how well I had done."

"But you passed your exams."

"Yeah. I did my best in *them*. I could do more than I ever produced in class. I would have been scuppered if it had been based more on coursework."

"Strange thing, isn't it?"

"What?"

"Being a teenager. You compete so much with others to prove to yourself that you're OK really."

"Yeah – both to yourself and others. It all stems from a lack of confidence. After all, teenagers haven't had much time in their lives to assess how they measure up to others. Most of them believe they are probably lacking, and want to try and give the impression that they are the complete item. It's all a sham, though. Most teenagers are in turmoil underneath."

"When you get to Dzeffi's age, you are supposed to be popular with boys… I never bothered. They all seemed such drips."

"All, until you met me."

"And that did me no good at all. Having a boyfriend on another planet doesn't count." Jalli giggled. "I wasn't really wanting a boyfriend."

"I must say that after I met you and you liked me, the whole lack of confidence thing completely disappeared."

"But Dzeffi is still in the middle of all the teenage angst. Too many decisions… I hoped I said the right things…"

★ ★ ★

The following morning, there was a gentle tap on the front door.

"I wonder who that could be so early? If it were one of ours, they would have just burst in."

Jalli opened the door and there stood Dzeffi. "I went to Parmanda Park," she said, "and met Mr Bandi, like you said. He was very kind. He never stopped talking about you and your husband… Jack. He asked me to give you this."

"Come in. Come through."

Dzeffi followed Jalli into the kitchen. "Dzeffi, this is my husband, Jack, and his mother, Matilda. Bandi and Yeka are still in bed… Dzeffanda from Wanulka City."

They stood and took Dzeffi's hand, and found her a chair at the table.

"Would you like some tea? Something to eat?" asked Jalli.

"Of course she would," said Matilda. "Let me get you some. Help yourself to that toast. I'll make some more."

"Mr Bandi. He gave me this to give you." She handed Jalli an envelope and a jar. The jar bore a picture of a parmanda with the Wanulkan words: "Best Parmanda Honey". Jalli smiled. It had come from the Parmanda Park visitors' centre. The envelope was addressed to Jallaxanya and Jack.

The note was a short one – dashed off in Mr Bandi's little office while Dzeffi had waited. He wrote that he and Pammy were well, and their Jalli was moving on to her new high school in a few months. This was a new school – not the one Jallaxanya Rarga had gone to – but it was nearer their home.

"You know, I do miss Mr Bandi," said Jalli, filling up. "I can't say I would know anyone else in Wanulka at all. I didn't have any real friends when I was living there."

"A bit like me," said Dzeffi.

"You don't need many," put in Matilda. "Just the right ones."

Jalli went and found her thesis. "Sorry to keep using you as a postie," said Jalli, "but would you give Mr Bandi this from me? Tell him I'm sorry it's not in Wanulkan. It's not about parmandas but bees – little creatures a bit like parmandas, but nowhere near as clever."

Dzeffi opened the bound wad of pages. "Somehow, it's magic, but I can understand this – or at least the words. You see them and then your brain, kind of, tells you what they mean in Wanulkan."

"Wonderful!" exclaimed Jalli. "If it's working for you, then it will probably work for Mr Bandi, too."

"I'll give it to him and if he can't read it, I will read it to him," decided Dzeffi.

"It's very long," said Jack. "You concentrate on your own studies. Don't get distracted."

"You sound exactly like my father."

"Do I?"

"Yeah, my dad – he's a proper dictator!" said Bandi from the doorway. "Hi, I'm Bandi."

"Like, *Mr* Bandi at Parmanda Park?"

"Yeah. Apparently I got named after him… so you must be the girl from Wanulka."

Then, there was a loud shriek from upstairs. Someone was feeling left out and was trying unsuccessfully to climb out of her cot.

35

Kakko dragged herself into the kitchen, trailing the belt of her dressing gown behind her. The house was full again. It was mainly full of Kakko. She couldn't help recounting the incident in which she floored the opposition. "Didn't know what hit him. It felt so good," she repeated. She fell into a chair and then spotted the jar – it was the picture of a huge bee-like creature that had attracted her. Jalli explained.

"Wow! Those parmandas really are big."

"No. It's supposed to be a close-up. They are about the same size as bees and do the same job."

"You'll leave that jar of honey for your mother to eat," ordered Jack. "It's packed with nostalgia."

"How'd you get it? I'd love to go to Wanulka," pondered Kakko.

"Well, so would your mother. But we are very pleased to have been visited by a very nice young lady who lives not far from where your mum grew up."

"Yay. How old is she?"

"Bandi's age, I guess."

"Yes," said Bandi, "she's sixteen."

"Another girlfriend! You can't have two girlfriends on two planets at the same time. It's not done!" objected Kakko.

"You'd be amazed to hear that since I've only met her once, and in this kitchen, she's not my girlfriend," said Bandi quietly.

"What's she look like?"

"Smaller than you – more delicate – but the same kind of features. Definitely Wanulkan," explained Jalli.

"She reminds me of your mother when I first met her," said Matilda.

★ ★ ★

They didn't have to wait more than a few days for Dzeffi to return. She was delighted to meet Kakko and Shaun, and was a natural with small children. Yeka delighted in the attention.

Dzeffi brought with her a photocopied document that Mr Bandi had given her. To her amazement, Jalli discovered it was her own school submission on parmandas to Mr Bandi all those years ago. He had photocopied it and kept it – which is more than Jalli had done with the original. An attached note ran:

Dear Jalli and Jack,

We are delighted to get this opportunity to exchange our news. You might be a long way away from us, but it seems that the Creator has allowed us to keep in touch.

You will remember our daughter, Jallaxanya. She is well and happy and wants to be remembered to you. You are her heroine, being the one after whom she was named. She has now started high school herself – not the one you and I were associated with, but a new one in the east of the city nearer our house. (There are now to be three high schools altogether. The city is growing tremendously fast. Dzeffanda will tell you about the western end where you grew up. She lives in what was fields of ibon when you were young.)

All is in good order in the park. Our visitor numbers are on the rise all the time. We cannot allow more than a third to go anywhere near the hives, which are visited strictly under supervision. Visits to the hives have to be booked well in advance. The rest of the people are kept well back and have to be content with the exhibition. It has, of course, changed the nature of the park – but we still get lots of compliments from our guests. Not so many of us remember those days when an individual could sit for hours in front of a hive and become absorbed into the surroundings. Not even I am allowed to do that these days.

I was pleased to meet Dzeffanda. Thank you for referring her to me. I don't know if I have helped with her deciding on what to study. If she were to decide on parmandas, she will find that they have been the subject of many a student's project since you did yours. I doubt whether, with all your moving around, that you still have your original, so I have asked Dzeffanda to leave this photocopy with you when she sees you. Did you know I had copied it at the time? I was that impressed with it.

I found your treatise amazing. It is every bit as detailed as the standard studies of the parmandas here. I guess you are among the first on your planet – it has all the hallmarks of a seminal paper. I know it is written in the local language, but the translation overlay is amazing. Somehow I have been able to understand every word. You still retain something of your style – the girlish enthusiasm is still there. It comes across, despite it being from a mature mind in a foreign language.

I got Dzeffanda on a hive tour and she came back full of questions, although she did not see a display – that is something that a comparatively few people have experienced. (I still can't get over how they displayed for you within minutes of your arrival when you last came.)

Tell your son, Bandi, that I hope he is doing well with his studies and his adventures. Tell him I am proud of sharing my name with him and I hope that one day I will be able to meet

him. If you have a picture of your family you can send back
with Dzeffanda, we will be pleased to receive it.
  Pammy sends her best wishes with mine,
  Paardi Bandi.

Jalli read the letter twice, the second time out loud for Jack
and the others.

"I told you," commented Jack, "a proud teacher."

"I have decided what I'm going to study," said Dzeffi.
"When I was there, at the park, there was a whole lot of little
flying beetles. Mr Bandi said they were very important to the
ecology of the park because they keep down the 'little green
monsters' – as he called them – that ate out the growing tips of
his plants and the buds of the flowers that feed the parmandas.
It's very interesting. The beetles keep down the little green
monsters, which feed the ants. Without the beetles, the park
would be short of flowers, and overrun with ants that invade
the hives. It all fits together. No-one is doing their project on
the beetles, which means no-one has taken out the books I
need from the library."

"So, problem solved," observed Kakko.

"Yeah, thanks to your mum."

"And the Creator," reminded Kakko, "who provides the
white gates and directs us to where he wants us."

"Yeah. Sure. Thanks be to God."

"But now I have to get down to some study, myself," stated
Kakko.

"A good idea," said Jalli, with a degree of relief. She knew
that good results did not just happen. "And I am off to the
college. Would you like to walk with me, Dzeffi? We can go
though the woods and you can see some of the natural things
we have here."

"I'd love to," replied Dzeffi, now trusting her white gate

would not disappear the moment she turned her back on it. "Er, actually... er... there is something I would like to talk to you about."

"Fire away. I don't have to go this minute."

"No... I mean... its a bit, well... I'd like to talk just to you about it... if you don't mind? No offence to anyone else..." Dzeffi was blushing, despite her dark complexion. "I don't mean to–"

"That's fine, Dzeffi," said Jack. "We quite understand. Some things are not suitable for general discussion. Why don't you two set off and take your time in the woods? I hope I will get to say goodbye later, but if not, I wish you well and hope to see you again soon."

Jalli and Dzeffi rose from the table and got ready to go out into the fine, bright morning.

★ ★ ★

By the time Jack got in later that day, Dzeffanda had gone.

"She didn't want to be away from home too long," explained Jalli. "She's a timid young lady – much shyer than I was when I was her age."

"Is she being bullied?" asked Jack.

"That's my discerning husband."

"Well, I guessed there was going to be more to her coming here than a biology project, important though that was to her."

"You're right. I was thinking that, too."

"She is too shy to share it with anyone in Wanulka."

"So it's not just about being bullied?"

"No. It's deeper than that. It's about her self-esteem. Bullies sense when people are vulnerable. They target them. Because bullies are themselves weak inside, they instinctively

371

go for those who they think they will win against. For them, it's about bolstering their own self-esteem."

"I remember only too well. Don't remind me. There was this kid with a limp we all used to pick on at school. He was one tough guy – he had to be. He had more self-belief than most of the rest of us put together. I recall thinking how much I secretly envied him… I used to think it was boys that bullied each other more than girls. Girls were less likely to brawl."

"You have no idea! Girls can be absolutely horrible to each other…"

That evening, Jalli was still thinking about whether she had said the right thing to Dzeffi. She and Matilda were alone in the kitchen.

"You're quiet, Jalli. Something on your mind?"

"It's Dzeffi… I don't suppose she would mind me telling you, but she wouldn't want this generally known. It's not just the bullying, although that is part of it. What it is with Dzeffi is that she is concerned that she isn't normal… her general appearance, everything about her body including… down below."

"And do you think she has a problem?"

"I very much doubt it. I asked if everything was working OK – did she have any pain or anything – and she said no."

"She didn't strike me as being abnormal in any way – not that I could see, of course."

"Nan, she's normal. She won't make a model – she hasn't the perfect figure – but–"

"What's perfect?"

"Exactly. She's judging herself against a sort of current ideal. I told her that fashions change anyway. But she is still worried that there's something… 'abnormal' about her body. And once you've got that into your head, it's not easily dismissed by just telling a person not to worry about it."

"She could get herself checked out by a doctor – then she could be reassured."

"I suggested that, but it isn't as simple as it sounds. She's only sixteen and she doesn't know where to begin without involving her parents. And her family doctor is a man – and for a sixteen-year-old that can be a problem. She doesn't like the idea of being examined by him. Then, he is the family doctor – she can't get an appointment without her parents and siblings knowing."

"Which means everyone."

"Teenage siblings are not naturally confidential. But the main thing is her relationship with her parents. They're quite overbearing, I gather. The last thing she wants to do is invite them into a discussion of her body."

"Oh dear. I can see the problem. I would have died rather than talk about my body with my mum when I was sixteen."

"Yeah. But that's where I come in. If you can come to a different planet somewhere else in the universe, and yet be able to talk in your own language to someone your mother's age, that's different. I don't know her parents and I am not likely to meet them sometime soon."

"So what did you do? What did you say?"

"I asked what made her feel like this? I told her she did not seem to have the symptoms of someone with physical problems. She just thinks… she just thinks she's the 'wrong shape'. I asked how she was sure that she was different. Apparently, these days things have changed on Raika. Pictures of naked girls abound – especially on computers and the social media. Raika is by no means what it was. It has changed so much… The place in which I was born hardly exists anymore."

"So she has seen many more pictures of naked girls than you did?"

"Certainly. She spends time online checking them out and comparing herself with them. But I asked her if she thought the pictures she saw were of normal people? Did everyone put pictures of themselves out there? No, she told me, of course not. So, I asked her who did?"

"And I bet she didn't know many people who did."

"None. Apart from one girl who had a nude picture of herself posted on the social media by her boyfriend – but that did not reveal much."

"So these pictures are of selected individuals."

"They are. That was exactly the point I made to her. *They* are the abnormal ones. And I bet most of them have been airbrushed, too."

"Airbrushed? What's that?"

"Pictures that have been changed. They can be, what they call, 'digitally enhanced'."

"I think I know what you mean. The negatives have been doctored."

"Yes. Except they don't usually have negatives these days."

"I think the girl's problem is that she's looking at these pictures too often," said Nan. "I doubt if there is anything really wrong with her."

"It's all in her head. What I told her – in so many words – is that if I were her, I would give up checking myself out. Take each day as it comes, and remember that kids are choosing to bully her because they secretly have the same doubts about themselves. And to remember that God has heard her prayers and opened up a gate into a special place – just for her. How cool is that? I asked her if she had a boyfriend, and, if so, what did he think about her body?"

"And has she?"

"She was adamant that she hadn't met anyone that she would like to be with – but, apparently, that wasn't normal either."

"That's nonsense. You don't have to have a boyfriend or a girlfriend at sixteen."

"Quite. I told her so. I told her that if she was meant to have a boyfriend one day, she would find one. The thing is, she's not really worried about the boys – it's all about how she measures up with the other girls. I told her to forget about people for a while – immerse herself in her beetles."

Nan laughed, "Dare to be different... like Jallaxanya Rarga."

"Grandma did a good job. I had enough confidence to stand out. Dzeffi's problems start at home."

"Where she can't talk to her parents without being embarrassed. I suggested she got on with the things that interested her and left the rest to God. I said a prayer with her."

"And was she happy with that?"

"Yes, I think so. I think that perhaps all she needed to do was talk about it... She went home a lot happier than she came anyway."

★ ★ ★

A few weeks went by, but they did not see Dzeffi again.

"I hope," prayed Jalli, "that that is because her problems have been addressed." She resolved that if ever she got the chance to return to Planet Raika, she would look her up.

36

"They've accepted it," announced Bandi. "They like my birth certificate with its English translation."

Bandi had applied to join the Longmead Sixth Form College, giving Abby's address. They had required his birth certificate and a transcript from his former school. He had translated both into English and Pastor Ruk had had it stamped with the same stamp that was on the originals. Abby's dad had given him a reference and mentioned that his father was born in Persham, but now lived away.

"So are you going to take it up?" asked Jalli. "What will you do – live in Persham?"

"It would make sense. If I wanted to go on and study philosophy, I would have to do it on Planet Earth. Living there would mean that I learned English quicker than coming home everyday."

"Are you sure that's what you want? Philosophy doesn't exactly lead into a job," said his father.

"Abby's dad said that with a philosophy degree, I could do a lot of things – it's a good grounding. He hasn't come across anyone with a philosophy degree that is unemployed. Anyway, I don't have to specialise just yet. I am going to have to do a foundation year at GCSE level, before going on to two years at A level."

"That's, like, starting again," said Shaun. "You're less than two years away from university here."

"But with philosophy, it's a broad foundation that is

important," explained Bandi. "Besides, my English isn't up to it. And I am going to need French and German, too."

"What about Greek and Latin?" wondered Jack. "I thought that most philosophers wrote in those languages?"

"Not the modern ones – the post-Enlightenment ones. But people usually do those old languages with their A level courses."

"What's the Enlightenment?" asked Kakko.

"The time on Planet Earth when they first began to make new scientific discoveries – beginning in the seventeenth century. Before that, they had not much idea of the way the universe worked – they mostly believed God micromanaged everything. But then they began to see new patterns – discover laws of nature."

"So nowadays God gets left out?" speculated Kakko.

"Mostly does, I'm afraid," said Jack. "But He doesn't have to be. Why shouldn't God work through the laws of nature?"

"No reason why He shouldn't," answered Bandi, "but most modern philosophers don't think God is 'essential' to understanding the universe. You can believe in Him if you choose, but the universe would still work if He wasn't there."

"I choose to believe in the Creator," stated Kakko, vehemently. "Without Her, I would be stuffed."

"Quite," agreed Bandi, "but, logically, since the Enlightenment, a Creator is no longer necessary."

"*I* think She is necessary. She is for me," insisted Kakko.

"It's about how you use the word, 'necessary'," explained Bandi. Kakko began to splutter.

Jalli intervened. "So you've got it all worked out, then – what you want to do and where you want to do it… But tell me one thing. I know you think highly of Abby – she's a lovely girl. Are you wanting to go to Earth to be with her or do you have a genuine desire to do this? I mean, if she weren't there, would you still want to study this Planet Earth One philosophy?"

"That's a good question," answered Bandi. "I have asked it myself. The answer is that I want both. But I am really interested in philosophy and would not give it up, even if Abby gave me up."

"Good answer," said Jack. "I think you ought to do this. So long as you don't retreat into some academic backwater, this could make you a really useful person."

"Thanks, Dad."

★ ★ ★

At the end of a British August, on a hot day in the late Persham summer, Bandi moved into the spacious new house that went with Rev Dave's new job. It was spacious, but not ginormous and draughty like the last one. They were reassured when their white gate had followed them. The house was a bus ride from Longmead, but more than doable. Abby was going into the upper sixth, with her boyfriend two years behind her. When they parted at the college gates, it felt to her as if he were younger, but later, after classes, he took her in tow like a big brother – it was as if they had been together forever. But neither Abby nor Bandi were your usual kind of teenager. His classmates supposed that that was how famous philosophers started in life. Bandi wasn't aware of how his enthusiasm for study rubbed off on the others, many of whom were repeating GCSE subjects they had failed the first time round. His tutors were delighted with him.

★ ★ ★

As the Smith family were getting used to Bandi's absence, Kakko was about to finish her course at the agricultural college and had applied for jobs up and down the coast. She didn't want to move too far from home, but jobs associated with farming tended to be scattered. Her preference had been the farm implement works on the other side of Joh City, next to the spacedrome. They weren't advertising any work – especially not the apprenticeship type of thing Kakko was looking for.

However, she decided it would not hurt to inquire, so she went down to the works and asked to see the human resources manager. He was very polite, but explained that they would not be taking on any new graduates for at least twelve months. He gave her a handful of literature and told her to come back the following year.

Kakko was disappointed, but hadn't expected much else. She walked back by the spacedrome and peered through the wire. There were a couple of Low Orbit Craft (LOCs) visible – one outside on the tarmac and a second through open doors inside a large hangar. She knew they also had a much larger craft that could leave orbit if necessary. It was currently in space, transporting a party of people to the mines on Joh's small moon. She wondered if they needed an agricultural engineer there, but since there was no atmosphere, it was hardly likely. She laughed at herself. She recognised the signs of impatience and schooled herself to be sensible. *Kakko, you said you were not going to become desperate,* she told herself. She walked on towards the main road, where she would pick up a bus. But as she was passing the spacedrome main gate, she spotted Professor Rob striding across the tarmac. He had been out inspecting the LOC on the tarmac. She had seen him under its wing, but he was quite a way from her and she hadn't recognised him. But *he* had recognised her. She was just outside the wire fence where he had met her the first time.

"Miss Smitt," he called.

Kakko turned. "Professor Rob."

"You remember me?"

"Of course. I'm amazed you remember me."

"No-one can forget *you*, Miss Smitt. I was trying to find you. I am looking for an apprentice engineer and you seem to me to have all the qualities I need. Only this morning, I phoned your college. They said you had finished lectures."

"I still have to present my project," explained Kakko, feeling suddenly light in the head. "All the rest is done – I have completed and passed the theory papers."

"Excellent. Come inside and I will give you an application form… If you would like to work here, of course."

"Work here? On those LOCs?"

"Yes. But mostly on the new-generation engine research. We are currently building a third-generation intrahelical polykatallassic engine from blueprints sent to us by the Thenits. Our task is to work with them to take it into a fourth generation. Interested?"

"Am I interested?! Wow, professor. But, I have only been doing agricultural engineering."

"As I said last time, an engineer is an engineer. You have as much experience in the space field as anyone coming straight out of college. But you have the enthusiasm, which counts for a lot. I have also heard that you are an excellent team worker and that is vital. Come in and get the forms."

Kakko couldn't remember walking to the bus stop from the spacedrome. Halfway home on the bus, she said, "Oh! God. Sorry, I should be thanking You. I can't believe this. I've never wanted to do anything more in my life… except perhaps be with Tam."

Kakko presented her project, which gained her a top-class certificate at the college.

★ ★ ★

The family were all in the garden, enjoying the sunshine and the scents of high summer. Suddenly, Yeka let out a scream. They all rushed to her to see what was wrong.

"Bee," she sobbed, holding out her hand. "Ow!"

Kakko got to her first. "Let me look... Oh, the bee has stung you. Did you try and pick her up?" Yeka nodded as tears rolled down her cheeks.

Matilda put her arms around her, while Jalli went to the medicine cupboard. She knew exactly what do for bee stings, of course. Soon, all three women were fussing around the little girl. She was sitting on Kakko's lap, Jalli was applying soothing cream and Matilda was proffering her a sweet. Yeka reached out to Shaun for a cuddle, too. Shaun thought of Wennai, Aril and Patia not having a mother. Yeka was a lucky girl.

"You like bees, don't you, Yeka?" said Jalli. "But you mustn't touch them. She was frightened. That's why she stung you. You are much bigger than her. Bees don't know you don't mean to hurt them."

Yeka snivelled. "Yeka not hurt bee."

"Of course not."

"Yeka sorry."

"I know you are. But you didn't understand. Now, you do. The sting is to remind you."

Half an hour later, Jalli watched Yeka who was back playing. The bees were still busy with the flowers. This time, she had her hands behind her back.

"Yeka sorry," she was saying.

Attracted by the bright colours on Yeka's T-shirt, one of the bees flew towards her. She settled on her chest for a fleeting second, decided there was no nectar to be had and returned to the flowers. Yeka felt forgiven.

Jalli watched this and smiled. Despite the sting, Yeka

was not put off. The bees still had a fan. She laughed as she watched them dancing in the breeze, as they moved from flower to flower, unknowingly being the means of new life – a new generation.

The soft breeze reminded Jalli again of the work of the Creator, the breath of God bringing order out of chaos. The winds could be both gentle or strong, but they were never still – creating, changing, giving, taking. The breath of the Creator could be alive and sharp, even violent; or soothing and soft, but, all the time, building a universe of wonders – from the tiny bee to the power of a galaxy with a trillion stars like the one in which she was born. *Wherever she is,* Jalli thought, *she is at home. Dear God, you are with us, whatever,* she said in her heart. *You always find a way to love us and give us what we need.*

★ ★ ★

At the end of a long day, a tired Jalli tucked Yeka into her bed and said a prayer.

"Tell me the story about Patta and the rainbow," begged Yeka.

"It's time for you to go to sleep, young lady," protested Jalli, with a smile.

"I know, but I like the story of the rainbow… and I promise I will go to sleep straight afterwards."

"Well, alright," Jalli bent over her daughter, and kissed her happy little face.

"Once upon a time, there was a daddy whose little girl, Patta, asked him where rainbows come from. Her daddy explained that rainbows come out to play only when both the rain and the sunshine are around together. Sometimes you can see where they start, and sometimes where they end.

"One day, Patta said goodbye to her mummy and her

brother, who were going to take the bus to the town. She and her daddy were going to join them later in the afternoon, when they had done all the shopping for her brother's new school uniform.

"In the middle of the morning, it started to rain. But the sun did not go away and soon a bright, new rainbow came out. It played among the clouds for a bit and then, all of a sudden, Patta saw where it started.

"'Daddy, Daddy,' she called. 'Look, the rainbow is starting by the wood.'

"'Come on,' said Daddy, 'let's go and climb it.' Her daddy found coats and scarves for them both, and, taking an umbrella, he led Patta up the hill to where the rainbow began. To her amazement, just at the bottom bit of the rainbow, she saw a flight of shiny, violet steps that led up the arc. They were very steep at first and her daddy helped Patti take them one by one. Soon, they were high enough up to look down on the valley below them and spot their house with its wet roof shining in the sunlight. Each step took them higher, and the higher they went, the shallower and less frequent the steps became, and soon Patti was skipping along, high in the sky, looking down at the road – a tiny silver thread – that led to the town.

"Then Patta looked up, but she could see no dark grey clouds. Above her was the rainbow with all of its colours… what are they, Yeka?"

"Red and yellow and–"

"You've missed one,"

"Erm…" Yeka smiled and began again. "Red and orange and yellow and green and blue and… and-indigo-and-violet."

"Right, only, from Patta's point of view, they were the other way up."

"But when she looked up, she didn't see violet, did she? It was white," said Yeka, who knew the story well.

"Yes, she saw all the colours of the rainbow blend in together and they made the most brilliant white you can ever imagine."

"What if you climbed the top of the rainbow instead of the bottom, and then looked up? What would you see then?"

"Then you would see the face of God. You can climb the steps on the top of the rainbow only once in your life and that's when you're on your way to heaven. But that's a different story. Patta and her daddy were underneath the rainbow… Soon they were right at the end of the stairs, and there was just a small curve there that led to the top of a slide."

"They're going to whiz down it!"

"They are indeed. The slide was long and smooth, but fast. It took them right to the end of the rainbow, which was in the happy valley of the park in the town. They landed – bump, BUMP – right in the sandpit. And that was just where they were to meet Patta's mummy and her brother."

"But then the rainbow disappeared…"

"Yes. It stopped raining. The sun shone brightly and began to dry up the puddles."

"Where do rainbows go?"

"They're always there in the sunshine, but they hide their colours until the rain comes out."

"Without the rain, the colours get all mixed together to make white," suggested Yeka.

"You're quite right. I can see you're going to make a good scientist one day."

"But you can't really climb a rainbow like Patta. That's only a story…"

"You can't climb a rainbow with your legs, but you can with your heart. There are rainbows made of God's love that you can climb, even if there is neither sun nor rain – heart rainbows that never go away."

"I know. Daddy can't see with his eyes, but he can still see the heart rainbows made of love… I like rainbows… I've seen a rainbow in the puddles before they got dried up. Why does Daan dry up the puddles?"

"Not now, little lady. It is time for you to sleep, and dream of rainbows–"

"I bet Patta's daddy made a big bump in the sandpit–"

"Goodnight, Yeka. More stories tomorrow," said Jalli, firmly, as she kissed her once more.

"Night, Mummy."

Jalli smiled. *I wonder what adventures lie ahead for us?* She shivered. *The older I get, the more I am aware of the dangers… but then, the longer I live, the more conscious I become of the fact that I am never alone. Not ever.*

THE WHITE GATES ADVENTURE SERIES

The Kicking Tree

The first in the series:

Meet Jack (18) from England on Planet Earth One and Jalli (17) from Wanulka on Planet Raika in the Jallaxa system (Andromeda Galaxy) as they discover the white gates, and each other, for the first time. Travel with them on their youthful adventures; engage with them as they face painful challenges.

Ultimate Justice

The second in the series:

Jack and Jalli now have teenage children of their own: daughter, Kakko (18), and sons, Shaun (16) and Bandi (14). Their base is Planet Joh in the Daan system, but they travel across the universe to adventures of all kinds, ranging from a children's day out on a lonely island to dodging bombs in Africa on Planet Earth. Kakko is into engines, Shaun discovers a talent as a midfield football player and Bandi befriends Abby, the daughter of a vicar.

Reviews for *The Kicking Tree*

"Wonderful story. Its a great adventure that made me cry. I love the two main characters who meet across the universe…" *Miss S (Amazon).*

"An interesting read. Was encouraged to read this book by a friend at church. Was not disappointed. An excellent way of putting Christianity in a modern perspective. Very thought-provoking too." *Aidie (Amazon).*

"… a perfect book for the adult-literacy teacher trying to encourage teens to read, with its strong narrative structure, simple vocabulary and positive, active role models. There are all too few authors who write well for this market, and Stubbs is one of them." – *Church Times.*

"Trevor Stubbs has an interesting philosophy of life: 'I hate injustice and oppression, especially against the weak and the vulnerable and want to speak out.' Trevor uses his undoubted skills as a master storyteller and a magical weaver of tales to bring about such justice." – *That's Books and Entertainment.*

"Five Stars. Very good. Suitable for young people. I am a bit old for it but enjoyed it nevertheless." *Glenys Brown (Amazon).*

"This book is one of the most special books I've ever read. In a good way. It's a love story. But it's not really a love story – it's about two people falling in love. It's an SF-book. But it's not really an SF-book: there is some time- (or perhaps wormhole-?) travelling going on and there are spaceships. It's also a fantasy story. But it's not really a fantasy story..." *Linn (Good Reads).*

"I think this book is amazing. I like the fact that almost nothing bad happens, but that you still want to read more. It is hard to put away and there is not a sentence in the book that is boring." *Ebba (Good Reads).*